Love in God's Timing

SERENITY CROSSING: THE HARTWELL'S
Book #4

Tara Baisden

STERLING RIDGE PRESS LLC

Dedication

For everyone brave enough to hope again.

And for the love that comes back — patient, steady, and choosing you today, tomorrow, and for every ordinary day that follows.

Always Love,
Tara

Contents

Chapter 1

The snow had been falling on Serenity Crossing for the better part of an hour, and from the window booth at Minnie's Diner, Rebecca Hartwell could see it collecting on the gazebo railing across the town square. Light flakes, the kind that dusted coats and melted in your hair before you could brush them off. January in the Smoky Mountains meant that sunlight disappeared early in the evening and long, wintry days. The diner was warm and snug, though. Plates clattered in the kitchen behind the counter, and a Patsy Cline song drifted low from the jukebox in the corner. The red vinyl booth where Rebecca sat with her best friend, Jenna Carver, had a comfortable, lived-in, cozy feel they both loved. They'd come here straight after closing the beauty salon, both too tired to cook.

"So I'm standing there with the toner already mixed, sectioning Linda Parson's hair off, and she shows me a picture on her phone." Jenna leaned forward across the booth, her dark auburn bob swinging against her jaw. "And it's not even the color she described when she first sat in my chair. Not even close. She told me warm caramel. Rebecca, this photo was fire-engine copper."

"She didn't."

"She absolutely did. And she's sitting in my chair looking up at me with those big hopeful eyes like I'm about to perform a miracle on a Friday afternoon."

Rebecca laughed and reached for her mug of coffee. "What did you do?"

"What do you think I did? I smiled, I pulled up three reference photos, and I walked her back to warm caramel so gently she thought it was her idea." Jenna sat back and picked up her mug of coffee. "She left happy. Tipped well. Booked her six-week follow-up."

"That's because you're good at what you do."

"That's because I've learned to read the person in front of me. You always say, match the energy and the person before you redirect them."

Rebecca smiled. She did say that. She'd been saying it to every new stylist she'd trained at her salon, the Fluff & Curl Beauty Salon, for six years, ever since she'd scraped together the savings and the nerve to open her own salon on Main Street.

"Doris Fielding came in this past Wednesday for her standing weekly hair styling appointment. By the time I had her in the cape, she was giving me her entire new theory about who's been stealing tomatoes from the community garden," Rebecca said.

"Was it interesting?"

"Oh yes, and very thorough, too. She now has a suspect list and a timeline."

Jenna nearly choked on her coffee. "I love this town."

"You and me both." Rebecca grinned and glanced toward the window, where the snow was coming down a little thicker now against the glow of the streetlamps. She loved these random Friday night dinners at Minnie's Diner. Not having to go home and cook for herself, the excellent coffee Minnie served, and Jenna across from her with her various stories that made her laugh until her sides ached. There was nothing fancy about any of it, and she wouldn't trade it for anything.

Amber Delaney passed their booth with a coffeepot in one hand and her ponytail swinging as she turned toward the couple two tables over. Rebecca had known Amber for years, both as a salon client and as a friend.

"So," Rebecca said, turning her fork through the last crumbles of Minnie's coconut cream pie. "Tell me about this date tomorrow night."

Jenna's face shifted. A slight lift at the corners of her mouth, a change in the way she held her mug. "His name is Grant. He came in last Saturday for a haircut. Walk-in, no appointment."

"And you just happened to be the one available."

"Of course. He sat down, he was polite, and he talked about moving here from Chattanooga recently." Jenna traced the rim of her mug with one finger. "He doesn't know anyone in the area yet. I gave him my number. Which I've never done with a client, before you say anything."

"I wasn't going to say anything."

"You were going to make a face."

"I was going to make an encouraging face." Rebecca grinned, and Jenna laughed. It was good to see her like this. Jenna had come back from Nashville three years ago with her heart broken after a bad breakup. The fact that she was willing to hand her number to a walk-in client said more than any amount of talking about it would.

"We've been texting all week," Jenna said. "He called me twice. Actual phone calls, Rebecca. Not just 'Hey, what are you up to' texts."

"Where is he taking you?"

"That Italian place in Pigeon Forge. Russo's, I think."

"Russo's is good. My sister Sarah and her fiancé Ethan went there last month, and she said the pasta was incredible." Rebecca set her fork down and picked up her coffee. "What are you wearing?"

"Haven't decided yet. I've got three options laid out, and I'll probably change four times before he picks me up."

"You're going to look great in whatever you decide on, and you know it."

Jenna lifted one shoulder, but the smile she was trying to hold back won.

"You're allowed to be excited, you know."

"I'm cautiously optimistic. Which, for me, is practically cartwheels." Jenna sipped her coffee and glanced toward the snow falling past the window. "What about you? What are you doing tomorrow night?"

"Laundry. A bath. Probably read a book," Rebecca shrugged.

Amber appeared at the edge of their booth with the coffee pot. "You two need a warm-up?"

"Please," Rebecca said, sliding her cup forward.

Amber poured; the dark stream curling against the white ceramic. "Minnie just pulled a fresh pecan pie out of the case if you want a slice, Jenna. I know it's your favorite."

"Don't tempt me, but thanks anyway. I'm stuffed from dinner," Jenna said.

"Well, if you change your mind, just wave me down." Amber smiled and moved on to the next table.

Rebecca wrapped both hands around her mug and let the fresh heat settle into her fingers. The diner hummed around her, low and familiar. Forks against plates. Amber's easy laugh carried from across the room. The snow coming down outside the window was peaceful. She was twenty-eight years old, and Friday nights like this one were the texture of the life she'd chosen. A good life. A full one.

She believed that most days.

Jenna was mid-sentence, talking about whether she should wear her hair up or down for her date, when the front door of the diner opened and a rush of cold air swept across the room. A man stepped inside and pulled the door shut behind him. He was tall and wore a dark wool coat with snowflakes dusting his shoulders.

Her hands went still around her mug as recognition hit her.

Rebecca watched him cross the checkered floor with one hand in his coat pocket and the other brushing snow from his sleeve as he made his way to the counter.

She knew him by the way he walked, by the set of his shoulders, and by the angle of his head as he leaned forward to greet Amber.

Conner Delaney.

Everything inside Rebecca rearranged itself in a single breath, the way a room shifts when someone opens a door you thought was locked up tight.

Amber handed Conner a to-go bag, and something she'd said made him laugh.

Rebecca looked away and fixed her eyes on the plate in front of her. A piece of pie crust sat on the white ceramic. She could count the layers in it. She could sit here and count every single layer and never look up again, and that would be fine.

"Rebecca? Is that..." Jenna didn't finish.

Rebecca gave a single nod and glanced back toward him as he turned away from the counter. His gaze swept the dining room, and his eyes locked on hers.

Rebecca watched as every part of him went still. His jaw shifted once. And in that half-second before his composure caught up with his face, she saw the same unguarded shock she was working so hard not to show. Then it was gone, tucked away behind an expression that was careful and composed.

He looked down at his bag and then back at her. His jaw worked once more, and Rebecca recognized the gesture from a version of him she hadn't been close enough to read in a decade.

He crossed the diner toward their booth at an unhurried, even pace.

"Jenna Carver," he said. His voice was the same, warm and unhurried, with a slight roughness underneath that ten years hadn't changed. "It's good to see you."

"Conner," Jenna said. "What a surprise seeing you."

He nodded. Then he turned to Rebecca, and the two seconds it took for his gaze to settle on hers lasted longer than any two seconds had a right to.

"Rebecca," he said. "How are you?"

"Good. I'm good. How about you?"

"Doing well." He glanced at the booth, at the two coffee mugs and the remains of their pie. "I'm sorry to interrupt."

"You're not interrupting," Jenna said. "We're just talking about work."

He smiled, and Rebecca watched the way it changed his face. His sandy brown hair was shorter than he'd worn it in high school. His jaw was sharper, more defined than the eighteen-year-old version she'd known. He carried himself with a quiet steadiness that hadn't been there when he was younger, a settled quality that suited him.

"Are you home visiting your family?" Rebecca asked.

He paused. His eyes dropped to his bag, then came back to hers. "No. I've actually moved back."

The sentence landed on her before she could brace for it.

Moved back. Not visiting. Not passing through. Back. As in permanently. As in living in this town, on these streets, in the orbit of every place she went and every person she knew.

"Oh," she said. "Wow. I didn't know that."

"I just got here Tuesday. Still settling in."

"Well, that's great," Rebecca said, and the smile she offered him was the one she used when a client showed her a photo of a haircut that wouldn't work with their texture. Warm. Convincing. Practiced enough that most people couldn't tell the difference. "Your family must be thrilled to have you home."

"They are. My mom's brought over enough food to last me through February." He grinned, and for a second he looked exactly like the boy she'd known at eighteen.

"Richmond, right? I think that's where I had heard you were living," Jenna said.

"Correct. I lived there for six years. After college, I worked for an inner-city church there. It was time to come home, though."

Jenna shifted in the booth and glanced at Rebecca. A look passed between them that held an entire conversation in a single second.

Rebecca turned back to Conner. "So what brings you back?"

He rubbed the side of his jaw with his free hand. "Actually, that's sort of what I was hoping to talk to you about. I'd been trying to figure out how to reach you. I thought about stopping by the salon, but I wasn't sure that was the right move. I thought about asking Pastor Warren for your number." He met her eyes. "Seeing you here tonight, it feels like maybe the Lord took care of it for me."

"What do you need to talk to me about?" she asked.

His gaze moved from her to Jenna and back. "Would it be all right if I sat down for a minute?"

Rebecca looked at Jenna. Jenna slid closer to the window and gestured to the space beside her. Conner set the to-go bag on the table and settled into the booth across from Rebecca.

A faint line sat at the corner of his left eye that hadn't been there at eighteen. His hands rested on the table with a stillness the younger version of him had never managed. There was a calmness around him now, a serene quiet that had settled into his face and his posture. The boy she remembered had always been in motion, always thinking ahead, carrying a restless energy as if whatever he had wasn't quite enough and the next thing was already calling him forward. That boy was gone. The man sitting across from her looked like someone who had finally arrived where he was supposed to be.

"I've accepted the assistant pastor position at Serenity Crossing Community Church," he said. "Pastor Warren reached out to me a couple of months ago. We talked it through, and the timing couldn't have been more perfect."

Rebecca nodded. She kept her face still and open. She'd known Pastor Warren was looking for an assistant pastor. She hadn't known the search had ended. She certainly hadn't known who it had ended with. And now the man sitting three feet away from her was telling her that he would be standing at the front of her church every single Sunday for the foreseeable future.

"That's wonderful, Conner. Pastor Warren's been hoping to bring someone on for a while now."

"He's a good man. I'm grateful he offered me the job." Conner looked at her directly, and his voice shifted into something more careful. "Part of my role, in addition to being the assistant pastor, will be leading the youth ministry. Building it up, developing new programming, and expanding outreach." He paused. "Which means we're going to be working together. Pastor Warren told me you're the youth coordinator."

The words landed one at a time, each one adding more depth and realization as to what Rebecca's world would soon become. Working together. Not just seeing him on Sundays. Not just polite nods across the fellowship hall. Planning sessions. Youth group nights. Side by side in the same room, week after week, building something that required trust and proximity.

"I am," Rebecca said.

He leaned forward, his forearms resting on the table. "I don't intend to come in and change everything you've built. I want to understand what's working first. I was hoping we could sit down and go over the program together. Maybe brainstorm some ideas."

"Of course. I'd be happy to walk you through it." The answer came easily because it was the professional answer, the generous answer, the Rebecca-who-runs-a-business-and-volunteers-at-church answer. It cost her nothing to say it. It was going to cost her everything to mean it.

"Would tomorrow work? I know it's short notice. I could meet you at the church, maybe around six? I'm sure Pastor Warren will join us as well."

Tomorrow. Saturday. Less than twenty-four hours from now. She would drive to the church and have to sit across from Conner Delaney while they talked about programming and outreach and volunteer schedules. She could do that. She had handled harder things.

"I could be there at six."

"Six it is then." He reached for the to-go bag and slid out of the booth.

"It was good seeing you, Jenna," he said.

"You too, Conner. And welcome home."

He turned to Rebecca. "It's good to see you, Becca."

The name went through her like a current. Becca. Nobody called her that. Nobody had called her that in ten years, and it landed in a place she'd sealed shut long ago. For a few unguarded seconds, her face must have shown something because his eyes held hers for a few moments before he looked away.

"It's good to see you too," she said.

He nodded, turned, and walked to the door.

"Well," Jenna said finally. "Isn't this interesting?"

Rebecca almost laughed. A breath that wanted to be a laugh and didn't get there. "Interesting? More like a shock to my system. He's going to be at church every Sunday. Every youth group meeting." She stared at her mug of coffee. "He will be everywhere."

Jenna flagged Amber for the check.

Amber set the slip on the table and squeezed Rebecca's shoulder before she walked away. Amber was married to Conner's oldest brother, Miles. She knew Rebecca's and Conner's history, and her silence just now was its own kindness.

They left money on the table to cover the bill and then bundled into their coats. Rebecca pulled on her gloves and wound her scarf around her neck while Jenna tugged on her red knit earmuffs. They pushed through the front door, and the cold hit them sharp and clean.

Main Street was quiet at this hour. The storefronts along the town square glowed with the warm light of shops that hadn't closed yet. Snow drifted down, each flake catching the light of the streetlamps before vanishing on the wet sidewalk. Christmas lights still hung on two of the buildings across the square. The white gazebo wore a thin coat of snow along its railings.

Jenna hooked her arm through Rebecca's. They walked the half-block to the Fluff & Curl without speaking, their breath visible in the cold. The salon was dark; the sign above the door unlit. Next to it, the narrow alley led to the back of the building, where the exterior staircase climbed to Rebecca's second-floor apartment.

They stopped at the bottom of the stairs, and Jenna turned to face her.

"Do you want me to come up? I could stay for a bit."

"No," Rebecca's voice was gentle. "I'm fine. I'll see you in the morning."

Jenna studied her for a second. Then she pulled Rebecca into a hug that was firm and warm.

"Call me if you need to," Jenna said.

"I will."

Jenna walked to her car nearby. Rebecca watched until her headlights came on, and then she turned and climbed the stairs. She reached her landing, unlocked her door, and stepped inside.

She turned on the lamp by the door and hung her coat on its hook. Her scarf went next, and she tucked her gloves into her coat pockets and stepped out of her boots, leaving them on the mat.

She walked across the hardwood floor in her stocking feet to the window that looked down on Main Street. The snow was still falling. The streetlamps lined the sidewalk in pools of amber. Across the town square, Minnie's sign still glowed red against the dark sky.

Conner Delaney was back in Serenity Crossing. He was going to be at church every Sunday, standing at the front of the room during every sermon. He was going to sit across from her tomorrow at six and talk about youth group programming while she pretended that his voice saying her name hadn't just undone ten years of careful, deliberate forgetting.

Becca.

She pressed her fingers against the window glass until the cold bit into her skin.

She'd never stopped loving him. She had tried. She'd made that phone call at eighteen with her back against her bedroom wall, her voice light and steady while her hand holding the receiver shook so badly she had to press it hard against her ear to avoid dropping it. She'd said the words she had rehearsed. She'd kept her voice even through every single one of them. And when she hung up, she sat on the floor of her bedroom for a long time, perfectly still, perfectly quiet, while the rest of her life rearranged itself around the hole she'd just made.

Ten years of polite nods whenever Conner came home to visit his family. Ten years of brief, careful exchanges that lasted less than two minutes and left her needing to go out and run six miles on a hard, tricky trail in the area to quiet what he'd stirred up. She'd buried her love for him so deep and so carefully that she'd almost convinced herself it was gone.

Tomorrow at six, she had to walk into church, sit across from him, act like she'd moved on, and that he didn't still hold a piece of her heart.

Rebecca dropped her hand from the glass. She stood there a moment longer, alone with her reflection and the handful of hours between now and Saturday at six.

She didn't have the faintest idea how she was going to do this.

Chapter 2

Warren Davis leaned back in his desk chair and held up a manila folder. "Rebecca put this file together before Christmas," he said. "Take a look."

Conner took the folder and opened it across his knee. Inside were neatly organized attendance records for the youth group. Handwritten columns listed the youth's names alphabetically, with check marks beside each Wednesday night they'd attended. Parent contact numbers filled the right-hand margins. Next to one name, a note read Moved to California, November. Next to another, in the same tidy handwriting, birthday Jan 22, loves chocolate cake.

He turned the page. More names, more check marks. Small, specific notes in the margins that turned a simple roster into a portrait of someone paying close attention to every youth in her care. The handwriting was neat and slightly rounded, and he recognized it.

She'd written him a letter once in that same hand, pressed into an envelope and mailed to his dorm. He still had that letter.

He closed the folder.

Warren's office was warm against the January cold outside. Bookshelves lined two walls, packed with study Bibles and commentaries stacked in no particular order. Family photos sat on every available surface between the books. A framed picture of Warren and his wife near the phone. Three school portraits of grandchildren on the shelf behind his chair. The desk was old and well-used, its surface covered in sermon notes and church bulletins. A lamp in one corner cast a warm circle of light across the clutter, and the radiator in the opposite corner clicked and pushed heat into the small room.

Warren adjusted his wire-framed glasses and nodded toward the folder. "Rebecca keeps contact information current for every family, recruits volunteers, and handles all the parent communication." He set his glasses back in place. "All volunteer. She runs a salon six days a week and still shows up every single Wednesday without fail."

"Her records are impressive," Conner said.

"She's been the backbone of this youth ministry for four years." Warren folded his arms across his chest. "I'll be honest with you, Conner. I haven't given her the support she deserves. I've been stretched too thin to lead the teaching side properly, and she's been filling gaps that weren't hers to fill. That's a big part of why I want you working on this program."

"I appreciate you telling me that."

"I'm telling you because I want this partnership to work," Warren leaned forward. "You've got the training and the experience. She's got the relationships and the knowledge. You need each other." A grin crept across his face. "And if you come in here like a bull in a china shop, I won't have to say a word. She'll handle you herself."

A quick, unguarded laugh broke out of Conner. "Fair enough."

Warren studied him for a second, his grin settling into something quieter. "She's good people, Conner. The kind you build with, not around."

His words landed with more weight than Warren probably intended. Or maybe exactly with the weight he intended. With a man like Warren, it was hard to tell sometimes.

"I know she is," Conner said.

A sound carried down the hallway. The church's front door opened, then closed. Footsteps followed on the hardwood, unhurried but purposeful, growing louder.

Warren glanced toward his office doorway. "Right on time."

Conner straightened in his chair. His hands went still on his knees. The woman walking down that hallway was the same woman whose face had stayed with him since last night when he'd spoken with her at Minnie's Diner. Her careful, composed voice saying, "I'm good" in a tone that meant the opposite. He'd lain awake in the parsonage until past midnight, turning that phrase over, listening to it from every angle the way you listen to a sound you can't quite identify in a quiet house.

Rebecca appeared in the doorway. She wore a cream-colored sweater over dark jeans, her blonde hair pulled back in a low pony-tail. A leather tote hung from her shoulder. She'd worked a full day at the salon and still managed to arrive looking sharp and prepared.

"Am I late?" she said.

"Right on time." Warren stood and gestured to the empty chair beside Conner. "Come on in. We were just getting warmed up."

Rebecca set her tote beside the chair and sat down. She pulled a small notebook from the bag, opened it to a page marked with a sticky tab, and balanced it on her knee. A faint scent reached him as she settled, something clean and warm that he couldn't name but that his memory recognized instantly.

"All right," Warren eased back into his seat. "Conner, walk Rebecca through what you've been thinking. Rebecca, I want your honest feedback."

Conner turned slightly toward her. She looked at him with friendly, professional attention, the same warm courtesy he'd felt at the diner. The same thin boundary sitting just behind it. Up close, in the lamplight of Warren's office, the boundary was easier to see. Her posture was open, but precise. Her smile reached her eyes and stopped exactly where she wanted it to.

"First," he said, "I want you to know I've looked at the atten-dance records you put together. They're thorough, and they tell me you've built something really amazing here. I've got no interest in tearing it down."

"Thank you," she said. "I appreciate hearing that."

"I mean it. These kids know you, and I'm sure their families trust you. What I'd like to do is build on this foundation that's currently in place. Add some structure to the teaching side and open up a few new opportunities."

"I'm listening," Rebecca said.

"First, I want to take over the Wednesday night teaching and make it consistent. From what Warren's described, the devotional portion has been rotating between different volunteers each week."

Rebecca glanced at Warren and then back at Conner. "The inconsistency has been a problem," she said. "We've had different people leading each week, and the quality varies. Some of them connect with the kids and make it meaningful. Some of them..." she trailed off.

"Read straight from a study guide without looking up," Warren said.

"I was going to be more diplomatic about it," Rebecca said with a grin that changed her entire face. Her guardedness had cracked open just enough to show something brighter underneath. Her grin reminded him so sharply of the girl who used to laugh at his jokes that he had to look down at his notebook before his face gave him away.

Warren chuckled. "Diplomacy is your department. I'm just stating facts."

"So I'd lead the teaching every Wednesday," Conner continued. "Build a consistent curriculum that actually connects with what these kids are dealing with. Not watered-down Sunday school material. Real conversations about identity and belonging. Faith that makes sense on any given day for these kids, not just inside the walls of this church."

"That would be a significant improvement," Rebecca said. She wrote something in her notebook. "What else?"

"I want to develop a mentorship program. I'm calling it Faith Foundations, but the name isn't set in stone." He opened his notebook and turned to a page of handwritten notes. "The idea is pairing adult volunteers with individual youths for ongoing, one-on-one support. Not formal counseling, just a consistent adult who shows up and builds a real relationship over time. Many kids don't usually have that outside their families. Some don't have it inside their families either."

Rebecca's pen stopped moving. She looked up from her notebook, and her expression softened into genuine interest. "How would the matching work?"

"That's where I'd need your help. You know these kids. You know the volunteer pool. I'd want your input on every pairing."

"I'd want to be involved," she said. "Some of these youths are in sensitive situations. You can't just pair them at random."

"Agreed. That's exactly why I wouldn't do it without you."

Something passed across her face when he said that. A flicker of something unguarded that arrived and left in the same breath. She looked back down at her notebook and wrote a note.

Warren leaned forward. "What kind of time commitment are we talking about for the volunteers? Because I'll tell you right now, the folks who volunteer at this church are already spread thin. Most of them work full time and serve in two or three ministries on top of raising families. If this feels like one more obligation, you'll lose them before you start."

"Once a month for a face-to-face, low-key meeting of some type, I'm envisioning that could take place during an activity or an outing," Conner said. "Maybe a check-in text or call during the week if it's needed. That's it. The point isn't building another program with meetings and sign-up sheets. The point is making sure every kid in this youth group has one adult who knows their name and pays attention."

Warren nodded. "I like that. Keep it simple. Keep talking."

"Last one, and this is the one I'm most excited about. I want to add regular monthly activities. Hikes, service projects. Maybe a camping trip in the spring." Conner sat back in his chair. "I spent six years in Richmond working with teenagers, and I learned something pretty quickly. Kids will sit in a circle and give you polite answers for an hour. But take them outside, put them on a trail, or give them something to do with their hands, and they'll tell you what's actually going on in their lives that may be bothering them, or they'll just ask honest questions about things they don't understand. The best conversations I ever had with various youths happened when we were outside the formal youth group meetings."

"Budget," Warren said.

"Minimal for the hiking and service projects. We'd need transportation and maybe some gear, but I can fundraise for that. The camping trip would take more planning, and I don't want to rush it. I'd rather get the weekly format solid first and build trust with the kids before I ask their parents to let me take them into the mountains overnight."

A smile crossed Rebecca's face. "You'd be surprised. Some of these parents would pay you to take their teenagers into the mountains for a weekend."

Conner grinned. "I'll keep that in mind when I'm writing the fundraising pitch."

Warren's laugh filled the small office, and for a moment the three of them sat in the warmth of it. The kind of easy humor that happens when people are doing work they care about. Conner let himself enjoy it. He'd missed this. Richmond had been good work, but it hadn't felt like home. Six years of building something meaningful in a city that never quite fit, and now he was sitting in a small-town pastor's office with a radiator clicking in the corner and a woman beside him whose laugh he would have recognized in a room full of strangers.

"Can I ask you something?" Rebecca said.

"Of course."

"The mentorship program. Faith Foundations. How soon are you thinking?"

"I'd like to start matching volunteers by mid-February. Then maybe by the end of February, have the mentors come to a youth group meeting and get that concept rolling."

Rebecca shook her head. "That's too fast."

Conner paused.

"These families need time to get to know you first." Her voice carried the steady certainty of someone stating a fact she'd earned the right to state. "You've been here less than a week. Some of the parents might remember you from when you were younger, but they don't know you now. They don't know how you lead or what your judgment looks like under pressure." She held his gaze. "If you ask them to sign their teenager up for a one-on-one mentorship program before they've watched you work, some of them will say yes out of politeness. Then they'll pull their kids out quietly when it doesn't feel right. Some will even say things out of earshot and compare notes with other parents, and I'm sure you remember how small towns work: gossip, fabricated stories, and tiny things becoming bigger than they need to be. You need to build trust first."

Warren sat with his arms folded, watching them both. He'd been in pastoral ministry long enough to know when a conversation was doing its own work, and he stayed out of the way.

Conner turned her words over. She was right. He knew it before she finished the sentence. He'd been thinking about Faith Foundations through the lens of Richmond, where he'd had six years of trust banked with the congregation.

"What timeline would you suggest?" he said.

"Maybe lead the youth group for a couple of months and let everyone learn who you are now and get used to you. Show up every Wednesday. Be consistent. Let the parents watch you with their kids before you ask for something deeper." She tapped her pen against the edge of her notebook. "By early April, they'll know who you are, and you will know which of these kids really need this the most. Then you roll out Faith Foundations with real buy-in instead of polite smiles."

"She's right," Warren said.

"She is," Conner said. He looked at Rebecca. "That's undoubtedly the kind of input I need. Thank you."

She accepted the compliment with a quick nod and looked down at her notebook, already moving past it.

"There's one more thing I should mention," Rebecca said. She turned a page in her notebook. "One youth in the group concerns me." She looked up. "Hannah Caldwell, she's sixteen, and she used to come consistently to youth group meetings and to church. Over the last few months, she's pulled back a lot. When she does come, she barely talks. We're talking this girl was so full of life, and now it's like she's withdrawing from something. I hardly ever see her in church on Sundays anymore."

"What's going on at home?" Conner asked.

"Her parents divorced about a year ago. Her dad remarried, and a new baby is on the way. Her mom is working two jobs, and I suspect her time is stretched thin." Rebecca paused. "And her best friend moved to California in November, right before Thanksgiving. She's the one I noted in the attendance records."

"I saw that note."

"Hannah still shows up sometimes. She's polite; she gives you answers that sound fine if you're not listening carefully." Rebecca's voice dropped half a register, and she leaned forward slightly in her chair, her notebook forgotten on her knee. "But she's pulling away, and I don't know how much further she'll go before she stops coming at all. I just feel as if something is going on in her life that is really troubling her."

Conner focused on what she had just said. She wasn't describing a name on a list. She knew this girl. The specifics of her family, the friend who'd moved, the way Hannah hid behind answers that sounded fine until you listened harder. Rebecca had been tracking all of it on her own, carrying concern for a kid who was doing her best to disappear from the sounds of it.

"I'll think about this situation," he said. "This coming Wednesday night I'll pay close attention and see if I can get a read on her if she attends. I want to handle this carefully; youths at this age have so many things going on, and sometimes adults forget what it's like being a teenager."

"She's a good kid, Conner. I think she just needs someone special right now. Someone to be her friend. Something is going on with her, and I'm not really sure what to do or say."

"Let's just take it a small step at a time. Maybe you or I could be that friend she might need right now."

Warren looked at his watch. "We've covered a lot of ground tonight. I think we've got a strong starting point." He turned to Rebecca. "I'd like you to take some time with what Conner's proposed. Think it through. If there are things that need adjusting or concerns I'm missing, I trust your instincts."

"I'll think on it," Rebecca said. She closed her notebook and slipped it back into her tote.

"Conner, plan on sitting down with me on Monday morning, and I'll fill you in a little more on what I know about Hannah's situation. Think on leading your first devotional this Wednesday," Warren said. He stood and reached for his coat behind the door. "Give these kids a chance to meet you properly, become their friend, and show them you are in their corner."

"Looking forward to it." Conner stood and tucked his notebook under his arm.

Rebecca rose from her chair and slung her tote onto her shoulder. "Thank you for including me tonight, Pastor Davis."

"Wouldn't do it without you," Warren said.

They walked down the hallway, past the bulletin board near the entrance and the coat rack in the foyer. Conner pushed open the front door and held it as the cold swept in.

Warren buttoned his coat and lifted a hand. "Good night, you two. See you both in the morning."

"Good night, Pastor Davis," Rebecca said.

"Night, Warren," Conner said as Warren started walking toward his car at the far end of the parking lot.

"Have a nice evening, Conner," Rebecca said as she began walking away.

Conner fell into step beside her as they crossed the lot.

"You don't need to walk me to my car," she said.

He nodded toward his truck, two spaces from the only other vehicle left in the parking lot. "I'm parked right there. I'm guessing that's your car, since it's the only other option."

"Solid detective work."

He smiled at that. "What time do you normally get to the recreation hall on Wednesdays to set up?" he asked.

"Six-thirty," she said. "Youth group starts at seven. That gives me enough time to get the room set up and put out snacks."

"Would you be willing to come in a little earlier? Say six? We could go over your thoughts on what I proposed tonight. Start mapping out the next few Wednesdays if we have time. Or we could grab dinner beforehand and talk through---."

"Six at the recreation hall is fine."

"Six it is," Conner said.

They reached their vehicles. Rebecca pulled her keys from her coat pocket and unlocked her door. "Good night, Conner. I'm glad you've got a clear vision for this."

"Night, Rebecca. Thanks again for coming tonight. Your input made every part of this better."

She gave him a small nod, got into her car, and pulled her door shut. Her headlights came on, and she backed out with a careful turn. He watched her taillights until they disappeared.

Conner stood beside his truck. Above him, the church steeple rose white against a sky full of stars. Wind moved through the pines at the edge of the property, and the quiet that followed it was wide and complete. The cold had found every gap in his coat and settled there, but he wasn't ready to climb into the truck yet. The stillness felt like something he needed to stand inside for a minute.

Six at the recreation hall is fine.

He played back the timing, not the words. She answered before he finished his sentence, her voice pleasant, her redirect smooth. Anyone paying less attention would've called it a scheduling preference and moved on.

Conner was paying attention. He'd spent ten years carrying this woman in his memory. The Rebecca Hartwell in that memory would've said yes to dinner without a second thought. She'd have laughed and asked where they were going.

The woman who just drove away was every bit as warm and every bit as capable. But guarded in a way that hadn't existed in the past. The speed of her redirect told him something no amount of polite conversation could. Something in the years he'd missed had taught her to close a door so gently and quickly, before anyone got close enough to step through.

He didn't know what, and he didn't have the right to ask.

But he knew this much. He had sat across from her tonight and watched her push back on his timeline with the gentle authority of a woman who had learned what trust looked like from the inside of a community she had never left. She had been right about every word of it. And the fact that she had earned that authority by being present, by staying, by doing the slow, faithful work of showing up week after week for four years, landed on a part of him that he had been carrying since he was eighteen years old.

She had stayed. He had left.

That was the truth underneath every polite exchange and every professional smile. He had followed his calling out of this town and into a life that had shaped him into the man he was, and he didn't regret it. But the woman who had just driven away had built something here, brick by brick and day by day, while he was gone. And the distance between her trust and his good intentions was measured in years he couldn't get back.

He opened his truck door and climbed in. The engine turned over, and cold air pushed through the vents. He sat while the cab warmed up, staring through his windshield at the church he'd driven four hundred miles to serve.

Wednesday at six. The recreation hall. Her terms and her timetable.

Every inch of trust between them was going to cost him something. And she was worth every single inch.

He put the truck in gear and pulled onto the dark two-lane road toward home.

Chapter 3

S unday morning light fell through the stained-glass windows of Serenity Crossing Community Church and laid colored patterns across the wooden pews. The sanctuary was nearly full. Families filled the rows in the comfortable, unhurried way of a congregation that had been gathering in this room for years. The organ played the prelude, low and familiar.

Rebecca sat in the fourth-row pew with her hymnal on her lap and her hands folded over it.

The Hartwell family occupied this pew every Sunday and had for as long as she could remember. Her father sat to her left, his suit jacket buttoned, his hands resting on his knees with the patient stillness of a man who arrived early to everything and never complained about waiting. Her mother sat beside him, her Bible open on her lap, her reading glasses perched low on her nose. Her brother Mike was on Rebecca's right, with his daughter Lizzie tucked between them, her patent leather shoes swinging six inches above the floor, her small hands busy folding and refolding the church bulletin into a triangle. The rest of the Hartwell siblings filled the end of the pew and the row behind it.

Pastor Warren stepped to the pulpit. He set both hands on its edges and looked out over the congregation with unhurried calmness.

"Good morning, church family. Before we get started this morning, I have something I've been looking forward to sharing with all of you." He adjusted his glasses. "When I took over as senior pastor years ago, I made a commitment to this congregation that I would always have an assistant pastor serve alongside me. We, as a church family, were blessed to have had Pastor Andrews serving alongside me for many years. His retirement had me seeking someone new to fill the role of assistant pastor that his departure left. I hoped for someone who could also lead our youth ministry and grow with this church into whatever the Lord has next for us. Well, I found that person. And many of you already know him because he grew up right here in Serenity Crossing."

Conner, who had been sitting behind him in a pew, rose and stepped forward to stand beside Pastor Warren.

Rebecca sat motionless in the fourth row.

"Conner Delaney has accepted the position of assistant pastor here at Serenity Crossing Community Church," Warren said. "He's coming to us from six years of ministry in Richmond, Virginia, where he served as youth pastor and then assistant pastor at one of the largest congregations in the city. He grew up in this town and in this church, and I want you all to know that I didn't make this decision lightly." Warren looked at Conner. "I prayed about it for a long time. And when the Lord made it clear, He made it very clear."

A murmur of approval moved through the congregation. Heads nodded. Someone behind Rebecca said, "Amen," in the soft, affirming way that small churches say it.

"Thank you, Pastor Warren. And thank you all for welcoming me home." Conner said. "As Pastor Warren said, I grew up in this church. My faith took root in this building, in this community, and I carry that with me everywhere I go. Being back here is an honor I don't take lightly." He paused and looked out over the congregation with an openness. "I'm here to serve alongside Pastor Warren and alongside all of you as well, and I'm grateful to be home."

The congregation responded with applause that was warm and genuine. Rebecca watched faces around the room soften toward him. The Fieldings in the second row. The Morrisons to her far left. Mrs. Patterson, who had taught Sunday school for the past thirty years, pressed her hands together with visible delight. Serenity Crossing was receiving him the way a small town receives one of its own who left and came back changed for the better. With pride and a kind of communal ownership that said, 'We raised him. We knew he'd turn out right.'

Warren invited Conner to read the morning Scripture, and Conner opened the Bible he'd carried with him to the pulpit.

"Ecclesiastes, chapter three," he said. "Verses one through eight."

Rebecca knew the passage before he read the first word. To everything there is a season. She'd read it a hundred times. She'd leaned on it during the years when the seasons of her life felt locked in a winter that wouldn't break.

Conner read without rushing. His voice moved through the familiar words with a reverence that wasn't performed. He read as if the passage mattered to him personally, as if he'd spent time with it recently and found something in it that he needed. When he reached the line about a time to embrace and a time to refrain from embracing, his voice didn't change. But his attention lifted from the page for half a second, and in the peripheral edge of Rebecca's awareness, she registered the direction of his glance.

Warren took the pulpit for the sermon. Conner moved to the pew he had originally been sitting on, where he sat with his Bible on his knee and his attention on Warren. He didn't fidget. He didn't scan the room. He listened to his senior pastor preach with the focused stillness of a man who respected the person he was learning from. The quality of that stillness said more about the man he'd become than anything he could have spoken from the pulpit.

Fifteen minutes into Warren's sermon, Bill Hartwell reached over and took Rebecca's hand. His fingers curled around hers with a gentleness that belonged to a man whose hands gripped tools and lumber six days a week and spent the seventh holding the people he loved. He kept his attention on the pulpit and said nothing.

Rebecca didn't look at him. She sat with her father's hand around hers, and the sting climbed into her eyes before she could catch it. He'd watched her during Conner's introduction. He'd watched her during the Scripture reading. And now, halfway through a sermon about God's faithfulness in seasons of uncertainty, he was holding her hand in the same pew where he'd held her mother's hand every Sunday of Rebecca's life. The gesture carried everything his silence held.

I see it, sweetheart; you're troubled and hurting. I'm right here.

She blinked twice, and the sting receded. She kept her face still and angled toward the pulpit and let her father hold her hand.

Lizzie leaned into Rebecca's side and rested her small head against Rebecca's arm. The child's warmth grounded her, pulling her back from the current that had been building since Conner had returned into her life. Rebecca freed her other hand and smoothed Lizzie's fine hair with absent, gentle fingers. Lizzie settled deeper against her, content to be close.

Warren finished his sermon, and the congregation stood for the closing hymn. Bill released Rebecca's hand and picked up his hymnal, and the absence of his grip left a cool spot on her palm that she closed her fingers around.

Rebecca's voice found the melody and held it, because singing in church was something she could do even when her mind was somewhere else. The organ carried the final verse to its close. Warren offered the benediction, his voice low and full of the particular blessing that comes from a man who has prayed over the same congregation for three decades.

"Go in peace," Warren said. "And carry His love with you into the week."

Pews creaked as people rose. Conversations began in a low, gathering hum of a congregation releasing itself from worship into fellowship. Bibles were closed. Children who had been patient for an hour found their voices.

Rebecca stood and smoothed the front of her skirt. She reached for her coat and put it on.

"Aunt Rebecca, can we go get a cookie?" Lizzie was on her feet, her bulletin triangle abandoned on the pew.

"In a minute, sweet girl. Let's wait for your daddy."

The Hartwell family began filtering out of the pew in the slow, sociable way families exit churches in small towns. Bill shook hands with the man in the row behind them. Olivia stopped to speak with a woman near the aisle for a few minutes. Eventually, Rebecca fell into the current of bodies filling the center aisle alongside her family, all of them headed toward the double doors at the rear of the church.

Warren and Conner stood at the doors, greeting the congregation as they filed out. Warren had his hand on the shoulder of a man Rebecca recognized from the building committee. Conner stood beside him, shaking hands with each person who passed. He looked like a natural here in the church, as if he'd always been here and had never left. He met each handshake with his full attention. She watched as Mrs. Patterson held both of his hands in hers and said something that made him laugh.

The line moved forward, and Bill reached them first. Warren clasped his hand. "Good to see you, Bill."

"Good sermon, Pastor." Bill nodded to Conner. "Welcome home, son. Glad to have you."

"Thank you, Mr. Hartwell. It's good to be back."

Mike shifted Lizzie to his other hip and shook Conner's hand. Lizzie studied Conner with the frank appraisal of a six-year-old and said, "Why are you here?"

"I'm the assistant pastor. Which means Pastor Warren is in charge, and I do what he tells me," Conner said with a smile.

"That's like me and my teacher," Lizzie said.

Conner grinned. "Exactly like that."

Rebecca stepped forward. She extended her hand, and Conner took it. His grip was warm and brief; his fingers closing around hers.

"Good to have you, Conner," she said.

"Thank you, Rebecca."

She pulled her hand from his, smiled, and walked through the double doors into the January cold.

The frigid air hit her face, and she welcomed it as she walked with her family across the parking lot toward the recreation building. She tucked her chin and kept pace with her family, letting the wind carry the heated flush from her face.

The recreation building was already semi-full when they stepped inside. Warm air, conversation, and the smell of fresh coffee met them at the door. The long table near the kitchen held two large coffee urns and an assortment of baked goods the congregation had brought. Betty Morrison's lemon squares sat beside a plate of oatmeal cookies. Someone had brought banana bread, sliced thick and fanned across a cutting board. Trays of various cookies and baskets of muffins filled the rest of the table.

People stood in groups of three and four, coffee in hand, voices rising and falling in the easy rhythm of a community that did this every week. Children wove between the adults. A toddler sat on the floor near the far wall, happily dismantling a muffin. The Fieldings had claimed the table closest to the kitchen, and two of their grandchildren were already working on their second cookies.

Rebecca poured herself a cup of coffee and added cream from the small pitcher beside the sugar bowl. She took a sip. It was strong and delicious.

She scanned the room and found Jenna near the windows on the far side, standing alone with a cup in one hand and her phone in the other. Jenna looked up as Rebecca approached.

"Well, how did your date go?" Rebecca asked.

"I wore my hair down," Jenna said.

"And?"

"And he told me I looked beautiful."

Rebecca smiled. "Tell me everything."

Jenna took a sip of her coffee. "He picked me up at seven. He opened my car door. He drove to Russo's without using his GPS because he'd already looked up directions beforehand." She paused for emphasis. "Beforehand, Rebecca."

"I heard you."

"The restaurant was packed, but he'd made a reservation, and we were seated without waiting. We split the bruschetta, and I had the mushroom ravioli. He had the chicken parmesan, and he didn't look at his phone once during the entire dinner. Not once."

"What did you talk about?"

"Everything. His family in Chattanooga, why he moved here, and what he's looking for." Jenna ran her thumb along the rim of her cup. "He asked me questions, Rebecca. Real ones. About the salon, about growing up here, about what I liked about living in Nashville, and about what made me come home. He listened to me, Rebecca... actually listened and responded. He remembered things I'd told him during his haircut and brought them back up."

"So he's the type that pays attention."

"It seems like he is." Jenna's mouth curved. "He walked me to my door at the end of the night. He didn't try to kiss me. He said he'd had a great time and asked if he could take me out again next weekend."

"What did you say?"

"I said yes before he finished the sentence."

Rebecca laughed, and for a few seconds the morning released its grip. Standing there with Jenna, listening to her describe a man who made reservations, opened car doors, wasn't addicted to his phone and asked real questions, she could almost forget the last hour. Almost forget the warmth of Conner's hand around hers at the church door, the two seconds that were still sitting in her fingers like a burning coal she couldn't set down.

"I'm happy for you, Jen."

"Thanks. I'm happy for me too." Jenna set her cup on the window ledge and looked at Rebecca. "How are you doing?"

"I'm fine."

"Rebecca."

"I'm fine, Jenna. It's a little strange having him here, but I'm adjusting. I'll get used to it... just give me a few days, or maybe a few months, more like it."

Rebecca looked down at her coffee and turned the cup slowly in her hands.

"This is hard," she said. Her voice dropped, and the brightness left it. "Having him here. Reading scripture, shaking hands with my father. I wasn't ready for how hard it would be."

Jenna unfolded her arms. "Nobody expected you to be ready... could a person ever be ready for something like this? He meant something to you at one time, Rebecca, and he still does."

"But I should be ready. It's been ten years. I shouldn't be feeling all torn up and confused like I am."

"That's not how it works, and you know it."

Rebecca took a sip of her coffee. She didn't have an answer for that, because Jenna was right, and they both knew it.

The recreation hall doors opened, and a gust of cold air swept through the room. Warren walked in first, unbuttoning his coat, followed by Conner. The hum of conversation shifted as people turned toward them. Warren moved into the room with Conner following, and within thirty seconds people began gravitating toward him. Doug Fielding crossed the room to shake his hand. Mrs. Morrison intercepted him near the coffee table. Someone called his name from across the hall.

Rebecca watched as he moved through the room without rushing, giving each person his full attention before turning to the next. He crouched down to talk to one of the Fielding grandchildren, his elbows on his knees, his head tilted to listen. The child said something, and Conner laughed, and the sound crossed the room and found her.

She looked away and took another sip of coffee.

He was working his way across the room. Not toward her specifically, but the hall wasn't large, and the distance between them was shrinking with every conversation he finished. In another five minutes he'd reach this side of the room, and she'd be standing here with Jenna and nowhere to redirect.

"I think I'm going to head out," Rebecca said.

Jenna looked at her. "You sure?"

"I'm sure. I'm tired, and I've got a full day of clients tomorrow. I just want to go home and rest. I really need to get out of this room now before I do or say something I regret."

"Do you want me to come over? I could bring lunch."

"No, I'm fine. Really."

Jenna studied her for a second. She didn't argue. She didn't push. She reached out and squeezed Rebecca's arm.

"Call me if you need me," Jenna said.

"I will."

Rebecca found her mother near the kitchen and told her that she was heading home. Olivia Hartwell looked at her with concern, hugged her, and kissed her cheek.

Rebecca waved to her dad, who lifted a hand from across the room without interrupting his conversation.

She didn't look for Conner. She kept her path straight and her pace easy, and she pushed through the recreation hall doors into the cold.

Rebecca walked to her car, unlocked the door, and got in. She pulled her door shut and sat in the cold silence of the cab.

Her hands were shaking as she gripped the steering wheel. She took a few deep breaths, and once she stopped shaking, she turned her key in the ignition and let the heat build while she sat staring through her windshield at the white steeple against the brilliant blue sky.

Wednesday. Six o'clock. The recreation building.

Just her and Conner in the same room, planning youth group, no congregation between them, no pew, and no family to anchor her. Three days from now she would go over youth group information and pretend that his return hadn't cracked something open in her that she'd spent years sealing shut.

She put the car in reverse, backed out of her space, and pulled onto the two-lane road toward Main Street. The church disappeared behind her in the rearview mirror, but the vision of him fitting so easily back into her world followed her all the way home.

Chapter 4

"You're having seconds whether or not you want them," Loretta Delaney said, and she was already lifting the lid off the Dutch oven before Conner could answer. Steam curled from the pot and carried the rich, savory scent of chicken and dumplings across the kitchen table. She spooned a generous portion into his bowl, the thick broth pooling around chunks of tender chicken and pillowy dumplings.

The Delaney kitchen hadn't changed much in the ten years Conner had been away. White cabinets with brass knobs lined two walls. A ceramic rooster stood on the counter beside the stove, one of a pair his parents had bought in Nashville before he was born. Its twin lived on the windowsill above the sink, standing guard over the herb pots Loretta kept there year-round. A wooden cross hung above the doorway into the living room.

Charles Delaney sat at the head of the table with his plate nearly clean and a glass of sweet tea half gone. Silver-haired and clean-shaven, he wore a flannel shirt tonight, untucked. On school days he wore pressed shirts and ties. He'd been the principal at the local high school for the past twenty years.

"Warren's sermon was strong this morning. He's been preaching on faithfulness all month, and it's been a good study," Charles said.

Conner broke a biscuit in half and spread butter across its warm center. His mother's biscuits were golden and flaky, the kind that practically melted in your mouth. "He doesn't waste a word. I've been in ministry long enough to know that's rare. Most preachers take twenty minutes to say what Warren says in twelve."

"Your father gives his morning announcements at the high school the same way," Loretta said. "Two minutes, tops. The students call him the Bullet."

Charles lifted one shoulder. "If you can't get to the point and say what you need to say in just a few minutes, you haven't thought about it enough."

Conner grinned. That line had followed him through childhood. Charles Delaney didn't lecture, didn't repeat himself, and didn't raise his voice. He stated things once, clearly, and expected them to land just the way they needed to. It had made him an effective principal. It had also made him the kind of father whose approval carried real gravity because he didn't hand it out for free.

"The congregation was really welcoming this morning," Conner said. He took a bite of the biscuit, and the butter dissolved on his tongue. "Mrs. Patterson grabbed both my hands after the service and told me she remembered when I asked if Noah brought mosquitoes on the ark."

Loretta laughed. "You did ask that. Gosh, that brings back memories... you must have been seven or eight at the time."

"I was genuinely concerned about it."

"You told her God should've left the mosquitoes behind."

"I stand by that."

Charles's mouth twitched at the corner. "Can't say I disagree, son. The world would be a better place without mosquitoes."

Conner laughed. "Doug Fielding came up to me after service this morning. He told me he's glad Warren hired a young pastor. He thinks the church and youth group could use fresh energy."

"Doug's not wrong," Charles said. "I think our church will benefit from having you as the assistant pastor, and the kids need someone who remembers what it's like to be their age. Warren's a fine pastor, but he's fifty-eight, and the last time he related to a teenager on their level was when Reagan was president."

"Charles," Loretta said.

"It's a compliment to Warren. He knows his limitations. That's why he hired the boy."

Conner shook his head and took another bite of chicken and dumplings. The boy. He was twenty-eight years old with a degree and six years of ministry experience, and his father still called him the boy. He didn't mind. Coming from Charles, it carried a tenderness his father would never attach to any other word.

Loretta reached for the dish of green bean casserole and served herself a small second helping. She'd made it with green beans from last summer's garden, canned by her own hand, topped with crispy fried onions. Everything on this table had a history. The Dutch oven had been a wedding gift. The butter dish had belonged to Loretta's mother. Even the salt and pepper shakers, a mismatched pair of ceramic lighthouses, had a story Conner had heard so many times he could recite it.

"Why didn't Miles and Adam come for dinner?" Conner asked.

"Your brothers have had a busy weekend between all their kids' activities and commitments. Miles called this afternoon and said that he and Amber were going to spend a quiet evening at home, order a pizza, and do nothing but relax. Their kids keep them running nonstop."

"What about Adam and Jenny?"

"Jenny's mother is visiting from Nashville, so they took her out for dinner." Loretta glanced at him. "I haven't had you to myself at this table in a very long time, so it's all good. I'll try to plan a family dinner soon."

"You've got me now, Mom," Conner said.

"I do." She smiled, and the warmth in it reached all the way to her kind eyes. Loretta had light-brown hair with soft highlights, and she wore a burgundy sweater tonight with small gold earrings.

"So tell me," she said. "How's the house? Are you getting settled in okay?"

"Getting there. I unpacked the last of the kitchen boxes yesterday. The living room's still a work in progress."

"Do you need anything? Towels, dishes?"

"Mom, I'm twenty-eight."

"And I'm your mother, which means I'll ask if you need anything until I'm ninety."

Charles pushed his plate forward an inch and leaned back. "Is the furnace working all right out there? That parsonage sat empty for a while."

"It runs fine. A little loud when it kicks on at night, but it heats the place. Warren had it serviced before I moved in."

"Good. Those old units can be stubborn sometimes." Charles folded his arms. "If you need anything looked at, just let me know."

"I appreciate that, Dad."

Loretta leaned forward and rested her forearms on the table, and looked at him. "I want to ask you something, Conner. And you don't have to answer it right now if you don't want to."

"Go ahead."

"What made you decide to come home?"

Conner set his spoon down and leaned back. "Plenty of things, and none of them happened all at once."

Loretta nodded and waited.

"I enjoyed living and working in Richmond. The church there was incredible; the people were great, and I learned more in six years than I thought possible. Everything on the surface of my life was fine." He picked up his glass of sweet tea and turned it in his hand. "But I hit a wall. Not with my work. I just reached a point where I started asking myself if fine was enough."

"Fine usually isn't," Charles said.

"No, sir. It isn't." Conner took a drink and set the glass down. "When Warren called and told me about the opening at church,

I didn't jump on it right away. I sat with it for a couple of weeks. I prayed about it. I talked to my senior pastor in Richmond and asked for his honest counsel."

"What did he say?" Loretta asked.

"He said that if I were even considering it, I should pay attention to that. He told me God doesn't usually plant restlessness in somebody without a reason." Conner paused. "And he was right. I'd been restless for months before that call came. I just didn't have a name for it yet."

Loretta's expression stayed open and steady. She was listening in the way she listened to the children in her classroom when they needed room to find their own words.

"My engagement to Lauren ending was part of it too," Conner said. "I won't pretend it wasn't. When that fell apart, it forced me to stop and really look at my life. Where I was and where I wanted to be."

Charles watched him with quiet attention, his arms still folded.

"Lauren didn't want the life I was offering," Conner said. "I knew that for a while before she said it out loud. When she ended our relationship, it saddened me. But I wasn't surprised. And that told me where my heart was."

"That sounds like a tough situation." Loretta said.

"It was, and it wasn't," he said. "She's a good woman, Mom. She just wasn't the right one. And staying in Richmond after that felt like standing in a room I'd already walked out of. Her ending our relationship was a beginning for me, really. A wake-up call, sort of. I started asking myself questions that I hadn't considered since college. What do I want out of life? Where do I want to be in a few years from now? Who do I want surrounding me while I live this life I've been given?"

Loretta reached across the table and covered his hand with hers. Her fingers were warm, and her grip was firm. She held on for a few seconds, then let go and picked up her tea.

"I missed you both," Conner said. He looked at Charles and then back at Loretta. "I missed my brothers and their families. I missed so many milestones in my nieces' and nephews' lives, and I regret that. I don't want to keep missing things. Phone calls aren't the same as being here."

"No, they're not," Charles said.

"So when Pastor Davis called, everything in my life just seemed to line up," Conner said. "The timing and the chance to come home and build something here. I prayed on it until I couldn't ignore the answer anymore. And here I am. Eating Mom's chicken and dumplings and getting called the boy by my father."

Charles almost smiled. "You'll always be the boy."

"I know, Dad."

"Well, I think God put you right where you need to be, and I'm glad He wants you here," Loretta said as she stood and began clearing plates. Conner pushed his chair back and reached for the serving dishes, but she waved him off. "Sit. You can help with the dishes after dessert."

"There's dessert?"

"Apple pie. I made it yesterday."

"You made apple pie and didn't lead with that information?"

"I wanted you to eat your dinner first." She carried the plates to the counter and set them beside the sink. "You're just like your father, and I know it. You would've skipped straight to pie if I'd told you I'd made your favorite."

"I would not have skipped dinner," Charles said. "I might have eaten faster, thought."

Conner laughed, and the sound filled the kitchen in a way that made something click into place. He'd missed this. Not just the food or the house, but the specific rhythm of his parents at their table. The way his mother orchestrated a meal and a conversation with equal attention. The way his father participated with economy and a dry warmth most people missed if they weren't paying attention.

Loretta cut three slices and brought them to the table on plates. The pie was golden brown with a lattice crust and a thin ribbon of cinnamon-sugar glaze across its top.

"This looks incredible," Conner said before he took a bite. The filling was warm and tart, balanced by cinnamon and a sweetness that wasn't overdone. His mother's crust crumbled under his fork. He closed his eyes for a second and let himself enjoy it.

"So, what are your plans for the youth program?" Charles asked. "Warren mentioned you've got some ideas."

"I do. What I want to build is a more structured program." Conner leaned forward. "I'm developing a mentorship initiative called Faith Foundations. The idea is to pair adult volunteers from the congregation with individual students for ongoing guidance.

Not tutoring, not counseling. Just consistent, reliable adults who show up for these kids on a regular basis."

"That's a good model," Charles said. "I've seen versions of it work in the school system. The kids who have consistency in their lives do better across the board."

"I also want to plan more group activities away from a normal, structured youth group meeting. Hikes, service projects, seasonal outings. Teenagers connect with each other better when they're doing things side by side instead of sitting in a circle of metal chairs."

"You were like that," Loretta said. "You never sat still in Sunday school. Your teachers used to tell me you answered every question correctly but answered them while wandering around the room."

"I retain information better when I'm moving."

"You retain information better when you're doing exactly what you want to do," Charles said.

Conner grinned. "Also true."

"How's it going to work with Rebecca?" Charles asked. "Warren told me the two of you will be running the youth program together."

"That's the million-dollar question, Dad. We're in kind of an odd situation with us having history, but I think it'll work out fine," Conner said. "She's coming in early Wednesday before youth group so we can sit down and go over the program some more. Figure out how we're going to work as a team."

"She's been running it on her own for a while," Loretta said. "She's really invested in those kids and has done so much with them over the past few years."

"She has," Conner met his mother's gaze. "I'm not wanting to come in and take over everything she has built. I can tell those kids mean a lot to her. She's built a good foundation. I'm coming in to lead the parts that need pastoral direction. The teaching, the programming. Rebecca's got the relationships and the institutional knowledge. We need each other for this to work."

Loretta nodded. "I just want you to be thoughtful about it. She's put a lot of herself into that ministry."

"I will be." He finished the last bite of his pie and set his fork on the empty plate. "Honestly though? It's a little strange. Being around her again after all this time. It isn't uncomfortable exactly, but it's different. We're different people now."

"Are you?" Charles asked.

Conner looked at his father. Charles watched him with the observant stillness he brought to everything. Not pressing. Just watching and waiting to see what his son would say when given room to say it.

"Yeah, Dad. We are. I'm not the eighteen-year-old kid who left this town, and she isn't the girl I basically left behind. She owns a business. She's a leader in the church. She's built a whole life here." He ran his thumb along the edge of his plate. "I respect that. And I think if we're going to work well together on this program, I need to let my respect for her lead instead of everything from the past."

"That sounds about right," Charles said.

Loretta picked up her tea and took a small sip while she watched her son speak.

Both of his parents knew that Conner and Rebecca had been in love once, and they knew how it had ended. They didn't know every detail, but they knew enough.

"She's been a little guarded with me so far, like she's protecting something," Conner said. "Which I understand. I showed up after ten years, and now I'm her partner on the youth program. That's a lot to adjust to."

"Give her time," Loretta said.

"I plan to."

"And give yourself time, too. You just got here, Conner; it's only been five days."

He smiled at that. Five days. It felt longer. The past week had been unpacking, meetings with Warren, preparing for this morning's service, and the particular disorientation of living in a town where everyone remembered the version of him that left. Serenity Crossing had a long memory, and it was welcoming him back into it one conversation at a time.

"I'm glad you're home, son," Loretta said.

Charles looked at Connor. "I'm glad, too. I've missed having you nearby."

"I've missed you both as well. I'm really in a good place in my life. I'm happy to be home; working in my home church feels right, and I'm looking forward to whatever God has planned for me."

Chapter 5

Conner had his laptop open on his desk and a legal pad beside it covered in notes when the idea finally clicked into place. He'd been circling the same question for an hour, scrolling through folders of sermon outlines and youth ministry curriculum he'd built during his six years in Richmond. Good material. Plenty of it. But none of it felt right for a first impression. He needed something that would land just right with a group of kids who didn't know him and had no reason to trust him yet.

He leaned back in his chair and looked at his legal pad. Three words were underlined twice near the top of the page. Chosen: an eight-week series. Below them, a rough sequence he'd sketched out over the past forty minutes. The arc started with a question he believed every teenager carried, whether they admitted it or not. Do I even matter? From there it moved through the noise of comparison, the cost of carrying labels other people put on you, and the slow work of understanding where worth actually comes from. The later weeks pressed deeper into what it means to feel overlooked and what it costs to let people see who you really are. It ended with a message he wanted to earn by the time he delivered it. You are not invisible.

He read through the sequence again. It was honest. It started where kids actually lived instead of where adults wished they lived. It built toward something real without rushing the spiritual framework into a space it hadn't earned yet. The faith was there, woven into the later weeks where it could arrive naturally rather than being imposed before the kids had any reason to receive it.

Wednesday, though, would be different. Wednesday was just the first meeting. He wanted to keep it simple. A chance for the students to size him up and for him to get a feel for the group's personality before he started teaching into it. If there was time at the end, he'd share something brief about who he was and why he was here. Enough to let them know he intended to show up consistently and that what they had to say mattered to him as much as anything he had to say to them.

He saved the file on his laptop and set his pen down. His office was quiet around him, a different kind of quiet than the hum of his office in Richmond. That church had been larger, the staff bigger. Somebody was always knocking on his open door with a question or a clipboard. Here, the hallway outside his door was empty. The church secretary didn't come in on Mondays, and Warren usually arrived closer to nine.

His office occupied a small room at the end of the hallway, two doors past Warren's. A single window behind his desk looked out onto the side yard of the church property. A row of bare oaks lined the edge of the parking area, their branches sharp and dark against the serene blue January sky. His desk was secondhand, solid oak, donated by a church member. It had a few scratches on its surface and a drawer that stuck if you pulled it too fast, but it was sturdy and it suited the room. Two bookshelves stood against the opposite wall, partially filled. His study Bible and a concordance occupied the top shelf beside a stack of commentaries he'd collected over the years. The lower shelves held his youth ministry binders from Richmond, labeled by year and series. A dog-eared copy of a leadership text his senior pastor had given him as a going-away gift leaned against the end of the row. A framed photograph of his family sat on the corner of the desk. Last Thanksgiving, taken in his parents' living room. Everyone was there except him. Amber had sent it to him the following week, and he'd kept it on his desk in Richmond as a reminder of what he was missing.

He still had a box in the corner that he hadn't unpacked. Books, mostly, and a couple of framed things he hadn't decided where to hang. The room was functional but still carried the temporary quality of a space waiting for its occupant to commit to it fully. He was getting there. A week wasn't long enough to make a room feel like it belonged to you, but every day it felt a little more like his.

He picked up his coffee mug from the desk and took a sip. Cold. He'd brewed it in the small kitchen down the hall over an hour ago and hadn't touched it since. He set it down and turned back to his legal pad. Beneath the "Chosen" outline, he'd written a short list of things he wanted to discuss with Warren this morning. The mentorship program timeline. Budget for youth activities. Wednesday night logistics. And at the bottom, a name circled once: Hannah Caldwell.

Rebecca had brought Hannah up during Saturday's meeting with a specificity that told him she'd been carrying this concern for a while. She hadn't presented it as a crisis or asked him to fix it. She'd laid it out plainly, the way someone does when they've been watching a situation develop and needed someone else to see it too. A sixteen-year-old girl was pulling away from every anchor in her life, and the adults around her were either too busy or too absent to notice. Rebecca had noticed.

What had caught him off guard since he'd been back wasn't Rebecca's competence or her professionalism. It was the depth of her investment in people. She tracked the kids in the youth group with an attention that went beyond attendance records and birthday reminders. She knew them. She carried them. And she did it on top of running a business and a life she'd built entirely on her own.

He wanted her input on the "Chosen" series. She'd see things in it he couldn't, because she knew these youths in ways he didn't yet. Their histories, the specific pressures they carried into that recreation hall on Wednesday nights. His curriculum was solid on paper. Her knowledge of the kids would make it land.

Footsteps in the hallway drew his attention to the open door. Warren appeared a moment later, carrying a white paper bag in one hand and two large to-go cups balanced in the other. He wore a navy sport coat over a button-down shirt with the collar open, and his wire-framed glasses sat slightly crooked on his nose.

"I come bearing gifts," Warren said. He set the cups on the edge of Conner's desk and held up the paper bag. "Apple fritters from Minnie's. Still warm."

"You didn't have to do that."

"I know I didn't have to. I wanted to." Warren pulled one of the two chairs across from the desk closer and settled into it. He opened the bag and set it between them on the desk. The smell of fried dough and cinnamon filled the small room. "Minnie asked about you this morning. She wanted to know if you've been eating enough."

Conner laughed and reached for one of the fritters. It was golden and warm, dusted with cinnamon sugar that stuck to his fingers when he picked it up. "I've been in town for a week. She's already monitoring my diet?"

"Minnie monitors everyone's diet. It's part of her civic duties." Warren picked up his coffee and took a slow sip. "She also told me she thinks it's wonderful that the church has a young pastor. Her exact words were, 'That boy needs to be fed properly and find himself a good wife.'"

"Naturally. Food and marriage, those are good priorities."

"Minnie has her priorities straight." Warren's grin settled into something quieter as he looked around the office. "How's the space treating you? Are you getting settled in here?"

"Getting there." Conner took a bite of the fritter. The pastry was light and sweet, and the cinnamon hit just right. Minnie's apple fritters were legendary in Serenity Crossing for good reason. "I've got my books up and my files organized. I still have a box in the corner I haven't gotten to."

"That box will sit there for six months. I had one in my office for two years before Mary finally unpacked it for me." Warren adjusted his glasses and nodded toward the laptop. "You look like you've been at it for a while this morning. What are you working on?"

Conner turned his legal pad so Warren could see it. "I've been putting a teaching series together for Wednesday nights. Not for this week. This Wednesday I just want to keep things loose. Let the kids meet me, get comfortable, and maybe share a short message at the end if the timing feels right. But I want to have something built for the weeks that follow."

Warren leaned forward and studied the legal pad. He read without rushing, his eyes moving down the page at a deliberate pace before responding.

"I'm calling it 'Chosen,'" Conner said. He set his fritter on a napkin and wiped his fingers. "Eight weeks. The arc starts with the question most teenagers are already asking themselves, but nobody's giving them permission to say out loud. Do I matter? And it builds from there. Identity, comparison, worth. Where those things actually come from instead of where the world tells them they come from. The faith component comes in gradually. I don't want to lead with theology and lose them before I've earned the right to speak into their lives."

Warren nodded slowly. He picked up his coffee and held it without drinking, his thumb resting on the rim of the lid. "That's a strong instinct. Starting where they are instead of where you want them to be."

"That's what I've learned works. In Richmond, every series I built that started with answers instead of questions fell flat. But the ones that opened with what the kids were already feeling? Those were the ones where I'd look up during a Wednesday night and realize nobody was checking their phones."

"Tell me about the back half."

Conner leaned forward. "Weeks five through eight go deeper. What it feels like to be overlooked. The difference between being chosen and what you expected being chosen to look like. And the last week ties it all back. You are not invisible. That's the landing point. By the time I deliver that message, I want these kids to have spent seven weeks peeling back the layers of why they believe nobody sees them, so when I tell them they are seen and known and chosen, it isn't just words. It's something they've walked toward."

Warren was quiet for a moment. He took a sip of his coffee and set it back on the desk. "You've done this before."

"Variations of it. I had a series in Richmond with a similar framework, but the content was different because the kids were different. This one I want to build specifically for this group. For this town. Which is part of why I want Rebecca's eyes on it before I finalize anything. She knows these young people. She'll know which weeks will land and which one's need adjusting."

"That's wise," Warren said. "Her perspective on these kids will save you from assumptions that look right on paper and miss the mark in the room."

Conner reached for his coffee and took a drink.

"So," Warren settled back in his chair and folded his hands loosely across his midsection. "Let's talk about Hannah Caldwell."

"She's been on my mind since Saturday."

"Mine too." Warren pulled a fritter from the bag and broke a piece off. He ate it slowly, and when he spoke again, his voice carried a careful, measured quality. "The Caldwells had been part of this church for a long time. Greg and Denise were married here. I officiated their wedding and baptized Hannah when she was an infant. They were consistent members for years. Good people. Active in the church."

"What happened?"

"What happens in a lot of marriages that look fine from the pew." Warren took another small bite and chewed it before continuing. "Cracks that nobody sees until the whole thing breaks open. I don't know the details, and I don't need to. What I know is that Greg and Denise separated over a year ago, and the divorce was finalized sometime last spring. Greg moved out, and Denise kept the apartment in the Town Center building with Hannah."

"Rebecca mentioned Hannah comes alone now."

"She does. For a while after the separation, Denise brought Hannah to church most Sundays. Then Denise started missing weeks. Then she stopped coming altogether." Warren paused and looked at the fritter in his hand as if he'd forgotten he was holding it. "From what I understand, Denise has been working longer hours and spending her free time with a new group of friends. I've heard she's dating somebody. I don't know the man, and I'm not going to speculate about any of that. What I can tell you is what I see, and what I see is a sixteen-year-old girl who walks to church by herself on Sunday mornings and sits in a pew where her family used to sit."

That image settled into the room like something physical. Conner didn't respond right away. He let it sit.

"Greg remarried," Warren said. "A woman from Knoxville, I believe. I've heard there's a baby on the way, or possibly already here. I don't know how much time he's spending with Hannah. I'd guess not enough, based on what I'm seeing, but I want to be careful about drawing conclusions I can't support."

"That's a lot of loss for a sixteen-year-old in a short window."

"It is. And there's more." Warren set his fritter on a napkin and brushed the sugar from his fingers. "Do you remember the Petersons? Dale and Karen?"

Conner searched his memory. The name was vaguely familiar but not specific enough to place.

"They were members here," Warren said. "Had a daughter around Hannah's age. The two girls were close. Best friends, from what I could tell. You'd see them sitting next to each other in youth group every Wednesday, whispering and giggling the way teenage girls do."

"What happened to them?"

"Dale got a job offer. A big one. Something in the tech industry out in California. It came fast, and they moved fast. They were gone before Thanksgiving." Warren shook his head slowly. "I barely had time to shake Dale's hand and wish them well before the moving truck was in the driveway. I don't think anyone realized how much that move would affect Hannah. But looking back, her attendance started dropping off right around that time. She lost her closest friend with almost no warning, right on top of everything else."

Conner picked up his pen and turned it between his fingers. The picture Warren was painting grew clearer with each detail, and it tightened something in his chest. Not a crisis in the way that triggers alarms and emergency meetings. Something quieter. A girl whose world had come apart in pieces over the course of a year, each loss compounding the last, pressing her into a silence that most people would mistake for moodiness or just being a teenager.

"Does she have anyone?" Conner asked.

"Her grandparents. Denise's parents. Good folks. The Turners, Howard and Glenda. They used to live here in Serenity Crossing and attended this church for years. They moved out to Pigeon Forge about six years ago." Warren picked up his coffee again. "I'd imagine they're still close with Hannah. They were devoted grandparents, the kind who showed up to every school play and every church program. If anyone is keeping that girl tethered right now, my guess would be them."

"Has anyone from the church reached out to Denise?"

"I've called several times and left messages. She returned the first call and was polite but brief. Thanked me for checking in, said they were doing fine, said Hannah was adjusting." Warren removed his glasses and cleaned them with the edge of his shirt, a habit Conner had watched him do a thousand times growing up. "I don't want to push Denise. She's an adult making her own choices, and I have to respect that, even when I don't agree with all of them. My concern is Hannah. That girl didn't choose any of this, and she's the one sitting with the consequences."

"I agree."

"Rebecca's the one person who is watching the situation closely. She flagged it before anyone else did, which doesn't surprise me at all." Warren put his glasses back on. "My suggestion is that you and Rebecca work on this as a team. Don't single Hannah out. Don't make her feel like a project. Just make sure she knows that when she walks into that room on Wednesday night, somebody sees her and somebody cares. That's the starting point. Everything else builds from there."

"I agree, and that's exactly how I'd approach it," Conner said. "The 'Chosen' series is designed to speak to kids like Hannah without putting a spotlight on them. If I do my job right, she'll hear herself in the material and know she's not alone in what she's carrying. But I won't push. I'll let the relationship develop at her pace."

Warren studied him for a moment, then nodded once. "Good."

They sat for a moment. Warren finished his fritter and wiped his hands on the napkin, then folded it neatly and set it aside. Conner took another sip of coffee and glanced at his laptop screen, the "Chosen" outline still open in the document window.

"Can I ask you something?" Warren said.

"Of course."

Warren crossed one leg over the other and settled deeper into his chair. His posture was relaxed, but something in his expression had shifted. "How are things going with you and Rebecca? Working together, I mean."

"It's going well," Conner said. "She's sharp and thorough. She cares about the program and the kids, and she's not afraid to push back on my ideas when she thinks I'm off base. I respect that."

"That's the professional answer," Warren said. His tone was gentle but direct. "I'm asking you as a friend."

Conner set his coffee down and leaned back. Through the window behind his desk, a cardinal landed on one of the bare oak branches and sat there, a bright red point against the blue sky. He watched it for a second before he spoke.

"It's been different from what I expected," he said. "Honestly, I'm not sure what I expected. I knew we'd be working closely. I knew it would be complicated, given our history. But it's not uncomfortable exactly. It's something else. Something I don't have a good word for yet."

Warren waited.

"I've been gone for ten years, Warren. And in that time, she built a life here. The salon, the youth ministry, and she has a place in this town. She didn't wait around. She got to work, and I respect that more than I can tell you." Conner picked up his pen again and turned it slowly between his fingers. "But being around her again, working beside her, it's brought up things I thought I'd put away a long time ago."

"What kind of things?"

"Regret, mostly. I left this town at eighteen, and I didn't look back the way I should have. When I'd come home for holidays or visits, I'd see her around town and we'd exchange a few words, and that was it. I never once sat down and had a real conversation with her. Never reached out. I let a decade go by and told myself that was just how things were, but the truth is I was too caught up in my own life to make the effort. She deserved better than that."

Warren nodded, a small motion that carried no judgment. "You were young when you left. You were building a life and a career. That takes a certain kind of tunnel vision, and there's no sin in it."

"Maybe not. But there's a cost." Conner set his pen on the desk. "She's very guarded with me. Protective is a better word. Not cold or unfriendly, just careful. And I understand why. I showed up after ten years, and now I'm her partner on the thing she's poured herself into. That's a lot to hand over to someone who hasn't been here."

"It is."

"What I want is to rebuild our friendship. That's what I keep coming back to. We were friends before we were anything else, and I'd like to find my way back to that. I've missed her, Warren. Not in a nostalgic way. I've missed who she is. The way she thinks, the way she says exactly what she means without softening it for your comfort. I missed that specific person, and I didn't let myself feel how much until I was sitting across from her on Saturday night."

Warren reached for the last piece of his fritter, ate it, and took his time chewing. When he swallowed, he picked up his coffee and held it in both hands, resting it on his knee.

"I remember you two in high school," he said. "I remember seeing you in church sitting next to each other, and it was one of those things where anybody with eyes could see it. You were a good match. Whatever happened between you, and I'm not asking you to tell me, the foundation was real. That kind of thing doesn't just disappear because a calendar turns over."

Conner didn't say anything. He didn't need to.

"I'll tell you something I've learned in thirty years of pastoring and thirty-six years of marriage," Warren said. He set his coffee on the desk and leaned forward, resting his forearms on his knees. "People get confused about the difference between patience and honesty. They think being patient means holding back, waiting for the right moment, letting things develop in their own time. And there's wisdom in that. But patience without honesty eventually turns into something else. It turns into distance. It turns into two people being polite with each other while the thing that actually matters sits in the room and nobody names it... they dance around it."

Conner listened. His chest felt tight in a way that had nothing to do with the coffee or the cold air leaking through the window frame.

"I'm not telling you what to do," Warren said. "I'd never presume to tell a man how to handle his business or his own heart. But I will tell you this." He straightened and met Conner's eyes. "If you care about someone, the kindest thing you can do is be honest about it. Not on their timeline. Not on yours. On truth's timeline.

And the bravest version of patience isn't holding back. It's being willing to stay in the room after you've said the honest thing."

The words landed somewhere deep, in a place Conner hadn't opened to anyone since he'd come home. He hadn't shared it with his parents at the dinner table or admitted it to himself in the quiet of the parsonage at night.

"That's good counsel," Conner said.

"It's free counsel, which means it's worth exactly what you paid for it." Warren's grin returned, and he slapped his hands on his knees and stood. "I've taken up enough of your morning. You've got a good plan for the youth group and a good head on your shoulders. Trust your instincts. They brought you home for a reason."

Conner stood and extended his hand. Warren took it and held it for a second, his grip firm and warm.

"Thanks, Warren. For the fritters and the conversation."

"Anytime." Warren stepped toward the door and paused with one hand on the frame. "I mean that. My door's always open, and so is Minnie's. If you ever need to talk, you know where to find me. And if I'm not here at the church, or at home, check the diner. I'll be the one with the coffee and the apple fritter pretending I don't know everyone in the room is listening to my conversations."

Conner laughed, and Warren disappeared down the hallway. His footsteps faded, and a moment later the distant sound of the church's side door opening and closing left the building quiet again.

Conner sat back down. The paper bag from Minnie's was still on his desk, folded over and empty except for a few crumbs and a dusting of cinnamon sugar. Warren's coffee cup sat beside his own, both nearly empty. His legal pad was where he'd left it, the "Chosen" outline still visible in his compact handwriting, and his laptop screen had dimmed to its screensaver.

He reached over and tapped the trackpad. The document came back up. Eight weeks of lessons mapped out in a framework he trusted, aimed at teenagers he hadn't met yet, designed to tell them the thing they most needed to hear. You are not invisible. You were chosen before you knew what being chosen meant.

But his eyes drifted from the screen to the window. The cardinal was gone. The oak branches were bare and still.

If you care about someone, the kindest thing you can do is be honest about it.

He'd told Warren he wanted to rebuild the friendship. He'd said it plainly, and he'd meant it . But sitting here now, alone with what that conversation had uncovered, he could feel the distance between what he'd said and what was actually true. Friendship was the word he kept reaching for because it was safe. Because it asked nothing of Rebecca and risked nothing of himself. It let him stand in the room with her and pretend that being near her after ten years was something he could manage with professionalism and good intentions.

It wasn't enough. The word wasn't big enough for what he carried in his heart, and calling it friendship didn't make it smaller. It just made him less honest.

He wasn't ready to say it out loud, not to his parents and certainly not to Rebecca, who had every right to her careful distance and every reason to keep it. But he could stop pretending, at least to himself, that what he wanted from her was something as simple and uncomplicated as friendship.

Warren's counsel sat in his chest like a stone he couldn't swallow and couldn't set down. The bravest version of patience isn't holding back. It's being willing to stay in the room after you've said the honest thing.

He wasn't there yet. But for the first time since he'd come home, he understood that eventually, he would have to be.

Chapter 6

Rebecca had the appointment book open on the reception desk and a pen between her fingers when Jenna called out from across the salon asking if there were more boxes of foils.

"Bottom cabinet, left side," Rebecca said without looking up. She turned the page and scanned Tuesday's column. Mrs. Hyatt at eleven-fifteen for a cut and style. Denise Palmer at noon for a full color. After that, a thirty-minute gap she'd earmarked for inventory, and then two back-to-back color appointments that would carry her through to close. A full day and a good one, and she still had forty minutes before Mrs. Hyatt walked in.

The Fluff & Curl Beauty Salon was a whirl of activity. Three of her six stylists were working today, and each of their stations was occupied. Jenna had a color client in her chair, with foil sections layered through the woman's hair. She painted highlights with careful, quick strokes, treating each section with the kind of attention that made her clients come back. At the station nearest the front windows, Claire Dawson worked a round brush through her client's damp hair while the blow dryer filled that corner of the room with a low, steady hum. Beside Claire, Stacy Marsh had her client's hair pinned up in sections and was trimming the layers, talking about her son's basketball game from last weekend. Her client laughed at a story about a referee who'd tripped over the scorer's table.

The salon filled the first floor of the building Rebecca owned at 106 Main Street. Large windows ran across the front, looking out onto the sidewalk and the town square beyond. The white gazebo sat under a blue January sky, and a few bundled pedestrians crossed between the storefronts. Inside, the space was warm and bright, with pale pink walls and white trim. Several styling stations lined the right side of the room, each with a wide mirror and a padded chair that swiveled. Framed prints of vintage hair advertisements hung between the mirrors, and a small shelf at each station held its stylist's personal tools and products. On the left side, two manicure tables were positioned, and along the back wall, a row of shampoo sinks. The floors were a light wood laminate that Rebecca had picked out herself during the renovation, and they caught the January light from the windows and reflected it back into the room.

The reception desk anchored the space near the front door. Rebecca had found it at an estate sale in Gatlinburg and refinished it herself, sanding it down and painting it a creamy white that matched the trim. A small glass jar sat on its corner, filled with peppermints. The last of the Christmas candy. She'd been meaning to swap them out for conversation hearts now that February was close enough to justify it.

Rebecca closed the appointment book and set her pen beside it. She leaned her hip against the desk. Claire's blow dryer hummed across the room, and Stacy's client was still laughing, and the quiet tap of Jenna's brush handle against her foil tray kept a rhythm underneath it all. Six years of building this salon from a gutted storefront, and the Fluff & Curl now had a waiting list at times, a loyal client base, and a staff she enjoyed working with. Every detail in this room was a choice she'd made, from the color on the walls to the candy jar she refilled each season because small things mattered to her.

She picked up her coffee mug from the desk and took a sip. It had gone cold an hour ago, forgotten between her first appointment and the phone call with her product distributor. She set it back down and glanced toward the front windows.

The town square was quiet for a Tuesday morning. A woman, Rebecca didn't recognize, walked past carrying two shopping bags. Her brother Jim's truck was parked in front of his hardware store across the square; a cardboard sign in his window advertised a sale on snow shovels. January in Serenity Crossing moved at a pace that suited her, slow enough to notice things and steady enough to keep her busy.

The front door opened, and Conner walked in carrying two to-go cups of coffee.

He wore a navy coat over a gray sweater, and the cold had put color in his face. His sandy brown hair was slightly wind-pushed, and he had a folded piece of paper tucked under his arm.

"Hey," he said. "I hope I'm not interrupting your morning."

"Not at all," Rebecca said. "I'm between appointments."

He crossed to the reception desk and held out one of the to-go cups. "I stopped by the Daily Grind on my way over. I wasn't sure if you still took your coffee with just a bit of creamer, but I took a chance."

Rebecca looked at the cup in his hand. A paper cup with a lid and a cardboard sleeve. She reached for it, and her fingers closed around its warm sleeve.

"I do," she said.

"Good," he smiled. "I was fifty-fifty on whether you'd switched to black by now."

"Never." She took a sip. The coffee was fresh and hot, with just the right amount of cream. Ten years, and he remembered how she took her coffee. She set the cup on her desk and folded her arms loosely. "What brings you by this morning?"

"Two things," he said. He pulled the folded paper from under his arm and opened it on the desk between them. "I've been working on a flyer for the youth group, and I wanted to get your thoughts before I finalize it."

Rebecca leaned forward and looked down at the page. A simple, clean design on white paper. Youth Group at Serenity Crossing Community Church ran across the top in bold letters. Below that, the meeting time and day, followed by a few lines about what the youths could expect: games, food, and real conversations about faith and life. A line at the bottom read, Questions? Contact Pastor Conner Delaney or Rebecca Hartwell, with the church phone number beside both names.

"You put my name on it," she said.

"Of course I did. You're the youth coordinator," he said. "If a parent has questions about the program, you're the first person they're going to want to talk to, more than likely. You know these families. They trust you. I can add your personal number if you like, or I can field all calls that come in for you at church and forward you the messages."

She studied the flyer for a few more seconds. Her name printed next to his, right there in black and white, as though they were a team that had been working side by side for years instead of a few days. Their names on a piece of paper that would hang in shop windows across town.

"The layout is good," she said. She tapped the middle section with her fingertip. "But this line here, where it says 'real conversations about faith and life,' that's going to sound vague to a teenager. You might lose them right there."

"What would you say instead?"

"Be specific. Tell them what they're actually going to get. 'A place to ask hard questions, be yourself, and figure out what you believe.' Teenagers don't want to be talked at. They want to know somebody's listening."

Conner pulled a pen from his coat pocket and wrote her words in the margin of the flyer. His handwriting was compact and angled slightly to the right. He captured the whole sentence without pausing. "That's good," he said. "That's much better wording than what I had."

"Where are you planning to put these?"

"Everywhere I can. I want to ask business owners around town if they'd be willing to hang them in their windows." He looked at her. "I was also going to talk to my father about posting them around the high school. If we can get them on the bulletin boards where students will actually see them, that's worth more than twenty copies placed around town."

"Your dad would do that in a heartbeat," Rebecca said. "If he puts these up, the kids will read them."

"That's what I'm counting on." Conner set his pen down and leaned his forearm on the edge of the desk. He was standing close enough that she could see the fine texture of his gray sweater and the way his collar sat against his neck. "Would you hang one here? In the salon window?"

"I'll hang two. One in the front window and one on the bulletin board by the shampoo sinks. Many of our clients are parents of teenagers."

"Perfect," he said. "That means a lot."

Behind them, Claire turned off her blow dryer, and the salon's volume dropped by half. Stacy's scissors made small, rhythmic sounds as she trimmed her client's layers. Jenna was at her station, intent on her foil work, but Rebecca caught the angle of her head. Jenna was tracking every word of this conversation, and she'd have opinions about it later.

"You said two things," Rebecca said. "What's the second?"

"Wednesday prep. I've been going over the devotional I'm planning, and I wanted to run a couple of ideas by you." He took another drink of his coffee and set the cup on the desk. "I know we're meeting at six at the recreation hall, but I figured if I was already coming by for the flyer, I might as well ask now."

"Go ahead."

"I'm going with a theme I'm calling 'Chosen.' It's a program I used previously in Richmond, and it's strong and effective. My first lesson will be about belonging. Not in the abstract Sunday-school sense, but the real version. What it feels like to walk into a room and wonder if anybody actually wants you there. What it feels like to fake being fine because the truth is harder to say out loud." He paused. "I want to start with a question. 'What's one thing about you that nobody in this room knows?' Let them sit with that for a minute before I open it up."

Rebecca considered it. "The question is good, but don't open with it. Let them settle in first. If you hit them with a question like that the second you start talking, they'll freeze up and give you safe answers. Give your lesson for ten or fifteen minutes. Get them comfortable with your voice and the way you teach. Then, toward the end, when they've had time to relax, ask the question."

He nodded, his eyes on hers. "Go on."

"The timing matters most of all with teenagers," she said. "They'll tell you the truth, but only when they're ready, and you can't rush that."

"I'm learning that about this town too."

She looked at him. He was leaning against her reception desk with his coffee beside the peppermint jar and his flyer spread open between them, and he looked at ease here. The boy she'd known at eighteen had never been still enough to lean on anything. The man in her salon was content to be right where he was.

"Can I hang on to this?" she picked up the flyer. "I want to read through it again before you print the final copies. I'll have a few more suggestions."

"Sure." He straightened from the desk and picked up his coffee. "I'll have notes."

He grinned. "I don't doubt it."

The work between them was easy, and she knew it for what it was. This was the version of Conner and Rebecca who could talk about fliers and devotionals and Wednesday logistics without any of the history pressing up through the floor. In this register, they were good, natural, and quick with each other in a way that would have taken most partnerships months to develop. She could do this version. This version was manageable.

It was the other version that kept her up at night. The version where he said her name the way he'd said it at Minnie's and her whole careful world tilted sideways.

Conner glanced around the room again, slower this time. "You've built an incredible space here, Rebecca. It feels like you."

"Thanks, I'm proud of it."

"You should be."

"Are you settling in all right? You've been here, what, a week now?"

"Just over a week. The parsonage is almost unpacked. I've still got a few boxes in the living room that I keep walking around instead of opening."

"What's in them that you're avoiding?"

"Avoiding? I'm not sure if I'm avoiding the boxes; it's more like what do I do with what's inside? Books, mostly. And a few things from my office in Richmond that I haven't figured out where to put yet." He smiled. "My mom keeps offering to come over and organize everything, and I keep telling her I'll handle it myself."

"Loretta would have that house sorted in two hours, and you know it."

"In two hours, with labels on every shelf and fresh curtains in every window." His eyes crinkled at the corners. "She's already brought me new rugs for the kitchen and bathroom floors. Yesterday evening she brought over new kitchen towels that she felt I had to have."

Rebecca laughed. Conner's mom sat in her styling chair every six weeks, and Rebecca knew the woman's generosity firsthand. Loretta brought homemade banana bread to her hair appointments for everyone to enjoy. The thought of her showing up at the parsonage with new rugs and towels was so perfectly Loretta that it bypassed every defense Rebecca had in place and reminded her, plainly, that she simply liked this man standing in front of her. She always had.

"How's it going otherwise?" she said. "Being back in your hometown… is it everything you thought it would be?"

Conner's expression changed as he set his coffee down on the desk. "Mostly," he said. "The town's about the same. Church feels right, and it's everything I expected. But some things have caught me off guard a little. Not in a bad way, just—"

The front door of the salon opened.

"Good morning!" Mrs. Hyatt called out as she stepped inside, pulling her wool scarf from around her neck. "I know I'm a little early, Rebecca, but it is colder than all get-out today, and I wasn't about to just walk around town to waste time in that wind."

Rebecca turned toward the door. "You're fine, Mrs. Hyatt. Come on in and get warm."

Conner picked up his coffee. He folded the flyer and slid it across the desk toward her. "I'll let you get to your client," he said. "Thanks for the feedback on the flyer and the advice. I appreciate it."

"Anytime," she said. "I'll have my notes ready for you."

He nodded to Mrs. Hyatt as he passed her. "Good morning, ma'am."

"Good morning, honey," Mrs. Hyatt said. She watched him walk out with the cheerful, appraising curiosity of a woman who knew every family's business in Serenity Crossing and considered that knowledge a civic responsibility.

Rebecca stood at the reception desk while Mrs. Hyatt chattered on about the weather. She wondered about what Conner hadn't finished saying when he'd been interrupted by her client arriving early.

She shook the thoughts from her mind and moved the coffee he had brought her to the shelf behind the desk.

"All right, Mrs. Hyatt. Let's get you taken care of."

Chapter 7

Conner pushed through the front door of the recreation building with a foil-wrapped container in one hand and his notebook under his arm. Rebecca was already inside, arranging metal folding chairs into a wide circle in the center of the room. Her blonde hair was pulled up in a loose twist, and she wore a fitted sage green sweater over dark jeans and boots. A canvas tote sat on one of the folding tables near the kitchen, its top open, a notebook and a manila folder visible inside.

The recreation building was still new to him. The church had built it a few years ago, and it had the functional look of a space designed for gathering rather than worship. High ceilings. A polished concrete floor. Windows ran along the south wall, but at this hour they showed nothing but the dark blue of a January evening. Overhead, fluorescent lights hummed in steady rows, and someone had hung framed prints of mountain scenery along the back wall to soften the industrial feel. Folding tables lined the west side. The kitchen occupied the far corner behind a long counter with a pass-through window.

"Hey," Rebecca said as she turned toward him.

"Hey yourself." He walked toward her and set his container on the nearest table. "I didn't realize you were already here. I was in my office working and would've come over sooner if I'd known."

"No worries. I figured I'd get a head start, so we'd have time to talk before anyone shows up. I've still got snacks in my car if you wouldn't mind helping me bring them in."

"Lead the way."

They walked out to her car in the parking lot. The cold January air bit through his flannel the second he stepped outside. Rebecca opened her trunk and handed him a case of water bottles and a gallon jug of sweet tea. She grabbed two bags of chips, a container of dip, and a fruit tray covered in plastic wrap. The tray looked homemade, strawberries and grapes and apple slices arranged around a cup of caramel dip in the center.

"Did you make that?" he asked, nodding toward the tray.

"I did. It's one of those simple things to make that just takes a few minutes."

"It looks like it took longer than a few minutes."

She glanced at. "Are you complimenting my fruit arrangement skills, Pastor Conner?"

"I'm acknowledging them."

She almost smiled at that and closed her trunk.

Back inside, they set the snacks out on one of the folding tables. Conner lined up the water bottles and the gallon of sweet tea while

Rebecca arranged the chips and fruit tray. They needed cups and paper plates from the kitchen, and he found them in the cabinet above the sink where she told him they'd be. He brought out a sleeve of cups and a package of plates and set them beside the tea.

Rebecca looked at his foil-wrapped container on the table. "What's in there?"

He peeled back the foil. Chocolate chip cookies sat in neat rows on a layer of parchment paper. "Chocolate chip."

Rebecca turned fully toward him and looked at the cookies, then at him. Her eyebrows lifted and stayed there. "You baked these."

"I did."

"You. Baked cookies."

He grinned. "From scratch."

"Conner Delaney." She shook her head. "I have known you since we were twelve years old, and I never once in all that time pictured you standing in a kitchen with a mixing bowl and a bag of chocolate chips."

"That's fair. When I left home, I couldn't boil water." He set the foil aside and slid the container toward the center of the table. "When I moved to Richmond, I had to learn how to feed myself, and somewhere along the way I figured out I actually enjoyed it. Cooking, baking, all of it... I find it relaxing."

"Relaxing," she said.

"There's something about following a recipe. Measuring things out, watching it come together. I enjoy it."

Rebecca studied him for a long moment. Her blue eyes moved across his face as if she were recalculating a file she'd closed years ago. Then she picked up one of the cookies, bit into it, and chewed.

"Well?" he said.

"These are really good."

"You sound surprised."

"I am surprised. I am genuinely, completely surprised." She finished the cookie and brushed a crumb from her lip. "What else don't I know about you?"

He could hear the curiosity in her tone of voice, real and unguarded, and the sound of it made him want to answer honestly enough to earn more of it.

"Quite a bit, probably," he said. "Ten years is a long time."

"It is." She picked up a napkin and wiped her fingers. Then she turned back to the snack table and adjusted the position of the fruit tray, and the moment passed.

They finished setting up the room. Rebecca had the chairs nearly done, and Conner helped her place the last few, spacing them the way she had shown him. Multiple chairs in a loose circle with enough room that a teenager wouldn't feel crowded by the person beside them.

When they finished, Rebecca pulled the manila folder from her tote and handed him the flyer he'd left with her at the salon yesterday. She'd written notes in the margins in blue ink, her handwriting small and tidy.

"I went through it again last night," she said. "Your layout is solid. I only have two things."

He took the flyer and read her notes. The first was a suggestion to add a line near the bottom that read Snacks provided, because, as she put it, a teenager would walk through a church door for free food before they'd walk through it for a devotional. He laughed. She was right.

The second note was about the contact information.

"Add my cell number if you still want to," she said. "If a new family or a youth sees this flyer and has questions, I'd rather they reach me directly instead of going through the church secretary and waiting for someone to pass along a message."

"Are you sure?"

"I'm sure. It makes sense."

He pulled a pen from his back pocket and held it over the margin. "What's the number?"

She told him, and he wrote the seven digits beneath her name in his compact handwriting. He capped his pen and slid it back into his pocket.

"Thank you," he said. "For the notes and for the number. I'll have the final copies printed by Friday."

"Let me know when they're ready, and I'll drop by and pick up a stack for the salon. I'll hang a couple and leave some on my receptionist's desk for anyone to pick up and take with them."

The gradual ease between them caught him off guard. When they discussed the program, the youths, and the work ahead, the distance Rebecca kept around herself thinned a little more each time. She was quick with her ideas and generous with them, and she listened to his with a directness that made him want to keep talking. In those stretches, the ten years between them compressed, and the woman standing across from him felt less like someone he'd lost and more like someone he was only beginning to find.

It was the other stretches that reminded him how much he didn't know. The stretches when she redirected a conversation drifting toward personal territory. He recognized the skill in it because he'd watched her use it at the salon yesterday, the moment he'd said something that landed closer than she wanted. She had a way of closing a door so gently that you almost didn't notice it had shut.

He noticed.

Conner set the flyer on the table beside his notebook and leaned against the edge. "Can I ask you something?"

"Sure."

"Yesterday at the salon. You asked me if coming back was everything I thought it would be, and I started to answer, and then your client walked in."

Rebecca met his eyes and held them before she answered. "You said some things caught you off guard. I was curious what you meant."

He nodded. He'd been thinking about how to finish that sentence since yesterday, standing in his kitchen at the parsonage, turning the question over while cookies baked. The truth was simple and complicated at the same time.

"The town is the same," he said. "The mountains, Main Street, the church. All of it looks and feels the way I remembered. I expected that." He paused. "What I didn't expect is how much the people have changed. Not everyone. My parents are the same. Warren is the same. But some people surprised me."

Rebecca stood near the circle of chairs with her arms folded loosely across her chest, watching him.

"You surprised me," he said.

"How?"

"I don't know how to say this without it sounding wrong. I didn't expect you to be the same person you were at eighteen. I know better than that. But the Rebecca I carried in my head for ten years was a version of you that stopped updating a long time ago." He rubbed his neck with one hand. "And the woman I've been working with this week isn't that version. You're more than I expected. Different in ways I'm still figuring out. And I don't mean that as flattery. I mean, I'm trying to understand who you are now, because I realize I don't know you the way I thought I did."

She didn't respond right away. Her arms stayed folded, and her expression was steady, but her eyes were searching his.

"People change, Conner. Ten years will do that."

"They will."

"You've changed too. The boy I knew at eighteen didn't bake cookies."

"No, he didn't."

She unfolded her arms and picked up a stack of napkins from the table. She carried them to the snack station and fanned them out beside the plates.

"I'm glad you told me," she said without turning around. "I was going to ask again if you didn't."

That was new. The Rebecca he'd known before would have let the unfinished sentence go, filed it away, and moved on. The fact that she intended to bring it up again, that she'd said so out loud, told him the ground between them had moved a fraction of an inch in a good direction.

"So," Rebecca said, turning back toward him. "Tell me your plan for tonight."

Conner picked up his notebook and opened it to his afternoon's work. He set the notebook on the table so that she could see it. "I want to use this first meeting to listen. Get a feel for where these kids are. Ask them what they like about coming on Wednesday nights, and what they'd change if they could. Let them direct the conversation."

"Good," Rebecca said. "I like where you're going with this."

"I'll introduce myself, tell them a little about my background, and give them a quick preview of the themes I want to build over the coming weeks if the vibes in the room feel right. But mostly I want them to talk."

Rebecca leaned forward and looked at his notes. Her eyes moved down the page, and he watched her read through what he'd written. She was close enough that he noticed the small gold hoops in her ears, a detail he'd missed earlier.

"You've got Tyler Brannigan and Josh Weaver in this group," she said, tapping a line in his notebook. "They're sixteen, best friends, and they'll test you in the first five minutes. Tyler will crack a joke to see how you react, and Josh will watch your face to see if you're real or if you're performing."

"What do you suggest?"

"Laugh at the joke if it's funny. Don't fake it if it isn't. And look Josh in the eye when you talk. He's the quiet one, but he's the one whose opinion the other boys follow."

Conner wrote that down. "Who else should I know about?"

"Emma Sorrells is fifteen, and she'll talk your ear off if you let her, which is fine because she's smart and she's got things to say. She just needs someone to listen." Rebecca straightened and folded her arms. "Caleb Hart is seventeen. He comes every single Wednesday. If you need a kid to help you carry a conversation early on, Caleb's your guy. And Megan Pruitt is fourteen and quiet, but she pays attention to everything. She probably won't say much tonight, but she'll go home and think about whatever you said and come back next week with questions."

He wrote each name as she spoke, adding her notes beside them.

"I also want to bring up Hannah Caldwell again," Rebecca said. Her voice dropped half a register, the way it had in Warren's office when she'd brought Hannah up the first time. "She may or may not come tonight. If she does, don't single her out. Don't ask her a direct question in front of the group. Let her sit where she wants and participate on her own terms."

"I remember what you told me. I'll follow your lead with her."

Rebecca nodded. She picked up the last chair from the stack against the wall and carried it to the circle, fitting it into a gap she'd been eyeing. "The other thing you should know is that these kids are used to a certain rhythm. For the past couple of years, I've been the one running Wednesday nights with a rotation of volunteers handling the teaching. The quality has been inconsistent, and the kids know it. Some of the volunteers connected with them. Some of them read straight from a manual without looking up." She set the chair in place and turned to face him. "What I'm saying is that you've got a real opportunity tonight. These kids are ready for someone who actually wants to be here. You've got a clean slate with them."

"That's encouraging and humbling at the same time."

"You'll be fine. You're good at this."

"You don't know that yet."

"I know enough." She walked past him to check the snack table one more time.

He stood there and watched her refold a napkin that had come loose from the stack. She moved through this room with a quiet, unmistakable ownership. Every detail she touched reflected a woman who understood that for teenagers, the small things built trust before the big things ever could.

He was aware of what was building in him when he watched her, and he couldn't pretend he wasn't. It had started at Minnie's on Friday night with that first jolt of seeing her across the diner. It had grown in Warren's office, through the salon yesterday, and now here, watching her tuck a napkin into place as if it mattered as much as a church sermon did. What he felt wasn't nostalgia. Nostalgia was warm and safe. This was the unsettling awareness that the woman ten feet from him was someone he wanted to know completely, and he was only standing at the edge of who she was.

The front door swung open at ten minutes before seven, and a burst of cold air and teenage voices filled the room.

Three boys came through first, two of them shoving each other's shoulders in the physical, easy way of fifteen-year-olds. The taller one had shaggy brown hair and a grin that marked him as the one who usually started trouble. The shorter one beside him had a buzz cut and a varsity jacket a size too big.

"Tyler, Josh, hands to yourselves; you're in a building," Rebecca said from across the room, her tone warm and completely unbothered.

"Yes, ma'am," Tyler said. He dropped his hands, and the grin widened.

Rebecca crossed the room to meet them. "Tyler Brannigan, Josh Weaver, Tucker Chase, this is Pastor Conner. He grew up right here in Serenity Crossing and went to the same high school you go to."

Tyler looked Conner up and down with the frank appraisal of a teenage boy deciding whether an adult was worth his time. "Did you play sports?"

"Football, basketball, and track," Conner said.

"What position in football?"

"Quarterback."

Tyler glanced at Josh. Josh raised an eyebrow. A flicker of respect passed between them, the kind earned with a one-word answer to a one-word question.

"Cool," Tyler said, and headed for the snack table.

More kids arrived over the next ten minutes, some in groups and some alone. A girl with dark curly hair came through the door mid-sentence, talking at full speed to the girl beside her about something that had happened at school. Rebecca intercepted her with a smile.

"Emma, breathe," Rebecca said. "You can finish your story in a minute. Come meet Pastor Conner."

Emma Sorrells looked up at Conner with the fearless curiosity of a thirteen-year-old. "Are you nice, and can you remember simple things?" she said.

"I try to be nice, and yes, most of the time I remember simple things," Conner said.

"Good. Because the last volunteer who led the lesson kept calling me Emily, and my name is Emma, and I corrected him three times, and he still got it wrong."

"Emma. Got it. I won't forget."

"We'll see," she said, and headed for the snack table with the confidence of someone who had just conducted a job interview.

Conner watched Rebecca greet every kid who walked through the door. She asked Caleb Hart about his midterm grades and told Megan Pruitt she liked her new sweater. She handed a boy named Derek a bottle of water and told him his mom had called that afternoon to let her know he needed to leave a few minutes earlier than normal tonight. She knew these kids, each one individually, and the teenagers responded to her with the ease of young people who trusted an adult completely. The younger ones stood close to her, hanging on her every word. The older ones talked to her with a casualness that said she'd earned her place in their world. She laughed at something Tyler said, and the sound crossed the room, clear and warm and unguarded.

By seven o'clock, fourteen kids had settled into the circle of chairs with plates of cookies and chips balanced on their knees. Conner stood near the edge of the circle with his notebook in his hand. The room hummed with the particular energy of teenagers in a group, and he loved it. This was the part of ministry that made everything else worth it. Not the meetings or the budgets, but this. A room full of young people who needed someone to show up for them and wanted to be there.

Rebecca was at the snack table, clearing a few empty plates, wadded-up napkins and used cups.

At a few minutes past seven, she straightened from the table and faced the circle. "All right, everyone, finish grabbing what you need and come sit down. If you haven't gotten a drink yet, now's the time."

The last stragglers found their chairs. Rebecca stepped into the circle and stood with her hands resting at her sides, her posture easy, her voice carrying across the room without effort.

"You all know me," she said. "I've been here every Wednesday night with you for quite some time now. But starting tonight, we've got someone new who will lead our group, and I want you to give him the same respect and honesty you've given me." She looked around the circle, making eye contact with several of the kids. "This is Pastor Conner, and he's got a very passionate heart for what we're building here. I want each of you to feel free to talk and be yourselves tonight. It's going to be a little different from what you're used to, and that's a good thing."

She turned to Conner and smiled.

It wasn't the practiced smile he'd seen her use at the salon or in church. It wasn't the careful warmth she offered when she was managing a moment. This smile was real. It came from somewhere behind the composure she wore like a second skin, and it reached her eyes and stayed there. It told him, without a single word, that she believed in what they were doing tonight and that she believed he was the right person to do it.

His whole mind went quiet. Every thought he'd been holding about tonight's lesson, about the teenagers watching him, about the names and notes in his notebook, all of it fell away for the length of that smile. What replaced it was a single, clear recognition that landed with the force of something he'd been circling for days without letting himself name: this woman still mattered to him in a way that no amount of time or distance had diminished, and standing here receiving her trust felt like the most important thing that had happened to him since he'd come home.

Fourteen kids in a circle of metal chairs stared back at him, waiting for him to speak, paper plates on their knees, and the fluorescent lights humming overhead.

He took a breath and stepped into the center of the circle.

"Thank you, Rebecca." He looked around the room, giving each face his full attention the way she'd just given him hers. "I'm Pastor Conner Delaney, but you are welcome to just call me Conner; I never expect any formalities. Some of your parents probably remember me from when I was about your age and getting into just as much mischief as you might be."

Tyler Brannigan grinned. Josh Weaver leaned back in his chair and watched his face.

"I'm not here to lecture you," Conner said. "I'm not here to read from a manual or talk at you for an hour while you pretend to listen. I grew up in this town. I went to your school. I sat in a chair just like yours, and I remember exactly what it felt like to have an adult tell me what to think instead of asking me what I actually believed."

He set his notebook on the empty chair behind him and put his hands in his pockets. "So here's what we're going to do tonight. We're going to talk. I'm going to ask you some questions, nothing too serious, nothing that requires a lot of thinking, just basic fun stuff so I can get to know each of you. I would appreciate it if you would answer truthfully if you'd like to. I will listen. That's it. No wrong answers. No judgment. Just a conversation."

Emma Sorrells sat up straighter in her chair. Caleb Hart gave a small nod from the front row.

And in the back of the circle, in a chair she'd slipped into while Rebecca was speaking, a girl sat with her arms wrapped around a worn journal pressed against her chest. She hadn't taken a plate of snacks. She hadn't spoken to anyone. She watched everyone around her with the careful stillness of someone who had learned how to sit in a room full of people without being noticed.

Conner didn't look directly at her. He didn't pause or change his expression. But he knew, with the instinct six years of youth ministry had given him, that this was the girl Rebecca had been carrying concern for since the fall. The one who was pulling away. The one whose quiet said more than anything.

"All right," he said, and let his voice settle into the warm, easy rhythm that came naturally to him when he stood in front of young people who needed someone to care. "Let's start with something easy. Tell me your name, how old you are, and one thing you wish an adult would ask you but never does."

Chapter 8

Rebecca had two foils left to do for the highlights she was putting in her sister's hair and a million and one thoughts running through her mind as Anna spoke, "I'm telling you, the vendor contracts from last year are gone. Not misfiled. Gone. And the spring festival is in three months, and I'm supposed to build a budget from scratch because Gail Hutchins kept half her records in a notebook that nobody can find."

"Did you check with the treasurer's office?" Rebecca sectioned off a thin piece of Anna's light-brown hair and laid it flat across the foil strip in her hand. She painted the lightener on with careful strokes, working from mid-shaft to the ends before going back to cover the roots. "Dave would have copies of any checks the Chamber cut to vendors last year."

"Dave was my first call. He pulled the payment records, but they only show amounts and dates." Anna held still while Rebecca folded the foil and pressed it into place. "No contracts, no terms, no vendor contact info. I need to know which vendors had exclusive agreements and which ones were open bids."

"Then start over," Rebecca said. "You planned the entire Christmas tree lighting ceremony last year and pulled it off in six weeks."

"That was different, and I wasn't under as much stress at that time."

"Then buckle up, sister, and focus on the goal at hand and set everything else going on in your life right now aside. This is your job, and you've got the entire Chamber of Commerce board behind you." Rebecca painted the last section, folded her final foil, and stepped back to check her work. Twenty-four foils, evenly spaced, each one catching the overhead light. "You've got this, Anna."

Her sister looked at her in the mirror. Anna wore a rust-colored cardigan over a white blouse, with a silver pendant necklace and small turquoise studs in her ears. Even sitting in a salon chair with foils stacked across her head, the youngest Hartwell managed to look even more beautiful and elegant than she already was.

"You sound like Mom," Anna said.

"Good. Mom's usually right."

Rebecca set her brush in the lightener bowl and peeled off her gloves. She checked the clock on the wall near the reception desk. "You've got about forty minutes before I rinse you. Do you want a bottle of water or a magazine?"

Anna reached into her bag on the floor and pulled out a paperback with a bent spine and a bookmark wedged near the middle. "I brought reinforcements."

"Of course you did." Rebecca dropped her gloves into the trash and wiped down her station with a clean towel as she glanced across the room.

All six stylists were working. Jenna was layering long sections of Carla Bennett's dark hair through her fingers and trimming the ends with her silver shears. Claire Dawson had a blowout going near the front windows, her dryer filling that corner with its low hum. Stacy Marsh was talking to her client about a recipe she'd tried over the weekend while she worked a flat iron through a stubborn section of bangs. Music played from the small speaker near the shampoo sinks, something soft and country that mixed with the layered conversations across the room. A Friday morning at the Fluff & Curl in full swing.

Rebecca headed toward the reception desk to check her afternoon schedule when the front door opened and Conner walked in carrying two to-go cups in one hand and a stack of printed flyers under his arm.

He wore a dark green jacket over a gray henley, and the cold had left color across his cheekbones. His sandy brown hair was windblown on one side. He was already smiling at her before the door closed behind him.

"Is this going to become a habit?" she asked.

"It just might." He walked toward her and held out one of the cups. "Same as last time."

She took it. The cup was warm through its cardboard sleeve. She lifted the lid and took a sip. The right amount of creamer, the same as Tuesday. She set it on the reception desk beside the glass jar of conversation hearts she'd swapped in yesterday.

"Thank you," she said.

He pulled the flyers from under his arm and set the stack on the desk between them. "Final copies. I made every change you suggested. The snack line is at the bottom."

Rebecca picked up the top flyer and looked it over. Clean layout, good spacing. Her cell number was printed beneath her name. The line at the bottom read, Snacks provided every Wednesday night.

"These look great," she said. "You didn't have to bring them all the way over here, though. You could've just given them to me Sunday."

"I could have." He leaned one hip against the edge of the reception desk.

She set the flyer back on the stack. "I'll hang up a couple of these right away."

"Sounds like a plan," he said.

Anna had her book open across the room, but her eyes were on the reception area. Two stations down, Jenna's hands were still moving through Carla's hair, but her gaze had drifted toward the front of the salon.

"Wednesday night went well, by the way," Conner said. "The kids responded better than I expected. Letting them drive the conversation made a real difference."

"Tyler Brannigan raised his hand to answer just about every question you asked," Rebecca said. She folded her arms and rested them on the edge of the desk. "That boy hasn't voluntarily participated in anything since he hit puberty."

Conner laughed. She watched his face soften when he laughed, the steadiness he usually carried giving way to something younger, and for half a second she saw both versions of him at once. The boy from senior year and the man in her salon.

"I also noticed Josh Weaver watching me with that look you warned me about."

"And?"

"You were right. He was deciding if I was real."

"Did you pass?"

"I think so. He found me afterward when you were speaking to Hannah and asked more about when I'd played football in high school."

"That's Josh's version of approval," Rebecca said. "If he's asking follow-up questions, you're in."

He took a drink from his cup and set it on the desk beside hers. "I couldn't have walked into that room the way I did without your help, Rebecca. The notes you gave me on each kid, the way you introduced me to the group. It mattered."

"You would've been fine without me."

"I wouldn't have been nearly as good."

She looked at him, and she knew he wasn't being polite.

"You're welcome," she said. "I'm glad it went well."

He picked up his coffee, took another drink, and set it down. "Do you have plans for lunch today?"

Rebecca's hands stilled on the edge of the desk.

"Why do you ask?"

"No particular reason. I just thought we could have lunch together."

"Just lunch," she said.

"Just lunch. I enjoy your company, Rebecca, and I'd like the chance to spend some time with you outside of church and meetings." He paused. "That's all."

I enjoy your company. Four words with no pressure behind them and no agenda. He wasn't asking for anything more than her presence. He was putting it plainly enough that she couldn't redirect it or file it away as professional.

She wanted to say yes, and the wanting surprised her. It was louder than it had been a week ago, louder than it had been that first Friday night at Minnies when he'd walked through the door and her whole world had rearranged itself in a single breath. But the part of her that had learned, twice now, what it cost to let a man in held its ground.

"I appreciate you asking," she said. "But I'm not sure about lunch. Maybe another time." She picked up her coffee and took a sip, giving her hands a task and her eyes a reason to look away from him. "Thank you for the coffee and for bringing these over. I'll see you Sunday."

His expression changed. The warmth stayed, but a flicker of hurt moved through his eyes before he steadied them and nodded.

Then he set his coffee down and pulled his phone from his jacket pocket, typed with his thumb for a few seconds, and hit send. He looked up at her and held her gaze.

Rebecca's phone buzzed at her stylist's station across the room. It was sitting right next to the bowl of lightener, and her sister, who was already looking down at its lit screen with wide eyes.

Anna picked up the phone and held it in the air. "You've got a message, sis," she said, grinning.

Rebecca looked back at Conner.

He smiled. It was quiet and unhurried, and it reached his hazel eyes. "Now you have my number too," he said. "If you change your mind, you know how to reach me."

He picked up his coffee, held her gaze for one more second, and walked out.

Rebecca stood at the reception desk and watched through the front windows as he walked down the sidewalk. She watched until he turned the corner past the gazebo, and then she walked back to her station.

Anna was still holding her phone. Jenna had stopped cutting and stood with her shears in one hand and her comb in the other, watching Rebecca cross the room.

Rebecca took the phone from Anna's hand and opened the text. Two words on the screen: Your turn.

She read it twice. Then she set the phone face down on her station and picked up a comb she had no use for.

"I cannot believe the nerve of that man," she said.

Anna turned in her chair. "What did the message say?"

Rebecca set the comb down, picked up her phone, and showed her sister.

Anna read it and pressed her lips tight, but the grin won. "That was smooth. You have to admit, Rebecca, that's the best response to being turned down I've ever witnessed."

"It wasn't smooth. It was bold."

"Bold is smooth when a man does it right." Anna shifted in her chair to face her fully. "So what's the big deal? He asked you to lunch. Why did you turn him down?"

"The big deal is he happens to be my ex."

Anna blinked. "So?"

Rebecca looked at her sister. "What do you mean, so?"

"I mean, that was ten years ago. You were both teenagers."

Rebecca turned toward her station and straightened a row of hair care products that didn't need straightening. "It's complicated."

"It didn't look complicated. It looked like a good man walked into your salon with coffee and flyers and asked you to have lunch, and you turned him down because of something that happened when you were eighteen."

"What did the message say?" Jenna called from two stations down.

"All he said was, 'Your turn,'" Rebecca said.

Jenna lowered her shears. "Well, the ball's in your court now. What are you going to do about it?"

Rebecca looked between them. "Nothing. I'm not going to do a single thing."

Anna set her book on the counter. The grin was gone. What replaced it was an expression Rebecca recognized from their mother, steady and stripped of any teasing, the kind of look that meant the next words would land whether Rebecca wanted them to or not.

"You're being stubborn," Anna said. "Mom and I spoke with him after church last Sunday during fellowship. You'd already left. He isn't the boy we knew in high school, Rebecca. He's interesting and kind, and his sense of humor had Mom rolling with laughter, and he genuinely cares about his work at the church. I spent twenty minutes talking to him about the youth program and about this town, and the man I talked to is someone worth knowing." She paused. "If my ex had walked in here with that kind of heart and asked me to lunch, I'd have said yes before he finished the sentence. I think whatever you've been carrying from ten years ago needs to be set down. That's a long time, sis."

The words found a tender place beneath Rebecca's composure and pressed against it. What she carried from ten years ago wasn't a grudge. It was the memory of loving someone with everything she had and watching him build a life that didn't include her. It was the quiet, stubborn fear that if she opened that door again, she'd end up standing in the same empty room she'd spent a decade learning to furnish on her own.

She looked at Anna and said nothing.

From Claire's station near the front windows, a woman leaned forward and looked past Claire toward Rebecca. "Excuse me for butting in, but was that Conner Delaney? As in the former star quarterback for the Wildcats?"

The woman was in her mid-twenties with auburn highlights and a round, friendly face. She looked familiar in the small-town way, where faces stayed stored even when names drifted.

"Yes, that was him."

"I'm Laura Simmons," the woman said. "I was a year behind you both in high school. I remember you and Connor. The whole school talked about you two."

Rebecca gave her a smile that was warm and polite, and perfectly measured. "That was a long time ago, Laura."

"It sure was. But he grew up to be a really handsome man, didn't he? My goodness... I wouldn't have been able to turn down lunch with him, honey." Laura settled back into Claire's chair. "I'm just saying."

Jenna caught Rebecca's eye and pointed at Laura with her comb. "I like her," Jenna said.

Anna laughed.

Rebecca closed her eyes and took a deep, steadying breath. She could hear Jenna's shears start up again, Claire's dryer humming, and Stacy talking her client through the plan for next month's appointment. Her salon on a Friday, doing what it did, full of women and warmth and the kind of truth that only got spoken in places where people trusted each other enough to say it.

She opened her eyes and picked up her phone. She read those two words one more time. Your turn.

She started typing. One sentence. She read it back, hit send, and then set the phone on her station and looked up.

Jenna was watching. Anna was watching. Laura Simmons had turned in Claire's chair. Carla Bennett had craned around in Jenna's chair to see what was happening.

Jenna raised her eyebrows. "Care to share?"

Rebecca looked at her best friend, then at her sister, then at the room full of women who had given up any pretense of minding their own business.

"I told him I'd be at Minnie's at noon if he cared to join me," she said.

Chapter 9

The jukebox in the corner of Minnie's Diner was playing a George Jones song that Conner remembered his mom and dad dancing to whenever it came on the radio. He looked around and realized the lunch crowd had filled most of the red vinyl booths along the windows as he'd been reading a John Grisham novel. He'd arrived fifteen minutes early and settled into a booth near the front with a clear view of the door. Minnie had poured him a cup of coffee, told him he looked as if he needed a good, healthy meal, and moved on before he could respond.

Plates clattered in the kitchen behind the counter. Two men in Carhartt jackets argued about a water heater from the spinning stools along the chrome-trimmed counter. A family of four occupied the booth ahead of him, and the youngest child was coloring a paper placemat with a level of concentration that would have put most of Conner's seminary classmates to shame. Framed photographs of Serenity Crossing covered the walls between vintage

Coca-Cola signs and yellowed newspaper clippings about championship football seasons from decades past. The black-and-white checkered floor gleamed under the overhead lights, and the glass pie case near the register held four different pies, each one cut into thick slices that Conner had been pretending not to notice since he sat down.

He read three more pages before the front door opened and Rebecca walked in.

She wore a dark plum coat over a cream-colored sweater and was pulling off a pair of brown leather gloves as she stepped inside. Her hair fell past her shoulders in loose waves, and the cold had left her cheeks flushed. She scanned the diner, found him, and her composure loosened just enough for him to catch it. The tight line of her mouth softened, and her shoulders dropped a fraction of an inch.

She crossed the room and slid into the booth across from him.

"You're early," she said.

"I'm always early."

Her eyes went to the paperback on the table. "What are you reading?"

"The Pelican Brief. John Grisham."

"Conner Delaney reading a novel." She set her gloves on the table beside her. "Since when are you a reader?"

"About four years now. A friend in Richmond handed me a copy of A Time to Kill and told me I didn't get to say I didn't like reading until I'd actually tried it."

"And?"

"And I finished it at two in the morning and went out the next day and bought three more."

She shook her head. "In high school, you wouldn't read the assigned books for English class."

"I read the Cliff Notes."

"That doesn't count."

"It counted enough to pass."

The smile she'd been holding back arrived, and it changed her whole face. Conner set the book beside him on the seat, out of the way.

Minnie appeared at the booth carrying a coffee pot and a white ceramic mug. She was a sturdy, bright-eyed woman with salt-and-pepper hair pinned up in a twist and an apron tied over a blue flannel shirt. She moved through her diner like a woman who had owned every square foot of it for years and didn't plan on letting go of a single one. She set the mug in front of Rebecca and filled it to the brim.

"Well, if it isn't Rebecca Hartwell gracing my establishment for a weekday lunch," Minnie said. "How ya doing, honey?"

"I'm great, Minnie. Busy morning at the salon, but nothing out of the ordinary."

"Your mama was in here Tuesday morning with her garden club ladies. She told me you did something different with her hair, and she's been getting compliments all week." Minnie pulled two laminated menus from under her arm and set them on the table. "I need to come see you soon because I look like I've been wrestling a push mower."

Rebecca laughed. "You look great, Minnie. But you know I'll take you anytime you want to come in."

"I know you will, sweetheart." Minnie tapped the menu with her finger. "Special today is meatloaf with mashed potatoes and green beans. Gravy's made from scratch this morning. Take your time, and I'll be back."

She moved on to the family behind them. Rebecca added a bit of creamer to her coffee and took a long sip. Her eyes closed for a second while she drank. When she opened them, she looked at him across the table.

"Minnie's coffee," she said.

"Best in town."

Rebecca set her mug down and unzipped her coat. She slipped it off and draped it over the back of the booth behind her. Her cream sweater had a small gold necklace resting against it, and she wore tiny gold studs in her ears. Her nails were painted a deep cranberry this week. Conner picked up his menu before his attention lingered on her any longer than it already had.

"Not much has changed on this menu," he said.

"Why would it? Everything she makes is good."

He looked over the top of his menu. "Are you still a chicken sandwich girl?"

She lowered hers. "I am. You remembered that, too?"

"I remember plenty of things. Is that what you're having?"

"I am. Let me guess yours. Cheeseburger."

"You guessed correctly, but I'm switching to sweet potato fries."

"Bold move, Mr. Delaney."

"I'm feeling adventurous."

They set their menus down. Rebecca folded her hands on the table, and the lightness from a moment ago faded. Her chin lifted, and her eyes found his with a directness that told him the small talk was over.

"What is this, Conner? What are we doing?"

He held her gaze. "This is lunch. You and I sitting across from each other having a meal."

She tilted her head. "You know what I mean."

He respected her too much to give her anything but the honest answer. He opened his mouth to offer it, but Minnie materialized at the end of the booth with her notepad.

"Are you two ready to order?"

"Chicken sandwich with fries," Rebecca said.

"Cheeseburger with sweet potato fries," Conner said.

Minnie wrote it down without looking at her pad. "Coming right up. Ten minutes, give or take." She collected the menus and headed toward the kitchen window.

Conner leaned forward and rested his forearms on the table. "Let's just enjoy lunch, Rebecca. I want to get to know you again. I've missed talking to you." He paused. "But I have one rule."

"You invited me to lunch, and now you hope to put conditions on it?"

"One condition."

"Let's hear it."

"Clean slate. You and me, right here, right now. No talking about our past. We get to know each other as if we're meeting for the first time."

"Are you serious, Conner Delaney?"

"One hundred percent. Are you game?"

She studied him across the table. The jukebox shifted into a Merle Haggard tune. Silverware clinked against plates in the booth behind them. Her eyes stayed on his while she turned it over and made her decision.

"Game on," she said.

Conner grinned and reached his hand across the table. "Conner Delaney. Assistant pastor and youth minister at Serenity Crossing Community Church. I'm glad you met me for lunch, Rebecca Hartwell. Tell me something about yourself. What do you like to do when you're not at work?"

She looked at his hand. Then she shook it with a grip that was firm and warm from the coffee mug, and she held it for longer than she needed to before she let go.

"Well now, Mr. Delaney, that's quite a question to ask someone you've just met." She picked up her coffee and settled back against the booth. "When my workday is done, it's done. I don't think about it; I don't bring it home with me. That's my one rule. Work doesn't get to follow me through my front door." She took a sip. "On any given evening, you might find me on my couch watching something funny on Netflix. Or I could be curled up reading a good historical romance novel, because I have a stack of them on my nightstand that never seems to shrink no matter how fast I read.

If neither of those sounds right, I might be in my kitchen making a batch of fudge because I have a serious sweet tooth, and when there's no ice cream in my freezer, somebody has to take matters into her own hands." She set her mug down and rested her elbow on the table. "Other nights I'll go for a run on one of the hiking trails outside town. I do my best thinking when I'm running. And if none of that appeals to me, I'm at my parents' house or at one of my brothers' or sisters' homes, because I come from a big family and there is always something going on with someone." She raised her eyebrows. "Your turn, Mr. Delaney."

He liked hearing her use his last name that way. It had a teasing quality that only appeared when she stopped thinking about whether to let her guard down and just let it happen.

"Well, it seems like you and I agree on one thing right out of the gate, because when my workday is done, the door closes and that's it. I'll watch whatever game happens to be on television. I'd choose a book over the TV any day of the week, unless the Tennessee Vols are playing, and if the Vols are on, nothing else in this world exists." He turned his coffee mug in a slow circle on the table. "I cook dinner for myself almost every night. Sometimes it's simple: eggs and toast or a sandwich. Other nights I'll get into a recipe that takes two hours and holds my attention from start to finish. I've gotten into trying things in the kitchen I've never attempted before, just to see if I can pull them off." He took a sip of his coffee. "If none of that suits me, I'll drive over to one of my brothers' houses and let their kids entertain me. Miles has four and Adam has three, and between the seven of them there isn't a dull moment in the family." He set his mug down. "But I'll be honest with you. In my calling, evenings aren't always mine. I might go visit a member of the congregation, just a chance to sit down with a good person or a good family and spend time with them. Other nights somebody from the church needs me, and I drop everything and go. But I don't look at those as interruptions. Some of the most meaningful moments I've had in ministry have come from those evenings. They remind me why I do what I do, and I wouldn't trade them." He looked across the table at her. "All right. Your turn. What is your favorite ice cream?"

"Butter pecan," she said. "And I don't want to hear a word of judgment about that."

"No judgment. Mint chocolate chip."

"Really?"

"But it has to be the right brand. There's a real difference between good mint chocolate chip and the kind that tastes like toothpaste."

She laughed, and the sound carried past their booth and into the diner. "There absolutely is a difference."

Minnie came back with two plates balanced along her arm. She set the chicken sandwich in front of Rebecca and the cheeseburger with sweet potato fries in front of Conner.

"Anything else I can get you two?"

"We're good, Minnie," Rebecca said. "Thank you."

Minnie topped off both their mugs from the coffee pot and moved on to a couple near the counter who were trying to flag her down.

Rebecca picked up her sandwich and took a bite. Conner bit into his cheeseburger. Hot off the griddle with a slight char at the edges. He'd been ordering the same thing every time he'd walked through this door since he was fourteen, and it hadn't changed.

"Since you mentioned cooking," Rebecca said, "what is the worst thing you've ever made?"

Conner set his cheeseburger down and shook his head. "My first attempt at homemade pizza. I was in my apartment in Richmond, and I decided I was going to make a pizza completely from scratch. The dough, the sauce, everything." He wiped his hands on his napkin. "The crust came out so hard I could have thrown it at a window and busted the glass. I took one bite, dropped the entire thing in the garbage, and called the local pizza place for delivery."

Rebecca pressed her hand over her mouth while she laughed. "You threw the whole pizza away?"

"After one bite. And honestly, one bite was generous. When I pulled the pan out of the oven and set it on the counter, it sounded like I was putting down a cinder block."

"Have you tried again since then?"

"I have, and I've gotten a lot better. But that first attempt is burned into my memory, and I'm fairly certain it's never leaving." He picked up a sweet potato fry. "What about you? What's yours?"

"A cake for my mama's birthday. Three layers, cream cheese frosting, decorated it perfectly. I was so proud of that cake I took a picture of it before we cut into it." She paused. "I forgot the sugar in the cake batter."

Conner stopped chewing. "You forgot the sugar in a birthday cake?"

"Every last bit of it. My mama took the first bite, and her face did something I have never seen before or since. She was trying so hard to be polite that she couldn't form a single word. My daddy set his fork down and said, 'Honey, I believe you left something out.'"

Conner laughed hard enough that the men sitting at the counter turned around. "What did you do?"

"I drove straight to the grocery store and came back with a bakery cake. We ate that instead." She shook her head. "My sister Sarah still brings it up at every family birthday we celebrate. Without fail."

"Your daddy's response is my favorite part of that story."

"That is exactly how Bill Hartwell handles every situation. Calm, direct, and specific."

They ate for a while, and the conversation settled into a rhythm that Conner hadn't expected to come so easily. Not once since she'd sat down had Rebecca redirected the conversation away from herself. She wasn't managing the moment or filling the silence with deflection. She was here, talking to him, answering with a kind of honesty that told him the clean slate had done exactly what he'd hoped it would do.

She asked if he was a morning person or a night person.

"Night," he said. "I do my best thinking after ten o'clock, and for some reason I can completely relax."

"I'm the opposite. I'm up by five thirty most mornings, even when I don't have to be."

"Five thirty on purpose?"

"On purpose. I love to watch the sunrise while I drink my coffee, and the day hasn't started telling me what to do yet."

"We'd have trouble sharing a morning routine. I need coffee before I can even focus on a sunrise," he said.

"Probably," she said, and she smiled and picked up a fry without looking away from him.

The jukebox shifted into a Dolly Parton song. Three women came through the front door, pulling off scarves and stamping snow from their shoes on the mat. Minnie greeted them by name from behind the counter and pointed toward an empty booth near the back.

Conner looked across the table at Rebecca, at the crumpled napkins and the ketchup packets scattered between their plates, and at the fry she was eating that she'd just stolen off his plate because she'd finished all of hers a few minutes ago. He couldn't think of anywhere in this town he'd rather be right now.

"All right," he said. He leaned back in the booth. "If you could go anywhere in the world for one week, where would you go?"

"Ireland," she said without a second of hesitation.

"That was fast."

"I've wanted to go since I was twelve years old. I saw a photograph in a magazine of green hills rolling down to the ocean with old stone walls running through the fields and a tiny village at the bottom. I can't explain it, but Ireland feels like somewhere I'm supposed to see." She picked up another one of his fries and dipped it in ketchup. "What about you?"

"Alaska."

"Alaska?"

"The wilderness up there seems unlike anything in the lower forty-eight. I want to stand somewhere so remote that the only sounds are wind and water. No roads. No buildings. Mountains and sky."

"That suits you perfectly."

"How so?"

"Conner Delaney standing alone in the middle of nowhere, surrounded by nothing but mountains. That is about as you as it gets."

He grinned. "I'll take that as a compliment."

"It was meant as one."

Rebecca wiped her fingers on her napkin and picked up her coffee. "My turn. What is the best piece of advice anyone ever gave you?"

"A pastor I worked with in Richmond told me something during my second year there. He told me, 'Conner, patience is a virtue, but patience without action is just avoidance wearing comfortable shoes.'"

Rebecca held her mug with both hands and looked at him over the rim. "That's deep... and a really good one."

"It took me a long time to understand what he meant. But once I did, it changed how I approach just about everything in my life." He set his mug down. "What about you?"

"My daddy." She set her coffee on the table. "I was twenty-two. I'd just broken up with Luke, a man I'd been seeing for a few months. He'd started trying to run my life. He had been trying to talk me out of buying the building where my salon is. I broke up with him the day I signed the paperwork to buy the building. I was scared out of my mind. I called my daddy and told him I thought I'd just made a mistake, that I'd just committed myself to owning a building and running a business, and I'd just ended a relationship all in the same day. And he said, 'Build your life with your own two hands, sweetheart. And when somebody comes along who's worth it, they'll add to what you've built. They won't try to replace it.'"

Conner looked at the woman sitting across from him. She'd quoted her father's words with the careful precision of someone who had carried them for six years and measured every man she'd met against them.

"Your daddy's a smart man," he said.

"He really is."

The lunch crowd had started to thin around them. Two of the counter stools were empty. The family ahead of them had paid and left. Minnie was wiping down their vacated table and humming along with the jukebox. The diner had settled into the quieter stretch between the noon rush and the midafternoon lull, and neither Conner nor Rebecca had noticed the room emptying around them.

Conner set his napkin on his empty plate. "What's one thing you want for your life that you don't have yet?"

Rebecca's hand went still on her coffee mug. She looked at him across the table, and every careful layer she'd been slowly setting aside since she walked through the door came off completely.

"A family," she said. "I want kids. I want a house that's loud and full. I want to come home at the end of the day to more than just my own company."

Conner held her eyes. "Same," he said. "A big family. Someone to build a good life with. Kids running through the house and getting into everything. I want all of it."

They looked at each other across the table. The jukebox played. A coffee mug clinked against a saucer somewhere behind the counter. Neither of them said what was obvious, and neither of them needed to. They'd both given the same answer to the same question, and they both knew that their answers hadn't changed since they had been teenagers.

Rebecca looked down at her watch. Her eyes widened. "We've been here for over an hour." She looked up at him. "I've got a client in thirty minutes."

"Time got away from us."

"It really did." She picked up her napkin, wiped her mouth, and set it beside her plate. "This was fun, Conner. I mean that."

"It was. I'm glad you changed your mind about lunch."

"So am I."

"Would you do it again?"

She looked at him. The diner hummed around them, Minnie's voice somewhere near the register, the jukebox fading between songs.

"I might," she said. "If you asked."

"Then consider yourself asked."

He caught Minnie's eye, and she brought the check. He picked it up before Rebecca could move.

"You don't have to do that," she said.

"I know I don't. I want to."

She looked at him for a long second, then let it go. "Thank you."

He left cash on the table, enough for the meal and a generous tip, and they slid out of the booth. Rebecca reached for her coat on the back of the seat, but Conner already had it. He held it open for her, and she paused for just a second before she turned and slid her arms into the sleeves. He brought the collar up and settled it across her shoulders, and his fingers grazed her neck where her hair fell over the fabric. She looked back at him over her shoulder, and the look she gave him was open and unguarded and gone in a breath. But it was long enough.

He pulled on his jacket and zipped it, and they walked out of Minnie's into the cold.

The January air was sharp, and the sky stretched flat and gray-blue above the rooftops along Main Street. A truck rolled past, and Rebecca raised a hand to the driver without breaking stride.

"I really did enjoy this," she said.

"So did I."

"And you were right, by the way. The clean slate was a good idea."

"I had a feeling it might be."

"Don't get smug about it, Delaney."

"Wouldn't dream of it."

They reached the Fluff & Curl. Through the front windows, Conner could see her salon's interior and all the activity going on.

Rebecca turned to him. "See you at church on Sunday."

"I'll be there," he said. "Oh, and hey, before you go. Lunch after church?"

She grinned. "I think that's a great idea. Where?"

"How about my place? An easy lunch, and we could go over some things for the youth group, maybe? I'd like your suggestions on a few things."

She nodded and smiled, then pulled the door open and stepped inside.

Chapter 10

The two-lane road out of Serenity Crossing narrowed past
the town limits, and the trees pressed closer on both sides.
The road curved gently to the left and followed the contour of
the mountains. Bare oaks and winter-stripped maples lined the
shoulder, their branches laced against a sky that had shifted from
this morning's bright blue to a softer shade. A split-rail fence ran
along the right side for a quarter mile, bordering a pasture. Three
horses stood near a round bale of hay, their breath visible in the
cold.

She'd driven this road a thousand times, but today she was paying closer attention to the mile markers.

Conner had told her three miles past the church, and she'd know
it by the gravel driveway on the left. She watched her odometer
and slowed when she spotted it. The driveway cut between two
mature oaks, and the parsonage sat back from the road on a slight
rise. A modest, single-story house with light gray siding, a dark

roof, and a small covered front porch. Conner's dark blue Ford truck was parked in the gravel area beside the house. The yard was open and winter-brown, with spots of snow here and there that hadn't melted yet. The property was bordered by trees that gave it a tucked-away feel. Beyond the treeline, the Smoky Mountains rose in layered ridges, their peaks faded to a blue-gray haze.

She pulled up beside his truck and cut the engine. The sudden quiet after the road noise and the heater's hum was startling. She sat for a few seconds and looked at the house through her windshield. This was where Conner lived. She'd driven past this property hundreds of times without a reason to turn into the driveway.

She had a reason now, and he had just walked out onto the front porch with his hands in the pockets of a charcoal pullover, watching her with a grin that said he'd been waiting.

Rebecca grabbed her purse from the passenger seat, stepped out onto the gravel, and walked toward the porch.

"You found it," Conner said.

"Three miles past the church, gravel driveway on the left. Your directions were pretty straightforward." She said as she climbed the two porch steps.

The porch was small, just wide enough for a couple of chairs, though there weren't any yet. A pair of work boots sat near the door, and a welcome mat that looked brand new was centered in front of the threshold.

"Come on in," he said, and opened the front door for her.

She stepped inside, and the warmth of the house wrapped around her. The front door opened directly into the living room, a rectangular space with two windows letting in the afternoon light. The walls were a soft off-white, and the hardwood floors showed a few scuffs in the high-traffic areas. A dark blue couch sat against the far wall with a knit throw blanket folded over one arm. A reading lamp stood beside it, and a paperback lay facedown on the side table. She could read the title from where she stood. The Firm. He was working his way through the Grisham catalog.

A bookshelf against the opposite wall was about three-quarters full. She recognized the spines of several novels alongside commentaries and study materials. A small television occupied the corner, and a braided rug in muted blues and grays covered the center of the floor. New, by the look of it, probably one of Loretta's contributions.

The room was lived in without being cluttered. Clean and organized in the particular way of a man who took care of his space without overthinking it. No decorations on the walls yet, but a framed photograph sat on the bookshelf beside a row of paperbacks.

"It's not much," Conner said behind her. "But it's home."

"It feels like you," she said, and she meant it. The room was warm and unpretentious, and it suited him.

"I'll take that as a compliment."

"You should."

He led her through the living room toward a short hallway. "Grand tour won't take long. The house has four rooms and a bathroom, so we'll be done in two minutes."

The hallway had two doors on the left and one on the right. The first door on the left was open, and she glanced in. A bedroom. A queen bed with a navy comforter pulled smooth, a nightstand with a lamp and a Bible. His Bible had a piece of paper tucked into the front cover, its edge visible above the leather binding. A dresser stood against the far wall with a few items on top.

"My room," he said. "Nothing fancy."

"You make your bed."

"Every morning. My mother trained that into me before I could tie my shoes."

"Loretta doesn't play around."

"No, she does not."

The second door on the left was a smaller room set up as an office. A desk and chair faced the window, with his laptop closed on the surface and a legal pad beside it. A bookshelf held binders labeled by year, study materials, and a few framed items propped against the books but not yet hung. A box sat in the corner with its flaps open, books visible inside.

"The famous boxes," Rebecca said.

He looked at her.

"You told me a few days ago you had boxes you hadn't unpacked yet, but I think you said they were in the living room."

"I opened most of them. That one's the holdout." He leaned against the doorframe. "It's mostly stuff from my office in Richmond. Pictures, a couple of plaques, things people gave me when I left. I haven't figured out where to put them yet."

"Or you're still deciding if this is where they belong."

"Maybe," he said. "I hadn't thought about it that way."

She moved on. The bathroom was across the hall, small and tidy with a white shower curtain and a dark blue bath mat.

The kitchen was the last stop, and it was the room that caught her off guard. Modest, with an L-shaped counter, standard appliances, and cabinets painted white. A window above the sink looked out onto the backyard and the tree line beyond. But the countertops told a different story than the rest of the house. A wooden knife block sat near the stove, beside a ceramic jar of cooking utensils. A small herb garden occupied the windowsill: three terra-cotta pots with green shoots labeled in Conner's compact handwriting. Basil. Rosemary. Thyme. A cookbook stood upright on the counter, propped open with a rubber band to a page near the middle. Beside the stove, a glass mixing bowl and a set of stainless-steel measuring cups sat on a folded dish towel, drying.

A small dining table with four chairs occupied the space between the kitchen and the living room, positioned near a window. The table was set with two plates, two glasses, and napkins folded beside each plate.

"You set the table," she said.

"I did. Are you impressed? He said with a grin.

"I am."

Rebecca stood in his kitchen and looked at the table he'd set, the herb garden on his windowsill, and the cookbook propped open on his counter. Something inside her chest loosened by a fraction. He'd prepared for her visit with quiet intention, and the fact that it came so naturally to him was the part that unsettled her most.

Her stomach chose that exact moment to announce itself. A low, unmistakable growl that she felt all the way to her ribs.

Conner turned and looked at her. His eyebrows went up. "Was that you, or is there a bear outside?"

"That was me. Geez, how embarrassing."

"That was louder than anything I've heard in this house since I moved in."

"Conner."

"I'm serious. I think the windows rattled."

She pressed her hand against her stomach and laughed. "I skipped breakfast this morning because I was running late for church. That's my punishment."

"Well, lucky for you, I've got lunch covered." He turned toward the refrigerator and opened both doors wide. "Come see what we're working with."

Rebecca stepped closer and looked inside.

The top shelf held a row of clear containers, each one neatly organized and labeled with strips of blue painter's tape. Sliced roast beef. Smoked turkey. Black Forest ham. Salami. The second shelf held another row: six different cheeses, sliced and stacked. She could see provolone, Swiss, sharp cheddar, pepper jack, and two others she'd have to open to identify. The door shelves held three different mustards: a classic yellow, a stone-ground, and a spicy brown. Two jars of mayonnaise, one regular and one of a brand she didn't recognize. A small glass bottle with a handwritten label that read balsamic vinaigrette sat beside them.

On the counter next to the refrigerator sat fresh bakery bread in a clear plastic bag. Beside it, a cutting board and two plastic-covered dishes, one holding sliced tomatoes and the other crisp lettuce leaves.

Rebecca looked at the refrigerator. She looked at the counter. She looked back at the refrigerator.

"Conner Delaney."

"What?"

"What do you mean, what? You have a sandwich shop in your refrigerator."

He pulled the container of roast beef from the top shelf and set it on the counter. "I like sandwiches."

"This isn't a man who likes sandwiches. This is a man who has a business license and a health inspection certificate hidden somewhere in this kitchen."

He laughed and reached for the turkey. "I get bored eating the same thing. If I come home for lunch during the week, I want to throw something good together fast and have options. So I keep my fridge stocked and rotate the meats every few days."

"You rotate the meats."

"And the cheeses."

"Of course you do."

He lined up the containers along the counter and pulled the rolls from the bag. They were soft, golden, and dusted with flour.

"These are from the bakery section at Valley Grocery. I picked them up yesterday."

Rebecca shook her head, but the smile on her face had settled in and wasn't going anywhere. "All right. Put me to work."

"Grab the mustards and the mayo from the door. And that bottle of vinaigrette."

She reached into the refrigerator and pulled out the condiments one at a time, lining them up on the counter beside the meats and cheeses. Conner sliced the rolls and laid them open on the cutting board.

"What's in the vinaigrette?" She asked, picking up the small glass bottle and tilting it. The liquid inside was dark and slightly thick, with flecks of herbs near the bottom.

"Balsamic vinegar, olive oil, a little garlic, oregano, salt, and pepper. I make a batch every couple of weeks."

"You make your own vinaigrette."

"It takes about three minutes. You put everything in a jar and shake it."

"You say that like it's normal."

"It is normal."

"Conner, most single men I know consider pouring salsa from a jar onto a plate of chips a major culinary accomplishment. You're standing here with homemade vinaigrette and six varieties of cheese."

He grinned and handed her a roll. "Build your sandwich. You've got options."

They stood side by side at the counter, and what followed was the most fun Rebecca'd had in a kitchen in longer than she cared to admit. She started with turkey and provolone on her roll and reached for the stone-ground mustard, but Conner intercepted her.

"Try it with the vinaigrette first," he said. "Just a little. Trust me."

She drizzled a thin line of the balsamic mixture across the turkey, added lettuce and a slice of tomato, and closed the roll. She took a bite. The tangy vinaigrette cut through the mild turkey and the sharpness of the provolone, with the fresh bread holding everything in place. She chewed slowly and closed her eyes for a second.

"Well?" he said.

"I'm never using mustard on a turkey sandwich again."

"Told you."

"Don't be smug."

"Too late."

She watched him build his own sandwich with the attention of someone who genuinely enjoyed the process. He layered roast beef and salami, added Swiss and a spread of spicy brown mustard, then topped it with lettuce, tomato, and a drizzle of vinaigrette. He pressed the roll closed and cut it in half with one clean motion.

"You cut yours in half," she said.

"Always."

"So do I."

He looked at her sandwich, still whole on the cutting board. She picked up the knife, cut it in half, and set it on her plate.

Conner poured two glasses of sweet tea from a pitcher in the refrigerator, and the ice clinked as he set them down on the table. They carried their plates and sat across from each other. The window beside the table looked out onto the side yard, where a pair of cardinals sat on the branch of a bare dogwood. The soft blue sky stretched above the treeline, and the mountains beyond were a wash of muted colors.

"This is really nice, Conner," she said. "All of it. The house, the lunch. You didn't have to go to this kind of trouble."

"It wasn't trouble. I eat like this anyway. You're just benefiting from my grocery habits."

She took another bite and shook her head. "Ten years ago, your idea of lunch was a gas-station hot dog and a Mountain Dew."

"I've evolved."

"You have."

They ate in an easy rhythm, the conversation moving between bites without effort. Conner asked about her path from high school to salon owner.

"I enrolled in cosmetology school in Gatlinburg and started in September after we graduated, but you already knew that," she said. "It was a year-long program, and I drove forty-five minutes each way."

"After I finished the program and got my license, I worked at a salon in Gatlinburg for about three years, and I learned a lot there. The owner was a woman named Pam Castillo, and she was brilliant. She taught me everything the school didn't, which was basically everything that actually matters. How to read a client, how to manage a chair, and how to build a reputation."

"Sounds like the cosmetology version of seminary."

She laughed. "Pam used to say that people sit in your chair and tell you things they'd never tell their doctor or their pastor. She was right. By my second year, I had clients who booked with me not because I gave the best haircut in the building, but because I made them feel like the most important person in the room for forty-five minutes."

"That's a gift, Rebecca. Not everyone can do that."

"I know, I've learned that by owning a salon and watching some of my stylists not understand how important it is to get to know their clients and talk to them while they are in their chairs," she said. "Anyway, I saved every penny I could for three years while I worked at that salon. I packed my lunch every day, I drove an old hand-me-down Honda that was on its last leg, and I didn't take a vacation. When the building at 106 Main came up for sale here in Serenity Crossing, I was ready."

"How old were you?"

"Twenty-two. I bought it using some of the money that my grandparents had left me and my savings. I spent six months renovating it alongside my sister Sarah's construction crew and opened the Fluff and Curl that September."

"That's impressive."

"It was terrifying," she said. "I was twenty-two years old with a small business loan and a building that needed more work than I'd budgeted for. I remember standing in the middle of the salon two days before the grand opening with sawdust on the floor and half the mirrors still wrapped in plastic, thinking, what on earth have I done?"

"And now you've got six stylists and a waiting list at times."

"I do. It's been a long six years, but it's been amazing," she said. "The first year was tight. Some months I wasn't sure I'd make payroll. But the clients came, and they kept coming, and by the second year I knew it was going to work."

"Do you ever wish you'd left Serenity Crossing? Gone somewhere else and seen what was out there?"

She set her sandwich down and looked at him. "No. Not once. I know that might sound small to some people, staying in the town you grew up in and never going anywhere else. But this is where I belong. My family is here. My business and church are here. Everything I've built is in this town, and I built it because I love this place."

There was a quiet certainty in her own voice that she recognized. She'd answered this question before, for herself and for ex-fiancée Nathan, and the answer had never changed.

"I don't think it sounds small," Conner said. "I think it sounds like a woman who knows exactly who she is and what she wants."

She held his gaze for a second longer than she needed to, then picked up her sandwich.

"What about you?" she said. "Tell me about college. Did you enjoy Liberty?"

Conner leaned back in his chair and picked up his tea. "I did. I was overwhelmed at first. The campus was huge, and the academic program was tougher than anything I'd dealt with in high school. I had to study harder than I'd ever studied in my life just to keep up."

"That doesn't surprise me. You were never a natural student."

"I was a natural athlete who happened to attend classes."

"That's the most accurate thing you've ever said about yourself."

He smiled. "But something clicked my second year. I started my ministry practicum, and for the first time, the classroom stuff made sense because I could see how it connected to real work. I was preaching at a small youth service near campus, working with about a dozen kids. Everything I was learning in theology and counseling suddenly had a place to land."

"And throughout your whole time there, you still knew it was the right path for you?"

"I did; my decision never wavered. I knew it was the right path for me my senior year in high school. And I still felt called to ministry through all the tough times of my freshman year at college. The first time I stood in front of a congregation and preached my first sermon, I was still confident that God had led me there."

Rebecca watched his face while he talked about it. The steadiness he carried with him everywhere gave way to something warmer, a quality that surfaced only when he talked about the work that mattered to him. She'd seen it at the youth group meeting on Wednesday. She was seeing it now across his kitchen table, and it stirred something in her that was harder to set aside each time she encountered it.

"What made you choose Richmond?" she asked. "Were there other offers?"

"Two others. A mid-sized church outside Nashville with a youth program already running and a small church in Roanoke starting one from scratch. Richmond was the biggest of the three and the most challenging. The senior pastor there, David Raines, called me directly after hearing me preach at a conference during my senior year. He told me the youth program was struggling, and he needed someone who could rebuild it."

"And you said yes."

"Not immediately. I prayed about it for three weeks. The Nashville offer was safer and closer to home. Roanoke was smaller and might've been a better first position. But Richmond was the one that kept me up at night. The challenge of it. A big church, a diverse congregation, a city where the kids were dealing with things I'd never encountered growing up here."

"What kinds of things?"

"Poverty. Violence. Broken families in ways that went deeper than divorce." He looked at his plate. "Kids who came to youth group on Wednesday night because the church was the only safe building in their neighborhood. One of my students, a boy named Milo, walked forty-five minutes each way to get to youth group every week because his mother didn't have a car and the bus route didn't run that late. He was fourteen years old, and he came every single Wednesday for three years."

"What happened to him?"

"He graduated from high school last spring. He's at Virginia Commonwealth on a partial scholarship." Conner's voice was steady, but his eyes weren't. "He called me the day he got his acceptance letter, and I sat in my office and cried after I hung up."

Rebecca was quiet for a moment. The man sitting across from her had spent six years in a world she'd never experienced, pouring himself into teenagers who needed him in ways that went far beyond a Wednesday night lesson plan. She'd built a salon. He'd built lives. Both things mattered, and both were real. The fact that he spoke about Milo with the same tenderness her father used when he talked about his own children told her something no amount of conversation could have.

"Do you miss Richmond?" she asked.

"I miss the people. I miss Milo and the other kids. I miss David Raines and his wife, Cheryl, who made enough food to feed the entire youth group every Wednesday and still had leftovers." He picked up his glass. "But I don't miss the city. I don't miss the traffic, or the noise, or the feeling of being surrounded by a million people and none of them knowing my name. I'm a small-town person, Rebecca. I always was. I just had to leave to figure that out."

"I figured it out without leaving."

"Some people are smarter than others."

She grinned before she ate the last bite of her sandwich.

He stood, walked to the kitchen, and came back with several containers, his homemade dressing, and two more rolls. He set them on the table between them.

"Round two?" he said.

"Round two."

They made second sandwiches right there at the table, passing the containers between them and arguing about whether pepper jack was superior to Swiss on turkey. Rebecca maintained that it was. Conner looked at her as if she'd suggested tearing down the church steeple.

"Pepper jack has no business being on turkey," he said.

"You're wrong."

"I'm a man who keeps multiple cheeses in his refrigerator. I think my opinion on cheese pairings carries some authority."

"Having a lot of cheese doesn't make you right about cheese."

"It makes me more qualified than someone whose cheese drawer at home is probably a single bag of pre-shredded cheddar."

Rebecca set her sandwich down and leveled her gaze at him across the table. "I have mozzarella sticks in my freezer. Those count."

"Those absolutely do not count."

She bit into her pepper-jack-and-turkey sandwich, looked him square in the face, and smiled.

"You're impossible," he said.

"I'm right, and you know it."

He laughed, and the sound filled his small kitchen in a way that made the room feel larger. She was laughing too, and the laughter had been coming easier all afternoon. She was sitting at a table in Conner Delaney's kitchen on a Sunday afternoon, eating a sandwich she'd built from his ridiculous deli refrigerator. Not only that, but she was having the kind of fun that made her forget about anything else going on in her life.

That was the thing she kept noticing. Not the house, nor the food, nor the conversation, though all of those were good. What she noticed was the absence. The careful, cheerful, competent version of herself that she wore like a uniform was hanging somewhere by the front door with her jacket. The woman sitting at this table was someone simpler. Someone who argued about cheese and didn't think twice about whether her laughter was too loud or her appetite was too obvious.

She hadn't felt this way with anyone since Nathan, but even with Nathan, there had been a layer of carefulness between them, a holding back of herself. With Conner, the layer wasn't there. It had never been there, not when they were teenagers. Whatever was building between them moved through her without resistance, and the ease of it was the most frightening thing about it.

Because the last time something felt this easy, she was eighteen. And the ease had been a lie that unraveled over the course of a winter and ended with a phone call on a Tuesday night.

But this wasn't the same because they weren't the same. The man across from her was not the boy who'd left for college with a plan and a calling that swallowed everything in its path. This man had come home. He'd set a table for her to enjoy a simple lunch. He kept basil on his windowsill, six kinds of cheese in his refrigerator, and a Bible on his nightstand. He spoke about a fourteen-year-old boy in Richmond with the same tenderness her father used when he talked about his children. This Conner had been built by the decade that separated them, and so had she. The people they'd become were more real and more worthy of whatever was happening here than the teenagers who'd loved each other simply because they hadn't known how not to.

"You're quiet," he said.

She looked up. "I'm thinking."

"About?"

"About how you've surprised me every day that we've been together the past few days."

He held her gaze across the table.

"You've surprised me too," he said.

They finished their second sandwiches and cleaned up. She rinsed the plates and put them in the dishwasher while he put the containers back in the refrigerator. They moved around each other in the small kitchen with a coordination that felt borrowed from a longer history than a little over a week.

When the kitchen was clean and the counters wiped down, they stood near the sink. The afternoon stretched out before them.

"So," Conner said. "I've got the youth group material spread out in my office. We can work at the table in here, or we can move to the living room."

"Living room," she said.

"Go make yourself comfortable. I'll grab everything from my office and be right there."

She walked into the living room and settled into the corner of his couch. The cushion gave beneath her, and the knit throw blanket was soft against her arm where it draped over the side. She pulled it across her lap without thinking, the way she would in her own apartment, and then caught herself. She was wrapping herself in his blanket on his couch in his living room, and it hadn't occurred to her to ask.

She looked around the room. The bookshelf, the Grisham novel on the side table, and the braided rug Loretta had probably picked out. The framed photograph on the bookshelf was visible from here, and she could see it now. A family photo. The Delaneys at Thanksgiving: everyone crowded into Charles and Loretta's living room. Miles and Amber, Adam and Jenny, the kids, and Charles and Loretta. Everyone except Conner.

Rebecca sat in the quiet of the living room with his blanket across her lap and the photograph of his family on the shelf across the room, and she let herself feel what she'd been circling all afternoon. She was comfortable here. Not the kind of comfortable that came from a warm blanket across your lap and a hot cup of coffee in hand, but the kind that came from being in a space that felt safe in a way she hadn't prepared for. She wasn't managing herself here. She wasn't smoothing anything over or filling the silence with brightness. She was just here.

His footsteps came down the hallway. She kept her eyes on the throw blanket across her lap and let the last few seconds of quiet hold before the afternoon moved into whatever came next.

Whatever this was becoming, she wasn't running from it today.

Chapter 11

Conner gathered his laptop and his legal pad with updated notes, then added two printed pages of the Week 1 outline he'd formatted that morning. He stacked everything against the binder, tucked the pile under his arm, and walked down the hallway toward the living room.

When he came around the corner, he stopped.

Rebecca was curled into the corner of his couch with his throw blanket pulled across her lap, her feet tucked beneath her. Her blonde hair fell loose over one shoulder, and the afternoon light caught her gold stud earrings.

She looked up when she heard him and smiled.

"You look comfortable," he said.

"I stole your blanket."

"I noticed."

"It's really soft."

"My mom made it." He crossed the room and set the binder and legal pad on the coffee table. His laptop went beside them. "She knitted it the Christmas before I moved to Richmond."

Rebecca ran her thumb along the blanket's edge. "Loretta's handiwork. I should've known."

Conner sat down on the opposite end of the couch.

"All right," he said. "Are you ready to see what I've been working on?"

"I'm ready."

He opened the binder and turned it so she could see. The first page was a title sheet he'd designed with clean formatting: Chosen: An Eight-Week Identity Series for Teens. A short paragraph beneath the title described the series' purpose.

"The basic idea is straightforward," he said. "Eight weeks, one theme per session, all building toward the same core message. Every kid who walks into that room on Wednesday night is carrying some version of the same question. Am I enough? Do I matter? The series meets them inside that question and walks them toward an answer that holds up."

Rebecca leaned forward and pulled the binder closer. Her eyes moved down the outline, and he watched her read it with her full attention, the way she did everything.

"Week one," she said. "Do I even matter?"

"That's the hook. If I can't get them engaged in the first session, the rest falls apart. So I'm starting with the most honest question I can ask. Not a Bible verse. Not a principle. Just the raw question most of these kids are living with, and none of them are saying out loud."

She nodded and turned the page. He let her read without interrupting. She moved through the second tab, the third, and the fourth. Her finger traced the margin of one page where he'd written a note in blue ink. She read it, glanced at him, and turned back to the outline.

"Week four is where you bring in a little more scripture," she said.

"Right. The first three weeks are all human experience. Feeling invisible, comparing yourself to everyone around you, and carrying labels other people gave you. Ease on the scripture. By week four, they've had three sessions of hearing their own stories reflected back at them. They trust their peers, and hopefully by then they will trust me. That's when I ask the bigger question. Who gets to decide what you're worth?"

"That's smart," Rebecca said. "If you start with heavy scripture, half of them tune out because they think they already know what you're going to say."

"Exactly. They've heard it all before. God loves you; you're special; be yourself. It bounces off because there's no foundation under it. I build the foundation first. I let them feel the question. Then, when faith and scripture enter a little more heavily, it enters as an answer to something they've actually been asking."

She turned to week five. Her eyes lingered on the description. What If You've Been Overlooked? Directly hits the emotional space of feeling left behind in family, friendships, and life.

"This one's for Hannah," she said.

"It is. But it's also for every kid in that room who's ever felt like the world moved forward without them."

Rebecca looked at him. Her expression carried something beyond approval. The flyer at the salon had been logistics. The Wednesday setup had been coordination. This was the substance of what he was building, and the way she was studying it told him she recognized its quality.

"Conner, this is wonderful."

"Thanks."

"I don't mean that politely. The structure is thoughtful, the pacing is intentional, and you've clearly done this before. The way you've sequenced it, building trust before you ask for anything real, that's not something someone puts together on a guess. You learned that."

"Six years of trial and error," he said. "The first series I ever wrote in Richmond was terrible. I tried to cover everything in four weeks. By week two, I'd lost half the group because I was moving too fast and asking too much."

"What changed?"

"A kid named Deshawn pulled me aside after youth group one night and told me I was confusing him and he didn't understand. He said I sounded like the guidance counselor at his school. He was fifteen, and honestly, he was right."

Rebecca smiled. "Teenagers will tell you the truth faster than anyone."

"They will. And they aren't always nice about it."

She turned through the remaining tabs. Weeks six, seven, and eight. He watched her read the final session, You Are Not Invisible, and her hand rested flat on the page for a moment before she closed the binder.

"The whole series is solid, Conner. The only thing I'd say is, for week three, the labels session, think about how the boys and girls in this group carry labels differently. The girls hear things like 'too quiet,' 'too dramatic,' or 'not enough.' The boys hear 'lazy' or 'weird.' If you can acknowledge that difference in the room, even briefly, they'll know that what you're saying is real."

"That's a good note. I'll work it in."

"And week seven. The vulnerability session. You'll need to go first. If you ask them to share something real and you haven't given them anything real from your own life, they won't trust it."

He nodded. "I always intend to go first. In Richmond, I used to tell a story about my freshman year of college. How I went from being the kid who knew everyone to being nobody in a school of thousands of students. It's honest, and it's low-stakes enough that they don't feel like I'm trying to match their pain."

"Good. These kids will read you if you're performing. They'll know."

"Believe me, I know they will."

She settled back against the cushion and pulled the blanket higher on her lap. "So what does week one actually look like? Walk me through it."

"You want the whole session?"

"I want to know how you'd deliver it. The outline is strong on paper, but paper doesn't talk to teenagers. Show me what it sounds like in the room."

He looked at her. She was sitting sideways now, one knee pulled up, her back against the armrest.

"All right," he said. "You want to be my test audience?"

"I want to be your youth group. Give me the lesson the way you'd give it to them."

He laughed. "You're going to sit there and pretend to be a teenager?"

"I'm going to sit here and tell you if it works. Pretend I'm one of those kids. Wednesday night, seven o'clock. I just walked in, grabbed a cookie from the snack table, and I'm sitting in one of those metal chairs wondering if this will be boring."

Conner set the printed pages on the coffee table and leaned back.

"Okay," he said. "Here's how I'd start."

He paused.

"So, I want to ask you guys something. And I want you to be honest. There's no wrong answer here. I just want to know what's true for you." He looked at Rebecca. "Have you ever walked into a room and felt like nobody noticed?"

She tilted her head. She was taking the exercise seriously.

"Sure," she said. "Lots of times."

"Where? Give me one."

She considered it. "School, probably. Walking into the cafeteria on a day when my usual group wasn't at our table. Just standing there with my tray, looking around, wondering where to sit."

"What did that feel like?"

"Awful. Like everyone else had somewhere to be, and I was the only one who didn't."

"Did anyone notice you standing there?"

"Probably. But it didn't feel like it."

He nodded. "That's the thing about feeling invisible. It doesn't matter how many people are in the room. What matters is whether any of them are looking at you. And not just looking, but actually knowing you. The real you. Not the version you put on when you walk through the door."

Rebecca's mouth curved slightly. "That'll land with them. The distinction between looking and knowing."

He held up one hand. "Stay in it. You're not giving me feedback yet. You're in the circle."

"Sorry. Go ahead."

"So here's what I think happens," he said. "I think most of us walk around carrying this question in our back pocket, and we never pull it out because we're afraid of what the answer might be. The question is simple. It's only four words." He held her gaze. "Do I even matter?"

"Some of you heard that question and thought, yeah, I've asked myself that. Some of you heard it and wanted to say, No, I'm fine; that's not me." He leaned forward slightly. "And some of you heard it, and something in your chest got tight, because the question isn't theoretical for you. It's Tuesday morning at your locker. It's Friday night when nobody texts. It's sitting at the dinner table while your parents talk about your brother's grades or your sister's game, and nobody asks about your day."

Rebecca was still. Her knee was still pulled up, her arm resting on it, but her fingers had closed around the blanket's edge. Her eyes were on his face, and the playfulness from two minutes ago was gone.

"So I'm not going to stand up here and give you five reasons why you matter," he continued. "I'm not going to quote a Bible verse and tell you God has a plan, because you've heard that before and it might not have fixed the feeling. What I'm going to do instead is ask you to be honest for the next few minutes. And I'll go first."

He leaned forward, his elbows on his knees. "When I was eighteen, I left this town. I left my family, my friends, everything I knew, and I went to college four hundred miles away. And the first month I was there, I sat in a dining hall full of people and ate lunch alone every single day. Nobody knew my name. Nobody cared that I'd been the starting quarterback back home. None of that mattered. I was just another freshman in a hoodie, and the loneliness hit so hard I called my mom and my girlfriend every day for the first few months because their voices were the only thing that reminded me I existed."

Rebecca's gaze moved from his face to the blanket and back. Her expression had changed: a softening along her jaw, a loosening around her mouth.

"That's strong," she said.

"We're still in the exercise, Rebecca."

She blinked. "Right. Sorry."

"So after I share that, I'd go around the room. Not forcing anyone. Just opening the door. I'd say, has anyone else felt like that? It doesn't have to be the same situation or even involve something that happened at school. Just the same feeling. That question sitting in your chest that you can't put down."

He watched her. She was rubbing the blanket's edge between her thumb and forefinger, a small repetitive motion, and her eyes had drifted toward the window.

"What would you say?" he asked. "If you were sitting in that circle."

She was quiet for a few seconds. The furnace kicked on somewhere in the back of the house, a low hum that filled the pause.

"I'd say yes," she said. "I've felt like that."

Her voice was steady. But the tone had changed. The brightness she wore so naturally, the warmth that made her the center of every room she walked into, had pulled back. What sat behind it was something simpler and more tender.

Conner noticed. He'd spent six years listening for exactly this kind of shift. The moment a practiced answer gave way to a real one. His instinct was so deeply trained that it registered instantly.

"When?" he asked.

"When I was eighteen."

She said it to the window. Her profile was turned partly away from him, and the light caught the small gold chain around her neck.

"What happened when you were eighteen?" he asked.

She turned back toward him, and her blue eyes found his.

"Someone I loved left," she said. "And for months, I carried that question around with me every day. Do I even matter? Not in a dramatic way. I wasn't sitting in a dark room feeling sorry for myself. I went to beauty school. I went to church. I smiled at people and showed up where I was supposed to show up. But underneath all of that, in the quiet moments, when I was driving home or lying in bed at night, the question was there."

"The worst part wasn't the leaving," she continued. "People leave. People go to college, people follow their dreams, and people do what they're supposed to do. I understood that. I wasn't angry about it." She paused, and when she spoke again, her voice was thinner. "The worst part was realizing that the life he was building didn't need me in it. That his world got bigger and mine stayed the same size. After a while, I stopped registering. I became background noise in a life that used to have my name all over it."

Conner sat with those words. They moved through him slowly, and each one left a mark. Background noise. She called herself background noise. The girl who had been the center of his world at eighteen, the girl whose laugh could fill a gymnasium, had spent years believing she'd faded to nothing in his life.

The guilt arrived. It came from the place it always lived, the deep interior room where he kept the ledger of things he'd done wrong in his life, and it pressed against his ribs. He'd felt it at twenty-two when he'd finally begun to understand what his absence had cost her. He'd felt it at twenty-seven when the older pastor in Richmond had asked him to name his deepest regret, and he'd said her name without hesitation.

But the guilt wasn't the only thing. Something else sat beneath it, quieter and more important. She had just handed him something fragile. Something she'd kept locked away from everyone, wrapped in cheerfulness and competence and the relentless brightness the whole town loved her for. She'd opened a door she hadn't opened for anyone. She'd opened it for him. And the fact that she'd chosen him to hear it wasn't a burden. It was a gift so specific and so undeserved that it made his throat ache.

"I'm glad you told me that," he said.

She looked at him with glassy eyes and a steady chin.

"I don't have a speech for this," he said. "I'm not going to try to explain it or fix it. It happened, and you carried it, and I'm sorry you had to carry it alone."

She watched his face as he said it. He could feel her looking for what she expected. The deflection. The theological redirect. The carefully worded pastoral response designed to make the moment manageable. He gave her none of it. He sat where he was, his hands between his knees, his eyes on hers, and he let the apology be small and honest and complete.

"You don't have to be sorry, Conner. It was a long time ago."

"I know. That doesn't mean it stopped hurting."

She looked away. Her thumb traced the blanket's edge again, and she swallowed once.

"I haven't told anyone that," she said. "Not like that. Not the actual feeling of it."

He nodded. He didn't ask why she'd told him. He didn't say any of the twelve things pressing against the inside of his chest.

Things about the boy he'd been. The phone calls between them that had shortened over time. The nights he'd been too tired to dial her number and too self-absorbed to notice what his silence was building on her end.

Those conversations would come. He could feel them waiting, lined up in the distance like fence posts along a road he hadn't traveled yet. But not today. Today, the only thing this moment needed was for him to stay in the room and hold what she'd given him.

"For what it's worth," he said, "you were never background noise. Not for a single day. I know that's hard to believe, given what happened. But it's the truth."

She nodded. "I think that answers your question about whether Week 1 would work."

He let out a breath that was close to a laugh. "I'd say it was effective."

"Maybe too effective." The corner of her mouth lifted. "You might want to warn people before you start asking questions like that."

"I'll create a flyer. Warning: this series may cause accidental honesty."

She laughed. "Can I see the Week 1 handout?"

He passed her the printed pages. She read through them while he sat with what had just happened. His hands were still clasped and his pulse was steady, but the rest of him felt rearranged. She'd told him something real. She'd let him look through a window into a room he'd always known existed but had never been allowed to see. The view was both simpler and more painful than he'd imagined.

Background noise. Two words that cut deeply.

She looked up from the handout. "The reflection questions at the end are good. Especially the last one." She read it aloud. "'If you could tell one person how you really feel, who would it be, and what's possibly stopping you?' That's the one that'll keep them up at night."

"That's the intention. I want them thinking about it between sessions. The best youth group material doesn't end when the meeting ends. It follows them home."

"It'll follow them all right." She set the pages on the coffee table and glanced at her phone. Her expression shifted. "Oh. It's after five."

"Is that a problem?"

"I've got dinner at my parents' house at six. I should go," she said. She pulled the blanket off her lap and folded it in half, then in half again, and laid it over the arm of the couch where she'd found it and stood.

Conner stood with her. "Thanks for going through all of this with me. Your feedback is exactly what I needed."

"Your material doesn't need much feedback. It's strong, Conner. Really strong."

She reached for her purse on the floor beside the couch and slung it over her shoulder, then she straightened and looked at him.

"Tell your folks I said hello," he said.

"I will." She started toward the door, then paused. "Conner."

"Yeah."

"Today was a really good day."

"It was."

She nodded once, small and certain, and walked out his door. He stood at the window and watched her cross the gravel to her car. She opened her door, slid into her seat, and started the engine. Her headlights came on, and she backed out of his driveway with a careful turn.

Her taillights disappeared around the curve where the oaks pressed close to the road.

Conner stood in his living room, thinking about what Rebecca had said.

I became background noise in a life that used to have my name all over it.

Chapter 12

Anna was telling the story about the fire chief and the inflatable snowman for the second time this month, and it was still funny. Rebecca dried a serving bowl and set it on the counter while her sister stood at the kitchen island with a dish towel over her shoulder. Anna had picked up a wooden spoon from the drying rack for no reason other than to gesture with it.

"So Chief Hayes calls me at eight in the morning and says, 'Miss Hartwell, I need to discuss a safety concern regarding the spring festival.' And I'm thinking, okay, this is about the fire lane near the food vendors. Legitimate concern. Happy to discuss." Anna paused for effect. "It was not about the fire lane. It was about the inflatable snowman from the Christmas tree lighting."

"What about it?" Sarah asked.

"He wants to know if I'm planning to bring it back for the spring festival. In April. Because, and I quote, 'That snowman caused a significant distraction for traffic on Main Street, and I would like to be prepared.'"

"A significant distraction," Rebecca said.

"A sixteen-foot inflatable snowman at a Christmas event was a significant distraction," Anna said. "I told him the Spring Festival doesn't typically include snowmen, and he said, 'You never know with the Chamber.' As if we're out here deploying rogue inflatables."

Rebecca laughed. The faint clink of dishes mixed with the low rumble of the television from the living room, where her father and her brother Dave sat watching the game. Her mother stood at the far end of the counter in the kitchen, wrapping the leftover pot roast in foil. The kitchen smelled of rosemary and roasted meat, and the coffeemaker was halfway through a fresh pot.

This was Sunday evening at the Hartwell homestead. Her brother Jim and his wife Grace had left an hour ago. Mike and his fiancée, Nicole, had followed shortly after.

"You handled the Christmas event well, Anna," Olivia said from the counter. She pressed the foil around the edges of the dish and opened the refrigerator. "The tree lighting was beautiful. Half the town told me so afterward."

"Half the town told you because you asked half the town," Anna said.

"I didn't ask. People volunteer opinions to me. I'm approachable."

"You're nosy, Mom," Sarah said.

"I'm informed," Olivia said. She slid the dish onto the top shelf and closed the door. "There's a difference."

Rebecca smiled and reached for the next dish on the drying rack. Her mother's kitchen was the heart of this house, a room that had fed six children and now expanded every Sunday to fit whoever showed up. A framed family photo hung near the pantry door, all eight of them from two Christmases ago, crowded around the Christmas tree.

The coffee maker beeped. Olivia pulled four mugs from the cabinet and filled them without asking who wanted one. She set them along the island counter with a small pitcher of cream and a sugar bowl, and the four of them migrated to their usual spots. Anna perched on one of the bar stools. Sarah leaned against the counter with her arms folded. Olivia settled onto the stool closest to the stove. Rebecca stood across from her mother and wrapped her hands around her mug.

Anna picked up hers and blew across its surface. "So, Rebecca."

"So, Anna."

"I've been patient."

"You've been nothing of the sort."

Anna grinned. "Fine. I've been waiting until now so I could ask without any of the males in this household chiming in. How was lunch with Conner on Friday? And don't give me the short version."

Sarah's gaze moved from Anna to Rebecca.

Rebecca took a sip of her coffee. The lunch date at Minnie's Diner was still embedded in her mind.

"It was good," she said.

Anna raised her eyebrows. "Good."

"Really good."

"There we go. Keep talking."

Rebecca smiled and set her mug down. A week ago, she would have redirected this conversation with a joke or a question aimed back at Anna. She'd done it a hundred times. She'd done it so well that her family had learned to let her, because pushing Rebecca Hartwell where she didn't want to go was like pushing against water.

"When we sat down at Minnie's on Friday, he told me he had one condition for lunch. A clean slate. No talking about our past. We get to know each other as if we're meeting for the first time."

"That's interesting," Olivia said.

"It was," Rebecca said. "We just talked so easily. He asked me what I do when I'm not working. I asked him about Richmond. We talked about several things, and at some point I forgot to be careful."

"What do you mean, 'by careful'?" Sarah asked.

"I mean, I've been managing every conversation with him. Keeping it professional. Keeping it friendly but holding back." She picked up her mug again. "On Friday, I stopped doing that. I just sat there and enjoyed being with him, and it felt good."

Anna's grin had softened into something warmer. "I'm glad you went out to lunch with him."

"Me too. We had lunch at his place today also," Rebecca said. "After church. He'd invited me over to go through some material for the youth group."

"You went to his house?" Sarah said.

"I did. He had the most ridiculous sandwich spread I've ever seen in a single man's refrigerator. Six kinds of cheese, assorted meats, three mustards, and homemade balsamic vinaigrette."

"Homemade vinaigrette," Anna said. "What kind of man is this?"

"The kind who keeps basil on his windowsill like Mom does and keeps his home clean but lived-in," Rebecca said.

Anna pressed her hand to her chest. "I think I'm in love with him."

"Get in line," Rebecca said.

"Tell us about the youth group material," Sarah said.

"It's a series called 'Chosen.' Eight weeks on identity, designed specifically for teenagers," Rebecca said. "He doesn't start with tons of scripture or a lecture. He starts by asking honest questions and letting the kids talk. By the time more scripture enters the conversation, they're already invested because they feel like he's been listening to them and they trust him."

"That's good ministry," Olivia said.

"It is. And the thing that struck me, Mom, is how much he cares about kids. He told me about a student in Richmond named Milo who walked forty-five minutes to get to youth group every Wednesday because his family didn't have a car. Milo's at Virginia

Commonwealth now on a scholarship." She paused. "Conner cried when that boy called to tell him he got in."

The kitchen was quiet for a moment. From the living room, her father's voice rose briefly at something on the screen, and Dave's followed, lower.

"He's changed," Rebecca said. "I keep coming back to that. The boy I dated in high school was fun and sweet, but he was eighteen. He didn't know about life yet, just like I didn't." She traced the rim of her mug with her thumb. "The man I spent the afternoon with today has matured. He's experienced life, and it's changed him. The boy I knew is still in there, but he's so much larger now and deeper. I can see it in how he talks to people, how he listens, and how he remembers what you said three conversations ago and brings it up when it matters."

Anna was still on her stool, her coffee untouched. "Rebecca, I need to say something, and I need you to hear it the way I mean it."

"Go ahead."

"This is the first time since Conner came back that you've really talked about him. I've watched you deflect every question and smile your way through every mention of his name. Tonight is different. What happened today?"

Rebecca looked at her sister. "You're right. I told him something today that I haven't told anyone. Not the whole story of why I chose to break up with him. Just a piece of it."

"What did you tell him?" Olivia asked.

Rebecca looked at her mother. "I told him that after he left for college, I spent a long time asking myself if I even mattered. And he was the reason I kept asking myself that question back then."

Sarah unfolded her arms. She was quiet for a long moment, which was unusual for a woman who processed everything at the speed of action. When she spoke, her voice carried something softer.

"What did he do when you told him?"

"He listened. He didn't try to fix it or explain it away. He just sat there and let me say it." Rebecca's throat tightened. "And then he told me I was never background noise. Not for a single day."

Anna's hand found Rebecca's on the counter and squeezed it once.

"I still care about him," Rebecca said. "I've dated since Conner. You all know that. Nathan and the others. None of them are still in my heart the way he is. I've often thought that something was wrong with me, that I was stuck on a boy from high school and needed to let go and move on. But it wasn't about being stuck. It was about knowing what fits." She looked at her coffee. "Conner fits. He always did."

"I'm scared, though," Rebecca continued. "I won't pretend I'm not. The last time I let myself want this, I was eighteen, and I knew then that he was the person I wanted to build my life with. Now, I know he's not the same person, and I'm not either. But fear doesn't care about logic. It just remembers."

"Fear never does," Sarah said. "But you don't build anything worth having by listening to it. You build it by showing up when you're scared and doing the work, anyway."

Rebecca looked at her sister. Sarah Hartwell, who ran a construction crew and bid on commercial contracts, and had once torn down a load-bearing wall to prove an inspector wrong. She spoke about courage the way she spoke about framing a house. It wasn't a feeling. It was a decision you made every morning, and then you picked up your tools.

"She's right," Anna said. "And for the record, you're not stuck on a boy from high school. He's a man now, and he's matured and become a better person. You're smart enough to know that he's always been the one for you. He matters to you. You're a woman who knows what she wants and has been too afraid to admit it and go after it."

Rebecca smiled. Her eyes stung, and she blinked it away. "When did you get so smart?"

"I've always been smart. You just never listen to me because I'm the baby of the family."

"You're not the baby. You're the youngest."

"Same thing."

"It is not the same thing, and I will have this argument with you until I'm old and gray."

Anna laughed and released Rebecca's hand.

Olivia sat on her stool with her mug in her hands, watching her daughters. "Rebecca, can I say something?"

"Of course, Mom."

Olivia set her mug down and folded her hands on the counter. "I've watched you take care of everyone in this family for as long as I can remember. You were the one who noticed when Mike needed someone after Jenny died, and you moved in with him for a month. You were the one who drove Anna home from Knoxville when she couldn't stop crying long enough to get behind the wheel because a man broke her heart. You show up for every person in your life with your whole heart, and you never once ask anyone to show up for you."

Rebecca's chest tightened. She hadn't expected her mother to turn the conversation there.

"That's not a compliment, sweetheart. That's the thing I worry about most." Olivia's voice was gentle but certain. "Because somewhere along the way, you decided that needing someone was the same as being weak. And I understand why. I watched you close yourself off after you broke up with Conner, and I watched you do it again after Nathan left, and both times you smiled through it so well that most people believed you were fine." She paused. "I never believed it. Not once."

"What you told us tonight," Olivia continued, "about carrying that question for ten years, about wondering if you mattered, that breaks my heart. Not because you felt it, but because you felt it alone. Because you thought you had to." Her eyes held Rebecca's without wavering. "You don't have to earn the right to want something, Rebecca. You don't have to be brave enough, or strong enough, or healed enough first. You just have to be honest enough to say, This is what I want, and let the people who love you hold that with you."

Rebecca's throat ached. She pressed her lips together and nodded because speaking wasn't possible yet.

"I don't know where things are going with Conner," Olivia said. "And neither do you, and that's all right. Only God knows the road ahead of you; all you need to do is to be willing to listen and follow. You don't need a guarantee before you let yourself feel something. That's not how any of this works." She reached across the island and covered Rebecca's hand with hers. "The bravest thing you've done in ten years isn't what you told Conner this afternoon. It's what you just told us. You let us in, and nobody had to pry the door open to get here."

Rebecca looked at her mother's hand on hers. Olivia's fingers were slender; her wedding band worn thin from thirty-five years.

"Love you, Mom," she said.

"I love you too," Olivia said.

Sarah pushed off the counter and picked up the coffee pot. She refilled Rebecca's mug without being asked and then Olivia's. She set the pot back on the warmer and looked at Rebecca. "So what happens next?"

Rebecca wrapped her hands around her fresh coffee. "I don't know; I'll see him on Wednesday for youth group." She took a sip. "If this is going somewhere, I'm gonna let it."

Anna raised her coffee mug. "I'll drink to that."

Sarah looked at her. "It's coffee, Anna."

"I know what it is. I'm making a gesture. Let me have this."

Rebecca laughed.

Chapter 13

The Fluff & Curl was busy when Conner walked through the front door. Three stylists were working; their stations occupied. Claire Dawson's blow dryer hummed from the far corner. Country music played low from the speaker near the shampoo sinks, and Stacy Marsh was telling her client something that made the woman laugh hard enough to tip her head back in the chair.

Rebecca's salon chair sat empty, angled toward the mirror, her tools lined up along the shelf, but she wasn't there.

Jenna had a client in her chair, and her brush paused mid-stroke.

"Well... hello, Conner. No coffee for Rebecca today?" Jenna asked.

"Very funny, Jenna, and good afternoon, by the way."

She nodded toward the back of the salon. "She's in the supply room doing inventory. The door on the left, past the break room."

"I appreciate it."

"I'm sure you do."

Conner walked through the salon toward the back. He passed the row of shampoo sinks and the shelves of product bottles lined in neat rows. A narrow hallway led past the break room with its small table and two chairs. Beside it, a door stood open. Through it, he could see shelves stacked with boxes and bottles, and Rebecca standing with her back to the doorway. She held a clipboard in one hand and a pen in the other, counting bottles on a middle shelf, her lips moving as she tallied. Her blonde hair was pulled up in a loose twist held with a clip, and she wore a soft blue top with her sleeves pushed past her forearms.

He knocked once on the doorframe.

She turned and smiled when she saw him.

"Hi," she said.

"Hey."

She looked at his hands. "No coffee today?"

"No coffee."

"No flyers?"

"Not a single one."

She tilted her head. "Then what brings the assistant pastor of Serenity Crossing Community Church to my supply room on a Tuesday afternoon?"

He leaned his shoulder against the doorframe. "I was finishing up at the church and thought you might like a break. I've had a taste for something sweet all afternoon, and Sweet Surrender's right next door." He nodded toward the wall that separated her building from the bakery. "Coffee and whatever looks good in those bakery cases. My treat."

Rebecca set the clipboard on the shelf beside a row of shampoo bottles and placed her pen on top of it.

"I could use a break," she said.

"Yeah?"

"This inventory isn't going anywhere." She pushed her sleeves down and straightened her top. "Let me grab my coat."

Rebecca pulled her coat from the hook near the break room and slipped it on, then told Jenna she'd be next door for a bit as they walked past her.

"Take your time," Jenna said without looking up. "The inventory can wait... especially when our favorite assistant pastor comes calling."

"I couldn't agree more."

"Enjoy yourselves," Jenna said with a wicked grin.

Rebecca caught Conner's eye and shook her head. They walked through the salon and out the front door into the cold.

The sidewalk between the two storefronts was roughly twenty feet of concrete. The smell of butter and cinnamon reached him before they got to the door. He held it open for Rebecca, and the bell above it jingled as she stepped inside.

Sweet Surrender Bakery was warm and bright in the January afternoon. Long glass cases stretched the length of the counter, packed with rows of glazed donuts, cinnamon twists, and apple fritters that featured apples grown locally at Thompson Orchards. Platters of cookies shared space with thick brownies and lemon bars cut into generous squares. At the far end, slices of pie fanned out on display. The seating area held sturdy wooden tables with mismatched chairs and a few upholstered benches near the front windows, where the afternoon light pooled across the worn surfaces. Framed black-and-white photos of Serenity Crossing lined the walls between handwritten recipe cards and a big community corkboard.

"All right," Conner said. "What are we getting?"

Rebecca was already at the glass case. He watched her study the rows with her full attention, her eyes moving from the donuts past the muffins and the lemon bars. Her gaze slowed on the cream puffs in the refrigerated display and finally landed on a slice of coconut cream pie near the end.

"That one," she said, pointing.

"Coconut cream pie... I didn't know you liked coconut."

"I adore coconut anything."

She ordered the coconut cream pie and a coffee with cream. Conner ordered a slice of apple cake and a black coffee. The woman behind the counter, a round-faced woman in a flour-dusted apron with a name tag that read Patti, set their plates on a tray and filled two ceramic mugs from the pot behind the register.

"Haven't seen you in here before," Patti said as she handed him his change.

"I'm new in town. Relatively."

"He's the new assistant pastor at the church," Rebecca said.

Patti looked him over with the particular appraisal of a small-town businesswoman meeting a new face. "Welcome to Sweet Surrender, Pastor. You come back anytime. We're here six days a week, closed Sundays."

"I'll be back," he said.

They carried their tray to a table near the front window. Rebecca slid into the chair facing the window, and Conner sat across from her. She picked up her fork and cut into the pie without hesitation. Her first bite made her close her eyes for a second.

"This is so good," she said. Then she took another bite and pointed her fork at his plate. "Try yours."

He cut a piece of the apple cake. Dense and moist, with a ribbon of cinnamon through the center and a thin glaze across the top. "It's fantastic."

"Everything they make here is good. I come in here at least once a week, sometimes more." She set her fork down and picked up her coffee. "Patti saves me a coconut cream slice on Fridays because they sell out by noon."

"She saves you a slice?"

"Loyalty has its privileges."

He smiled and took a sip of his coffee. "So, you were doing inventory when I dragged you away from the salon. How's that going?" he asked.

"Slow. I'm about halfway through. We're running low on a few permanent color lines and some other supplies." She took a sip of her coffee and set it down. "I actually need to make a run to Gatlinburg tomorrow. There's a beauty supply warehouse I use for the colors and some supplies we can't get through our regular distributor."

"Gatlinburg," he said. "I haven't been out that way in years."

"It's changed a lot. More tourist shops, more traffic. But the supply warehouse is on the outskirts, so I usually don't have to deal with most of it."

"Would you like some company on the drive?"

She looked at him across the table. "Are you offering?"

"I'm offering. I'll drive. We could grab lunch out there while we're at it."

"I have two appointments in the morning. I can leave around noon, and we need to be back in time to set up for youth group."

"Plenty of time. Leave at noon, forty-five minutes out, pick up your supplies, grab lunch, and forty-five minutes back. We'd be home by four at the latest."

She turned her coffee mug in a slow circle on the table. "All right. That sounds good."

"Yeah?"

"I'll text you when my last morning appointment wraps up, and you can come get me."

He nodded and took another bite of his apple cake.

"Have you heard the forecast for Thursday?" she asked.

"Six to eight inches of snow. Maybe more, depending on which direction the front moves."

"That's a real snow. Not the dusting we got last week."

"You sound excited about it."

"I love a good snow. When it's heavy enough that the whole town goes quiet and everything slows down. When I was a kid, my daddy would take all six of us out to Henderson's Hill the morning after a big storm. We had three sleds between us and had to take turns. There were arguments."

"Henderson's Hill." Conner set his fork down. "I haven't thought about that place in years."

"We spent plenty of time on that hill."

"We did." The memory came back without effort, sharp and clear. "Senior year. Christmas break. That big storm that dropped almost a foot overnight... do you remember that?"

"I remember."

"You and I used that old wooden toboggan my grandpa kept in the barn."

"We hit that bump near the bottom," she said with a grin.

"We hit that bump, and the sled went one direction and we went another. I landed face-first in a snowbank, and you rolled about twenty feet past me."

She laughed, and the sound filled their corner of the bakery. "I had snow in places snow should never be. My coat was packed with it. I couldn't get up because I was laughing too hard."

"I remember... I couldn't either. We just lay there laughing hysterically."

"You crawled over and pulled the snow chunks out of my hair."

"You had about a pound of it between your neck and the collar of your coat, too."

Her whole face lit up with a smile, the kind that changed her eyes and softened the line of her jaw. "That was a good day."

"It was a really good day."

Rebecca glanced at the clock on the bakery wall. "I should get back. That inventory won't finish itself, and I have two more color clients this afternoon."

"I understand." He picked up their tray and carried it to the counter. Patti thanked them and told Rebecca she'd save her a slice Friday. Rebecca said she'd hold her to it.

They walked back out into the cold. The twenty feet of sidewalk passed in a few steps, and Rebecca stopped at her salon's front door.

"I'm glad you dropped by," she said. "I could get used to these kinds of breaks. See you tomorrow, Conner."

"I can easily arrange regular breaks for you, and I mean it," he said. "See you tomorrow, Becca."

Chapter 14

Conner's truck was idling at the curb in front of the Fluff & Curl when Rebecca stepped out of the salon and pulled the door shut behind her. The January air caught her immediately, sharp against her cheeks, and she tucked her chin into the collar of her coat. He was already out of the cab and rounding the front bumper, and he reached the passenger door before she got to it. He opened it and held it with one hand while she climbed up onto the seat.

"Thank you," she said.

"Yes, ma'am." He closed her door and walked back around to his side.

She set her purse on the floorboard near her feet and buckled her seatbelt.

Conner pulled away from the curb and turned left at the end of Main Street. Two blocks later they were past the town limits, the last storefront shrinking in his side mirror, and the road narrowed to two lanes.

"How were your appointments this morning?" he asked.

"Good. Tabitha Miller came in for her color at nine, and Anita Woodson followed her at ten-thirty for a cut and color. Both easy appointments." She adjusted her coat across her lap. "Anita brought me a jar of pickled okra from her garden this past summer. She brings me something every visit."

"Pickled okra."

"She makes it herself. It's actually good."

"High praise from a woman who grew up eating Olivia Hartwell's cooking."

"My mama would approve of Linda's pickled okra. She'd also ask for the recipe and then change three things about it and call it her own."

Conner laughed. He drove with one hand on his steering wheel and his left arm resting against his door. His flannel shirt was rolled up to his forearms, and his watch caught a glint of pale light from his window.

"What about your morning?" she asked.

"I met with Warren for about an hour. We went over the schedule for February and talked about the men's breakfast the deacons want to do the first Saturday of next month. After that, I spent some time in my office working on the Week Four lesson for the youth series."

"How's it coming?"

"Slow. Week Four is where more scripture comes in and more focused study for the kids when they go home. I want the transition to feel earned. If I bring it in too early, the kids will check out, I'm sure."

"You'll get it right," she said. "You've been thinking about it long enough."

The road curved to the right and began its climb into the foothills. Winter-bare trees pressed close on both sides, their branches laced overhead like lattice. The pavement followed the ridgeline. Through gaps in the tree cover, Rebecca could see the mountains layered in blue and gray, each ridge a shade lighter than the one in front of it. A thin cloud cover had moved in since morning, and the landscape carried the soft, muted look of a watercolor left to dry.

She'd driven this road hundreds of times during her years working at Pam Castillo's salon in Gatlinburg. Forty-five minutes each way, five days a week for three years. She knew every curve, every spot where the cell signal dropped, and every pull-off where she used to park on summer evenings just to watch the sky change colors as the sun set over the ridgeline. But today the passenger seat gave her a different angle on a familiar road, and the company beside her made the miles feel shorter before they'd even started.

"Have you heard the updated forecast for tomorrow?" Conner asked.

"Jenna checked it this morning. They bumped it up to eight inches, possibly more overnight into Friday."

"That's a real storm."

"I hope it is. I love a heavy snow. Everything gets quiet, and nobody expects you to be anywhere."

"You and snow," he said. "You talked about it the same way yesterday at the bakery."

"Because I mean it. Some of my best memories involve snow-storms." She turned slightly in her seat to face him. "Can I tell you about the time I got snowed in at Pam Castillo's house?"

"Of course, you can tell me anything."

"It was my second winter working at her salon. It was early February, and the forecast called for two or three inches, nothing serious. I drove to work like normal, and by noon it was coming down so hard you couldn't see the parking lot from the front window. It kept going all afternoon. By four o'clock there were nine inches on the ground, and the roads were a mess."

"And you had a forty-five-minute mountain drive home."

"Yep. Pam took one look at the road and said, 'You're not driving home in this. You're staying with me.' She lived about ten minutes from the salon on a back road, and we barely made it there. Her driveway was uphill, and her car fishtailed twice trying to get up her hill. We ended up leaving the car at the bottom of the hill and having to walk up to her house."

Conner glanced over at her. "How long were you stuck?"

"Two and a half days. The plows didn't get to her road until early in the morning on our third day." Rebecca smiled at the memory. "We ate everything in her pantry. She made this tomato soup from scratch the first night, using whatever she had on hand. We ate it with saltine crackers and sliced cheese because her bread was frozen solid."

"Frozen solid?"

"She kept her bread in the freezer. I didn't know anyone did that until I stayed at her house."

"My mom does the same thing."

"It's a generational commitment, apparently." Rebecca shifted her purse with her foot and settled deeper into her seat. "The second day we stayed in our pajamas until dinner. Pam made pancakes at two in the afternoon. We sat at her kitchen table, and she taught me how to read a profit-and-loss statement. She pulled out her salon's actual books and walked me through every line. Revenue, cost of goods, overhead, payroll. I learned a lot about running a business in those two and a half days."

"She sounds like the kind of mentor who doesn't waste a single opportunity."

"She didn't waste anything. Not time, not a teachable moment." Rebecca looked out of her window. The trees thinned along a stretch where the ridge dropped away and a narrow valley opened below. "We also watched three movies back to back the second night. She had a whole shelf of old films. Doris Day, Audrey Hepburn. She made popcorn on the stove in a big pot with real butter. We sat on her couch in our pajamas and didn't move for the rest of the evening."

"That sounds like a good snow day."

"It was one of the best."

The road dipped into a hollow and crossed a small bridge over a creek. The water below was dark and narrow, moving fast between mossy rocks. On the far side, the road climbed again, and the trees thickened.

"Speaking of snowstorms," Conner said. "I thought about Henderson's Hill last night after I got home. That entire day came back to me. More of it than I expected."

"Me too," she said. "I was lying in bed last night, and I started remembering things I hadn't thought about in years."

"Like what?"

"Like how after we wiped out at the bottom, we walked back up to go again. And Tyler Knox and Brooke Simmons showed up with their sleds. Then Kevin Barker came, and then the Weber twins. By the end of the afternoon, there were probably fifteen of us out there."

"Tyler brought that green plastic sled that was cracked down the middle."

"And he rode it anyway. He made it halfway down before it split in two, and he just slid the rest of the way on his back."

"I remember that." Conner shook his head. "He stood up at the bottom, covered in snow, and held up both halves of the sled like he'd won a trophy."

"Brooke was yelling at him from the top of the hill to stop being ridiculous, and he yelled back, 'This is the best day of my life.'"

"That was Tyler."

"It was; he was such a happy-go-lucky type of person." She smiled and let the memory settle. "Do you remember the drive home that night?"

He glanced at her. "I do."

"I was so tired. We'd been out there for hours. I got in your truck, and your heater was going, and I remember thinking I'd just close my eyes for a minute."

"You were out before we hit the main road."

"I remember. I woke up when you parked in my parents' driveway, and it took me a second to figure out where I was." She paused. "But here's what I'm not sure if I remember right or not. My parents' house is ten minutes from Henderson's Hill. I remember looking at the clock on your dash when I woke up because it was pitch-black outside, and we'd been driving for over an hour. Did we go somewhere else, or am I remembering wrong?"

Conner kept his eyes on the road.

"No, you're remembering right. I drove around town and then took a drive through the mountains."

"Why?"

He was quiet for a few seconds. The road curved gently through a stand of bare birch trees, their white trunks pale against the winter woods.

"You looked peaceful," he said. "You had your coat bundled up against the window like a pillow, and you were deep asleep. I didn't want to wake you up yet. But eventually, I had to get you home in time for your curfew... otherwise I would have just kept driving around to let you sleep."

Rebecca turned her face toward her window. The mountains moved past in their slow procession, ridge behind ridge, each one a lighter shade of gray than the one before it. She pressed her lips together and let the ache of that image move through her. Eighteen years old and asleep in his truck. And he'd driven who knows how many miles just so she could rest.

"That was a perfect day," she said quietly.

"It was."

The road straightened for a long stretch, running parallel to a split-rail fence that bordered a cattle farm. Black Angus stood in clusters near a frozen water trough, their dark shapes stark against the brown pasture. A barn with a rusted tin roof sat at the far edge of the field. Smoke rose from the chimney of the farmhouse beside it, a thin column that dissolved into the low clouds.

"You said you were lying in bed last night remembering things," Conner said. "What else came back?"

Rebecca looked at him. She liked that he'd been listening closely enough to circle back to something she'd said ten minutes ago. "A lot, actually. One memory kept pulling up the next one." She smiled. "A favorite of mine was a trip I took a few years ago. My mama took me, Sarah, and Anna to Asheville for a long weekend. No, Dad, no brothers. Just the Hartwell women, as my mama called it."

"Where'd you stay?"

"A little bed and breakfast near downtown. Two rooms, one with a fireplace. Anna and I shared the fireplace room, and Mama and Sarah took the other one." She turned her hands over in her lap, and her coral-painted nails caught the light. "We spent three days doing whatever we wanted. We walked through every shop on those downtown streets. Mama bought a ceramic vase that she fell in love with. Anna found a bookstore and stayed in it for an hour while the rest of us went to a cafe next door."

"Anna in a bookstore for an hour. That sounds about right."

"She came out with a bag full of books and a grin on her face." Rebecca smiled. "The second day we hiked in the Blue Ridge Mountains. Mama kept stopping to take pictures of every wild-flower she saw. Anna was ten steps ahead the entire time because she walks like she's trying to set a land-speed record. Sarah and I stayed in the middle and just talked."

"What did you talk about?"

"Everything. Her construction business, my salon, and what we wanted for the next few years. Sarah doesn't open up easily, but when she does, she's wonderful to talk to. She told me that weekend that she admired what I'd built with the Fluff and Curl. That she was proud of me." Rebecca looked down at her hands. "Sarah doesn't say things like that usually. It meant a lot because I look up to her."

"Your sisters are lucky to have you. Your whole family is."

"I'm the lucky one," she said. "That trip is another one of my favorite memories. We shared plates at every restaurant that caught our eye and laughed at Anna for putting hot sauce on everything. On the last morning, Mama made us all sit on the porch of that bed and breakfast with our coffee, and she said, 'I want you three to remember this. Whatever life brings you, you've always got each other.' And then she cried, and we all cried, and Sarah said, 'Mama, it's seven-thirty in the morning.'"

Conner laughed. "Your mama is something else."

"She is. I cherish that trip more than they probably realize."

They passed a green road sign that read Gatlinburg, 14 miles. The road began a gradual descent, switching back through a series of curves that followed the contour of the mountain. Conner took them easily, his hand steady on the wheel. The trees changed as they dropped in elevation. More evergreens appeared among the hardwoods, dark green against the bare gray branches.

"Can I ask you something?" Rebecca said.

"Of course."

"You told me about Richmond. The ministry, the work you did there. But what about the rest of your life? When you weren't at the church, what did you do?"

He thought about it for a second. "Honestly, the first couple of years, there wasn't much separation between work and the rest of my life. I went home, I ate, I slept, and I went back to work. Richmond was consuming in the beginning."

"But it got better?"

"It did. I'd say around midway through my second year, I'd started to find my rhythm. I cooked a lot. I started hiking on my days off and found some good trails outside the city." He adjusted his grip on the steering wheel. "But the best thing I did outside of church during those early years happened my second fall in Richmond. My college buddy Derek called me out of the blue on a Monday night and said he was driving down from D.C. and wanted to know if I could take a couple of days off. He wanted to go to the Outer Banks."

"The Outer Banks?"

"Yep, neither of us had ever been. I talked to Pastor Raines the next morning, told him I hadn't taken a day off in over a year, and he practically pushed me out of the building. Derek picked me up that afternoon. We hit the North Carolina border, and his GPS took us on some back road through rural countryside that added an hour to the trip. We missed a turn and ended up in a town that had one gas station, a post office, and a church, and nothing else."

"That sounds like a great start to a vacation."

"We stopped at that gas station and bought the saddest-looking pre-wrapped sandwiches you've ever seen. Turkey and cheese on half-stale white bread. And we sat on the curb outside and ate them, and Derek said, 'This is gonna to go down in the record books as the best vacation ever... I can feel it in my bones.'"

"Did you make it to the beach?"

"Eventually. We got lost a second time trying to find the campground, and drove past it twice because the sign was hidden behind a bush. We set up the tent in the dark and woke up the next morning to the sound of the ocean."

"That's a good way to wake up."

"It was. We spent two days on that beach doing absolutely nothing. Swimming and sitting in camp chairs, staring at the water. We tossed a football around a bit. But we had no schedule. No one needed anything from either of us." He paused. "I think about that trip sometimes. Derek and I lost touch a few years back, but those days have stayed with me."

"Because it was a simple vacation with nothing planned."

"That and because I didn't have to be anything for anyone. I was just a twenty-something-year-old man sitting on a beach with a buddy without a care in the world."

Rebecca looked at him. "Can I ask you something else?"

"I'm an open book."

"What was the hardest part about Richmond?"

He didn't answer right away. The road curved left, and a stand of tall pines cast long shadows across the pavement. He took the curve and let his truck straighten before he spoke.

"Sunday evenings," he said. "The church services were over. I'd drive home to my apartment, and I'd sit on my couch with leftovers and whatever was on television, and it would hit me that the whole week was going to reset in the morning, and I'd do it all again." He kept his eyes forward. "The work was good. I loved the work. But Sunday evenings were when I noticed the emptiness in my life. On Sunday evenings, I missed my family in the worst way because growing up, Sundays were always family days. We'd go to church and then home and enjoy family time. Sitting alone in that apartment in Richmond was tough."

Rebecca didn't respond right away. She watched the mountains through his windshield, the way they opened and closed around the road as it descended. A hawk circled above a cleared field to the left, riding a thermal in slow spirals.

"I know what that feels like," she said.

Conner glanced at her.

"Saturday nights," she said. "That's when it gets to me. Not always. Most Saturdays I'm fine. I close the salon, I go upstairs, and I make dinner. It's a good routine." She traced the seam of her coat with one finger. "But sometimes, it seems like everyone but me has somewhere to be. The town square is alive; couples are out enjoying the evening, and my friends are out on dates or with their spouses. Saturday nights are when I notice the emptiness."

They drove without talking for a minute.

Rebecca watched a farmhouse pass on the right, its windows lit against the gray afternoon. A child's swing set stood in the side yard, motionless in the still air.

"Come to dinner Saturday," she said.

Conner looked at her.

"At my place," she said. "I'll cook."

He nodded. "I'd like that."

"Good."

"What if we did this?" He said. "I'll pick you up after you're done working for the day. We can run by the grocery store and grab what we need and cook together."

"I'd like that."

The road leveled out as the descent eased, and Gatlinburg appeared ahead of them. A gas station on the left. A souvenir shop with a wooden bear carved out front. The traffic thickened as the two-lane road widened and a few side streets branched off toward the main tourist strip.

"Have you eaten at Brick and Vine?" Rebecca asked.

"Not that I recall. What is it?"

"A wood-fired pizza place on the east side of town. Small, nothing fancy. The crust is thin, and they use fresh mozzarella. It's one of my favorites out here."

"Are you suggesting that for lunch?"

"I am. Unless you had something else in mind."

"I had nothing in mind. You know this town better than I do."

"Then Brick and Vine it is. There's also a grocery store about two blocks past the restaurant. We should stop there and grab snacks and drinks for the youth group tonight. I meant to pick some things up yesterday, but the bakery sidetracked me."

"I'll take partial credit for that."

"You should take full credit."

He grinned and slowed his truck as they approached a stoplight. The main strip of Gatlinburg stretched out before them. Tourist shops lined both sides of the road, their signs advertising taffy and T-shirts. A family in matching jackets crossed at the crosswalk. Beyond the storefronts, the mountains rose, their ridgelines softened by the low clouds.

The light turned green, and Conner eased his truck forward.

"The beauty supply warehouse is on Birch Street," she said. "Take the second right past the pancake house."

"Copy that."

She settled back in her seat and let the familiar streets pass. Saturday. Her kitchen. A meal from scratch with the man sitting beside her. The thought of it sent a thrill of excitement coursing through her.

Chapter 15

Rebecca dropped a box of spaghetti into the cart and kept walking. Conner picked it up, read the label, and put it back on the shelf.

She turned around. "What are you doing?"

"We're not using that." He scanned the row above it and pulled a different box. "This one. Bronze-cut. It holds the sauce better."

"Conner, it's pasta."

"This is better pasta." He set the box in the cart and pushed it forward. "Trust me."

Valley Grocery on a Saturday evening had the unhurried feel of a town winding down its week. A few families moved through the aisles with loaded carts. Hank Morrison's teenage son restocked canned goods near the front with his earbuds in, nodding along to something only he could hear. The warm smell of fresh bread hung in the air near the deli, mixing with the faint sweetness of the cookie display that had been picked over since morning.

Rebecca walked beside the cart with her coat unzipped and her purse slung over one shoulder. Her hair was down, loose past her shoulders, and her nails today were a deep winter berry that caught the fluorescent light every time she reached for something on a shelf. She'd changed out of her salon clothes before he picked her up, and the jeans and cream-colored sweater she wore softened her whole presence in a way that made it hard for him to look anywhere else for long.

"All right," she said. "What else do we need?"

"Chicken breasts, mozzarella, Parmesan, and the ingredients for the sauce. Garlic. Basil if they have it fresh. And bread for the garlic bread."

"There's frozen garlic bread in aisle six."

"We're making it from scratch."

She stopped and turned to look at him. "You want to make garlic bread from scratch when there's a perfectly good frozen loaf thirty feet from where we're standing."

"Frozen garlic bread has no business being in the same kitchen as homemade chicken Parmesan," he said.

"That is so dramatic."

"And I stand by every word of it."

She shook her head, and he pushed the cart toward the produce section, and for the next fifteen minutes, they moved through the store with the easy rhythm of two people who had nowhere else to be. He picked out Roma tomatoes and a bulb of garlic while she grabbed a bag of mixed greens for a salad. They debated olive oil brands in aisle three, Conner holding up two bottles and explaining the difference between first-press and blended while Rebecca told him he sounded like a cooking show host. She reached past him for a block of Parmesan from the cheese case, and her arm brushed his as she pulled it from the shelf. Neither of them said anything about it. She set the cheese in the cart and kept walking.

At the bread display near the bakery, Conner picked up a loaf of Italian bread and tested the crust with a gentle squeeze. Rebecca stood beside him with her arms folded.

"Are you interviewing the bread?"

"I'm checking the freshness."

"It was baked this morning. I can see the date on the tag."

"The tag and the bread don't always agree." He set the loaf in the cart. "This one's good."

"I'm relieved."

He turned the cart toward the checkout lanes, and as they walked, he caught their reflection in the glass of the freezer case along the far wall. The ordinariness of what he saw made him smile.

They loaded the items onto the belt, and Conner reached for his wallet, but Rebecca's card was in the reader before he got it out of his pocket.

"You didn't have to do that," he said.

"My kitchen, my groceries."

"I'm the one who vetoed half your choices."

"And I let you, which means I've already been more generous than you deserve." She signed the screen with her finger and took her receipt from the girl at the register, who smiled at both of them without saying a word.

They carried the bags across the parking lot to his truck. The January air had sharpened since they'd gone inside, and the sky above the parking lot had deepened to a cold, clear navy. A handful of stars were already visible past the reach of the lot lights. Conner opened his rear door and set the bags on the back seat, then walked around and climbed into his side while Rebecca settled into the passenger seat and pulled her door shut.

He started his engine and pulled out of the Valley Grocery lot, turning onto Oak Street. The heater pushed cold air across his dashboard for a few seconds before it warmed up . Two blocks south, he took a right onto Main, and the storefronts along the town square appeared on both sides, glowing in the early evening. The white gazebo sat under a layer of snow that reflected the nearest streetlamp. A couple walked arm in arm past the bookstore with their breath trailing behind them, and a man in a heavy coat was turning the deadbolt on the front door of Jim Hartwell's hardware store.

Conner drove past the Fluff & Curl, the salon windows were dark, the Closed sign visible behind the glass. He turned at the end of the block and followed the narrow side street, then turned again into the alley.

He parked beside a wooden staircase that climbed the rear of her building to a second-floor landing. He stepped out into the cold and opened his rear door to gather the grocery bags, two in each hand. Rebecca came around his side of the truck and took one of the bags from his left hand.

"I can carry all of them," he said.

"I know you can. I'm choosing to help."

They crossed the small patch of snow-covered asphalt behind her building and reached the bottom of the stairs. Conner looked up at the landing above them. The deck was wide enough for the two cushioned chairs and a small table he could make out in the dim light. Beyond the railing, the rooftops of Main Street stretched in both directions, and the mountains rose behind them as a dark, uneven line against the last color in the sky.

He followed Rebecca up the stairs.

Rebecca set her bag down on the deck table and unlocked her door. She pushed it open and reached inside to flip a switch, and warm light filled the doorway.

"Go on in," she said.

Conner stepped through her door and into the apartment for the first time.

The space opened directly into her living room, and the warmth reached him before anything else. Her walls were a soft ivory that held the lamplight close, and the room had the particular glow of a space lit by lamps rather than overheads. A cream-colored sofa sat against the far wall, with a sage green throw draped over one arm and two blush-pink pillows tucked against the cushions. A small coffee table held a candle in a glass jar and a short stack of books. Beside the sofa, an upholstered chair in a muted coral faced the windows that looked down onto Main Street.

Her floors were a light wood that ran the full length of the apartment, and an area rug in soft neutrals anchored the seating area. Framed prints hung on the walls, florals in quiet colors that matched the sage and blush she'd carried through the room. A built-in shelf near the windows held a row of books, and he recognized them immediately. Historical romance novels, a dozen or more, their spines creased from reading and rereading. Beside them, a framed photograph sat propped against the end of the row. Bill and Olivia Hartwell, surrounded by their six children, everyone dressed for a holiday, Rebecca near the center with Anna beside her, both of them grinning.

Her kitchen was to his right, separated from the living room by a short counter with two stools tucked beneath it. The space was smaller than his kitchen at the parsonage, with an L-shaped counter, white cabinets, and brushed gold hardware that caught the lamplight. A ceramic utensil holder sat beside her stove, and a small potted herb occupied the windowsill above her sink. Her counters were clean, everything in its place. A dish towel with a floral pattern hung from her oven handle.

Past the kitchen, a small round dining table with four chairs sat near the window. Two cloth napkins were folded beside two plates, and two glasses waited beside them.

He smiled and carried the grocery bags to her kitchen counter. The windows at the far end of her apartment looked down onto Main Street, and from this angle he could see the gazebo, the front of the bookstore, and the storefronts that were still open. She woke up to this view every morning. She came home to it every night.

She'd chosen it, and she'd designed every detail of the surrounding space with the same care she brought to her salon, her clients, and her family.

Everything in this apartment told him who she'd become while he was gone. A decade of choices, each one hers alone, and the result was a home that was warm and beautiful and entirely Rebecca's .

She hung her coat on a hook beside the door and joined him in the kitchen. She stood across the counter from him and started unpacking the bags.

"So," she said. "Chef Delaney. Walk me through the plan."

He pulled the chicken breasts from the bag and set them on her counter. "I'll bread and fry the chicken. While that's working, I'll build the sauce from the tomatoes and garlic. Once the chicken's done, it goes in a baking dish with sauce and mozzarella, and we finish it in your oven."

"And my job?"

"Salad and garlic bread. You're on side duty."

"Side duty." She raised her eyebrows. "You've been in my home for two minutes, and you've already demoted me."

"I've promoted you. Garlic bread is the most important part of the meal. Slice the Italian bread lengthwise, mix butter with minced garlic and a little parsley if you have it, spread it on both halves, and we'll broil it at the end."

She opened a drawer and pulled out a cutting board. He found her knives in the block beside her stove and chose the chef's knife, testing its edge with his thumb.

They fell into a rhythm that built itself without planning. When he stepped toward her stove, she shifted back toward the counter. When she reached past him for the olive oil on the shelf above the range, he moved to give her room. Her kitchen wasn't built for two people cooking at the same time, and the closeness was constant and unhurried. Each time she moved beside him, he was aware of the small space between them.

Conner had sliced the chicken breasts thinly and set up a breading station using three of her shallow bowls. Flour in the first, beaten eggs in the second, and breadcrumbs mixed with grated Parmesan in the third. He dredged each piece through the line while the olive oil heated in her largest skillet.

"Where did you learn to do that?" she asked. She'd been slicing the Italian bread on her cutting board beside him, and she'd paused to watch his hands work through the breading.

"A cooking channel on YouTube," he said. "I spent about a year watching videos every night and then trying whatever I'd seen. Chicken Parmesan was one of the first things I got right."

"You taught yourself to cook from YouTube."

"YouTube and a lot of failed attempts. The pizza I told you about at Minnie's was early in the process."

"The cinder block pizza."

"That was rock bottom. Everything improved after that."

She went back to slicing the bread, and he laid the first pieces of chicken into the hot oil. The sizzle filled her kitchen, sharp and immediate, and the smell of frying breadcrumbs rose from the skillet. She opened the window above her sink an inch, and a ribbon of cold January air slipped in and mixed with the warmth from her stove.

"Smart," he said.

"I've set off that smoke detector before. It's sensitive, and I'd rather not explain to my neighbors why my building is screaming on a Saturday night."

He turned the chicken with a pair of tongs from her utensil holder. The coating had browned to a deep golden, the edges crisp and even. He transferred the pieces to a plate lined with paper towels and started the second batch.

While the chicken fried, he filled a pot with water and set it on her back burner for the pasta, then turned to the sauce. He heated olive oil in a smaller pan, dropped in the minced garlic, and let it soften until the smell filled her kitchen. The chopped tomatoes went in next, and he stirred them down with a wooden spoon, added a pinch of red pepper flakes and a torn handful of fresh basil, and let the sauce simmer low while he finished the second batch of chicken. Rebecca had the garlic bread assembled on a baking sheet beside him, the butter and garlic mixture spread in an even layer across both halves. She covered it with foil and set it near her oven for later. Then she moved to the salad, tearing greens into a wooden bowl she pulled from the cabinet above her refrigerator.

"Do you have vinegar?" he asked. "I'll make a quick dressing."

"Cabinet to your left. Top shelf."

He opened the cabinet and found red wine vinegar beside a bottle of apple cider vinegar and a small jar of honey. He pulled the red wine vinegar and the olive oil from the counter along with some herbs and mixed a simple vinaigrette in a coffee mug, whisking it with a fork.

"You and your homemade dressings," she said.

"It's vinegar and oil. Takes sixty seconds."

"Most people just buy a bottle, Conner."

"Most people haven't met Mrs. Benedetto."

"Who?"

"My old neighbor in Richmond. Italian woman who lived two doors down from my apartment. She told me the secret to any good vinaigrette was to stop buying it in a store." He drizzled the dressing over the salad and tossed it with two forks. "She fed me dinner at least once a week for two years and treated me like a grandson."

Rebecca covered the salad and put it in her fridge while Conner assembled the baking dish. Sauce on the bottom, chicken layered in, more sauce over the top, sliced mozzarella covering everything. He slid the dish into her oven and set the temperature.

"Fifteen minutes for the cheese to melt," he said. "I'll drop the pasta when we're close."

She leaned against her counter with her arms folded. "While we wait, you owe me a question."

"I owe you a question?"

"Yep... come on, play along. Fifteen minutes. Clock's running."

He leaned against the opposite counter, three feet from her, and took a sip of the sweet tea she'd poured from a pitcher in her refrigerator.

"All right," he said. "What did you want to be when you were a kid?"

"A teacher," she said. "Like my mama."

"Really?"

"From the time I was about seven until I was thirteen, I was convinced I was going to teach second grade. I used to line my stuffed animals up on my bed and give them lessons." She picked up her glass of tea and settled against the counter behind her. "I had a grade book I made out of a composition notebook. I graded those stuffed animals on participation and behavior."

"Did any of them fail?"

"A bear named Captain. He had a terrible attitude and wouldn't stay seated."

Conner laughed. "What happened to the teaching dream?"

"I started doing hair," she said. "My mama let me practice on her when I was thirteen. French braids, updos, anything I could find in a magazine. Anna was my second test subject because she'd let me do whatever I wanted without complaining. By the time I was fifteen, I was doing hair for every girl in my class before school dances, and I just knew."

"From stuffed animal teacher to stylist."

"The common thread is that I've always wanted to take care of people. The method just changed."

He let that settle. It ran through everything she'd built. The salon, the youth group, the way she remembered what people needed before they asked for it.

"What about you?" she said.

"I wanted to be a park ranger."

Her eyebrows lifted. "A park ranger."

"Dead serious. From about age ten to age fifteen, that was the only future I could see. I spent every free hour in the mountains. I knew every trail within ten miles of our house, and I'd hike until my legs gave out and then sit on a ridge watching the valley until it got dark." He turned his glass in his hand. "I told my dad when I was twelve that I was going to live in one of those ranger cabins in the Smokies. He looked at me and said, 'Sounds like a fine life, son.'"

"That's very Charles Delaney," she said.

"It is. He didn't try to redirect me or suggest something more practical. He just let me have it."

"When did your calling to become a pastor happen?"

"Gradually. Our youth pastor at church was the first person who made faith feel like something I could build a life on. He didn't talk down to us. He talked to us as if we were smart enough to handle real questions." He glanced at her oven timer. Eight minutes left. "By the time I was sixteen, I knew. The mountains weren't going anywhere, but the work Steve was doing with us, that was something I wanted to give to other people."

"Do you ever miss the park ranger version?"

"Sometimes. When I'm on a trail and it's quiet and there's nothing but trees and sky for miles, I think about what that life would've looked like." He smiled. "But I wouldn't trade what I do. The ranger version of me would've been happy. The version of me that stands in front of a congregation or a room full of youths on Wednesday nights is fulfilled in a way I don't think the ranger would've been."

Her oven timer showed five minutes. Conner pushed off the counter and dropped the spaghetti into the pot of boiling water on her back burner, stirring it once with a long fork. Rebecca refilled both their glasses from the pitcher and set his on the counter beside him.

"My turn," he said. "What are you most proud of in your adult life that has nothing to do with the salon?"

She looked at him for a moment. Then her gaze moved across her apartment, traveling from the living room to the windows to the walls she'd painted and the furniture she'd chosen.

"This," she said. "This apartment. The salon is my business, and I love it, but this space is mine in a different way. I designed every inch of it. I picked every color, every piece of furniture, every detail down to the hardware on those cabinets." She traced her finger along the edge of her counter. "Sarah's crew did all the major construction, but every decision came from me."

She paused, and her expression shifted into something quieter.

"It was the first thing I ever built that was just for me," she said. "The salon is for my clients and my team. The youth group is for the kids. My family gets everything I've got, and I give it gladly. But this apartment is the one place where I'm only taking care of myself, and I gave it everything I had because I wanted to prove that I deserved the same effort I give everybody else."

"It shows," he said. "Every bit of it."

Her oven timer went off. Conner pulled the chicken Parmesan out and set it on her stovetop. The mozzarella had melted into a golden layer across the top, and the sauce bubbled at the edges of the dish. He drained the spaghetti in her colander, then slid the garlic bread under the broiler and crouched in front of her oven window, watching until the edges turned golden and the butter sizzled across the surface of the bread.

He divided the pasta between their plates and set a piece of chicken over each bed of spaghetti, spooning extra sauce from the baking dish over the top. Rebecca carried the salad and the bread to the table. They sat across from each other at her small, round table near the window. Main Street lay below them, quiet and lit by streetlamps.

Rebecca cut into her chicken and took a bite. She chewed slowly, her eyes on her plate.

"Well?" he said.

"This is excellent, Conner."

"You don't have to sound surprised."

"I'm not surprised. I'm impressed. There's a difference." She took another bite. "The sauce is fantastic. What did you put in it besides the obvious?"

"A pinch of red pepper flakes and a half teaspoon of sugar to cut the acidity."

"Sugar in tomato sauce."

"Mrs. Benedetto's rule. She told me the secret to any good red sauce was a little sugar and the patience to let it cook slow."

Rebecca smiled and tore a piece of garlic bread from her half. "This bread is good, too. I'll give you that."

"Better than frozen?"

"I'm not answering that."

"That's an answer."

She pointed her piece of bread at him. "Don't push your luck, Delaney."

They ate without rushing, the conversation moving between bites the way it did every time they sat across from each other.

"What are you most proud of?" she asked. "Same question. Outside of ministry."

He set his fork down. "The relationship I have with my brothers."

"Miles and Adam?"

"About three years ago, they both drove to Richmond without telling me they were coming. They showed up at my apartment on a Saturday morning and told me we needed to talk." He picked up his glass. "I thought somebody was sick. I thought something had happened to my parents. But they sat me down at my kitchen table and told me the truth, which was that I'd disappeared from the family."

Rebecca set her fork down and listened.

"I hadn't been home in over a year. Adam said our mama cried after every phone call because the calls kept getting shorter and further apart. They told me their kids missed me and wanted to know why I never came to visit them. Miles's son had asked him why I didn't like them anymore and if they'd done something to make me mad." He turned his glass on the table. "They told me I'd gotten so consumed by my life in Virginia that I'd forgotten I had a family in Tennessee. And they weren't gentle about it. Adam told me I was being selfish, and Miles told me I was hurting our parents, and I sat there and listened because every word of it was true."

"What did you do?"

"I got mad and defensive at first. I told them they didn't understand the demands of ministry, that I was building something important, that I couldn't just drop everything and drive four hours every other weekend." He shook his head. "Miles looked at me and said, 'Conner, Dad drove to Knoxville every Saturday for six months when Grandpa was sick. He taught school all week and made that drive every single weekend because that's what family does. Don't tell me about demands.'"

"Ouch... I bet that hurt."

"It did, and it shut me up. I spent about a month being angry, and somewhere in the middle of it I realized they were right. I'd built my entire life around the church, and I'd let my family become the thing I got to when I had time. I'd become the brother who sent a text on birthdays instead of showing up. The son who called on Sundays and kept it to ten minutes." He looked at her. "So I drove home one weekend and apologized. To both of them and to my parents. And I changed what I could. I made the phone calls longer and more often. I started using my vacation time to come home instead of filling it with church events. I showed up for holidays when I could work it around my schedule." He turned his glass on the table. "It wasn't enough. I still missed too much. I still wasn't there the way I should've been. But I stopped treating my family like something that would always be there when I had time."

"That's why you three are so close now."

"It is. And I'm proud of it because it would've been easy to stay angry and tell myself they didn't understand. But they understood better than I did. They saw what I couldn't see from inside my own life."

They finished dinner and cleared the plates. Rebecca rinsed them in her sink while Conner dried, and they worked through the small stack in a few minutes. He folded the dish towel and hung it on her oven handle where he'd found it, and her kitchen returned to its clean, ordered state.

Rebecca moved to the living room and picked up a small remote from her coffee table. A moment later, soft music came from a speaker on her bookshelf. Something acoustic, a woman's voice over a guitar, low enough to live in the background of a conversation.

"Coffee?" she asked.

"Please."

She crossed to her counter and pulled two mugs from the cabinet, then set a pod into the Keurig beside her refrigerator and pressed the button. While the first cup brewed, she opened her freezer and pulled out a carton of ice cream. She set it on her counter and reached into the cabinet for two small bowls.

Conner saw the carton from the kitchen doorway. Green lid. The brand he'd named at Minnie's three weeks ago when she'd asked him his favorite ice cream and he'd said mint chocolate chip, but it has to be the right brand.

She scooped two bowls without ceremony and set them beside the mugs on her counter.

"You remembered," he said.

"You were very specific about it."

She said it simply, the way she'd say she'd picked up the youth group snacks and beverages. But she'd gone to the store before tonight and found the exact brand he'd mentioned over lunch at Minnie's.

She swapped the full mug for the second and let the Keurig run again. She carried everything to the coffee table on a tray.

He took a bite of the ice cream as he sat on her sofa, and Rebecca sat beside him, one leg tucked beneath her.

They talked while enjoying the ice cream, and the coffee cooled. She told him about a trip to Nashville two years ago to visit a friend from cosmetology school. She'd spent an afternoon in the Ryman Auditorium, sitting in an empty pew while a band ran their soundcheck on the stage below.

"There's something about hearing music in a space that was built for it," she said. "The wood, the height of the ceiling, the way the sound reaches the back row without trying. I sat there for an hour and forgot I was supposed to meet my friend for dinner."

He told her about a hiking trip in Shenandoah, his third year in Richmond. Three days alone on a ridge trail with nothing but his backpack and the wind. He'd come back to his apartment afterward and sat on his couch for an hour without turning on a single light because the silence had followed him home, and he wasn't ready to let go of it.

"That sounds like the park ranger version of you," she said.

"He's still in there."

"I can tell."

The music on her speaker changed to something slower. Their empty bowls sat on the coffee table beside their half-finished mugs.

"My last year in Richmond, my mentor asked me a question I couldn't answer. We were sitting in his office after a Wednesday night service, and he looked at me and said, 'Conner, what are you building your life around?'"

Rebecca's hands stilled around her mug.

"I sat with that question for three weeks," he said. "I turned it over every morning and every night, and the answer I kept coming back to was the same one. Ministry. My schedule was built around the church. My friendships were built around the congregation. My identity was built around the work." He looked down at the empty ice cream bowl. "There was nothing outside of it. My apartment was a place I slept. I ate dinner alone most nights and told myself that was fine because the work was good and the work was enough."

"Was it?"

"For a long time, I believed so. My mentor. He told me a man who builds his whole life around one thing, even a good thing, is standing on a very narrow foundation."

"Wow... that's deep," she said.

"It is." He lifted his eyes and met hers. "But the answer turned out to be simpler than I expected."

Conner reached across the cushion between them and held his hand open, palm up, beside hers.

She looked at his hand. Then she looked at him. And she slid her fingers into his and closed them.

His hand tightened gently around hers, and the warmth of her palm settled against his own.

"Rebecca, I want you to know something. The life I'm building here isn't just about the church. It isn't just about ministry." He paused. "You're part of what brought me home."

She didn't look away. She didn't pull her hand back or redirect the way she would have days ago. She sat beside him on her sofa, her fingers laced through his, and her eyes held steady on his in the lamplight of the apartment she'd built for herself.

Her thumb moved once, slowly, across the back of his hand.

"I'm glad you're home, Conner," she said.

Chapter 16

"My first year in Richmond, I went to a youth ministry conference in Northern Virginia," Conner said. He was sitting in the circle with the kids who had gathered for the youth group. "About three hundred youth pastors from across the United States. People who had been doing this for fifteen, twenty years. Programs with full-time staff and buses that picked kids up from five different neighborhoods. One church had a youth building with a rock-climbing wall."

Tyler Brannigan leaned forward. "A rock-climbing wall?"

"In the youth building. Floor to ceiling."

"That's insane."

"I saw pictures; it was impressive," Conner said. "I sat in that conference for two days watching these pastors present their programs, and by the time I drove home, I was convinced I was the worst youth pastor in the state of Virginia. I had twelve kids, a folding table, and a budget that covered pizza if I bought the store brand. I walked into my apartment that night and sat on my couch and thought, what am I even doing?"

Rebecca watched him from her chair on the far side of the circle. The recreation hall was full tonight. Seventeen kids filled the chairs. The snack table along the west wall was picked over, half-empty bags of chips beside a fruit tray with most of the strawberries gone.

Conner had been talking for about twenty minutes. Week two of the Chosen series, and the topic was about why comparison messes with you.

"What happened after that?" Caleb Hart asked. He sat two chairs from Conner with his arms folded loosely across his chest.

"I spent about a couple of weeks comparing everything I was doing to what I'd seen at that conference," Conner said. "I looked at my twelve kids and saw a number that wasn't big enough. I looked at my lesson plans and saw material that wasn't polished enough. I measured my church and its little youth room against every program I'd seen or heard about, and I came up short every single time."

"So how'd you get past it?" Caleb asked.

"My senior pastor asked me a question I wasn't ready for. He said, 'Conner, can you tell me the name of every kid in your group?' I said yes because I could. I knew all twelve of them. He said, 'Can the man from the church with the rock-climbing wall say that?' I didn't have an answer for that. But the question changed something. It made me realize I'd been so busy looking at what everybody else had built that I stopped paying attention to what was right in front of me."

He let the room sit with that for a few seconds. Emma Sorrells was nodding from her chair near the snack table. Josh Weaver had his eyes on Conner with a careful, evaluating stillness. Megan Pruitt sat with her hands folded in her lap, her gaze steady.

"So here's what I want to talk about tonight," Conner said. "Comparison. Not the textbook version. The real version. The one that runs in the background of your brain when you're scrolling through your phone on social media or sitting in the cafeteria or walking through the hallway at school. The voice that says, Everybody else has it figured out, and I don't."

He looked around the circle. "I'm not going to ask you to raise your hand or put you on the spot; feel free to share if you'd like to. But I want to know where comparison hits you the hardest. What's the version of it that gets under your skin? Because everybody in this room has one. Including me. Including Rebecca."

Rebecca gave a small nod when a few of the kids glanced her way.

Tyler spoke first, which didn't surprise her. "My brother's a senior, and he's got a full ride to UT for baseball. Every time I walk through the school, somebody asks me if I'm as good as Trent, or they compare me to him. Teachers, coaches, kids I barely know. It's like I showed up on the first day of school with his name on my forehead, and it's stuck ever since."

"That sounds exhausting," Conner said.

"It is. I'm not even that into baseball. I play because my dad wants me to, and I'm decent, but I'm never going to be Trent."

Tyler shrugged. "The thing that messes with me the most is that I don't even want to be Trent."

Emma went next. "Social media is the big one for me. I know everyone says that, and I know it's kind of obvious, but it's true. I follow girls my age who post these perfect photos with their perfect friend groups, and their comments are full of people telling them how amazing they are." She pulled her sleeves over her hands. "And I'll be sitting in my room on a Friday night doing nothing, looking at that, and I just feel like I have no life. Like my life is boring, and everyone else is out there living something better."

"Do you think they actually are?" Conner asked.

"Probably not. But it doesn't matter if I know that in my head, because my feelings don't care what my head knows."

Conner pointed at her. "That's one of the smartest things I've heard anyone say in a long time. Your feelings don't care what your head knows. That's exactly right. Comparison isn't a logic problem. You can't think your way out of it, because it doesn't live in the thinking part of your brain. It lives in the feeling part. That's why it's so hard to shake."

Rebecca had heard Conner talk to adults. She'd heard him talk to Warren, to her family, and to her. But watching him with these kids was something else. He wasn't delivering a lesson from above and waiting for the right answers. He was sitting in a circle of folding chairs on a Wednesday night in February, asking teenagers to tell him something real, and then treating what they said like it mattered. She could see it on their faces. These kids were used to adults who talked at them. Conner was talking with them, and the difference had changed the room.

Caleb spoke again. "I think the worst kind of comparison is when you're not even comparing yourself to another person. You're comparing yourself to some version of your life you thought you'd have by now. Like you had this picture in your head of where you'd be at seventeen, and the reality doesn't match, and you don't know whose fault that is."

"Can you say more about that?" Conner asked.

"I don't know how to explain it exactly. It's like everyone else is on schedule. They've got the grades, the girlfriend, and the plan for after graduation. And I'm just kind of here. I don't have a plan. I don't know what I want to do." Caleb unfolded his arms and rested his hands on his knees. "Sometimes it feels like I'm the only person who doesn't have it figured out, even though I know that's probably not true."

"It's definitely not true," Conner said. "But I hear you. That feeling is real, and it's heavy, and you shouldn't have to pretend it isn't."

The room was quiet for a moment. The heater clicked on somewhere behind the far wall, and its low hum settled into the background.

Then Hannah spoke. Her brown hair was tucked behind her ears, and she wore a gray hoodie with the sleeves pulled past her wrists. She'd been quiet all evening, her arms folded across her stomach, her gaze on the floor more often than not.

"It's not comparing myself to people online," Hannah said. Her voice was low but steady. "I don't care about that. The comparison that gets to me is when your own dad starts a new family and posts pictures of them on Facebook, and you can see in the pictures that he's happy. Really happy." She paused. "And you can't stop yourself from thinking that maybe the first family was the rough draft, and this one is the version he actually wanted."

The room went still. Emma turned in her chair. Tyler looked at the floor. Megan Pruitt's hands tightened in her lap.

Conner didn't rush. He let the silence hold for exactly long enough, and then he leaned forward in his chair. "Hannah, thank you for saying that. I mean it. That took a lot of courage, and what you just described is one of the hardest versions of comparison there is. It comes from inside your own family, and you didn't choose it."

Hannah nodded once without looking up. Her arms stayed folded, but something in her shoulders loosened by a fraction.

Rebecca sat still. Her hands were folded in her lap, and she was aware of the steady press of her own pulse against her wrists. Hannah's words were specific to Hannah's life, to her father, and to the ache of watching a parent build a new family and wondering where you fit inside it. But the structure underneath those words was something Rebecca knew from the inside. The rough draft. The version someone actually wanted. She'd never used those words about herself. But she'd lived inside that feeling at eighteen, sitting on the edge of her bed after a phone call with Conner where she'd counted the sentences before he said he had to go, he was busy, he had to study, or whatever the excuse at the time had been. She'd lived inside it again years later when Nathan, her ex-fiancé, had packed for Florida, and she understood that she hadn't been enough to make yet another man stay.

A few more kids spoke. A girl named Sophie talked about comparing herself to her older sister. A boy named Allan said he compared his family's house to other kids' houses and hated himself for caring. Conner listened to each one and responded without rushing.

Near the end, he brought it home. "There's a verse I want to leave you with tonight. Galatians 6:4. 'Each one should test their own actions. Then they can take pride in themselves alone, without comparing themselves to someone else.' I'm not going to unpack that for you, because I think it says what it says. Your story is yours. It's not behind. It's not ahead. And the only measuring stick that matters is the one between you and God, and He's not grading on a curve."

He reached beside his chair and picked up a short stack of printed pages from the table. "Before we wrap up, I've got something for next week." He handed the stack to Tyler, who took one and passed the rest. "Next Wednesday, weather permitting, we're not meeting here. We're meeting at Bill and Olivia Hartwell's place." He glanced at Rebecca with a grin. "Rebecca's parents."

"The bonfire," Caleb said.

"You remember."

"I remember the s'mores."

"We'll have s'mores again. And hot chocolate. We'll build a fire out on their property, like some of you who've been in youth group for a while may remember doing in past years. Bill and Olivia have invited us back."

Emma was already smiling. Tyler nudged Josh and said something about the creek behind the property.

"For those of you who don't drive yourselves here on Wednesday nights, make sure your parents know the location so they can get you out there," Conner said. "The address and directions are on the sheet. We'll start at seven, same as usual."

He looked around the circle one more time. "Good night, everybody. Thank you for being honest tonight. I mean that. We ran a little longer tonight than I had planned, but if you have the time, go enjoy some more snacks if you want, or hang out and chat; that's fine too."

The room broke apart. Kids stood, pulled on coats, and gathered backpacks. Tyler and Josh headed for the door first, still talking about the creek. Emma stopped at the snack table for one more cookie and waved at Rebecca on her way out. Caleb shook Conner's hand near the door and told him the lesson was good, then pushed through into the cold. Parents' headlights swept across the windows as cars pulled into the lot. Within ten minutes, the room had emptied down to three people.

Hannah was standing near her chair. She held the bonfire handout in both hands, reading it again, and she hadn't put on her coat. Rebecca walked over. "Hey, Hannah."

"Hey."

"You okay?"

"Yeah. I just had a question about next week." She glanced at the handout. "The Hartwell property. I don't know where that is. I normally walk here from my apartment."

"It's about four miles outside of town," Rebecca said.

Hannah nodded slowly. "My mom works evenings. I don't have anyone who could drive me."

"I'll pick you up," Rebecca said. "It's my parents' house. I'm driving out there, anyway. I'll swing by your building around six-thirty. That gives us plenty of time. I'll text you when I'm on my way. Is your number still the same one we have on file?"

Hannah looked at her. A quick, careful assessment of whether this offer was real or the kind of thing adults said and then forgot about. Rebecca held her gaze.

"Yes, ma'am, it's still the same number. Thank you."

"Of course. I'm glad you want to come."

Hannah pulled on her coat and zipped it up . She folded the handout and slid it into her pocket. At the door, she turned back.

"What he said tonight about comparison," Hannah said. "About it living in the feeling part of your brain. That's true."

"I know it is," Rebecca said.

Hannah pushed through the door, and the cold rushed in for a moment before it swung shut behind her.

Conner was stacking folded chairs into the metal rack along the far wall. Rebecca watched Hannah through the window, a slim figure crossing the parking lot toward the road, her breath trailing behind her in the cold.

"Hannah just asked about next week," Rebecca said as she walked toward Conner.

Conner turned. "The bonfire?"

"She wants to come, but her mom works evenings. She doesn't have a ride."

"What did you tell her?"

"That I'd pick her up."

He set another chair in the rack. "Good."

"She almost didn't ask. I could see it. She was standing there thinking and trying to decide if it was worth saying something or if she should just let it go."

"But she didn't let it go," Conner said. "I'm glad she asked for a ride."

Rebecca picked up the fruit tray from the snack table and carried it toward the kitchen. A few apple slices and a cluster of grapes were all that remained around the rim. She set it on the counter beside the sink and started gathering the paper cups scattered across the table.

Conner followed with the sweet tea jug and the chip bags. He set the jug on the counter, folded the empty bags flat, and dropped them in the trash can near the kitchen door. They moved through the cleanup the way they'd done every Wednesday for weeks now.

"She was brave tonight," Conner said, standing beside her at the counter. "What she said about her dad."

"It was more than brave. What she described isn't really a comparison. Not the way Emma was talking about it, or Tyler."

"What do you mean?"

Rebecca turned off the water and leaned her hip against the sink. "Emma's comparing herself to strangers on a screen. That's hard, but there's distance in it. She knows those people aren't real, even if it still hurts. Tyler's comparing himself to his brother, which is closer, but it's about performance." She picked up a towel from the counter and dried her hands. "What Hannah described is about being replaced. It's watching someone who was supposed to choose you every single day build a new life that doesn't include you. That's not a comparison. That's a wound, and that hurts... that cuts deep."

Conner turned toward her. "You're right. The word comparison doesn't cover it. What she's feeling is closer to being measured against something she can't compete with, because the thing she's being measured against is a whole new family."

"And the worst part," Rebecca said, "is that she's not angry about it. Did you notice that? She wasn't upset when she said it. She was calm. She said it like it was a fact she'd accepted a long time ago. Like she stopped expecting anything different."

"That's what concerns me most," Conner said. "When a six-teen-year-old talks about her own father with that kind of calm, it means she's already done her grieving. She's decided this is just how things are, and that in itself is sad."

Rebecca folded the dish towel and laid it across the edge of the sink.

"I think most people carry some version of that," she said. "A different situation, maybe, but the same feeling underneath it. Measuring your life against the one you thought you'd be living by now and coming up short. Watching someone else get the thing you wanted and telling yourself you're fine with it because the alternative is admitting you're not."

"Yeah," he said. "I think you're right. And I think the people who carry it the quietest are usually the ones carrying the most."

Rebecca looked up, and he was watching her with the same steady, unhurried attention he'd given Hannah in the circle tonight. "You were good with them tonight," she said. "Those kids trust you already."

"They trust you too," he said. "Hannah didn't ask me for a ride next week. She asked you."

"She knows I'll show up."

"She does." He held her gaze across the small kitchen. "So do I."

Chapter 17

Conner turned off the two-lane road onto the paved driveway and followed it uphill through a corridor of bare oaks and tall pines. The Hartwell property opened in front of him as the trees thinned. The house sat at the top of a small rise, lit from within against the gray February sky. Trucks and cars lined the driveway, and a thin thread of smoke rose from the stone chimney into the cold air above the roofline.

He pulled in beside Mike's truck and turned off his engine. The Smoky Mountain ridgeline stretched behind the property in layered shades of blue and charcoal. When he stepped out, the air carried the clean bite of February and the faint smell of wood smoke from the chimney. Rocking chairs lined the porch, all empty in the cold, and a welcome mat sat in front of the heavy wooden door.

Olivia had caught him in the recreation hall after church this morning. He'd had a cup of coffee in his hand and Rebecca beside him, and Olivia had asked if he had plans for the evening. His parents were on vacation in Savannah. Both Miles and Adam had plans with their families. Olivia had said, "Then you're coming to dinner at our house," in the tone that Olivia Hartwell used when a decision had already been made and the other person simply hadn't been informed yet.

He hadn't sat at their table in ten years.

The front door opened before he reached it. Lizzie Hartwell stood in the doorway in a purple dress and striped leggings, holding a crayon in one hand.

"Hi," she said.

"Hey, Lizzie. Your grandma invited me for dinner."

She studied him with the frank appraisal he'd come to expect from her. "I know you silly Pastor Conner. Grammy asked me to open the door for you. We're having roast and potatoes. And Grandma made two pies and a cake."

"Two pies and a cake... really."

"One pie is chocolate. That's my favorite." She stepped back and held the door open with her whole body, and the warmth and noise of the Hartwell home rolled over him before he crossed the threshold.

The house smelled of roasted meat and coffee. Coats hung on hooks near the door, and boots and shoes were lined along the wall in a row. From the kitchen, Olivia's voice carried above the clatter of serving dishes, and from the family room, a basketball game murmured on the television.

"Conner," Bill Hartwell said as he appeared from the hallway with a coffee mug in his hand. His silver hair was combed, and he wore a flannel shirt. He extended his free hand, and Conner shook it.

"Thank you for having me, Mr. Hartwell."

"Glad you could make it. Coffee's in the kitchen. Olivia's about ten minutes from putting everything on the table."

"Can I help with anything?"

"You can try. She'll tell you no."

Conner smiled and followed Bill toward the kitchen. The main living area opened as he moved through the house, the kitchen flowing directly into a large family room with comfortable furniture and a stone fireplace. Family photos covered the walls and lined the mantel in mismatched frames, years of Hartwell history arranged in no particular order.

The kitchen was full. Olivia stood at the counter, transferring roasted potatoes from a baking sheet into a large serving bowl. Anna was beside her, taking biscuits from a baking pan and stacking them in a cloth-lined basket. Rebecca stood at the sink, rinsing lettuce in a colander, and when Conner came around the corner, she turned her head and smiled at him.

"Hey," she said.

"Hey yourself."

She was wearing a soft blue sweater and jeans, her hair down past her shoulders. Her nails this week were a pale pink, and a thin silver bracelet caught the light as she shook water from the colander. She looked comfortable and in her element here, standing in her mother's kitchen with her sleeves pushed up and a smile on her face.

"Conner, welcome." Olivia set the serving bowl down and crossed the kitchen to hug him. Her embrace was firm and unhurried. "I'm so glad you came. Are you hungry?"

"Starving."

"Good. We've got enough food to feed the entire town." She released him and turned back to her counter. "Anna, hand me that trivet, please."

"Do you need any help, Mrs. Hartwell?" Conner asked.

"Absolutely not. You go and sit down and relax. We girls have everything under control."

Anna caught his eye as she passed the trivet to her mother. "She says that, but if you stand around this kitchen for too long, she'll give you a job, anyway."

"That's how mothers work," Olivia said. "Now go tell your brothers dinner's almost ready."

The dining room sat adjacent to the kitchen, separated by a wide archway. A long table filled the space, already set with plates and cloth napkins. Extra leaves had been added to extend it, and chairs of various styles were pulled up on every side.

In the family room, Bill had settled into his chair near the fireplace. Dave sat on the couch with his legs crossed, a glass of iced tea on the end table beside him. He wore a pressed button-down shirt even on a Sunday evening. His wire-framed glasses reflected the television screen where the basketball game played on low volume.

Jim stood near the window with his arms folded, and his wife, Grace, sat on the arm of the couch next to him, her posture relaxed, watching the game on television with a smile on her face.

Mike appeared from the hallway, carrying Amber on one hip. Nicole followed with Alicia holding her hand, and Lizzie trailed behind all of them, her crayon replaced by a stuffed animal she carried by one ear.

"Delaney," Mike said with a nod. His voice was quiet, and his handshake was firm when Conner extended his hand.

"Good to see you, Mike."

"Likewise. You met Nicole?" He shifted Amber to his other hip.

"Briefly, at church. Good to see you again, Nicole."

Nicole smiled. "You too, Conner. The girls have been asking about you since your sermon illustration last Sunday."

"The one about the fishing trip?"

"They want to know if the fish was really as big as you said."

Conner looked at Amber, who was watching him from the safety of Mike's arms. "It was bigger. I had to leave that part out because Pastor Warren said nobody would believe me."

Amber considered this with the seriousness of a six-year-old evaluating an adult's credibility. "Mike caught a big fish once."

"Did he?"

"It was this big." She held her hands about fourteen inches apart.

Mike smiled. "It was about that big."

"That's a good fish," Conner said.

The front door opened behind them, and Sarah came in, pulling off her coat, with Ethan right behind her. "Sorry we're late."

"You're not late," Bill said from his chair. "Your mother hasn't called us to the table yet."

"When she does, nobody better be slow about it because I'm starving," Sarah said. She hung her coat and nodded at Conner as she passed. "Hey, Conner."

"Hey, Sarah."

Ethan shook Conner's hand on his way through. "Good to see you."

"You too, Ethan."

Olivia's voice carried from the kitchen. "Dinner's on the table. Everybody, come sit down."

The migration from the family room to the dining room took several minutes. Chairs scraped across the hardwood. Glasses were filled from a pitcher of iced tea and a second pitcher of water. The three girls were seated at one end of the table on cushions stacked on their chairs to bring them up to the right height. Conner sat beside Rebecca on the long side of the table, with Anna on his other side. Jim and Grace sat across from them. Dave was beside Grace. Sarah and Ethan filled the chairs at the far end, and Mike and Nicole bracketed the girls on either side. Bill sat at the head, and Olivia took the chair nearest the kitchen.

Bill said grace. The table went quiet, and every head bowed. His prayer was brief and unhurried. He thanked God for the food and for the hands that prepared it. He thanked Him for bringing the whole family to this table tonight, including their guest. He asked for grateful hearts and continued blessings. He said amen, and the room returned to motion immediately.

Dishes traveled around the table in both directions. The roast was tender and seasoned with rosemary and garlic. The potatoes were golden and crisp at their edges. Green beans with slivered almonds, fresh rolls, a boat of gravy, and a bowl of coleslaw rounded out the spread.

"Mrs. Hartwell, this roast is incredible," Conner said.

"Thank you, sweetheart. It's Bill's mother's recipe. She wrote it on an index card in 1962, and I've been using her recipe ever since."

"The edges are brown and the ink's fading," Anna said. "But Mom won't copy it."

"If I copy it onto a new card, the roast won't taste the same," Olivia said. "I don't make the rules; I just live by them."

"Superstition," Dave said.

"Tradition," Olivia corrected.

Bill cut another piece of roast and said nothing, but the corner of his mouth lifted into a partial grin.

The table settled into overlapping conversations. Three discussions ran at once, weaving in and out of each other with the ease of people who'd been talking over each other for years. Jim asked Dave about the tax filing deadline for the hardware store. Sarah told Ethan she needed his opinion on a structural issue at a renovation site on Pine Street, and Ethan said he'd stop by tomorrow before his first client meeting. Anna launched into a story about the Chamber's planning committee and a disagreement over the spring festival stage dimensions.

Rebecca leaned slightly toward Conner while Anna was talking. "She does this every Sunday," she said, her voice pitched low enough to belong only to the two of them. "By the end of the story, you'll feel like you were in the meeting."

"I already do."

"Welcome to my life."

He liked sitting next to her at this family table once again. He had many fond memories of sitting here as a teenager, enjoying the loud chaos of a Hartwell family dinner.

"So, Conner," Jim said from across the table. He set his fork down and leaned back in his chair. "I heard you've been running the youth group, and it's turning out to be quite successful. Wednesday nights, new curriculum, the whole operation."

"Rebecca's the one running the operation. I just show up and talk."

"That's not true," Rebecca said.

"It's mostly true."

Jim looked between them with a measured gaze. "You playing any ball these days? I remember you were a decent point guard back in high school."

"Decent," Conner said. "That's generous."

"I'm being polite. You traveled every third possession."

Dave glanced up from his plate. "He did travel a lot."

"I didn't travel a lot."

"You traveled," Mike said from down the table without looking up.

Rebecca pressed her lips together, and Conner caught her doing it. "You think so too?"

"I'm not getting involved," she said. "But yes. You traveled."

The table laughed, and Conner held up both hands in surrender. "I want the record to show that I averaged twelve points a game senior year."

"And four traveling violations a game," Jim said.

"Three at most."

Bill looked up from his plate. "It was three."

The table went quiet for a second, and then Jim laughed, and the rest followed. Bill returned to his roast without another word. Conner grinned and picked up his fork. He hadn't been ribbed like this in years. His brothers did it, but the Hartwell version had its own rhythm, a rotation of voices that built on each other until the target had nowhere left to go. That they were doing it at all told him more than any formal welcome could.

Dinner continued. The three girls were conducting a negotiation at the end of the table about which nail polish colors they wanted Rebecca to use later. Lizzie was lobbying for purple. Amber wanted pink. Alicia wanted both, which Lizzie declared wasn't how it worked. Nicole intervened with the calm authority of a first-grade teacher and told them Rebecca had enough colors for everyone to pick whatever they wanted.

"Aunt Rebecca, are you going to do our nails tonight?" Lizzie called down the table.

Rebecca turned toward her. "After dinner. We'll set up in the family room."

"Can you do sparkles?"

"Of course, sweet cheeks, you know I love me some sparkly nail polish."

Lizzie's whole face lit up, and she turned to Amber and Alicia with the breathless urgency of breaking news. The three of them went back to their conversation at a higher volume.

Rebecca turned back and caught Conner watching her. "What?"

"Nothing."

"You're smiling."

"Am I not allowed to smile?"

"You're smiling at me like I did something."

"You always did love nail polish with sparkles in it. I had forgotten that little detail about you."

She bumped his shoulder with hers and reached for her glass of iced tea.

Dave set his fork down and looked across the table at Conner. "Are you planning to play on the church softball team this spring?"

"Absolutely. Warren already mentioned it. I asked him to put me on the roster."

"What position?" Jim asked.

"Outfield, ideally. I played on a men's league in Richmond for a few years, and I spent most of my time in center field."

Jim leaned forward. "We could use another outfielder. Last year we had to put Dave in right field, and he caught exactly one ball the entire season."

"I caught three," Dave said.

"One of those bounced off your glove and hit you in the chest," Sarah said.

"It was still an out. The runner didn't advance."

"Because he was laughing too hard to run," Mike said.

Dave adjusted his glasses. "The result is what matters."

Conner grinned and looked at Rebecca. "You play?"

She turned toward him with her eyebrows raised, and the competitive edge that surfaced was instant and unmistakable. "You better believe I do. I wouldn't miss the church softball games for anything. I've played every year since they started."

"She's not exaggerating," Jim said. "She plays shortstop, and she'll tag you out before you see her coming."

"All the Hartwells play," Bill said from the head of the table. "Except Anna."

Anna held up both hands. "Sports were never my thing. I keep the score book and bring the snacks."

"She also heckles the other team from the bleachers," Sarah said. "Which honestly contributes more than Dave's fielding."

"I'm sitting right here," Dave said.

"I know," Sarah said.

Rebecca looked back at Conner, and the competitive spark hadn't left her face. "Fair warning, Delaney. The Hartwells don't play for fun. We play to win."

"I wouldn't expect anything less," he said.

"Good. Because Jim still brings up the year we lost to Pigeon Forge Baptist, and that was four years ago."

"They had a ringer," Jim said. "That pitcher transferred in from Knoxville two weeks before the first game."

"He was their associate pastor," Grace said.

"He threw a seventy-mile-an-hour fastball. That's a ringer."

The table laughed, and the conversation drifted into favorite moments from past seasons. Sarah recalled a play where Mike had turned a double play unassisted from second base. Mike credited it to instinct, and Sarah said it was the only athletic instinct he'd ever shown. Conner listened and added the church softball season to his mental calendar alongside Wednesday youth group and Sunday dinners and every other thread that was stitching him deeper into the fabric of this town.

Eventually, Olivia began clearing the dinner plates. Rebecca and Anna stood to help, and Conner started to rise, but Olivia pointed at him and said, "Sit." Grace carried a stack of plates to the kitchen, and within a few minutes the table was cleared. Olivia returned with two pies on a wooden cutting board and a chocolate cake on a glass stand. A tub of vanilla ice cream followed, and Anna brought out dessert plates and forks.

"Chocolate pie, pecan pie, and the chocolate cake is Grace's contribution," Olivia said.

"Grace, you made this?" Anna asked, looking at the cake.

"I did. It's a new recipe. Three layers with chocolate buttercream."

"It looks like it belongs in a bakery window," Anna said.

"Well, I'm not sure my cake decorating skills are good enough for a bakery window yet, but thanks, Anna," Grace said.

Dessert plates were filled. Bill took a slice of pecan pie and a scoop of ice cream. Dave took the smallest possible piece of chocolate cake and said he was watching his sugar. Conner chose the chocolate pie because Lizzie had recommended it, and one bite confirmed her judgment.

The conversation slowed as the meal reached its final stretch and plates were pushed aside. Coffee appeared, and steam rose from each cup in the kitchen light.

Conner rested his arm along the back of Rebecca's chair. She leaned slightly into the space he'd made, and the fabric of her sweater brushed the inside of his forearm.

Jim cleared his throat and stood up. Grace set her fork down and looked up at him with a grin.

"Grace and I have something we'd like to share with you all," he said.

Olivia's hands went still on her coffee mug. Bill leaned back in his chair and looked at his oldest son.

Jim glanced at Grace. She nodded, and her smile widened until it changed her whole face.

"We're expecting," Jim said.

The silence lasted about two seconds. Olivia's hand went to her mouth. Anna made a sound that fell somewhere between a gasp and a laugh. Rebecca pushed her chair back.

"Wait," Grace said. She held up one hand, and the room paused. "There's more."

Jim put his hand on Grace's shoulder. "It's twins."

The room fell apart.

Olivia stood up so fast her chair fell over behind her. She rounded the table with her arms open, reached Grace first, and pulled her into a hug that lasted long enough for tears to start. Then she turned to Jim, held his face in both her hands, and kissed his forehead. Bill rose with the quiet deliberation of a man who didn't rush for anything. He crossed behind Olivia and wrapped his arm around Jim.

Rebecca was on her feet with tears on her cheeks. She waited until Bill released Jim, and then she hugged her brother hard enough that he rocked back on his heels.

"I am so happy for you," she said into his shoulder.

"Thank you, Bec."

She let him go and turned to Grace. Grace laughed and wiped her eyes. "We just found out this past week. I've been trying to keep a straight face all through dinner."

"I knew something was up. I just knew it. "You've had a smile on your face the entire night, Grace, and Jim has been more quiet than usual," Rebecca said.

The laughter that followed carried the joy of a family receiving the news of two blessings to look forward to. Mike reached across and shook Jim's hand. Nicole's eyes were bright, and she squeezed Grace's arm when Grace sat back down. Sarah walked to Jim and hugged him without saying a word, which, from Sarah, was the equivalent of a five-minute speech. Ethan shook Jim's hand and told him, Congratulations.

Dave sat in his chair and looked at Jim. "Twins."

"Twins," Jim said.

"That's going to require a revised budget. Have you sat down and figured out what this is gonna cost? Buddy, you better start a couple of college savings plans right away.

"Dave," Anna said.

"What? I'm asking a practical question and thinking ahead."

"We've got time," Jim said. "But I wouldn't mind sitting down with you on it."

Dave nodded. "I'll put something together this week... and congratulations to you both."

The girls had picked up on the energy even if they didn't understand all of it.

"Two babies? Twins like Amber and Alicia?" Lizzie asked.

"Just like Amber and Alicia," Grace said.

Lizzie turned to Amber and Alicia. "You're twins, and now Uncle Jim's going to have twins too." The three of them processed this with the rapid excitement of first-graders encountering new information, and within thirty seconds they were discussing names, none of which were practical.

Conner watched all of it from his chair. He watched Olivia sit back down and dab her eyes with her napkin while Bill put his hand on the back of her neck and stood beside her.

Rebecca sat back down beside him. Her cheeks were flushed, and her eyes were still damp. She reached over and put her hand on his forearm, where it rested on the table.

"Two babies," she said.

"Two babies, what a blessing," he said. Her hand was warm through the fabric of his shirt, and she didn't move it.

The evening softened from there. Olivia refilled the coffees and began wrapping the leftover pie in foil. The conversation drifted, and the youth group bonfire came up naturally. Olivia mentioned she'd already started baking cookies for it and had been freezing batches all week. She planned to have chips and dip, and she and Bill were ordering pizzas for the kids, along with water, pop, and juice.

"There's plenty of firewood stacked in the barn already," Bill said.

"I'll come early and help you get the fire set up," Conner said.

Bill nodded. "I'd appreciate that. Say around five?"

"I'll be here at five."

"I'll be here a little after six-thirty," Rebecca said. "I'm picking up Hannah first. She doesn't have a ride. Then Hannah and I can help Mom carry things out."

"That's the girl who walks to youth group that you mentioned before?" Olivia asked.

"That's her. She lives over in the Town Center Apartments."

"Poor thing, walking in this cold, but I guess you could look at it this way: the child is determined if she walks to youth group every week," Olivia said. "You tell her we're glad she's coming."

The girls claimed Rebecca shortly after. Lizzie appeared at her elbow and announced it was nail time, and Amber and Alicia flanked her on either side like a small, determined delegation. Rebecca laughed and pushed her chair back and told them to go pick their spots in the family room.

He could see her from where he sat. Lizzie was in her lap. Amber sat cross-legged on the floor with her hands extended, fingers spread wide. Alicia stood behind the couch and worked a small brush through Rebecca's hair with the careful concentration of a child performing surgery. Rebecca held Amber's tiny hand steady and painted each nail with slow, even strokes. She was talking to all three of them at once about colors and sparkles and whether butterflies or flowers were better, a debate she mediated with the seriousness of a Supreme Court justice.

The lamplight caught the side of her face. Her laughter carried across the room, uncomplicated and full, as the three girls orbited her.

The men had migrated to the kitchen. Jim and Mike were discussing the lumber mill's equipment maintenance schedule for March. Ethan was telling Dave about a renovation he'd designed for a bed-and-breakfast near Pigeon Forge. Dave was asking about the permitting timeline with the meticulous interest of a man who found county zoning regulations genuinely fascinating. Bill stood at the counter with his coffee, listening without contributing, letting his children fill the room while he held the center of it simply by being in it.

Conner carried his plate and Rebecca's to the sink and turned on the water. He washed them and set them on the drying rack, then reached for the serving bowls stacked on the counter.

Bill appeared at his elbow with a dish towel. He picked up the first plate from the rack and dried it without comment.

"How's the youth group series coming?" Bill asked.

"Good. It's going better than I imagined it would. The kids are engaged, and I think I've gained their trust."

"I've heard good things. Mrs. Pruitt told Olivia that her granddaughter comes home now every Wednesday night and tells her and her parents all about it. She said you were making quite an impression on her granddaughter because she never talked about church or the youth group before without being prompted."

"I'm glad to hear that," Conner said.

Bill dried another plate and set it on the counter. He folded his towel once and draped it over his shoulder.

"Conner."

"Yes, sir?"

Bill looked at him. "Olivia and I are glad to have you in our home again. You're welcome here anytime, son."

"Thank you, sir. That means more than I can tell you."

Bill held his gaze for a second and went back to drying dishes.

Later, Conner said his goodbyes. Olivia hugged him at the door and pressed a foil-wrapped plate of leftovers into his hands. Anna waved from the kitchen. Jim shook his hand and told him to keep up the good work with the youth. Mike nodded. Bill lifted his mug from across the room.

Rebecca walked him out.

The porch was cold, and their breath showed in the air between them. The mountains were invisible against the dark sky, but the trees along the driveway stood in silhouette against the faint glow from the house windows. The noise from inside was muffled by the closed door, and the quiet of the property settled around them.

"You handled a Hartwell family dinner rather well. You fit right back in as if you never left," Rebecca said. She stood with her arms folded against the cold, her sweater too thin for a February evening on a mountain porch.

She was standing close enough that he could see the faint pink still on her cheeks from the warm house.

"I had a really good time tonight, Rebecca."

"I'm glad." She looked up at him. "My family likes you. They wouldn't have given you that hard a time if they didn't."

She held his eyes for a long second, and then she reached out and slid her fingers into his. Her hand was cold from the February air, and he closed his around it, lifted it, and pressed his lips to the back of her fingers.

"Drive safely," she said. "I'll see you Wednesday."

"I'll be here at five o'clock for firewood duty."

She smiled and stepped back through the door.

Chapter 18

"All right," Conner said, leaning forward in his camp chair with his elbows on his knees. "Here's what I want to know tonight. What's one thing people assume about you that isn't true?"

The fire crackled between them, sending sparks upward into the dark February sky. Twelve teenagers sat in camp chairs arranged in a loose circle around the pit, their faces lit by shifting orange. The air held at about forty degrees, mild enough for February, and the fire did its job providing warmth. Beyond the circle, the Hartwell property stretched into the darkness. The treeline stood as a black edge against a sky scattered with stars.

He and Bill had been out here since five o'clock. They'd hauled firewood from the barn in Bill's wheelbarrow, stacking some nearby. Bill had shown him his preferred configuration for a fire: split oak on the bottom with kindling layered underneath, and two larger logs set across the top at an angle. He'd handed Conner the matches and let him light it. The fire caught on the first try, and Bill had given him a nod that said good enough without saying anything at all.

Tyler shifted in his chair two seats to Conner's left. He scratched the side of his neck and glanced at Josh beside him.

"I'll go," Tyler said.

"Go ahead."

Tyler leaned back and folded his arms. "People think I'm the class clown. Like that's my whole identity. Tyler's the funny guy; Tyler's the one who never takes anything seriously." He looked at the fire instead of the circle. "But most nights after school, I'm at home watching my little brother and sister. My mom and dad both work in the evenings during the week. I make sure they eat. I check their homework when I can. I get them to bed by eight-thirty so they're not wrecked the next morning. The only reason I can come to youth group on Wednesday nights is because our neighbor comes over and sits with my brother and sister." He shrugged one shoulder. "Nobody at school knows that. They just know the kid who cracks jokes in the back row."

"Tyler, thank you," Conner said. "That took guts to share, and I appreciate you trusting us with it. That's a lot of responsibility for a young man."

Bill sat across the fire in a heavy canvas jacket, a mug of coffee balanced on his knee. His silver hair caught the firelight. Olivia was beside him in a quilted vest, her hands wrapped around a mug of hot chocolate. Their chairs were angled slightly toward each other, close enough that his boot rested a few inches from hers. They looked natural here, at ease on their land, part of the circle the way two old oaks are part of a yard.

Bill looked at Tyler. "I know a little about that young man," he said. His voice carried the unhurried quality of a man who didn't give words freely and didn't waste the ones he gave. "I started working at my family's lumber mill when I was fourteen because my daddy needed the help. School came second. My grades slipped, and my teachers figured I didn't care." He took a sip of his coffee. "Nobody saw the kid keeping the family business from going under. They just saw the kid who fell asleep in third period, and then later I joked it off with my buddies as having stayed out too late the night before."

Emma spoke next. She sat with her knees drawn up, her sneakers balanced on the front edge of her chair, and her jacket pulled down over her hands. "People assume I'm confident because I'm outgoing. Because I talk a lot and I raise my hand first." She laughed. "The truth is I second-guess almost everything I say. I'll send a text and then stare at my phone for twenty minutes wondering if what I said was weird. I'll answer a question in class and spend the rest of the period convinced I sounded ridiculous or dumb." She looked around the circle. "Being outgoing and being confident aren't the same thing. I'm just loud naturally, but I'm almost always unsure… I have a hard time trusting my judgment sometimes."

A few of the girls smiled in recognition. Sophie piped up and said, "Same," and Emma pointed at her with a grateful grin.

"That's a really important distinction, Emma," Conner said. "A lot of people confuse volume with confidence."

Olivia leaned forward in her chair. "Emma, can I tell you something?" Her voice carried the particular warmth of a woman who had spent years in a classroom and never stopped encouraging children who needed it. "The fact that you question yourself means you're thinking about how your words land on other people. That's not a weakness, sweetheart. That's kindness with a backbone."

Emma's expression softened. "Thank you, Mrs. Hartwell."

"You're welcome, honey."

Caleb went next. He sat straight in his chair with his hands in his jacket pockets. "Kids at school call me 'the church kid.' They say it like it's supposed to bother me. Like it's a joke I should be embarrassed about." He looked around the circle. "Freshman year, it did bother me. I spent a lot of time trying to be somebody different on weekdays so I could fit in. But I got tired of pretending." He shrugged. "So now I just wear it. You want to call me the church kid? Go ahead. I know who I am, and I know whose I am."

"Caleb, that's about as solid as it gets," Conner said.

"I stopped caring about everybody's approval, and I'll admit, my mama and daddy helped me understand that," Caleb said. "Life got a lot simpler once I got that through my thick skull."

Tyler grinned from across the fire. "You realize you just sounded like a forty-year-old, right?"

"I've been told that before," Caleb said, and the circle laughed.

The fire had settled lower, the flames finding new heat in the embers. Two more kids shared. A junior named Simon talked about people assuming he was angry because he was quiet. Sophie said people thought she had it all figured out because her grades were good, but most nights she lay awake convinced she'll never get into college.

Conner watched the way these kids listened to each other. No phones out. No fidgeting. No cross-conversations. They sat in their camp chairs and gave each other what most adults failed to give teenagers: their full attention.

He glanced to his right. Rebecca sat one chair over, her blonde hair pulled back, her jacket zipped to her chin. Hannah Caldwell was beside her, hands tucked between her knees, her gaze fixed on the fire.

The honesty around the circle had built something Conner could feel. The kids leaned in rather than back. Their voices had softened without getting smaller. Tyler's admission had opened the door, and the others had walked through it, and the air around the fire carried the quality of a space where people had decided that the truth wouldn't break anything.

"I don't really have a label," Hannah said. Her voice was quiet but clear. "Nobody at school calls me anything. I'm just kind of there." She paused. "But if I had to pick a label for myself, I'd say lonely."

"My best friend moved to California right before Thanksgiving," she continued. "Before she moved, we talked every day. We'd walk to school and walk home, and she'd come over after, and now we text sometimes, but it's different." She swallowed. "My parents got divorced a year ago, and my dad got married again, and he's got a baby on the way with his new wife, and she already had two kids of her own. My mom works two jobs, so most nights I'm home by myself. I'm not mad about any of it. I don't really know who I'd be mad at. I just miss how things used to be. All of us in the same house. My friend down the street. My mom and dad both home at night." She looked at the fire. "Lonely just seems like the most honest word for a label I'd give myself."

Nobody spoke, and Conner took a moment to fully grasp what Hannah had said. A sixteen-year-old child who labeled herself as lonely, and that in itself bothered him. He knew very little about this girl, but he could sense she needed a friend, she needed someone to lean on, and she wanted her parents.

Sophie and Mary, who were on the far side of the circle, stood and picked up their camp chairs. Then they carried them around the outside of the circle and set them down on either side of Hannah with the chair arms touching hers and sat back down.

Conner felt his throat tighten. He had watched teenagers do careless things and thoughtless things. He had also watched teenagers do things that were completely unexpected as what he'd just witnessed. Move toward someone's hurt without instruction. Sit closer because closer was the only thing they could offer, and it was the right thing.

"Hannah," Conner said. "What you just shared took real courage. I want you to know you are not alone."

Hannah nodded once without looking up, but her shoulders had dropped, and the rigid line of her posture had eased by a fraction. The two girls beside her didn't move.

"I want to read something," Conner said. "First Samuel, chapter sixteen, verse seven. 'People look at the outward appearance, but the Lord looks at the heart.'"

"Tonight some of you named a label somebody else gave you. The class clown. The confident one. The church kid. The quiet kid. The one who's got it all figured out." He looked around the circle. "Those labels come from what people see in a few seconds. A glance in the hallway. A single conversation. And a snapshot never tells the whole story."

He leaned forward. "God doesn't read the label. He reads the whole story. Every chapter. Every page you haven't shown anybody else. He knows Tyler goes home and takes care of his brother and sister every night. He knows Emma questions herself after every conversation. He knows Caleb chose to be who he is even when it cost him at school. He knows Hannah is carrying more than most adults could manage, and she's doing it with grace." He looked at the fire. "The world gives you a label based on what it sees in five seconds. God knows every page. And He isn't confused about who you are."

"All right," he said. "Tonight you all made my life richer and more meaningful by being here and speaking openly. I appreciate every one of you. Let's let the rest of this evening just be about fun and enjoying our time here with good people. The s'mores and pizza are up on the back porch. Mrs. Hartwell has been baking cookies for tonight as well. She's been baking since last week."

"Since before last week," Olivia said. "I've got three kinds up there, and I expect them to disappear."

"You heard the lady," Conner said. "Go eat."

The circle came apart with the speed of teenagers released from reflection into food. Chairs scraped against the packed earth. Tyler and Josh were first to the porch, Tyler taking the steps two at a time. Emma followed Sophie, Mary, and Hannah; the four of them were already talking as they walked. Caleb stretched and wandered toward the s'mores station, where Olivia had arranged graham crackers, chocolate bars, and marshmallows on a tray beside a bundle of long roasting sticks.

Bill stood and picked up an iron poker. He shifted two of the remaining logs and settled a fresh one across the coals. The fire accepted it with a low hiss and began working at the bark.

Conner stood and rolled his shoulders. The cold had crept into his back while he'd been sitting, but the fire's warmth pushed it away as he stepped closer. He looked up. Stars covered every visible inch. No streetlights. No glow from Main Street. Just the fire below and the sky above and two hundred acres of Hartwell land holding it all.

The back porch glowed. Olivia had arranged the food across a folding table covered with a cloth weighted at its corners with small river rocks to keep the slight February breeze from lifting it. Pizza boxes stood open in a row. Bowls of chips flanked by containers of dip. Plates of cookies and the hot chocolate urn she'd borrowed from the church sat at the center, its red indicator light on, steam curling from its spout every time someone filled a cup. Water bottles and cans of pop and juice boxes lined the far end.

Kids moved through the line with paper plates, loading them with pizza and cookies. A few had already migrated back to the fire with marshmallows on long sticks. Tyler had one so thoroughly blackened it was barely holding onto the stick, and Josh was telling him it was ruined. Tyler ate it anyway and declared it perfect.

Conner poured himself a cup of hot chocolate and leaned against the porch railing. From here he could see the fire pit, the clusters of teenagers scattered across the yard, and the dark stretch of property that ran toward the mountains. He could hear laughter and the low murmur of conversation and, beneath it, the steady crackle of the fire Bill kept fed.

Rebecca stood near the far end of the porch. Hannah was with her, holding a cup of hot chocolate in both hands. They stood by the railing, their conversation carrying the easy rhythm of two people enjoying each other's company.

"What's it like being a beautician?" Hannah asked. "Like, what do you actually do all day? We had career day at school last week, and I keep thinking about what I'd want to do when I'm done with high school."

Rebecca leaned her shoulder against the porch post. "Well, it depends on the day. Some mornings I'm booked from eight until five. Cuts, color, highlights, blowouts. I do nails too: manicures and pedicures. The occasional facial when somebody's in the mood to be pampered." She smiled. "Other days are slower, and I catch up on inventory or rearrange my station, which is really just me organizing the same products in a different order because I like things a certain way."

"Do you like it?"

"I love it; my job suits me. I look forward to going to work every day... I don't really even think of it as a job because I honestly enjoy what I do. I get to talk to people all day, which suits my personality perfectly. And there's something about watching someone sit down in your chair looking tired or stressed and then watching them leave an hour later standing a little taller. That part never gets old. I love making other people feel good about themselves."

"Did you always know you wanted to do it?"

"Not always," Rebecca said. "I knew for sure by the end of my junior year of high school that I wanted to be a beautician. I liked working with my hands; I liked people, and I liked the idea of making someone feel better about how they looked. I love styling hair. I always enjoyed painting my friends' fingernails and doing their makeup." She paused. "Not everybody thought it was a real career, though, back when I was in high school. Some adults would comment that I would never be able to support myself. I overheard a kid at school one time saying people who did hair only chose that kind of job because they weren't smart enough to do something worthwhile. But I was strong enough to know what I wanted, and I stayed with my gut instinct. Now I own the building where my salon is, and I built the business from nothing, and every client who sits in my chair is there because they trust me. I wouldn't trade that for anything."

Hannah took a sip of her hot chocolate. "That's cool. I like that you built it yourself."

"You should come by the salon sometime," Rebecca said.

Hannah looked at her. "Really?"

"Really. I'll give you the full tour. Show you how everything works—the stations, the products, all of it. And then we'll do a girls' day. I'll do your hair and your nails, and we'll play music and just have fun."

"You don't have to do that."

"I know I don't. I want to. You'd be doing me a favor, honestly. I love having company in the salon. Ask anybody in town, and they'll tell you I talk their ears off." Rebecca grinned. "What do you think?"

Hannah held her cup with both hands and looked down at the steam rising from it. When she looked up, she was smiling. "Okay," she said.

"Awesome. Come by after school on Friday. My last client is at 1, and by the time you get there, I'm free for the rest of the day."

Conner took a sip of his hot chocolate and looked out over the yard. Rebecca had just done what she did better than anyone he'd ever known. She'd found the specific thing Hannah needed and offered it without ceremony, without pity, without making it feel like a project. She'd given her a reason to walk through a door. A place to go. And she'd done it so naturally that Hannah would remember it not as charity but as an invitation from someone she obviously looked up to.

The evening wound down. Headlights swept across the yard as parents pulled up the long driveway. Derek, Tyler, and Josh climbed into Derek's truck, and he honked once as he swung around near the barn. Emma's mom idled by the fence, and Emma jogged to the car with her coat half-zipped. Simon and Sophie left with Simon's older sister, Mary. Two more cars collected the remaining kids, their taillights tracing red lines down the driveway through the bare trees.

Caleb found Conner near the fire and extended his hand.

"Good lesson tonight," Caleb said. His handshake was firm.

"Thanks, Caleb. I appreciate your being here. Drive safe."

"Yes, sir."

Within fifteen minutes, the property had cleared down to five. Conner. Rebecca. Hannah. Bill. Olivia. The noise drained away, and what replaced it was the sound of the fire settling into itself and the deep quiet of nature at night.

Olivia appeared at the top of the porch steps and looked down at Hannah, who sat on the bottom step with her empty cup between her hands.

"Hannah, sweetheart, would you mind helping me carry a few things inside? I've got a whole table to clear, and an extra pair of hands would be a blessing."

Hannah stood immediately. "Yes, ma'am."

"Thank you, honey. You grab the chip bowls, and I'll get the pizza boxes." Olivia held the screen door, and Hannah followed her across the porch and into the warm light of the house.

Bill picked up his coffee mug from the flat stone beside his chair. He looked at Conner across the fire, gave a single nod, and then he turned and walked toward the porch, following his wife inside.

Rebecca stood a few feet from the fire with her hands in her jacket pockets. The firelight moved across her face, catching the loose strands of blonde hair that had pulled free from her ponytail over the course of the evening. She was watching the flames, and her expression was open in a way Conner had only seen a handful of times since he'd come home. The careful structure she usually kept in place had been set down, and what was left was simply Rebecca. Present and still.

"This was a good night," she said.

He moved beside her. The fire was lower now, working through the last of the larger logs, and the heat reached them in slow waves. "It was; I think, the kids had a good time."

"They did." She was quiet for a moment. "Tyler surprised me. I didn't know his parents worked in the evening."

"He carries a lot for a sixteen-year-old. More than he lets anyone see."

"Emma too. She's so bright when she walks through a door that you'd never guess she's questioning every word that comes out of her mouth."

Conner nodded. He watched the fire and thought about every kid who had spoken tonight, every label they'd named and set down in front of the group. Then his thoughts returned to where they'd been circling all evening.

"Hannah got to me," he said.

Rebecca looked at him. "Me too."

"When she said lonely was the label she'd give herself, I could hear a year of loss packed into that one word. Her friend. Her parents. Her mom gone every night. All of it compressed into a single sentence, and she said it like she was reading off a grocery list."

"Because she's rehearsed it," Rebecca said. "Maybe not out loud. But in her own head, she's told herself that story so many times the edges have worn smooth. It doesn't cut the same way on the outside anymore."

The fire crackled low. A log split in half and settled deeper into the coals, sending a brief rush of sparks upward before the darkness absorbed them.

"Conner, when Hannah said that word. Lonely. It hit me, and it hit me hard."

He turned toward her.

"Because that's the word I would have used for myself," she said. "After you left for college."

Rebecca pulled her hands from her pockets and folded her arms against the cold. "I didn't feel like your girlfriend anymore, Conner. The calls got shorter and shorter every time we talked. The conversations grew thinner. You'd tell me about your classes and your professors and these new friends I'd never met, and I could hear your world getting bigger." She looked at the embers. "Every time we'd talk, it was bigger. And mine was exactly the same. Same town. Same people. Same everything."

"I could feel you pulling into your new life," she continued. "And I was standing still, watching you go. The worst part was that I didn't think you even knew you were doing it."

A gust of wind pushed through the yard and stirred the fire. Sparks scattered sideways, and the heat flared briefly before settling.

"I broke up with you because I already felt alone in the relationship," she said. "Ending it was easier than sitting on my bed every night waiting for a phone call that felt like I was an obligation." She looked at him. Her eyes were clear. She wasn't crying. She wasn't angry. She was a twenty-eight-year-old woman telling a twenty-eight-year-old man what it had felt like to be eighteen and losing the person she loved most. "I'm not blaming you. I made the call. I picked up the phone and said the words. That was my decision to break up with you, and I own it." She held his gaze. "But I wanted you to fight for me, Conner. I wanted you to say, 'No, Rebecca, I'm coming home this weekend, and we're going to work this out.' And you didn't. You just let me go. You didn't fight for me. That's what hurt the most."

"I get it," he said. "You're right. About every bit of it. I did pull away. I was eighteen, trying to be mature when I really wasn't. I was consumed with school and my calling and everything happening in Lynchburg, and I told myself you understood. I told myself what we had was strong enough to survive and what I was doing at school was for us. I was trying to build a future for us." He shook his head once. "I didn't see what it was costing you. Not until it was too late. And by then you'd already made your decision, and I thought the right thing to do was let you go because you'd asked me to."

"You didn't fight for me," she said.

"No. I didn't. I've known for a long time that I should have. Honoring your decision was tough on me. I told myself I was being respectful, and that I was giving you what you wanted." He turned toward her fully. "But the truth is I was scared, and I used respect as a cover. I should have driven home. I should have knocked on your door and told you I was sorry and that I was going to be a better person and make the time for you that you deserved." His voice didn't waver. "I should have fought for us, Rebecca. And I didn't. And I've carried that with me every day since."

The fire burned lower. The embers glowed beneath the remaining wood, orange and deep red, and the heat pressed outward against the cold February air that surrounded them on every side.

"I'm not telling you this to make you feel guilty," she said. "We were eighteen. We didn't know what we were doing. I didn't know how to say what I needed, and you didn't know how to hear it."

"I know," he said. "But being young doesn't undo the fact that you were hurting and I wasn't paying enough attention."

"I want you to know something," she said. Her eyes held his without hesitation. "I'm not lonely anymore."

"Neither am I," he said.

He reached for her hand. Her fingers were cold from the February night, and she closed them around his without hesitation. He drew her closer, his arm settling around her shoulders, and she leaned into him.

Chapter 19

Jenna was at the reception desk with her last client of the day, flipping through the scheduling book while Mrs. Weatherford fished through her purse for her wallet. Rebecca stood at her station, wiping down the counter with a damp cloth and returning bottles and brushes to their places. The other stylists had left an hour ago.

"Same time in three weeks, Doris?" Jenna asked.

"Make it four. My daughter's coming from Knoxville that third week, and I'll be too busy entertaining to sit in a chair for two hours."

"Four weeks it is." Jenna penciled in the appointment and tore off the reminder card. "Tell Linda I said hello."

"I will. She still talks about that updo you did for her daughter's wedding." Mrs. Weatherford said as she tucked the card into her purse and waved at Rebecca on her way to the door. "Have a good weekend, girls."

"You too, Doris," Rebecca said.

The door closed, and the salon dropped into its Friday-afternoon quiet. Jenna leaned back against the reception counter and stretched her arms over her head.

"That's it for me. I moved Mom to tomorrow morning so we'd have the rest of the afternoon free."

"You didn't have to do that."

"I wanted to. I told her about our special guest we have coming in, and she said, and I quote, 'Well, of course, move my appointment and show that precious child a good time.'" Jenna reached beneath the counter and pulled out a small speaker she kept near the appointment book. She connected her phone, and upbeat country music filled the salon at a low, easy volume. "There. Now it feels like a Friday."

Rebecca smiled and hung her cloth on the hook beneath the counter. She checked her watch. A little after three-thirty. Hannah's school let out at three, and the walk from the high school to Main Street ran about fifteen minutes.

She looked around the salon. The stations were clean and the refreshment bar was stocked. The candy jar on her reception desk was full of conversation hearts and foil-wrapped chocolates in shades of pink and red.

The front door opened, and Hannah stepped inside.

She wore jeans and a pink pullover sweatshirt with her backpack over one shoulder. Her brown hair was tucked behind her ears. She stopped just inside the doorway, her gaze traveling across the styling stations, the mirrors, the product shelves, and the wash area toward the back.

"Hey, Hannah," Rebecca said, crossing the salon toward her.

"Thanks for inviting me." Hannah shifted her backpack strap and looked around again. "It looks different in here than it does through the window."

"Bigger, right?"

"Yeah. And it smells really good."

Rebecca laughed. "That's the diffuser I have running. Citrus and vanilla today." She gestured toward the reception area. "You can set your bag down anywhere. This is Jenna; you might know her from church."

Jenna extended her hand to Hannah. "We've seen each other at church, but I don't think we've officially been introduced."

Hannah shook her hand. "Nice to meet you. You have pretty hair."

"Thank you. Rebecca's been talking about you coming in all day today. I hope you're ready, because we've got plans for you."

Hannah glanced at Rebecca. "Plans?"

"Good plans," Rebecca said. "Come on. Let me show you everything."

She started the tour at the reception area, explaining how the scheduling worked, how clients checked in, and how the candy jar had been a tradition since the salon opened six years ago. She walked Hannah along the product wall and pulled down a couple of bottles to explain the difference between a sulfate-free shampoo and a clarifying wash. Hannah turned a bottle of leave-in conditioner in her hands and studied the label.

"How do you know which product to use on which person?" Hannah asked.

"Hair type, texture, what they're trying to achieve. It took me a while to learn. My first year in cosmetology school, I put a volumizing mousse on a client who already had thick hair." Rebecca set the bottle back on the shelf. "She walked out looking as if she'd been caught in a windstorm."

"Rebecca's being humble," Jenna said. She'd followed the tour at an unhurried distance, leaning against door frames along the way. "She was top of her class in cosmetology school, and she built this business from nothing. The building was a wreck when she bought it. Show her the picture."

"She doesn't want to see the picture."

"Yes, I do," Hannah said.

Rebecca pulled out her phone and scrolled until she found it. A photo of 106 Main Street before the renovation. Peeling paint, a faded awning, and a front window with a crack running diagonally from corner to corner.

Hannah looked at the photo and then looked around the salon. "You did all this?"

"My sister Sarah's construction crew did the heavy lifting. I told them what I wanted, and Sarah made it happen. But the design and the layout were mine, and I helped with a lot of the renovation work to keep my costs lower."

"Wow, that's cool."

They moved to the styling area, and Rebecca walked Hannah through the stations, showed her the tools at each one, explained the difference between shears and thinning scissors, and let her hold a flat iron and feel its heft. She showed her the wash sinks in the back, tilted one of the chairs so Hannah could see how the reclining mechanism worked and walked her through a color treatment step by step.

"What's the hardest part of the job?" Hannah asked. She stood near one of the styling chairs with her hand resting on its leather armrest.

Rebecca considered it. "Saying no to walk-ins when I'm already booked solid. I want to help everybody, and turning someone away goes against every instinct I have. Jenna's better at it than I am."

"Because I have boundaries," Jenna said. "Rebecca would work until midnight if nobody stopped her."

Hannah smiled, and it reached her eyes.

"All right," Rebecca said. She pulled out her styling chair and patted the seat. "Your turn. Have a seat."

"Wait, right now?"

"Right now. Jenna and I are going to style your hair. No cut, just a full blowout and waves. A real salon treatment."

Hannah looked between them. "You really don't have to do all this."

"We know," Jenna said. She was already pulling a fresh cape from the cabinet. "We want to. Now sit down before Rebecca starts listing all the reasons you should let people do nice things for you, because that speech takes about ten minutes."

"It does not take ten minutes."

"It took twelve the last time you gave it to me."

Hannah laughed, an open, unguarded sound that came out before she could rein it in, and she sat down in the chair. "You two are so cool."

Rebecca draped the cape around Hannah's shoulders and ran her fingers through her hair, feeling the texture. "You've got great hair, Hannah. Healthy, and the texture is just right for waves. How do you feel about loose curls?"

"I've never really done much with it. I usually just let it air dry and leave it alone."

"Well, not today." Rebecca caught Jenna's eye in the mirror. "I'm thinking soft waves with some volume at the roots. Maybe a side part."

Jenna came around and gathered a section of Hannah's hair between her fingers. "Agreed. And some texture spray to hold it. You want to start on the left or the right?"

"I'll take the left."

They set up on either side of Hannah's chair. Rebecca plugged in her curling wand while Jenna sectioned Hannah's hair with clips. The music played behind them, and the light through the windows had shifted to a warmer amber as the afternoon thinned toward evening.

"So, how was school today?" Rebecca asked, wrapping a section of hair around the barrel of her wand.

"It was okay. We had a history test that I think I did all right on. And Ms. Cooper assigned a new poetry project in English that's actually kind of interesting."

"Poetry?" Jenna said from the right side of the chair. "What kind?"

"We get to pick a style and write three original poems. I'm thinking about doing free verse."

"You write poetry?" Rebecca asked.

Hannah paused. "Sometimes. In a journal. It's not anything serious."

"I think that's wonderful," Rebecca said. "Do you enjoy it?"

"Yeah. It helps me think through stuff. When something's stuck in my head and I can't figure out how to say it out loud, writing it down helps." She glanced at her hands in her lap. "That probably sounds weird."

"It doesn't sound weird at all," Jenna said. "It sounds like you've found your way of processing. Everybody needs one. Rebecca's is running. Mine is reorganizing my apartment, which is a really boring way of saying I rearrange furniture when I'm stressed."

"You moved your couch four times in one weekend last March," Rebecca said.

"And it ended up back where it started. But I felt better, and that's what matters."

Hannah's shoulders had loosened. She was settling into the chair and into the conversation, and the stiffness she'd carried through the door was gone.

Rebecca released a finished curl and moved to the next section. "So, tell me about your week. Did anything good happen?"

Hannah was quiet for a second, then looked up at Rebecca in the mirror. "Actually, yeah. Something kind of good happened."

"Tell us."

"You know Sophie and Mary? The two girls who moved their chairs next to mine at the bonfire on Wednesday?"

"I remember," Rebecca said.

"They sat with me at lunch yesterday. At school. I was at a table by myself, and they just showed up with their trays and sat down." Hannah picked at the edge of her cape. "Sophie asked me if I was going to youth group next week, and Mary started talking about how she thought Tyler was cute, and we just talked through the whole lunch period. Nobody's sat with me at lunch in a while. Not since my friend moved."

Rebecca met Hannah's eyes in the mirror. "Hannah, that's great. Sophie and Mary seem nice."

"Emma talked to me too. In the hallway between second and third periods. She's in the grade below me, but we have lockers on the same hall. She came up and asked for my number, and we've been texting." Hannah's voice picked up speed, the way it does when someone is telling good news and gaining confidence in it. "She's actually coming over to my apartment tonight. We're going to watch a movie."

Jenna looked at Rebecca across Hannah's head and raised an eyebrow. Rebecca returned a quick smile.

"What movie?" Jenna asked.

"I don't know. Emma said she'd bring snacks, and I told her I'd pick the movie, but I don't know what to choose. I've been overthinking it."

"If she said she'd bring snacks, she's already committed," Jenna said. "The movie is secondary. She wants to hang out with you, so don't worry too much about finding the perfect movie."

"You think so?"

"I know so. That's how girls work. The movie is the excuse. The hanging out is the point."

Hannah considered this. "I guess you're right. It's been a while since I had plans with somebody on a Friday night."

"Well, you've got two sets of plans today," Rebecca said. "Us right now, and Emma tonight. That's a pretty solid Friday."

They worked through the rest of Hannah's hair in easy conversation. Jenna told a story about a client in Nashville who had asked for platinum blonde and cried in her chair when she had finished because she felt beautiful. Hannah asked what the worst hair disaster Rebecca had ever seen was, and Rebecca told her about a woman who had tried to do her own highlights with a box kit from the drugstore. She ended up with orange stripes that took three sessions to correct. Hannah asked how much cosmetology school cost and how long it took, and Rebecca walked her through the timeline, the licensing process, and what the tuition had cost when she had gone to school. Hannah listened with the attention of a girl mentally filing information she might need later.

Jenna finished her side first and stepped back to assess. Rebecca completed her final curl, misted a light texture spray through the full style, and used her fingers to separate the waves and give them movement.

"All right," Rebecca said. She turned Hannah's chair toward the mirror. "Take a look."

Hannah went still.

Her hair fell in soft, loose waves past her shoulders, parted to the side with volume at the crown that framed her face. The texture spray gave it hold without stiffness, and it moved when she turned her head.

She reached up and touched the side near her ear, then pulled her hand back.

"You can touch it; you won't ruin it at all," Rebecca said.

Hannah ran her fingers through the waves and watched them fall back into place. She studied herself in the mirror for a long moment, turning her head one way and then the other.

"You look beautiful, Hannah," Jenna said.

"I do?" She tilted her chin and watched the waves shift again. "It looks so different."

"Same hair," Rebecca said. "Just shown off a little. You've got natural texture that most people pay good money to get with a perm."

Hannah looked at Rebecca's reflection. "It's different, but... I think I kind of love it. I'm not used to feeling pretty."

Rebecca squeezed her shoulder. "Now. Are you ready for nails?"

"Nails too?"

"I told you we had plans."

They moved to the manicure station at the side of the salon. Rebecca pulled up two stools so she and Jenna could sit on either side of Hannah, each taking one hand. The small table between them held a row of polish bottles, cotton pads, a bottle of remover, and a set of files.

"Pick your color," Rebecca said. She gestured toward the polish display on the wall. "Anything you want."

Hannah walked to the display and leaned closer to read the names on the bottles, her newly styled hair falling around her face.

"What color are your nails?" Hannah asked, looking back at Rebecca.

Rebecca held up her hands. Her nails were a soft coral, neat and even. "This is Sunset in Savannah. One of my favorites."

"I like it." Hannah turned back to the display, reached for a bottle, hesitated, then picked it up. A rich, warm berry shade. She held it out. "What about this one?"

"Blackberry Fizz," Rebecca read. "Good choice. That's going to look great on you."

They settled back into the manicure station. Rebecca took Hannah's left hand, and Jenna took her right. Rebecca filed first, shaping each nail with quick, careful strokes while Jenna matched her pace on the other side.

"Have you ever had your nails done professionally?" Jenna asked.

"No. I've painted them myself a few times, but I'm terrible at it. My right hand always looks decent, and my left hand looks like a toddler did it."

"That's everyone's experience with their non-dominant hand," Rebecca said. "The secret is thin coats and patience. And not trying to do it while watching TV, because you will smudge every single nail."

"Speaking from experience?" Hannah asked.

"Multiple experiences. I ruined a good manicure during a tense episode of a cooking competition show once. Smeared three nails reaching for the remote."

"She threw a pillow at the television, Hannah," Jenna said.

"I didn't throw it. It slipped."

"It slipped across the room."

Hannah laughed as Rebecca applied the first coat of Blackberry Fizz to her left hand, painting each nail with steady, even strokes. The color was rich against Hannah's skin. Jenna matched her pace on the right, and within a few minutes all ten nails had their first coat.

"Let that dry for a minute, and then we'll do the second coat," Rebecca said.

Hannah held her hands out in front of her and spread her fingers, tilting them in the light. "They match," she said. "Both hands actually look the same."

"That's the professional difference," Jenna said. "And now you know what to do if you ever want to apply for a job at a salon. Walk in, show them your nails, and say, 'Both hands match. Hire me.'"

"Is that really how it works?"

"No," Rebecca said with a laugh. "But it would be a memorable interview."

They finished the second coat and a quick-dry top layer. Hannah's nails gleamed under the station lamp, all ten of them neat and polished in the deep berry color she'd chosen.

"How do they feel?" Rebecca asked.

"I like it; they make me feel pretty, too." Hannah held her hands up again.

"Give it about five more minutes, and then you're good to go," Jenna said.

Hannah was grinning from ear to ear when the front door opened.

All three of them looked toward it.

A woman walked in carrying a bouquet wrapped in pale pink tissue paper and tied with a satin ribbon. A dozen roses, soft pink, arranged with sprigs of baby's breath and greenery. The woman holding them was smiling, and her eyes were twinkling with mischief..

Shelby Prescott owned Prescott's Florals over on Beech Street and had graduated from Serenity Crossing High School the same year as Rebecca and Jenna. Her dark hair was pulled into a ponytail, and she wore her green shop apron over a flannel shirt.

"Delivery for Miss Rebecca," Shelby said.

"Shelby, what on earth?" Rebecca said.

Shelby crossed the salon and placed the bouquet into Rebecca's hands. A full-sized envelope was tucked between the stems, secured with a small clip. "I'm delivering these in person because the man who ordered them asked me to make sure they were perfect. And honestly, I wanted to see your face." She stepped back and folded her arms with visible satisfaction. "Conner Delaney came into my shop on Tuesday and ordered these. He picked the color himself."

Rebecca looked down at the roses. Soft, pale pink, just barely opened, the petals layered in tight spirals that would unfurl over the next few days. The scent reached her before she brought them close, sweet and clean.

"Honey, that man is a keeper," Shelby said. "I didn't even know he'd moved back to town until he walked into my shop. And he's a pastor now." She shook her head. "A very fine-looking pastor, if I do say so myself." She pointed at Rebecca with the confidence of someone who had known her since the ninth grade. "Don't let that one go again, Rebecca. I mean it. Hang on to him."

"Thank you, Shelby," Rebecca said.

"You're welcome." Shelby waved at Jenna and then at Hannah. "Hey, Jenna. Hi, sweetheart. I hope ya'll have a fabulous Valentine's Day tomorrow!" Then she walked out the door and pulled it shut behind her.

Rebecca stood in the middle of her salon, holding the bouquet. The tissue paper crinkled as she adjusted her grip and looked at her pretty flowers. The envelope sat between the stems, white and square, with her name written across it in Conner's compact handwriting.

Jenna was leaning forward on her stool. "Rebecca. Open the card."

"I'm looking at the roses."

"They're beautiful. Open the card."

Hannah watched Rebecca from her chair, her freshly painted nails held in front of her. "Wait," she said. "Those are from Pastor Conner?" Her eyes went wide. "Are you two dating?"

Rebecca looked at Hannah and nodded.

"Open the card, Rebecca," Jenna said. "I'm serious. If you don't open it in the next five seconds, I'm opening it for you."

Rebecca shifted the bouquet to one arm and pulled the envelope free with her other hand. She slid her thumb under the seal and opened it.

The card made her laugh before she had read a single word.

On the front was a whimsical illustration of two kids bundled in winter coats and scarves, sitting on a toboggan and flying down a steep, snow-covered hill. Their mouths were open wide, and snow sprayed up behind them in a white arc.

Henderson's Hill. Senior year. Tyler's cracked green sled and Brooke yelling from the top of the hill. Conner's warm truck afterward and the long drive through the mountains while she slept against the window.

"Come on, Rebecca... the suspense is killing me... read the card out loud," Jenna said.

Rebecca took a breath and opened the card.

"Rebecca, I'd like to cook dinner for you tomorrow night. Be at my place around six. I'm making something you'll love, and I promise the kitchen won't catch fire. After dinner, we can drive into town and see a movie, or walk around the square, or just sit and talk. Whatever you want. Happy Valentine's Day a day early. Love, Conner."

Jenna pressed both hands over her mouth. She held them there for three seconds and then dropped them. "That is the sweetest, most romantic thing ever. He's cooking for you. On Valentine's Day. Rebecca."

"This is incredibly sweet of him," Rebecca said.

"And he's giving you options for afterward. He's not planning the whole night without asking. He's letting you choose." Jenna put her hand flat on the counter as if she needed something solid under her. "We both have dates on Valentine's Day. Praise the good Lord, we are not sitting home alone this year."

Hannah looked from Jenna to Rebecca, her berry-colored nails still held carefully in front of her. A smile was spreading across her face, and she shook her head once with the plain, unfiltered honesty of a sixteen-year-old who saw exactly what she saw.

"Wow," she said. "Pastor Conner is really into you."

Rebecca laughed as she looked down at the card in her hand: the two kids on the toboggan, and the handwriting she'd known since she was seventeen. The roses filled her other arm.

"He's a really good man, Hannah."

Chapter 20

The gravel driveway crunched beneath her tires as Rebecca pulled in beside Conner's truck and cut the engine. The parsonage glowed from within against the February dark.

She sat for a moment with her hands in her lap. The roses he'd sent yesterday were in a vase on her kitchen counter at home, their petals already loosening into a full bloom. The card with the two kids on the toboggan was propped against the vase where she could see it from her couch.

Rebecca picked up her purse from the passenger seat, checked her reflection in the rearview mirror, and stepped out into the cold. She'd changed outfits several times before leaving her apartment. She'd settled on a cream-colored sweater, jeans, and the small gold earrings her mother had given her for her twenty-fifth birthday. Simple and comfortable.

She climbed the two steps up to his front porch, knocked, and Conner opened the door within seconds.

He wore a dark green Henley and jeans. A dish towel hung over one shoulder. His sandy brown hair looked as if he'd pushed it back from his face more than once, and the grin he gave her when he saw her changed his entire face.

"Hi," he said. "You look beautiful."

"Thanks, you don't look so bad yourself."

He laughed and stepped back to let her in. The house was warm, and the smell surrounded her immediately. Smoky and sweet, layered with butter and something she couldn't quite place. The living room was the same modest space she remembered from her visit before. Blue couch. Loretta's knit throw blanket was folded over the arm. The bookshelf against the far wall.

But the dining table had been transformed. A white cloth covered its surface, and two candles burned in simple glass holders, their flames steady in the still air. Two place settings sat across from each other with cloth napkins and glasses of sweet tea. And in front of the plate nearest the window, a single pink rose lay across the table's edge, its stem trimmed, its petals just beginning to open.

Rebecca stood in the doorway between the living room and the kitchen and took it in. The candles. The rose. Every detail was placed by a man who had thought about this evening long before she arrived.

"Can I take your coat?" Conner asked.

She slipped it off and handed it to him. He hung it on the hook near the front door beside his jacket and came back to her.

"Are you hungry?"

"Starving."

"Good." He took her hand and led her to the table. He pulled her chair out and waited while she sat, then tucked it in gently. She looked up at him, and the care in his expression was so focused and so deliberate that it made her smile.

"Don't move," he said. "I'll bring everything out."

"Can I help?"

"No, ma'am. Not tonight. You sit right there."

He disappeared into the kitchen, and Rebecca picked up the rose from the table. She turned it slowly in her fingers. Soft pink, the same shade as the dozen he'd sent to the salon. She breathed in its scent, clean and faintly sweet, and set it beside her plate.

Conner came through the doorway carrying a large platter, and when he set it on the table, Rebecca grinned.

BBQ ribs. A full rack, dark and glazed, the sauce caramelized along the edges.

"Conner," she said.

He was already heading back to the kitchen. He returned with a bowl of corn on the cob, golden and glistening with butter, and set it beside the ribs. Then he went back and came out with a heavy ceramic bowl of mashed potatoes. She leaned forward. Flecks of garlic and green herbs ran through the creamy surface, exactly the way his mom made them with ranch and garlic and butter stirred through.

"Are those your mama's mashed potatoes?" she asked.

"Yes, I called her and asked for the recipe, and she told me not to skimp on the butter."

Rebecca laughed as he went back to the kitchen one final time. He came back carrying a basket of cornbread wrapped in a cloth napkin and a Mason jar of pickles. He set the cornbread near her plate and placed the jar between them.

She stared at the table. Every dish held a memory. Every single one.

The ribs she used to ask for on her birthday because they were her absolute favorite. The corn on the cob they used to eat at church picnics, racing each other to see who could finish a full ear first. Loretta's mashed potatoes, that Rebecca had loved so much that she'd always had a second helping at a Delaney family dinner, which made Loretta beam for the rest of the evening. The honey-buttermilk cornbread Loretta baked every Sunday, the recipe Rebecca had tried to replicate in her own kitchen and never gotten right because she couldn't nail the ratio of honey to buttermilk. And the pickles. Loretta's canned pickles that she put up every summer from cucumbers in her own garden, the ones Rebecca used to eat straight from the jar on the Delaney porch after school.

He remembered. Not one thing. All of it.

"These are all my favorites," she said. Her voice was steady, but her eyes weren't. She blinked twice and looked up at him.

Conner sat down across from her. "I know they are." He reached across and turned the jar of pickles so that the label faced her. Loretta's handwriting on a small white sticker: Bread & Butter Pickles. "Mom sent those home with me last Sunday. I had told her I was making you dinner for Valentine's Day, and she handed me the jar and said, 'Rebecca always loved these. Put them on the table.'"

Rebecca pressed her fingers against the edge of the tablecloth. She had spent years perfecting the art of giving. She gave her time at the salon, her attention to her clients, her energy to her family, her Sunday afternoons to anyone who needed her, and also her time and attention to the youths on Wednesday nights. Giving was the part she knew by heart. It was receiving that was hard for her.

Conner reached his hand across the table, palm up.

"Let me say grace," he said.

She placed her hand in his. His fingers closed around hers, and he bowed his head.

"Lord, thank You for this meal and for the hands that grew and made the food on this table. Thank You for second chances. Thank You for being patient with us when we weren't patient enough with each other and for bringing us back together after all these years. Guide us as we walk this road You've set before us, and help us to be brave enough to follow where You lead. Bless this food and bless this evening. In Your name, amen."

"Amen," Rebecca said.

He squeezed her hand once before letting go, and the warmth of his grip lingered on her fingers.

Conner served the ribs and placed two ears of corn on her plate. She scooped mashed potatoes and took a square of cornbread from the basket. The cornbread was warm and dense, golden at its edges. She opened the jar of pickles, fished two out with a fork, and set them beside her ribs.

She took her first bite of the ribs and closed her eyes. Tender and smoky, the sauce sweet with a low-heat underneath, the meat pulling clean from the bone.

"These are incredible," she said. "Conner, seriously. Where did you learn to make ribs like this?"

"Trial and error, mostly. My first attempt in Richmond was so dry you could've used it as a doorstop. I've been adjusting the recipe ever since. This version uses a dry rub overnight and a low, slow cook with the sauce going on at the end."

"You practiced."

"I practiced a lot. My neighbors in Richmond benefited from many of my experiments."

She tried the mashed potatoes. The ranch came through first, then the garlic, then the butter Loretta had told him not to skimp on. She broke off a piece of cornbread, and the honey sweetness hit her right away, rich and warm with the tang of buttermilk underneath.

"This cornbread," she said. "This is just like how your mama makes it."

"I followed her instructions to the letter. She told me to use real buttermilk, not the powdered kind, and to warm the honey before I added it to the batter. I called her back once during the mixing to make sure I had the proportions right, and she talked me through it like she was coaching a surgery. She also informed me that if I burned it, she'd come over and make it herself, and I'd never live it down."

Rebecca smiled and ate another bite. She picked up a pickle, and the crunch was crisp, and the familiar sweet-tart brine of Loretta's recipe carried her back to a dozen afternoons on the Delaney porch. She and Conner sitting on the steps after school, her legs stretched out in front of her, a jar of pickles open between them, talking about nothing and everything while the afternoon stretched long.

"Do you remember our graduation party?" she asked.

Conner set his corn down and wiped his hands on his napkin. "I do."

"This meal reminds me of it. Your mama and my mama put that whole thing together, and they had ribs and chicken and corn and every side dish you could think of spread across three folding tables in my parents' backyard."

"My dad handled the grilling," Conner said. "He and Bill stood at that grill for four straight hours."

"They didn't let anyone else touch it. My brother Jim tried to take over at one point, and your daddy waved him off with the tongs and said, 'Son, this is a two-man operation, and we've got it covered.'"

Conner laughed.

"The whole church came. The Davise's, the Morrisons, the Fieldings. Minnie brought three pies." Rebecca leaned back in her chair. "And all our friends from school. Everybody out in the yard playing volleyball. Remember when Trent Fisher spiked the ball so hard it went over the fence and into the pasture, and your brother Miles had to go chase one of Daddy's cows away from it?"

"Miles was not happy about that. He was wearing new shoes."

"He came back with mud up to his ankles and cow manure on his left shoe, and your mama made him take them off, rinse them in the creek, and leave them on the porch to dry out."

"And then we all went for a swim," Conner said.

"That pool was the highlight of every summer. I think half the youth group learned to swim in my parents' backyard." Rebecca picked up her glass and took a sip of her sweet tea. "Do you remember the diving contest?"

"Justin Williams did a belly flop that echoed across the entire yard."

"He turned bright red from his chest to his chin, and he got out of the pool and said, 'I meant to do that,' and everyone knew he absolutely didn't mean to do that."

They were both laughing, and the sound filled the small dining area and bounced off the kitchen walls. The candle flames bent slightly from the movement of air between them, and the food was warm on the table, and the February night pressed against the windows while they sat inside a glow that belonged only to them.

"That was another good day," Rebecca said. "One of the best days. Everyone we loved was in the same place at the same time. I remember standing on the back porch of my parents' house that evening, watching the ridgeline go purple behind the mountains and thinking that I wanted to remember every single second of it."

"I remember that too," Conner said. "You were standing at the porch railing with a plate of watermelon, and the light was behind you, and I remember looking at you and thinking I was the luckiest guy in this whole town."

Rebecca held his gaze across the table. The candlelight caught the gold flecks in his hazel eyes.

"That was a special day I'll always cherish," she said.

They ate for a while, the conversation moving between bites, and their plates emptied slowly. Conner refilled their glasses from a pitcher on the kitchen counter, and the evening loosened into the particular rhythm of two people who hadn't a care in the world.

"My turn for a question," Conner said. He set his napkin beside his plate and leaned forward with his forearms on the table.

"Hit me with it; I'll be honest."

"Where do you see the salon in five years?"

Rebecca tilted her head. "Well… that's an interesting question. My salon's solid. I've got a strong client base, good stylists, and we stay booked. I'd like to hire a full-time manicurist so I can take that off my plate and Jenna's. But honestly, the salon isn't the thing I've been thinking about most lately."

She paused. This was something she hadn't shared with many people. Jenna knew. Her mama knew. She hadn't said it out loud to anyone beyond them because saying it made it real, and real meant it could fail.

"I want to open a second business here in Serenity Crossing," she said. "A day spa."

Conner's eyebrows lifted, and interest sharpened across his face. "A spa. Tell me about it."

"Something completely separate from the salon. The salon is energy and conversation and music and people coming and going all day. I love that. But there's a market here for something quieter. Facials, massage therapy, body treatments, aromatherapy. A space where somebody can walk in feeling worn out and walk out feeling like they've had a full reset." She picked up her glass and turned it in her hand. "I've been researching it for months. I have a notebook at home with layouts and cost projections, and service menus. I've looked at the old Calloway building on Birch Street. It's been empty for two years, and the square footage is right, and it's got good natural light."

"You've looked at a building."

"Twice. Sarah walked through it with me the second time and said the bones are good. It needs work, but she could do most of it."

"Rebecca, that's incredible. You've been carrying this around and haven't said anything?"

"I'm careful about sharing things before they're ready. I don't want to talk about a dream until I know it has legs."

"It sounds like it already has legs," he said.

She laughed. "It has a notebook and a lot of sticky notes."

"That's how some of the best dreams start."

"What about you?" she asked. "What kind of pastor do you want to be over the next few years?"

Conner leaned back and crossed his arms loosely. "Long term, I'd like to take over for Warren whenever he decides to retire. He and I have talked about it in general terms, and I think that's where this road leads if God keeps pointing me in this direction."

"Warren would love that. He's said as much to my parents. I think the church congregation expects it as well."

"Beyond Sunday mornings, I've got some things I want to build. I would like to develop the adult Bible study program into something deeper and more consistent. Right now it's a Thursday night group that rotates leaders, and the content varies depending on who's teaching, similar to what the youth group had been in the past. I'd like to create a structured curriculum that goes book by book through Scripture. Something people can follow and grow with over months."

"That's needed; I think the congregation would like that," Rebecca said.

"I also want to start a monthly church dinner. Not a random potluck after service. Something dedicated. A Saturday evening once a month when families come and bring a dish to share and sit down together. Fellowship with no agenda, no program. Just people being together because being together matters."

"My mama would be first in line for that, and she'd bring enough food for twenty people."

"I'm counting on it." He smiled. "And there's one more thing I've been turning over. I want to start visiting the retirement home here in town regularly. Once a month, maybe twice. Bring a small group from the church, have the choir come sing, and hold a short service. But I don't want it to just be a service and then we leave. I want it to be a real visit. Sit with people. Read to them. Play games. Let them know their church family hasn't forgotten them just because they can't make it to the building on Sunday."

"I love that, Conner," Rebecca said. "Those folks in that retirement home are some of the sweetest people in this community, and a lot of them don't get many visitors."

"Ministry isn't just what happens inside the church walls. It's what you carry outside them."

She looked at him across the candlelit table. Every plan he'd described was rooted in Serenity Crossing, in their church, and in this community. He wasn't chasing a bigger pulpit. He was planting himself here, and every seed he'd just named would take years to grow. None of it required leaving.

"We both want the same kind of life," she said.

"I think we always did," he said. "We just weren't ready for it at the same time."

She picked up a pickle and ate it, and the quiet between them was easy and full. After a moment, she looked at him.

"Do you ever think about what would've happened if we hadn't broken up?"

Conner turned his glass in his hand and was quiet for a few seconds.

"I used to think about it a lot," he said. "I think we would have struggled a lot. I think we had a lot of growing up to do. I sometimes question if we would've made it, Rebecca."

"I have too," she said.

"I wasn't ready back then, and I know that now. My intentions were good, but I didn't have the maturity to see what was right in front of me while I was chasing what I thought was ahead of us. I was so focused on school and building a future that I thought was for both of us that I didn't know how to make room for our relationship while I was doing it. I wanted to be able to give you a good life someday, and I lost sight of the life we already had." He held her gaze. "I didn't see us falling apart because I was too busy looking at the road in front of me to notice you were standing behind me."

"We were eighteen, Conner. Still babies."

"I know. But I was the one who pulled away and didn't realize I was doing it. That's not something I can put on being young alone. I wasn't emotionally ready for the depth of what we had, and I didn't see that until years later."

Rebecca reached across the table and laid her hand on his. His fingers turned beneath hers and held on.

"You're right that we might not have made it," she said. "And I've thought about my side of it too. Back then, my entire world revolved around you. You were my number one, and everything else came second. School, my dreams. I never stopped to think about what I really wanted for myself." She rubbed her thumb along the side of his hand. "The years apart taught me who I am. I built a business. I figured out what I'm good at and what I want from my life. I learned how to stand on my own and not need someone else to make me feel complete." She paused. "I think the woman sitting at this table tonight is ready for a deeper and more meaningful relationship than the girl who made that phone call ten years ago and let you go. Because I know who I am now, and I know what I bring to a relationship, and I'm not going to disappear into somebody else's life and lose myself again."

"You wouldn't," he said. "And I wouldn't let you."

"I know you wouldn't."

The candles had burned lower, the wax pooling in their glass holders, and their plates sat mostly empty now.

"I'm confident God knew what He was doing with us," Conner said. "I think He looked at two kids who loved each other deeply and weren't ready, and He said, 'Not yet. But soon.' And He spent ten years getting us both ready for this."

Rebecca squeezed his hand. "I think so, too."

Conner stood and began clearing the table. She started to rise, and he pointed at her chair.

"Sit, I've got this."

"Conner, let me help."

"You are helping. You're keeping that chair warm, and just you being here makes me happy." He stacked the plates and carried them to the kitchen. She heard the water run briefly and the plates settle into the sink. He came back and took the serving bowls, and she watched him move through his kitchen with the ease of a man who loved cooking and loved cooking for her even more.

He returned carrying a white bakery box and a small rectangular package wrapped in brown craft paper with a thin ribbon tied around it. He set the bakery box on the table and lifted the lid.

A whole coconut cream pie. Tall whipped topping, toasted coconut flakes scattered across its surface, and the golden crust crimped around the edges.

"Is that from Sweet Surrender?" she asked.

"Patti saved it for me. I called her on Wednesday and asked her to set one aside."

"You called Patti and ordered me a whole coconut cream pie."

"Of course, it's your favorite. You told me at the bakery that Patti saves you a slice on Fridays because they sell out by noon. I figured if one slice makes you that happy, a whole pie might make your entire week joyful."

Rebecca looked at the pie and then at him and shook her head slowly. "You are something else, Conner Delaney."

He cut two generous slices and set one in front of her. The filling was thick and smooth, and the toasted coconut on top smelled warm and sweet. She took a bite, and it was perfect. Cool and creamy, the coconut flavor layered through, and the crust flaked against her fork.

"Now," he said. He slid the wrapped package across the table. "This is your Valentine's gift."

She set her fork down and pulled the package toward her. The brown paper was neatly folded, and the ribbon was tied in a simple knot. She untied it and peeled the paper back.

Inside was a small booklet, roughly the size of a greeting card, made from heavy cardstock and bound with twine through two holes punched along the left edge. The cover read, in Conner's compact handwriting: Coupon Book. No expiration, good for a lifetime.

She looked up at him.

"I made you one of these our senior year," he said. "For Valentine's Day. You probably don't remember."

"I remember," she said. "One free piggyback ride. One night where I picked the movie. One batch of my favorite cookies, which you couldn't bake at the time but said your mama would help you make. That coupon book is in a scrapbook I made the summer after we graduated from high school."

Conner set his fork down slowly. "You made a scrapbook?"

"I did. I put everything in it. Every card you ever gave me, the coupon book, movie ticket stubs, that note you wrote me on the back of a napkin at Minnie's the night you asked me to be your girlfriend." She smiled. "Some of the flowers you gave me. I pressed them and taped them to the pages. And lots of pictures of us."

"You kept all of that?" he said.

"Every bit of it. I pulled the scrapbook out a few days ago, actually. I sat on my couch and went through the whole thing page by page." She looked at the coupon book in her hands. "I thought about getting rid of it a few times over the years. I couldn't do it. Something in me wouldn't let go of it."

Conner looked at her across the table, and the expression on his face was tender, full of a kind of awe that had nothing to do with the scrapbook itself and everything to do with what keeping it meant. Ten years. She'd held on to every piece of them for ten years.

"Open it," he said.

Rebecca opened the coupon book to the first page. His handwriting filled each card, neat and compact.

One Saturday morning breakfast at Minnie's Diner. I'm buying. You pick the booth.

She turned the page.

One hike to anywhere you choose. I'll pack the water and the snacks.

One evening of your Netflix picks. Zero complaints. I promise.

One batch of chocolate chip cookies, from scratch, delivered to the salon on the day of your choice.

One quiet walk around town when you need to get out of your head.

One run on a trail when you need to think and want a shoulder to lean on.

One long break from work because your sweet tooth is getting the best of you and coconut cream pie is calling your name.

One midweek lunch break. No errands, no rushing. Just sitting together.

One trip to Henderson's Hill to act like kids again and go sledding.

One evening where I plan everything. You just say the word.

One slow dance, wherever we happen to be.

She turned to the last page.

Revolving coupon: One chance every day to show you what you mean to me.

Rebecca ran her finger along the edge of the last card. The handwriting was the same boy who'd made her the first coupon book at seventeen, but the man behind these pages had filled them with things that told her he knew who she was right now. The morning breakfast at Minnie's because he knew she loved that diner. The hike was because she'd told him she wanted to spend more time outdoors. The walk around town or a run because he understood that sometimes her thoughts got loud, and she needed to move. The slow dance because he was the kind of man who'd dance with her in a kitchen or a parking lot, and he wasn't afraid to put it in writing.

She closed the booklet and held it against her chest.

"Every single one of these is personal," she said.

"Every single one was written for you."

"The slow dance."

"Whenever you're ready. I'll be there."

She looked at the coupon book in her hands. Then at the coconut cream pie. Then at the pink rose beside her plate and the candles that had burned low. The man sitting across from her had spent days thinking and building an evening around who she was at eighteen and who she'd become at twenty-eight. She had spent years believing that this kind of love, the kind that was specific and daily and personal, was something other people got to have. Her parents had it. She'd watched it her whole life. She'd wanted it with a quiet, steady ache she'd buried so deep she'd nearly forgotten it was there.

It was sitting across the table from her in a green henley with BBQ sauce on his napkin.

"Conner," she said. "Thank you. For all of this. The dinner, the pie, the coupons. Everything. You are such a special man."

"You don't have to thank me."

"Yes, I do. Because I want you to know that I see what you did tonight. You didn't just make me dinner. You told me you remember who I was, and you're paying attention to who I am now, and both of those things matter to me more than I can say."

He reached across the table and took her hand. His thumb traced a slow line across her knuckles.

"What would you like to do with the rest of our evening?" he asked.

She didn't hesitate. "Let's walk around town. I want to see what the shops have in their windows. I want to walk around the town square, holding your hand. I just want to be out with you on a Saturday night."

"That sounds perfect," he said.

He stood and walked to the hooks near the front door where her coat hung beside his. He lifted hers off the hook and held it open, and she crossed the room and turned so he could slip it over her shoulders. His hands rested there for a moment, warm and steady through the fabric, before he reached for his own jacket.

Rebecca tucked the coupon book into her coat pocket, where she could feel its edges against her hip. A Valentine's Saturday in Serenity Crossing with the man she'd loved since she was seventeen, and not a single part of her wanted to be anywhere else.

Chapter 21

Conner had turned his chair away from his desk and was watching a single squirrel navigate the bare oaks along the edge of the church parking area. The branches were stripped clean for February, dark and angular against a blue sky. His Bible sat open on the desk behind him. His legal pad beside it, half a page of notes in his compact handwriting for tonight's youth group lesson. He was supposed to be choosing a verse. Instead, he'd been stuck on a single word he'd underlined twenty minutes ago.

Overlooked.

Lesson Five. "What If You've Been Overlooked?" He'd written the session description a few years ago in Richmond, built the discussion questions and the opening exercise, and the small-group breakout. He'd fine-tuned it in January for the kids here in Serenity Crossing, adjusting the examples to fit what he knew about their lives. He'd been fine-tuning this particular lesson with Hannah Caldwell in mind. The girl whose father started a new family. The girl whose mother worked every evening and came home after midnight. The girl who labeled herself lonely with the flat delivery of someone reading from a list she'd memorized a long time ago.

The lesson was good. The framework was solid. And none of that was the problem.

The problem was that the word kept circling back to him.

He picked up the legal pad and read his own notes. Overlooked doesn't always look like cruelty. Sometimes it looks like distraction. Sometimes the person doing it doesn't even know. He'd written that line for a room full of teenagers. For kids who'd been passed over by busy parents, forgotten by friends who moved on, lost in classrooms where the quiet ones never got called on. It was a good line for them.

It was also his own story.

He set the legal pad down and rubbed his thumb along the edge of his jaw.

He hadn't overlooked Rebecca with cruelty. What he'd done was subtler and, in its own way, harder to forgive. He'd overlooked her with the particular blindness of an eighteen-year-old boy whose world expanded while hers stayed the same size. His calls shortened. His attention narrowed to the life unfolding around him in Lynchburg. She became someone he checked in with instead of someone he chose to walk alongside, and the distinction had been invisible to him until it was too late.

Every lesson in this series has been pressing on the same bruise. Circling back to the place where his failure and her pain met. He hadn't designed it that way. The curriculum existed before he came home, before he knew he'd be standing in a church recreation hall on Wednesday nights beside the woman he'd loved since he was eighteen.

He turned his chair back to the desk and looked at his Bible. The leather was worn soft along its spine, the page edges dulled from years of handling to a faded amber. He'd had this Bible since college. His mother's careful handwriting filled the front page with his name and the date she'd given it to him, the summer before he left for Liberty.

He turned to Matthew 10 and read the passage he'd bookmarked with a thin slip of paper. *Are not two sparrows sold for a penny? Yet not one of them will fall to the ground outside your Father's care. And even the very hairs of your head are all numbered. So don't be afraid; you are worth more than many sparrows.*

Good verse for the lesson. Concrete. The kind of thing a teenager could carry in a pocket and pull out on a bad Tuesday.

He turned to Psalm 139 and read his other option. *You have searched me, Lord, and you know me. You know when I sit and when I rise; you perceive my thoughts from afar. You discern my going out and my lying down; you are familiar with all my ways. Before a word is on my tongue, you, Lord, know it completely.*

Beautiful. True. But abstract for a room full of kids who needed something they could hold in their minds.

He leaned back and set his pen on the desk. Two good options, and he couldn't commit to either because his mind wouldn't stay in the lesson plan. It kept drifting back to the bonfire and to the look on Rebecca's face when she told him she broke up with him because she felt alone. To the Valentine's dinner ten days ago when they'd sat across from each other and talked about the breakup with the honesty of two people who'd finally stopped protecting themselves from the truth.

A knock on his open office door pulled him back.

Rebecca stood in the doorway holding a white bakery box in one hand and a cardboard drink carrier with two cups in the other. Her blonde hair was down, falling in loose waves past her shoulders. She wore a soft blue sweater with small white flowers printed across its fabric, jeans, and the silver earrings she'd been wearing lately caught the low light from his window. Her nails were a deep berry color this week.

"Hey," she said.

"Hey." He stood from his chair and crossed the small office in two steps. "This is a nice surprise."

"I finished with my last client about thirty minutes ago, and I had a thought that involved cake." She lifted the bakery box.

He took the drink carrier from her and set it on his desk. She stepped past him into the office, and something floral and clean followed her in, the same scent he'd noticed a hundred times.

"Sit," he said, pulling the spare chair closer to the desk for her.

She set the bakery box on the edge of his desk and opened the lid. Two slices of cake on small cardboard plates. The one on the left was dark, layered with thick chocolate frosting between three dense layers. The one on the right was lighter, golden-brown with a ribbon of cinnamon through its center and a thin glaze across its top.

"Triple chocolate for you," she said, sliding the dark slice toward him. "And the apple cake for me."

Conner looked at the chocolate cake.

"My mama used to bake something like this. Chocolate cake is a favorite of mine," he said.

"I know she did. Every birthday, every special occasion, and sometimes on a random Saturday just because you asked." Rebecca pulled a napkin from the bakery box and handed it to him.

"You went to Sweet Surrender Bakery for me."

"I'll be honest, I went to Sweet Surrender because I wanted apple cake, and while I was there, I saw the triple chocolate in the case and thought of you." She picked up one of the coffee cups from the carrier and handed it to him. "Black."

"Thank you," he said. "This is really thoughtful."

"You're welcome." She crossed one leg over the other and settled into the chair as if she'd already decided this was where she planned to spend her Wednesday afternoon. She picked up her fork and cut into her apple cake. "So, what are you working on?"

"Tonight's lesson for the youth group," he said, gesturing at the legal pad.

Rebecca took a bite of her apple cake and looked at his notes.

"What If You've Been Overlooked," she read from the top of the page. She looked at him. "This is the lesson you were talking about, adjusting a little with Hannah in mind."

"It is." He took a sip of his coffee and set it down. "But I've been sitting here for the last hour, and I can't get past the prep work. I'm supposed to be picking a verse, and my thoughts keep drifting."

"Where are they drifting to?"

He looked at her across the desk. She was holding her coffee cup near her chin, her blue eyes on his, and the afternoon light from the window fell across her shoulder and caught the silver of her earrings.

"To us," he said.

She set her coffee down and held his gaze.

"Go on, I'm listening," she said.

Conner leaned forward with his forearms on the edge of the desk. "Every lesson in this series has been doing something I didn't plan for. I built the Chosen curriculum in Richmond for the youth group there. I fine-tuned it for the kids here. Every discussion question, every opening exercise, every verse—all of it designed for teenagers who need to hear that they matter." He paused. "But week after week, the conversations you and I have had after the meetings have been opening doors neither of us expected. The lessons land on the kids, and then they land on us."

Rebecca set her fork down and leaned back in her chair. "I've noticed it too. The first week, when you told those kids about sitting alone in a college dining hall. About calling your mom and your girlfriend every day because their voices were the only thing that reminded you that you existed." She looked at him. "I was standing in the back of that room, and I heard you say that, and all I could think about was every night I sat on my bed waiting for a phone call that came later and later as time moved on. And then shorter and shorter. Until eventually I stopped expecting your calls as much."

"And the lesson on labels," she continued. "When Hannah said lonely. When she described her parents and her friend moving away and the house being empty every night. I stood there listening to that girl tell her story, and afterward, when we were cleaning up, I told you I would've used the same word for myself at eighteen." She picked up her fork and turned it in her hand. "That wasn't a coincidence, Conner. The lesson drew it out. I wouldn't have said that to you on a random Wednesday if we'd been talking about anything else."

"I know," he said. "The comparison lesson did the same thing. What Hannah described wasn't comparison. It was abandonment dressed up in a quieter word. When you said that, I went home and sat in my living room for an hour thinking about how I'd done the same thing to you. I pulled into my new life and left you standing in the old one, and I didn't look back to see what it was costing. I was so full of myself and my needs and wants."

Rebecca reached across the desk and laid her hand on his legal pad, her fingers resting near the word he'd underlined. Overlooked. She looked at the word and then at him.

"Each lesson has landed on the kids and then landed on us," she said. "You're right. It's been happening every single week."

He covered her hand with his. Her fingers were warm from the coffee cup, and she turned her palm up beneath his.

"Help me pick the verse for this week," he said.

She smiled. "You have options?"

"Two." He reached across with his free hand and turned his Bible toward her. "Matthew 10:29–31. The sparrows passage. And Psalm 139:1–4."

Rebecca pulled the Bible closer and read the Matthew passage first, her lips moving slightly as her eyes tracked the words. She turned to the Psalm and read it the same way, careful and unhurried.

She looked up. "The sparrows."

"Tell me why."

"Because it's concrete. A teenager can picture it. A small bird that nobody pays attention to, and God sees it anyway. That's the kind of image a youth can catalog in their mind and pull out when they need it." She tapped the page gently. "The Psalm is beautiful, and it's true, but it's abstract. 'You perceive my thoughts from afar' is going to sail over most of their heads. They need something they can envision and feel."

"That's exactly what I was leaning toward," he said.

He nodded and picked up his pen. He wrote Matthew 10:29–31 beside his Lesson Five notes on the legal pad.

"These conversations we've been having. Before youth group. After youth group. At the bonfire. At my table on Valentine's night. They've meant something real to me, Rebecca. All of them. Every Wednesday night when the kids leave, we stay behind and clean up and end up talking about what the lesson stirred up." He leaned forward. "The truths we've spoken to each other about being young and the mistakes we made and what the breakup cost both of us—those conversations have been freeing me from guilt

I've carried for ten years... some of which I hadn't really known I was carrying."

She set her coffee down and gave him her full attention.

"The remaining lessons are going to keep pressing on us," he said. "Lesson Six is 'Being Chosen Doesn't Always Look the Way You Think.' Lesson Seven is 'Letting People See the Real You.' Those topics will land on us the same way every other one has. We both know it."

"I know," she said.

He leaned closer. "Would you be willing to sit down with me before each youth group meeting going forward? A real conversation. Go through the lesson material, work through the content, and pick the verses. And if the topics bring more honesty between us, more healing, we welcome it instead of running from it or dismissing it."

"We lay everything on the table," he continued. "We could do dinner, or meet here at the church, or the rec hall, or the salon. Anywhere. I just want us to keep doing what we've been doing, except deliberately instead of accidentally."

She was quiet. She looked at their hands on the desk. Then at his Bible. Then at the legal pad with his notes for a lesson called "What If You've Been Overlooked?"

"What's been happening between us through these lessons isn't accidental," she said. "You built this curriculum for teenagers. You built it to help kids who feel invisible understand that they matter. But God's been using it for more than that. He's been using it on us."

"I think so, too."

"I believe God works through ordinary things," she said. "Wednesday nights in a church rec hall with a group of teenagers who have no idea that the two adults standing at the front of the room are being healed by the same material." She squeezed his hand. "Every week, you stand up and teach these kids something true, and every week that truth turns around and teaches us. I don't think that's a coincidence. I think that's God doing what He does best, using the thing you built for one purpose to accomplish something bigger than you planned."

Something loosened in his chest. The slow easing of a knot he'd been carrying so long he'd stopped noticing it was there.

"So, yes," she said. "I'll sit down with you before every meeting. We go through the material. We pick the verses. And whatever the lessons bring up between us, we stay in it. We don't change the subject, and we don't save it for later; we tackle this head-on."

"Thank you," he said.

"Don't thank me." She smiled. "I'm getting just as much out of this as you are. Maybe more."

She held his hand for another moment, and then she let go and picked up her coffee. She took a long sip and set it down.

"Lesson Six," she said. "Being Chosen Doesn't Always Look the Way You Think. When were you planning to start prepping that one?"

"Next Monday, probably. I usually start early in the week and refine through Wednesday."

"Then I'll come by Wednesday afternoon... in fact, let's just meet early in the rec hall."

"Sounds like a solid plan."

"I hate to cut this short, but I promised Mom I'd come by her house before youth group. She's planning on turning my old bedroom into a nursery and wants my opinion. She's so excited about Jim and Grace's twins coming and wants help deciding how she should decorate it." She picked up her coffee and her purse from the back of the chair. At the doorway, she turned.

"For what it's worth," she said. "The guilt you've been carrying. You can set it down. I'm not holding it against you, and I haven't been for a while now. We were eighteen. We did the best we could with what we had." She held his gaze. "And the man sitting in this office right now is not the boy who left. I like who you are, Conner. Right now. Today. Very much. What happened in our past happened. We can't change it. All we can do is keep building toward a future that I think both of us have always wanted together."

She tapped the doorframe once with her palm, turned, and left.

Conner sat in his chair and looked at his desk. The two coffee cups. The bakery box. His Bible, open to Matthew 10. His legal pad with the verse reference written in fresh ink.

He'd built this series for teenagers. Every lesson, every discussion question, and every verse selected and sequenced for kids who feel invisible and need to hear that they are known and valued. He'd designed it in Richmond, fine-tuned it in Serenity Crossing, and delivered it week after week to a room full of teenagers who were just beginning to question who they are and understand life. Chosen was the title he had named this series long ago.

But the two people leading this youth group needed these lessons just as much as the youths that came to a simple meeting in a church recreation hall.

God sure works in mysterious ways.

Chapter 22

Rebecca pushed through the door of the recreation hall with two grocery bags balanced against her hip and her purse strap sliding down her shoulder.

Conner was near the front of the room, arranging two folding chairs side by side, angled slightly toward each other. A small table sat between the chairs with two to-go coffee cups on it. His Bible and legal pad rested beside the cups. He looked up when the door closed behind her, and the smile that crossed his face was immediate.

"There she is," he said.

Rebecca set her bags on the snack table and crossed the room toward him. She didn't slow down or second-guess it. She walked straight to him and wrapped her arms around his shoulders in a hug that she held for a good solid minute before pulling back.

"I've missed you," she said. "These have been the longest past few days."

"It has." His hand rested on her arm for a moment before he let go. "Between sermon prep, two hospital visits, and a trustees' meeting that lasted three hours, I feel like I haven't come up for air since Sunday."

"My week wasn't much better. Three color corrections back-to-back on Tuesday, a wedding party consultation yesterday morning, and a pipe leak under my shampoo sink that took the plumber two full days to sort out." She stepped back and looked at the two chairs, the coffee, and the table arranged with care. She picked up the cup nearest to her and took a sip. "How long have you been here?"

"About twenty minutes. I wanted to get the chairs set for the kids and the snack table ready before you got here so we'd have time to sit and talk." He nodded toward the long table against the wall where a case of water bottles and a gallon of sweet tea were already arranged. Beside them, a plate of cookies sat covered in plastic wrap. "I made peanut butter chocolate chip cookies. My mom's recipe."

"Loretta's peanut butter chocolate chip cookies." Rebecca looked at him. "Those kids are going to lose their minds."

She went back to the snack table and unpacked her bags. Two large bags of tortilla chips, a container of spinach artichoke dip she'd picked up from the deli counter, and a glass bowl of trail mix she'd put together that morning with peanuts, raisins, M&M's, and pretzels. She arranged everything beside his cookies and the water bottles, adjusting the layout until it looked good.

"This is a solid spread," she said, stepping back to survey the table.

"Between the two of us, these kids are going to think we're running a catering operation."

Rebecca laughed and picked up her coffee from where she'd left it on the small table. She sat down in the chair closest to the wall, tucked one leg beneath her, and settled in. Her blonde hair was down tonight, loose past her shoulders, and she'd worn a soft burgundy top with small gold buttons at the collar, jeans, and her favorite pair of gold hoop earrings. She'd changed twice before leaving her apartment, which was ridiculous, and she knew it was ridiculous, and she'd done it anyway.

Conner sat in the chair beside her and picked up his coffee.

"All right," she said. "Lesson Six. Walk me through it."

Conner leaned forward with his forearms on his knees and turned the legal pad so she could see his notes. "The title is 'Being Chosen Doesn't Always Look the Way You Think.' The core idea is something I've seen play out in every youth group I've ever worked with. People build a picture in their heads of what love is supposed to look like, what being wanted is supposed to feel like. And when love shows up in a form that doesn't match that picture, they don't recognize it. Sometimes they push it away because it doesn't look right."

Rebecca ran her finger along the rim of her coffee cup. "Give me an example. How would you frame that for a teenager?"

"A few ways. A parent who shows love through rules instead of affection. The kid thinks the parent doesn't care, but that parent is up at midnight checking grades and packing lunches because that's what they do as a parent. Or a friend who tells you the truth when you don't want to hear it, instead of agreeing with everything you say." He glanced at his notes. "A father who can't bring himself to say 'I love you,' but he's at every single game, every recital, every school event, sitting in the third row with his phone out taking pictures. Or a teacher who comes across as strict and demanding, but what she's really doing is refusing to let you settle for less than she knows you're capable of. The love is in every one of those. It just doesn't match the version the kid built in their head."

"That's strong," Rebecca said. "Concrete enough for them to grab onto."

"The discussion question I want to build toward is this: Has someone ever loved you in a way you didn't recognize at the time? And if so, what did you think it was instead?"

"That question." She set her coffee on the table between them. "I need to answer it before I can sit in that circle tonight and listen to you ask those kids the same thing."

He closed his legal pad and set it aside, and gave her his full attention.

"When I was eighteen," she said, "I had a very specific picture in my head of what being chosen and wanted or loved was supposed to look like."

She paused. Not because she was gathering courage, but because she wanted the words to come out right.

"When you were at college before we broke up, I expected to be chosen and needed. Coming home on weekends when you could.

Calling me first thing in the morning instead of last thing at night. Showing up at my door when things got hard between us and saying, 'I'm here, and you come first.'" She held his gaze. "I wanted to be your priority again. Right beside your classes and your calling and everything else. The way I'd been during our whole senior year, when there wasn't anything pulling you away from me."

"And I know now that the things I resented weren't things I should've resented. Your classes, your professors, your friendships, your calling. All of that was good. All of that was God working in your life. I can see that as an adult." She pressed her thumb against the seam of her jeans. "But at eighteen, I didn't have that kind of perspective. I was a girl who was deeply in love with a boy she knew in her bones was the one for her. And that boy's world was getting bigger every day, and mine was staying exactly the same size, and I could feel myself slipping further and further down his list. I wasn't trying to hold you back from your future. I just wanted to be a part of it. I wanted to matter enough that pursuing your calling and loving me didn't have to be an either-or. So I broke up with you. But here's the part I haven't said out loud. To you or to anyone." She looked at the floor for a moment, then back at him. "The breakup was a test."

"I wanted you to fail it," she continued. "I wanted to say, 'It's over,' and I wanted you to say, 'No, it's not.' I wanted you to drive home from Lynchburg and knock on my door and tell me you weren't going to let me walk away. That's what I was waiting for. Every day after that phone call, I was waiting for you to show up." She pressed her palms flat on her knees. "And when you didn't, I told myself it proved what I was already afraid of. That I wasn't worth fighting for. You no longer wanted me in your life. You no longer needed me. That you could let me go without it costing you anything."

"Rebecca—"

"Let me finish." She said it gently, and he nodded.

"I've carried shame about that for ten years. Because testing someone is manipulative. I know that now. I'm a grown woman, and I can look back at what I did and call it what it was. I set a trap. I gave you an ultimatum I didn't mean and then punished you in my heart for honoring it." She shook her head once. "I've sat in church pews and listened to sermons about honesty and integrity and thought about that phone call several times. I wasn't honest with you, Conner. I told you I wanted to break up when what I really wanted was for you to need me again. I wanted to be your priority. Me. Just me."

"But here's what I've been working through this week," she said. "The test was wrong. The way I went about it was wrong. But what I wanted underneath it wasn't."

She leaned forward.

"What I wanted was to be chosen first. The way my daddy has chosen my mama every single day for thirty-five years. He didn't choose her when it was convenient. He chose her when the lumber mill was struggling and money was tight, and there were six kids running through the house. He chose her first because that's what love looks like when it's real. He comes through the door at the end of every day, and she is the first person he goes to. Before he sits down. Before he takes off his boots. He finds her. That's what I grew up watching. That's what I thought love was. That's what I still think love is."

She sat back in her chair and let herself breathe.

"And you taught me that too, Conner. During our senior year, I was your priority. I was your person. When you had a free afternoon, you spent it with me. When something good happened, I was the first call you made. When something hard happened, I was the one you told. I wasn't competing with anything because there was nothing to compete with. You chose me clearly and simply, and I built my whole understanding of what love feels like on that too." Her voice was steady, and she held his gaze without flinching. "Then you went to college, and over time, I wasn't that anymore. I wasn't first. I wasn't even close. And I watched the distance between us grow larger each week. In my selfish teenage mind, I ended it and tested you and expected you to come running back to me, and all along I had this video playing in my mind that you would. And I'd act all unsure at first just to test you again and have you beg for me to be your girlfriend again. Then I waited for you to come after me, and you didn't, and I spent the next few years telling myself I was foolish for wanting you. Telling myself that I wasn't good enough for you and that you no longer wanted me in your life."

"I'm twenty-eight years old," she said. "And I'm done being ashamed of wanting to be chosen first. What I wanted at eighteen wasn't immature. It wasn't needy. It was what every person who has ever loved someone deserves to feel. I want to matter enough that the man who loves me would fight to keep me. I want to be important enough that if everything in his life is pulling him in different directions, I'm the thing he refuses to let go of. That's what I want. That's what I need. And I've spent ten years apologizing for it inside my head, and I shouldn't have. I shouldn't make myself feel bad for what I want. I believe when two people love each other, they are both each other's priority, and there should never be any doubt of that in either person's mind."

Conner sat with his hands clasped between his knees. He hadn't moved through any of it. He'd listened with the full measure of his attention, and when she finished, the quiet that followed wasn't strained. It was a man letting the truth settle where it needed to go.

"I called you," he said. "The morning after you broke up with me. The next morning. I sat on the edge of my dorm room bed, and I picked up my phone, and I called your number."

She stared at him.

"It rang five times," he said. "I sat there counting every ring. Five rings. Then it went to voicemail, and I hung up. You didn't answer the phone, Rebecca, and I told myself that was your answer. That you didn't want to hear from me. That you'd made your decision, and the kindest thing I could do was let you have it."

"Conner, I didn't know you called. I would've answered. If I'd seen your number, I would've picked up. Why didn't you call again?"

"You didn't answer my call the first time, and I used that as permission to stop trying." He rubbed his thumb across his knuckles.

"I told myself I was being respectful. That you'd asked me to let go, and I was honoring what you wanted. And that was true, but it wasn't the whole truth." He looked at her. "The whole truth is that I was scared. I was terrified that if I called again, and you answered, you wouldn't take me back. That you'd say the words a second time, and I wouldn't survive hearing them twice. So I used respect as a shield, and I let the silence become the story."

"I was a scared eighteen-year-old kid who loved you more than he knew how to say and couldn't face the possibility that loving you wasn't enough to keep you," he continued. "I should've called again. I should've called ten times. I should've gotten in my truck, driven home, stood on your front porch, and told you I was an idiot and that I was going to do better. And I didn't. And I have to live with that."

Rebecca pressed her fingers against her temples. She wasn't crying. She was holding back the particular pressure that comes from learning something that rearranges a story you've told yourself for a decade.

"One missed phone call," she said, lowering her hands.

Headlights swept across the windows on the far side of the room, white beams tracking across the cinder block.

Conner looked at her. "We're not going to be able to finish this tonight."

"No," she said. "We're not." She straightened in her chair and picked up her coffee. She took a long sip, set it down, and looked at him. "But we're not done here."

"Not even close," he said.

The side door opened, and Tyler's voice carried into the room before the rest of him appeared. Josh was behind him, followed by Derek and Allan. Emma came through next with Sophie and Megan, their conversations overlapping as they shed jackets and moved toward the snack table. Caleb walked in alone, nodded at Conner, and took a seat in the circle. Tucker followed a minute later with Simon, and Mary came in behind them. Hannah arrived last, stepping through the door quietly with her jacket zipped to her chin. She found a seat between Emma and Sophie without hesitation, sat down, and Emma leaned over and said something that made her smile.

Rebecca stood and moved to her usual spot on the edge of the circle. She greeted the kids as they settled in, asked Tucker about his basketball game last Friday, told Megan she liked her new sneakers, and smiled at Hannah.

Conner let the room fill for a few more minutes. Kids grabbed water bottles and cookies from the snack table. Tyler took a handful of trail mix and dropped into his chair. Josh grabbed cookies and sat beside him. The noise rose and settled into the particular pitch of teenagers at ease.

A little after seven o'clock, Conner stood in the center of the circle.

"All right, everybody. Welcome back. Grab your seats, and let's get started."

The room quieted. Chairs scraped. Last conversations trailed off. Rebecca settled into her chair and folded her hands in her lap, and Conner opened his Bible to the page he'd bookmarked.

"Tonight's lesson is called 'Being Chosen Doesn't Always Look the Way You Think,'" he said. "And I want to start with a question before I say anything else." He looked around the circle. "Has anyone in this room ever gotten something they wanted, but it came in a package they didn't recognize? Maybe it didn't look the way you expected. Maybe it showed up at the wrong time or from the wrong person. And because it didn't match the picture in your head, you almost missed it."

Rebecca sat on the outer edge of the circle and listened. She heard every word Conner said, and beneath them, she heard the conversation they'd been having twenty minutes ago running like a second track underneath the lesson. Being chosen doesn't always look the way you think. She'd built a picture at eighteen of what Conner's love was supposed to look like. Grand gestures. Her on a pedestal like some kind of princess. Urgency. Unmistakable proof that she mattered above everything else. And when his love had arrived in a different form, steady and quiet and woven into phone calls that shortened because his world was pulling him in directions he didn't know how to manage, she hadn't recognized it. She'd looked at his faithfulness and called it neglect because it didn't match the picture in her mind.

That didn't erase what she'd told him tonight. She still wanted to be chosen first. That want was real and right, and she stood behind every word of it. But the lesson was pressing on a different bruise now, one she hadn't expected. The possibility that Conner had been choosing her the whole time, in the only way an eighteen-year-old boy away from home for the first time knew how, and she'd been too hurt, insecure, and thoughtless to see it.

She watched him move through the lesson. He was good at this. Better than good. He read the room with an instinct that came from years of standing in front of teenagers and learning which silences to fill and which to leave alone. He called on Josh, who talked about his older brother joining the Marines and how their mom cried for a week, and Josh thought she was sad, but really she was proud. Emma talked about her grandmother, who never said "I love you" but sent a card every single birthday with five dollars inside and a note that said, "Keep being you." He drew Caleb out on the subject of his youth pastor in middle school, a man who'd been tough on him and held him accountable, and whom Caleb hadn't appreciated until years later.

Rebecca watched Hannah during these exchanges. Hannah sat between Emma and Sophie and listened to everyone speak with a quiet attention that reminded Rebecca of herself at that age. Taking everything in. Measuring it against her own experience. Filing it away.

Twenty minutes passed. Then thirty. Conner opened his Bible and read from Matthew 10:29–31. "'Are not two sparrows sold for a penny? Yet not one of them will fall to the ground outside your Father's care. And even the very hairs of your head are all numbered. So don't be afraid; you are worth more than many sparrows.'" He closed the Bible and held it at his side. "A sparrow is small and common. Very few people stop to notice one. But God does. He sees every single one, and that's the thing about being chosen. It doesn't always look the way you'd expect. God didn't choose eagles for this verse. He chose sparrows. The ones most people overlook. The ones most people walk right past." He looked around the circle. "Some of you feel like sparrows. Small. Easy to miss. But God isn't missing you. He's paying attention to every detail of your life, down to the number of hairs on your head. That's what being chosen looks like. It's not loud. It's not flashy. It's someone caring enough to notice what everybody else walks past."

Rebecca's mind kept returning to the same place. He called the next morning. He sat on the edge of his bed and dialed her number. She hadn't known. For ten years, she'd told herself a story in which Conner accepted the breakup, pushed her aside, and moved forward into his new life without looking back. That story had shaped everything. Her previous engagement to Nathan. Her reluctance to let anyone close enough to disappoint her since then. The careful, cheerful armor she wore in front of the whole town.

She looked at him standing in the center of the circle, his Bible in his hand, his voice warm and measured and given entirely to the youths sitting around him. This man wasn't the boy who'd left. The boy who left had been at college and had been careless without realizing it, consumed by a future he thought he was building for both of them. The man standing here had spent six years in Richmond learning how to show up for people. Learning how to see those who were slipping through the cracks.

He was steadier now. More careful with his attention. He noticed things: the shift in a teenager's posture, the change in a kid's voice when the conversation got close to something real. She'd watched him do it week after week, and every time, the distance between who he'd been and who he'd become struck her again.

Conner wrapped up the lesson and asked the kids to spend a minute thinking about one person in their life who'd loved them in a way they didn't recognize at the time. He didn't ask them to share. He let the question sit.

The room was quiet for a long moment. Then he closed his Bible and smiled.

"All right," he said. "That's our lesson for tonight. The snack table is loaded, thanks to Miss Rebecca and her trail mix, which I'm told has M&M's in it."

"It does," Rebecca said from her chair.

"Then go eat before Tyler gets to the M&M's first."

"Too late," Tyler said, already standing.

The circle broke apart, and the room shifted into the loose, warm chaos of teenagers moving toward food and conversation.

Conner came to stand beside her near the front of the room. He had a cookie in one hand and coffee in the other. They stood there talking about the lesson and how the kids had responded.

As they were talking, Hannah walked up to them.

"I need to tell you both something," she said.

"Go ahead," Conner said.

"That question you asked about someone loving you in a way you didn't recognize." Hannah looked at Rebecca and then at Conner. "My dad. I thought being his daughter was supposed to look a certain way now that I'm a kid with divorced parents. Him being at my school stuff. Him coming to pick me up when he's supposed to. Him calling me just to check in on me. It doesn't look that way. He chose a different family, and for a long time I thought that meant I had done something wrong. That if I'd been a better daughter, he would've paid attention to me." Her voice was even, and her eyes were dry. "But I didn't do anything wrong. I'm still his daughter. He's the one who forgot that. He's the adult, and he needs to step it up. Him, not me. That's not love. My mom works two jobs and comes home late at night, but she takes the time to write me a note that tells me to 'have a good day,' or 'keep my chin up,' or 'smile, it's Friday.' She sets it on the kitchen table so it's the first thing I see when I eat breakfast in the morning. That's love showing up in a different way, and I see that now."

Hannah looked at both of them when she was done speaking. Then she stepped forward, put her arms around both of them, and held on for a few seconds. She let go, turned, and walked back to where Emma, Sophie, and Mary were waiting for her by the far wall. Emma handed her a cookie, and the four of them picked up their conversation as if nothing had happened.

Rebecca turned to Conner. "That took a lot of courage for Hannah to come and say that to us. That child amazes me. Let's go enjoy the rest of the evening and spend some time with these kids."

"Wait," he said. "Can we get together tomorrow evening? I want to finish what we started talking about tonight... before the kids arrived."

"Come to my apartment," she said. "Around six. I'll order pizza and have it delivered."

"I'll be there."

"Good."

She turned toward the room full of teenagers, toward the noise and the laughter and the easy warmth of a Wednesday night that mattered more than most of these kids would realize for years. And beneath all of it, quiet and enormous, the thing Conner had told her earlier pressed against the center of her chest. He had called the next morning. He had picked up his phone and dialed her number.

Chapter 23

Rebecca had changed out of her salon clothes and into leggings and an oversized sweatshirt that fell past her hips. She'd ordered the pizza at four-thirty from Tony's on the square, loaded with everything, because that was how they'd both eaten pizza in the past. Pepperoni, sausage, mushrooms, onions, green peppers, black olives, and extra cheese.

She had spent the whole day at the salon, telling herself she was fine. Her nine o'clock had been a simple cut and blow-dry. Her ten-thirty wanted a fresh color. Rebecca had mixed the formula and painted the foils with steady hands and talked about the woman's daughter's dance recital and listened and smiled and been exactly the Rebecca Hartwell that Serenity Crossing expected her to be. By lunchtime she'd had two more clients, and by three o'clock Jenna had looked at her across the salon and said, "You've been checking your phone every ten minutes since noon. You want to tell me why, or do I have to guess?"

The truth was that she'd been thinking about one phone call all day.

One phone call, ten years ago, that she had missed.

She had been playing the what-if game in her mind from the moment she woke up this morning.

What if she had a cell phone back then?

What if someone had been home or had taken the time to pick up the landline at her parents' home and talked to Conner and taken a message for her?

What if he'd left a voicemail, and she'd called him back and said, "I didn't mean it, Conner. Come home."

What if she had gotten in her hand-me-down car and driven to Lynchburg, Virginia, and visited him?

What if she had just taken the initiative and spoken up instead of testing the boy she loved and believed in?

Or more importantly, what if she had never broken up with him in the first place?

A knock came from her front door, and she crossed her living room, past the coffee table where the coupon book Conner had made her for Valentine's Day sat beside a candle and a short stack of books.

Conner stood on her landing with his Bible in hand.

She noticed it before she registered anything else about him. She'd seen it a hundred times at church, at youth group, and on his desk at the parsonage. But he wasn't here for ministry tonight. He wasn't here to plan a lesson or prepare a devotional. He was standing on her landing, coming into her home for a conversation about the two of them, and he'd brought his Bible.

"Hey," she said.

"Hey. I'm early." He smiled, and the smile carried an edge of nerves beneath its warmth.

"You're fine, come in."

She stepped back and held the door open. He walked past her into the apartment, and she caught the clean scent of his cologne. He set his Bible on the coffee table and shrugged off his jacket.

"Here, I'll take it," she said, and he handed it to her. She hung it on the hook beside her door, next to her own coat.

She heard footsteps on the staircase outside and opened the door again. A teenage boy in a Tony's Pizza jacket appeared on the landing holding a large pizza box, his breath trailing in the cold evening air.

"Delivery for Hartwell?" the boy said.

"That's me." She handed the boy cash and a tip from her sweatshirt pocket. "Thank you."

"Yes, ma'am. Enjoy."

The boy turned back down the stairs, and Rebecca nudged the door shut with her hip.

"I'm starving," she said, setting the box on the counter.

He lifted the lid and looked inside. "That's a serious pizza."

They filled their plates and carried them to her small, round dining table near the window. They sat across from each other, and Conner reached for her hand across the table and bowed his head.

"Lord, thank You for this food and this evening. Thank You for the honesty You've given us courage for and for conversations that bring us closer to truth and to each other. Guide us tonight. In Your name, amen."

"Amen," she said.

The pizza was good. The crust was thin and crisp at the edges, the cheese melted into the toppings, and every bite carried a different flavor because there was so much loaded onto it.

"How was the salon today?" he asked.

"Easy day, actually. My clients were low-maintenance, and I had a gap in the afternoon. I spent about an hour working on my spa plans."

"The Calloway Building?"

"Yes, I pulled up the floor plan again and started sketching a treatment room layout. Four private rooms for massage and facials, a relaxation lounge in the center, and a small retail area near the front." She picked a mushroom off her slice and ate it. "Sarah said she could have a crew in there by late summer if I'm ready to pull the trigger on financing."

"You're going to make that happen, Rebecca."

"I'm getting closer to believing that." She wiped her fingers on her napkin. "How was your day?"

"Long. Good, though." He took a drink of his sweet tea. "Warren and I spent most of the day going through plans for the adult Bible study program. We mapped out week plans, book by book. Genesis through Ruth. He's excited about it, and I think it's going to be the kind of thing people actually commit to showing up for week after week because there's real structure behind it."

"And the monthly church dinners?"

"The first one is tentatively set for the third Saturday in April. Warren wants to announce it from the pulpit this Sunday and start getting families to sign up. I told him your mama would bring enough food for twenty people, and he said, 'I'm counting on Olivia Hartwell's potato salad.'"

Rebecca smiled.

They finished eating, and Conner helped her clear the table. She wrapped the leftover pizza in foil and slid it into her refrigerator while he rinsed the plates in her sink.

Rebecca made two mugs of coffee, carried them to the living room, and sat on her sofa.

She pulled one leg beneath her and turned toward him. "I thought about that one phone call you made to me all day."

Conner turned his coffee mug in his hands but didn't drink. "I figured you might."

"I played the what-if game from the minute I woke up." She shook her head once. "I keep thinking about how close we came to a completely different ten years."

"I've thought about it too," he said.

"The what-ifs will eat you alive if you let them. I know that. I keep telling myself that looking backward doesn't change any-thing. But knowing that and feeling it are two different things."

He set his mug on the table. "They are."

She let the quiet sit for a moment, then looked at him. "I want to tell you about something else that was on my mind a lot today. My ex-fiancé, Nathan Whitaker. He was from Pigeon Forge and worked in finance. I met him when I was twenty-three, and we dated for a year. He proposed right here in this living room on a Saturday evening, and I said yes."

Conner was quiet. His hands rested on his knees.

"I said yes because he was kind and steady, and he wanted the things I told myself I wanted. A family. A home." She paused. "I had made some wedding plans. I had an idea of the wedding dress I wanted. I told my family I was happy, and I believed it, because I'd made believing it a decision."

"What happened?" he asked.

"He got a job offer in Florida. He came over one evening and told me about it like it was the best news in the world. A bigger city, bigger opportunities, a considerable salary, a fresh start. He assumed I'd go with him." She looked towards the window. "I listened to him describe the life we could have in Florida, and somewhere in the middle of it, I knew I didn't want that. I didn't want to leave the salon I built, or my family, or my friends."

"I told him I'd think about it. I didn't sleep for a week. And when I finally told him I couldn't go, I expected him to stay. I expected him to say, 'Then I'll turn down the job.' That's what the men in my family would've said. That's what my daddy would've said to my mama without thinking twice. I needed to be the thing that mattered more than a job to Nathan. He told me he was sorry and that he had to take it and hoped I understood." She smoothed her sweatshirt fabric across her knee. "I took off the ring and gave it to him and told him I hoped he'd be happy. He looked at me with a stunned look on his face, then he got up and left without saying another word. Then I sat on this floor and cried for a few minutes." She looked at Conner. "But not as long as I should have. And that's the part I've never really sat and thought about."

"What do you mean?"

"I mean that the next morning, I opened the salon, and by lunchtime I felt something I wasn't prepared for." She held his gaze. "Relief. Not happiness. Not joy. Just a quiet, surprising lift, like I'd been carrying something heavy, and I'd finally set it down and I could breathe again." She pressed her palm flat against the sofa cushion. "Relief isn't what you're supposed to feel when your engagement falls apart, Conner. You're supposed to be devastated. I felt lighter. And the lightness shamed me because it told me that I had been settling. That Nathan was a good man, and I cared about him, and none of it was enough because he wasn't you." The words came out plain and unvarnished, and she didn't look away from him. "I wanted a replacement for what I'd lost, and no man was ever going to fill that space. I compared every man I dated to you, and if I'm being honest, to my father too. The way Daddy loves Mama. The way you loved me when we were teenagers. That was the measuring stick, and Nathan never reached it. Nobody ever did."

Conner sat with his hands clasped between his knees and didn't move.

"I've never told anyone that," she said. "Not Jenna. Not my mama. Nobody knows that I felt relief when my engagement ended. I've carried it for four years like a secret I was ashamed of, because what kind of woman says yes to a good man and then feels lighter when he leaves and simply carries on with life?"

Conner was quiet for a long moment. Then he leaned forward, his forearms on his knees.

"The kind of woman who was honest enough to put an end to it because in her heart she knew it wasn't right," he said.

She looked at him.

"I know because I've carried something similar," he said.

Rebecca stared at him. "What?"

"I was engaged once, as well. That's a part of my life that I very seldom talk about. Her name was Lauren," he said. "She owned a clothing boutique a few blocks from my church in Richmond. We dated for about a year, and I proposed in October when I was twenty-six."

He rubbed his thumb across his knuckles. "Lauren came from a broken family, Rebecca. Her father left when she was nine. Her mother was a raging alcoholic and went through three more marriages after that, and none of them were good situations. Lauren grew up in that, and she'd built her adult life on sheer willpower. The boutique, her home, and a handful of friendships she held onto with everything she had. Her faith was new and fragile. She started coming to my church because she wanted to belong somewhere."

"And you saw that in her," Rebecca said.

"The first time I met her. I'm a pastor. I'm trained to see it." He looked at his hands. "And that's where I got it wrong. I cared about her. I liked her. She was funny and she made me laugh. But my caring for her wasn't romantic. It was pastoral. I saw a woman with a wounded history and a fragile faith, and a part of me believed that loving her might help her heal. That if I were steady enough, she'd grow into someone stronger." He shook his head. "You don't ask someone to be your wife to save them, but at the time, I told myself what I felt was enough."

"What happened?"

"By Christmas, she was pulling away. She got quieter. She made excuses to skip church. She flinched every time someone asked about the wedding or what life would look like as a pastor's wife." He paused. "I could see it coming. I knew she was going to end it. And here's the part I'm ashamed of. I kept it going anyway because I wanted to bring her closer to God and fix all the pain she held onto from her youth. I was attempting to build a life with the wrong woman and for the wrong reasons. Lauren ended it in February. She told me she couldn't be a pastor's wife and her faith wasn't where mine was, and she didn't think it ever would be. She told me she was sorry." He was quiet for a moment. "I held her hand and told her I understood. And I did."

"What did you feel?"

"Sadness. I was deeply saddened for her because she was a good person who deserved more than what life had given her." He met Rebecca's eyes. "And then, underneath the sadness, slowly, the same word you just used. Relief. A quiet knowing that I'd been standing in the wrong place for a long time and I was finally free to stop pretending." He leaned back against her sofa. "I didn't love her the way a man should love a woman that he wants to spend the rest of his life with. In a full year of dating Lauren, I'd never once felt for her what I had felt for you."

Rebecca pressed her hand to her mouth. She held it there for a few seconds, then lowered it to her lap.

She looked at his Bible on the coffee table. The worn leather. The faded page edges. The book that had traveled with him from Liberty to Richmond to Serenity Crossing.

Conner followed her gaze. He leaned forward, reached for the Bible, and held it in both hands for a moment. Then he opened the front cover.

Pieces of paper lay against the inside of the cover, folded along creases that had gone soft from years of handling. The paper was notebook-ruled. The folds were worn to a cottony softness, the kind that comes from being opened and closed again and again. He opened them both and set them on the coffee table.

"You wrote me two letters," he said.

Rebecca looked at the folded papers, and for a moment her mind went still.

She recognized her handwriting before she fully understood what she was looking at. The blue ink. The slightly rounded letters. The way her g's curved below the line and her t's crossed a little too high.

"This one," he said, touching the paper on the left, "is the letter you wrote me the night before I left for college. You told me to read it after I crossed the Virginia state line." He touched the paper on the right. "This one is the letter you wrote after you broke up with me. I received it about a week after your phone call."

"You kept them all this time."

"They've stayed in the front of my Bible, and they've traveled from Liberty to Richmond and back home here to Serenity Crossing."

Rebecca stared at the two pieces of notebook paper on her coffee table, and then she reached for the letter on the right. The breakup letter. The blue ink had faded, but the handwriting was sharp, each letter formed with the careful control of someone holding herself in one piece.

Dear Conner,

I want you to know that the time we had was the best time of my life. Senior year with you was everything I thought love was supposed to be. You made me feel important. You made me believe that I was the kind of girl a boy would build his whole world around, and I will carry that with me for the rest of my life.

I'm not angry with you. I need you to know that. You are doing exactly what God called you to do, and I would never want to be the reason you stopped. You were meant for this, Conner. Ministry, school, all of it. You were meant for greater things than what Serenity Crossing could hold, and watching you step into that calling has been one of the greatest privileges of my life.

But I can't keep being the girl who waits by the phone anymore. I can't keep making myself smaller so I fit into the spaces you have left. That's not fair to you, and it's not fair to me.

Please don't call. I know that sounds harsh, and I'm sorry. I just need space to figure out who I am without you in the middle of every thought I have. Please respect that.

I'll always root for you. I'll always pray for you. I'll always believe that God has incredible plans for your life. Go after them. Follow your calling. Be the man I already know you're going to become.

Love, Becca

Rebecca read the last line twice. Love, Becca. She'd signed a breakup letter with love. Asking for space and signing off with love. Letting go and holding on, compressed into a single signature.

She set the letter back on the table, and then she reached for the other letter. The good letter. The one she'd written the night before Conner left for Liberty College.

The handwriting was different from that of the breakup letter. Looser. Wider. The letters leaned forward as if the hand writing them couldn't move fast enough.

Conner,

You're not allowed to read this until you've crossed the state line. I mean it. If you're reading this in your driveway or on Route 25, you better fold this right back up and wait. I'll know if you cheated, and you know I will.

Okay. Here's what I need to say to you.

I am so proud of you. I don't have words big enough for how proud I am. You have known for some time now that God was calling you to something, and instead of running from it or pretending you didn't hear it, you said yes. You said yes when your friends were picking colleges based on football programs and party weekends. You picked Liberty not because you were given a full-ride scholarship but because you believed it was where God wanted you, even though it meant you'd be farther away from home. That takes a kind of courage that most people never find in their whole lives, and you found it as a young man.

I want you to remember something when the classes are hard, the homesickness hits, and the dorm room feels too small. I want you to remember that night on my parents' porch last June when the lightning bugs came out, and we sat on the top step and you told me about the sermon you wanted to preach someday. You said you wanted to stand in front of a room full of people and tell them that God doesn't love them because they earned it. He loves them because He can't help it. You said it just like that, with your elbows on your knees and a glass of Mama's sweet tea in your hand, and I sat there listening to you, and I knew. I knew right then that you were going to change people's lives. I knew it as surely as I've ever known anything.

And I want you to remember the night of the homecoming game, our senior year. Fourth quarter, you threw that pass to Jake Ridley in the end zone, and the whole stadium went crazy, and after the game you found me on the sideline and picked me up and spun me around, and you smelled like grass and sweat, and you were grinning so big I thought your face would split open. And then I grabbed your face with both hands and said, "That's my boy." And you said, "Always." Do you remember that? Because I will never forget it. That was the night I knew you were the person I wanted beside me for the rest of my life. Not because of the touchdown. Because of the way you looked at me afterwards. Like I was the only person in that whole stadium who mattered.

Here's what I want, Conner. I want you to go to Liberty and become everything God made you to be. And when you're done, I want you to come home to me. I want us to have a porch like my parents' porch, with steps wide enough for two people and sweet tea in the evening. I want Sunday dinners where our kids run through the yard while we sit with our families and laugh until our sides hurt. I want a dog. A big one that sleeps at the foot of our bed and goes everywhere with us. I want to sit in the front pew of our church here in Serenity Crossing and watch you do the thing you were born to do. I want to know that when you look out at the congregation, your eyes find me first. Every single time.

I want to build a life with you. Ordinary days full of all the small things that add up to something beautiful. I want morning coffee and grocery trips and arguments about what to watch on TV, and long drives in the mountains on Saturday afternoons. I want all of it. Every bit of it. With you.

You are my person, Conner Delaney. I have known that for a long time now, and I will know it when I'm a hundred. Nothing about college or distance, or time is going to change that. You are the one. You are my person. You've always been the one.

Go be amazing. I'll be here when you get back.

Love, Becca

Rebecca held the letter in both hands. Her vision blurred; she blinked, and the words sharpened again. The handwriting of an eighteen-year-old girl who'd never been hurt. The confident, wide-open certainty of a girl who had no reason to believe that love could fail her.

She read the last lines again. You are the one. You are my person. You've always been the one.

She'd been ashamed of this girl for a decade.

She'd spent ten years calling this girl naïve. A girl who wanted too much, who believed too hard, who wrote a love letter on notebook paper the night before her boyfriend left for college and actually believed every word of it. She'd built an entire adult life to prove she was smarter and more careful than that girl. She'd turned herself into the woman who gave everything and asked for nothing, the woman who filled silences before they could become vulnerable, the woman who would rather lose love than admit she wanted it. All of it built to protect herself from being the girl who wrote that first letter and got her heart broken.

And he'd kept it. He'd carried it for ten years. She remembered him telling her that he had read the letter that she had sent him off to college with while sitting in a gas station outside Roanoke, where he'd pulled over to fill up with gas. He'd grabbed a gas station sandwich and read the letter in the parking lot, and then he had put his forehead on the steering wheel and prayed that he had made the right decision.

He'd carried both of these letters through four years of college. Through ministry in Richmond. Through a broken engagement and then back home to Serenity Crossing. These letters had lived in the front of his Bible for an entire decade.

"Why did you keep them?" she asked.

Conner looked at the two letters on the coffee table. "Because they're the most honest things anyone has ever written to me."

She pressed her lips together and nodded once.

"How often do you read them?"

"I used to read them more often; now, not so much." He looked at the letters. "But I know they're there."

"Why keep them?" she asked again. "You could've thrown them away. Why hold on to them for ten years?"

He was quiet, and she watched as he rubbed his thumb along the seam of his jeans, reaching for something honest, something past the surface answers.

"Because they were a reminder of the cost of my calling. That I needed to remember what following God's path had cost me so I'd never take it for granted. Those letters were a reminder to stay humble. That I was the boy who lost the girl he loved because he wasn't paying attention, and I needed to keep that lesson close. I simply couldn't bring myself to throw them away."

Something opened inside Rebecca's chest, slow and warm, like ice thinning over a creek in early spring. The kind of breaking that doesn't destroy. It reveals what's been moving underneath all along.

She looked at the good letter on the table. The wide, eager handwriting. The girl who wrote about a porch and Sunday dinners and a dog and a life built side by side. The girl who said, You are my person, and meant it with every cell in her body.

She'd been hiding from that girl for ten years. She'd buried herself under competence and cheerfulness and the particular armor of a woman who gives to everyone and asks for nothing. She'd called that girl foolish. She called her young and needy. She'd told herself that the girl who wrote a love letter on notebook paper with that much certainty was someone to outgrow, someone to be embarrassed by.

But that girl wasn't naïve. She was brave. She loved without reservation. She knew what she wanted, and she knew her own worth, and she knew that the boy sitting on her parents' porch step talking about the sermon he'd preach someday was the man she wanted beside her for the rest of her life.

And the man sitting on her sofa had recognized what those words were worth. He'd carried the proof of her bravery in the front of his Bible for ten years.

"I've been ashamed of the girl who wrote those letters, especially the first one," Rebecca said. Her voice was steady now. "I spent years calling her naïve... needy... even selfish. I told myself she wanted too much and believed too hard and didn't know how to let go. I built my whole adult life trying to prove I was stronger and wiser than the girl who poured her heart onto notebook paper and signed it with love."

Conner reached for her hand. His fingers closed around hers, warm and deliberate, and he held on.

"That girl wasn't naïve, Rebecca. She was the bravest person I've ever known. She loved me with everything she had, and she put it in writing, and she wasn't afraid of any of it. She knew exactly who she was and exactly what she wanted, and she said it plainly."

The tears slid down her cheeks, and she didn't wipe them away.

The girl who wrote the good letter wasn't a weakling. She was the part of Rebecca that had always known what love was supposed to look like. The part that believed in porches and Sunday dinners and a man whose eyes found hers first across a crowded room.

Rebecca's gaze drifted to the Bible, still open on the table where Conner had left it after pulling out the letters. A folded piece of paper sat there, and she could read the words from here.

Lesson #7: Letting People See the Real You

"In a way... we're doing our homework tonight," she said as she pointed at the paper.

Conner looked at the lesson outline in his Bible, then back at her. A slow recognition moved across his face.

"We are," he said.

He lifted their clasped hands from the cushion and pressed his lips to the back of her hand. The gesture was quiet and deliberate, warm against her skin, and he held there for a moment before lowering their hands and keeping them joined.

Chapter 24

Conner had his Bible open to Colossians 3 and his legal pad angled beside it. The passage he was considering for tonight's youth group was strong. Set your minds on things above, not on earthly things. A good anchor verse for this lesson. Concrete enough for teenagers to hold on to and broad enough to carry everything he wanted to say tonight.

Lesson 8. You Are Not Invisible. The last session of the Chosen series, and the one he'd been building toward since week one. Eight Wednesdays of sitting in a circle of metal chairs with a group of kids who'd come in not knowing him, and slowly, week by week, he'd earned their trust.

He'd written this curriculum in Richmond for a youth group three times this size, and it had landed well enough in that room. But here, in Serenity Crossing, the material had done more than he'd planned for. Every session had pressed on the same nerve in the teenagers and then turned around and pressed on the same nerve in him and Rebecca. Identity and worth. What it means to be chosen when the choosing doesn't look the way you expected. They'd spent eight weeks teaching it to the kids and learning it themselves, and neither of them had planned on that.

Tonight was the capstone. He'd spent the morning reviewing his notes and tightening the discussion questions, and he was satisfied with where it sat.

His phone buzzed on the desk beside his Bible. He glanced at his screen expecting Rebecca's name, but the caller ID read Bill Stevenson.

Conner picked up. "Bill. How are you?"

"Conner Delaney." The voice on the other end carried the easy energy of a man who genuinely enjoyed people. "I was starting to think you'd forgotten me."

"I've just been terrible about calling people back, and I apologize for that."

"You've been busy. I heard through the grapevine you finally made the move."

"I did. I've been in Serenity Crossing since mid-January." Conner leaned back in his chair and set his pen on the legal pad. He and Bill had been in the same ministry cohort at Liberty, and the friendship had held through the years. The last time they'd spoken, Conner had still been packing boxes in Richmond. "How are you? How's Claire?"

"Claire's great. She's been substitute teaching at the elementary school near the church, and she loves it. The kids adore her." Bill paused. "Actually, Claire is part of the reason I'm calling."

"Everything okay?"

"More than okay. We've been praying about something for about two years now, and we finally said yes. We're committing to a year of missionary work in Central America. There's a ministry network in Guatemala that's been building schools and training local church leaders. They've been asking us to come for a while. We leave in June."

Conner sat forward. "Bill, that's incredible. A whole year?"

"A whole year. Claire and I talked it through from every angle. We prayed about it until we couldn't ignore the answer anymore, and the answer was go."

"I'm proud of you both. That takes real courage."

"It takes a wife who's braver than I am, is what it takes." Bill laughed. "Claire was the one who said yes first. I was still doing research and taking notes."

Conner smiled. "So what happens with Grace Community while you're gone?"

"That's the other reason I'm calling." Bill was quiet for a second. "My church needs a lead pastor, Conner. Not an interim. Someone permanent. The elder board and I have been talking about it for the past month, and your name came up early and keeps coming up."

His hand stilled on the arm of his chair.

"Grace Community is a good church," Bill continued. "Three hundred and twenty members, solid elder board, strong family ministry. The staff is small but committed. We've got a worship director who's been with us for five years and an administrative assistant who runs the building tighter than anyone I've ever worked with. The congregation is established and generous, and they're ready for someone with fresh energy and a pastor's heart."

Conner looked at his legal pad on the desk. His notes for tonight's lesson, the underlined verse, and the closing statement he'd been refining all morning.

"Bill, I'm honored. I mean that."

"I know you do."

"Tell me more about the congregation. What are they looking for in a lead pastor?"

"Someone relational. Someone who preaches from experience and not just from a commentary. Someone who can connect with young families and still earn the trust of the older members who've been in those pews for years. I told the elders that the best pastor I know for that job is a guy who grew up in a small town in Tennessee and spent six years in Richmond building one of the strongest youth programs I've seen."

"Who else are you considering?"

"Two other names have come up. Both solid." Bill paused. "But you're the one I want to replace me."

Conner leaned back in his chair again and looked up at the ceiling of his office.

"Bill, I appreciate this more than I can tell you. The fact that you'd think of me for something like this means a lot. But I'm where I'm supposed to be. I came back to Serenity Crossing because everything in my life pointed here. My family's here. This is my home church. I'm building a youth ministry that's just hitting its stride, and my senior pastor is mentoring me toward a future in this congregation. My heart is in this town."

"I hear you," Bill said. "And I respect that. But I'm going to ask you to do one thing for me."

"What's that?"

"Don't give me a final answer today. Sit with it for a couple of days. Pray about it, and if the answer is still no on Friday, then it's no, and I'll move forward with one of the other candidates. I just don't want you to close a door before you've given yourself time to look through it."

Conner was quiet for a moment. "I'll sit with it, but I don't expect my answer to change."

"I understand; call me Friday."

"I will."

They talked for a few more minutes. Bill told him about the mission organization in Guatemala and the school they'd be helping build outside Antigua. Claire was already learning Spanish from an app on her phone and practicing on the barista at their local coffee shop. Bill said the barista was endlessly patient and possibly entertained. Conner laughed and told Bill about the youth group and the Chosen series wrapping up tonight. Bill said he'd pray for the session, and they hung up.

Conner set his phone on the desk.

Lead pastor at Grace Community Church in Charlotte. Three hundred and twenty members. A solid staff and an established congregation ready for new leadership. The kind of position most pastors worked years toward. The kind of opportunity that validated everything he'd been building since his first clumsy sermon in a Richmond church.

He thought about Bill and Claire packing their lives into suitcases and flying to Guatemala for a year. Two people in their late twenties, stepping away from everything familiar because they believed God was asking them to go. He admired that. The faith it required to leave a congregation you loved and a home you'd filled with years of small daily living. That kind of obedience was its own form of courage, and he respected it deeply.

But his own obedience had taken a different form. God had brought him home. And the life he was building in Serenity Crossing wasn't the safe option dressed up as a calling. It was the calling itself. Warren's mentorship and the succession plan they'd discussed. The youth group he'd spent weeks pouring into. His parents and his brothers and their families living a few miles down the road, close enough to be part of each other's ordinary days instead of voices on a phone.

And Rebecca.

Rebecca, whose name had been in his thoughts more and more since he'd returned home. Rebecca, who'd sat on her sofa two weeks ago and read her own eighteen-year-old handwriting and stopped being ashamed of the girl who'd written it. The distance between them had narrowed. What remained was open ground, and he was standing in the middle of it with his hands unclenched and his heart unhidden.

Charlotte had a church that needed a pastor. Serenity Crossing had the life he was building and the woman he wanted to build it with.

He pulled his legal pad closer and wrote a note in the margin beneath tonight's lesson plan. Think about pastors to recommend to Bill. Paul Kessler from the Richmond network? Matt Preston from the Roanoke church plant? He'd spend some time on it before Friday and give Bill a name or two worth considering.

A knock on his open door made him lift his head. Warren stood in the doorway with his reading glasses pushed up on his forehead and a manila folder tucked under one arm. He looked at Conner for a second, then walked in and sat down in the chair across from his desk.

"You've got a look on your face," Warren said.

"Do I?"

"The kind that says something is going on in that mind of yours, and you're trying to decide where to put it. What's going on?"

"I just got off the phone with a friend from college. Bill Stevenson. He's the lead pastor at a church in Charlotte."

Warren nodded and waited.

"He and his wife are committing to a year of missionary work in Guatemala. They leave in June." Conner leaned forward. "His church needs a lead pastor, and he wants to recommend me for the position."

Warren's expression stayed level, giving Conner nothing to read in either direction. "What did you tell him?"

"I told him I'm honored and that my heart is here. He asked me to sit with it for a couple of days before I give him a final answer. I agreed."

"That's fair." Warren adjusted his glasses on his forehead. "What draws you to the offer?"

"Honestly? Charlotte doesn't pull me. But the fact that Bill thinks I'm ready for a lead role. That part landed."

"It should land. You are ready."

"I appreciate you saying that."

"I'm not saying it to flatter you," Warren leaned back. "You're ready, Conner. The question isn't whether you're ready. The question is, where."

Conner met Warren's eyes across the desk.

"So let me ask you this," Warren said. "What would you be walking toward in Charlotte?"

"A bigger platform. The chance to lead a church from the front and build an established church into something more."

"And what would you be walking away from here?"

The answer came without hesitation. "You. This church. The youth ministry. My family and Rebecca."

Warren nodded. "Is your certainty about staying rooted in what you're building here or in what you're afraid to leave?"

"What I'm building," he said. "If God told me to go to Charlotte, I'd go. But He brought me back to Serenity Crossing for a reason. Everything that's happened since January confirms it. The ministry, the people, this church. I'm planted here."

Warren was quiet for a moment. Then a small, satisfied expression settled across his face. "The pastors who last in ministry aren't the ones chasing the bigger pulpit. They're the ones who recognize when they're already standing where God put them." He tapped the folder on his knee. "You can spend your whole career looking for the next door, or you can build something worth staying for in the room you're already in. You're building something worth staying for."

"I believe that with everything in me, Warren. Thank you for saying that."

"Don't thank me. Thank the Lord for giving you the sense to see it." Warren stood and tucked the folder back under his arm. "Now. Before I forget. Sunday morning. Your first sermon on our rotation. What are you thinking?"

Conner leaned back in his chair. "I'm going to build off the Chosen series I'm wrapping up with the youth group this evening," he said. "Not reteach it, just carry the core idea into Sunday. We've spent weeks talking about identity, how easy it is to let other people or circumstances decide your worth. And I kept thinking that doesn't stop when you grow up."

Warren folded his arms and listened.

"So I want to speak to that. What it actually means to be chosen, and how most of us don't live like we believe it. How we keep trying to prove something God already settled." Conner glanced up. "Just something simple. Something that meets people where they are and shifts how they see themselves a little when they walk out."

"I like that," Warren said. "Keep it personal. Your best preaching comes from the same place your best teaching comes from. Experience, not abstraction."

"That's the plan."

Warren moved toward the door, then turned. "Mary's got a pot roast waiting for me at home, and if I'm late again, she's going to give my portion to the dog." He pointed at Conner. "Have a good evening. Go finish strong with those kids tonight."

"Yes, sir."

Warren's footsteps moved down the hallway at their unhurried pace, and the front door of the church opened and closed behind him. The building settled back into its late-afternoon quiet.

Conner picked up his pen and made a final note on his legal pad, a reminder to print the reflection handout for tonight's session.

His phone buzzed with a text. Rebecca's name on his screen: *Hey — I'm so sorry, but I can't come early tonight. My friend Carla called and asked if I could squeeze her in for a quick color touch-up, trim, and manicure. She's leaving early tomorrow morning for Nashville—she has a job interview and wants to look her best. She's a dear friend, and I couldn't say no. I'll be there by 7. I'm sorry!*

He typed back: *No worries at all. I'll run to the grocery store and grab all the snacks and drinks for tonight so you don't have to worry about it.*

Her response came quickly: *Thanks! You're the best. See you this evening.*

He set his phone on the desk and looked at his lesson notes. His passage from Colossians and the closing statement he'd written and rewritten three times until it said what he wanted it to say.

The Charlotte offer crossed his mind one more time. Not the job itself, but whether to tell Rebecca about it.

He'd tell her because his answer was already made, and she deserved to hear it from him. He'd tell her because a man who'd spent years learning what silence costs doesn't choose silence again. The life he was building in this town had her in every corner of it, and the Charlotte offer was nothing more than confirmation of what he already knew. His place was here. His calling was here. And the woman he wanted beside him was here.

Chapter 25

Rebecca watched from her place on the far side of the youth group circle. She'd arrived after seven, slipping through the side door when Conner was already ten minutes into the lesson. He'd glanced up when the door opened, met her eyes across the room, and given her a small nod before returning to what he was saying.

The snack table along the west wall was fully stocked. Chips, cookies, water bottles, a tray of vegetables with ranch dip, and a bowl of trail mix. Conner had handled all of it tonight because she'd been at the salon until six forty-five finishing Carla's color and manicure. He'd texted her a photo of the snack table around six forty-five with the message: *Snack game is strong. No judgment on the vegetable arrangement. I did my best.*

She'd laughed at the photo. The vegetables were arranged in uneven rows, carrots, and celery sticks pointing in different directions, the ranch cup slightly off-center. The kind of effort that looked like a man who cared enough to try and was honest enough not to pretend he was good at it.

Conner turned a page on his legal pad and looked around the circle. "So here's the thing about invisibility," he said. "We've spent seven weeks talking about identity. Who gets to decide what you are worth? What happens when you carry labels other people gave you? What it means to be chosen when the choosing doesn't look the way you expected." He paused. "Tonight I want to talk about the part nobody brings up. The part where you make yourself invisible."

Tyler shifted in his chair. Emma's hands tightened slightly in her lap.

"I'm not talking about being ignored by other people," Conner said. "That's real, and we've covered it. I'm talking about the thing that happens inside you when you decide that small is safe. When you stop raising your hand because it's easier to sit in the back. When you stop telling people what you actually think because you've convinced yourself your opinion doesn't matter." He looked around the circle. "When you shrink on purpose because somewhere along the way, you started believing that shrinking is all you deserve."

Conner looked at his Bible. "Colossians 3, verses 1 through 3. I want to read this, and then I want you to sit with it for a second before we talk." He read from the page. *"Since, then, you have been raised with Christ, set your hearts on things above, where Christ is, seated at the right hand of God. Set your minds on things above, not on earthly things. For you died, and your life is now hidden with Christ in God.'"*

He closed his Bible and held it at his side. "Hidden with Christ in God. I want you to hear that word. Hidden. There's a difference between hidden and invisible. Invisible means nobody sees you. Hidden means you're held somewhere safe by Someone who sees everything." He let the words sit in the room for a few seconds. "You aren't invisible. You've never been invisible. The God who made you has known you from the moment you were conceived. There hasn't been a single second of your life when He lost track of you." He looked around the circle. "What I'm asking you tonight is this: are you going to keep making yourself small? Or are you going to stand in the space God already gave you and let people see who you actually are?"

Rebecca looked at the teenagers around the circle. These weren't the same kids who'd walked in here eight weeks ago. Tyler wasn't slumped in his chair with his phone hidden under his leg. Caleb wasn't staring at the floor with his jaw set. Emma wasn't sitting with her shoulders curved inward, making herself as compact as possible. Hannah wasn't in the back with her jacket zipped to her chin and her eyes on her shoes.

They were leaning forward. They were listening. They trusted this man, and they trusted this room. Both of those things had been built one Wednesday at a time over two months. Rebecca had watched it happen from the inside. She'd helped build it. She'd brought the snacks and set up the chairs, and stood in the back while Conner taught. She'd sat beside him afterward while they cleaned up and talked about what the lesson had opened. She'd watched him earn the trust of these teenagers with the most uncomplicated tool in the world: he showed up, he was honest, and he treated every one of them like they mattered.

She was proud of what they'd built in this room. It was specific and earned, and sitting here watching it reach its final session before beginning a new topic next week, she felt the pride settle in her chest with the quiet certainty of a woman who'd been part of something good.

Conner shifted into the closing discussion. He set his legal pad on his chair and looked around the circle with his Bible tucked under his arm.

"Two questions," he said. "And I want you to actually think about these before you answer. Don't give me the Sunday school version. Give me the real one." He held up one finger. "First. What's one thing you could do this week to let someone in your life know they matter to you? That you see them." He held up a second finger. "And second. What's one thing you could do to stop making yourself invisible? To let someone actually see the real you, even if it's uncomfortable."

He gave them a moment. The room was still, and Rebecca could hear the building's heating system pushing warm air through the vents near the ceiling.

Simon spoke first. "I'm gonna eat dinner with my grandparents," he said. "Like, actually sit down at the table with them instead of taking my plate to my room and watching videos on my phone. They cook every night, and most of the time I just grab my food and disappear. That sounds kind of terrible when I say it out loud."

"It's honest," Conner said. "That's what I asked for."

"My grandma makes really good meatloaf," Simon said. "I should probably tell her that, too."

A few kids laughed, and Simon grinned.

Caleb was next. He sat forward and rubbed his palms on his jeans. "I'm gonna stop pretending I don't care about my grades," he said. "I do care. I just don't act like it because the guys I hang out with treat school like its something to survive. But I check my grades every night on my phone, and when I get a good score, I don't tell anybody because I don't want to be the kid who tries." He shrugged with one shoulder. "That's dumb. I'm done doing that."

"Good," Conner said.

Emma raised her hand halfway, then lowered it and just spoke. "There's a girl in my grade who eats lunch alone in the library every day. Her name is Waverly. She moved here from Knoxville a few weeks ago, and I don't think she's really made friends yet." Emma glanced at Sophie. "I'm going to ask her to sit with us tomorrow."

The room loosened, and a few more kids offered answers. Tucker said he was going to call his older brother, who was stationed at Fort Campbell and hadn't heard from Tucker in a month. Megan said she was going to tell her mom she appreciated everything she did because she'd never said it out loud.

Then Hannah spoke.

"I'm going to talk to my mom," Hannah said. "My mom works two jobs almost every day. She waitresses in the evenings out near Pigeon Forge, and she doesn't get home until after midnight most nights." She paused. "I miss her. I miss sitting with her and talking about school and watching TV on the couch and just being with my mom. I know she's working hard for us. I know she's tired. But I'm lonely, and she doesn't know that because I've never told her. I want her to know that I need more time with her. I want her to know I'm not okay with being alone all the time." She looked around the circle. "I hope she listens."

Rebecca looked at the girl sitting across the circle from her and saw two people layered over one another. The sixteen-year-old who'd walked into this room on the first night of the Chosen series with her jacket zippered to her collar and her gaze fixed on the floor. And the young woman sitting here now, who'd just told a room full of her peers what she needed.

Eight weeks ago, Hannah wouldn't have said any of this. She wouldn't have trusted her peers, and she wouldn't have trusted herself. What had changed wasn't one single thing. It was the accumulation of small, specific moments that had added up to something larger. The curriculum had given her the language to name what she was carrying. The friendships with Emma, Sophie, and Mary had shown her that speaking up didn't always end in rejection. And Conner's consistent presence, week after week, had given her a model of an adult who actually paid attention.

Rebecca caught Hannah's eye across the room and smiled. Hannah held her gaze for a second and then looked away.

"That's our last session of the Chosen series," he said. "Eight weeks. You all showed up. You were honest. You trusted each other, and that's not a small thing." He looked around the circle. "If any of you ever need to talk about anything, I'm here. Pastor Warren is here. Day or night. You know where to find us. Next week we'll start a new series, and I'm certain you'll enjoy it; we're going to be focusing on faith." He gave them a nod. "Go eat."

The circle broke. Kids stood and moved toward the snack table, and the focused quiet dissolved into the loose, warm noise of teenagers who were comfortable with each other and ready for food.

Rebecca stood from her chair and watched the room. The kids weren't forming isolated clusters the way they had in January. They moved between groups, talked across the space, and called to each other by name. Tyler wandered over to where Megan and Simon were standing and said something that made Megan throw a piece of popcorn at him. Caleb walked past Hannah's group and stopped to say something to Emma, who laughed and shoved his shoulder gently. The community that she and Conner had built over two months was visible in how these teenagers occupied the room. They belonged to each other now, and they knew it.

Conner appeared beside her with a cookie and a water bottle. "You hungry?" he asked.

"Starving. I haven't eaten since lunch." She picked up a plate from the stack on the snack table and loaded it with vegetables, ranch, and a handful of trail mix. She ate a carrot stick and looked at him. "That was a good lesson, Conner. These kids trusted you with real answers tonight, once again."

"It comes from both of us, Rebecca. You built the ground they're standing on."

She ate another carrot stick and didn't argue the point, though a warm flush climbed into her cheeks.

She walked over to where Hannah stood with Emma, Sophie, and Mary. The four girls had their heads close together , and Hannah was showing something on her phone to Sophie.

"Hannah," Rebecca said.

Hannah looked up. "Hey, Miss Rebecca."

"How's the poetry project going? Did you finish your free verse poems?"

Hannah's face brightened. "I did. I turned them in last week. I got an A."

"An A? That's wonderful."

"Ms. Cooper wrote a note on the last one. She said it showed real emotional depth, and she'd like me to consider submitting it to the school's literary newspaper."

"Are you going to?"

Hannah tucked a strand of hair behind her ear. "Maybe."

"I'd love to read them sometime," Rebecca said. "If you ever feel like sharing."

Hannah looked at her for a moment with the careful assessment of a girl still learning which offers from adults were genuine. Then her expression relaxed. "Maybe," she said. "I'll think about it."

"No rush. Whenever you're ready."

She left the girls to their conversation and moved back toward the snack table. Kids eventually started leaving in small groups. Parents' headlights swept through the windows as cars pulled into the lot. Tyler and Josh were the first out the door, Tyler calling something over his shoulder to Conner about next week. Caleb shook Conner's hand near the door, their Wednesday night routine, and Tucker followed him into the parking lot. Megan, Simon, Derek, and Allan left in a cluster, still talking. Emma hugged Rebecca on her way out, a quick, tight squeeze that carried more warmth than most sixteen-year-olds gave away. Sophie and Mary followed, and then Hannah pulled on her jacket, zipped it halfway, and stopped at the door.

"Goodnight, Miss Rebecca," Hannah said. "Goodnight, Pastor Conner."

"Goodnight, Hannah," Conner said. "Text me after you talk to your mom. I want to know how it goes."

"I will." She pushed through the door and walked into the March evening, and the last set of headlights turned out of the parking lot and disappeared down the road.

Conner picked up a trash bag from the roll near the kitchen and started collecting cups and napkins from the snack table. Rebecca grabbed a second bag and worked the other end. They moved through the cleanup without speaking for a few minutes.

She was carrying two folded chairs toward the metal rack along the far wall when she stopped. She set the chairs down and turned to face him.

"Conner."

He looked up from the chair he was folding. "Yeah?"

"I missed not being here earlier tonight. Our pre-session conversations. Going through the lesson material, picking the verses, and talking about what the topics stirred up in us. That time with you has become one of the best parts of my week, and I look forward to it."

He set his chair down and gave her his full attention.

She crossed the distance between them and reached for his hand, wrapping her fingers around his, and held on. His fingers closed around hers without hesitation.

She looked at their joined hands and then at his face. His hazel eyes were steady on hers, and the full measure of his attention was on her.

"For most of my adult life," she said, "I was the woman who made sure everyone else in the room mattered. I noticed who was hurting. I smoothed things over. I showed up first and left last. And somewhere along the way, I stopped letting anyone do that for me." She held his gaze. "I made myself small because small was safe. If I didn't need anyone, no one could disappoint me. If I didn't ask for anything, I never had to hear no."

She took an even breath. "These Wednesday nights changed that. Watching you teach. Sitting in honest conversations with you before and after. Letting the curriculum land on both of us and not running from what it brought up." She squeezed his hand. "You helped me want to stop being small, Conner. You made me want to be known. Not the bright, cheerful version I've been performing for years. The real me. The one who wants things she's been afraid to name."

His thumb moved across her knuckles in a slow, gentle pass. "Getting to know you again, the real you, underneath all of that, has been the best part of coming home."

They stood in the quiet of the half-cleaned room with their hands joined. The tenderness of what she'd said rested between them, unguarded and true. Then she squeezed his hand once more and started to turn back toward the remaining chairs.

"Rebecca. Hold on. Look at me for a second."

She stopped and turned back. She tilted her head slightly. "Everything okay?"

"Everything's fine. More than fine. But there's something I want to tell you, and I want your full attention when I say it. I got a phone call today," he said. "From my friend, Bill Stevenson. We were in the same ministry cohort at Liberty."

"Okay."

"Bill and his wife, Claire, are leaving for missionary work in Guatemala. They leave in June, and they'll be gone for a year. Bill's the lead pastor at a church in Charlotte. Grace Community. Three hundred and twenty members. Bill wants to recommend me to replace him."

The word Charlotte landed in her chest before she could brace against it. Her mind assembled the pieces of what he was saying with speed and precision. A bigger church. A bigger city. A trajectory that pointed away from Serenity Crossing and toward the kind of future that expanded until everything small fell off its edges.

She heard him keep talking. She could see his mouth moving and registered the cadence of his voice and knew that more words were coming. He was saying something about not hesitating. About his heart being here. About Charlotte never being a real question. About his calling being in Serenity Crossing, in this church, in the life he was building.

But the words arrived muffled. They passed through a filter that had been installed in her nervous system at eighteen and never fully removed. The filter took Charlotte and cross-referenced it with Liberty College and produced a conclusion in her mind she couldn't override: his world could get bigger again.

She knew it wasn't true. The rational part of her brain was still functioning, and that part understood clearly that the man standing in front of her had just said his answer was no. That he'd said his heart was here. That Charlotte was never a real question. She heard all of that in pieces. But the rational part wasn't the part that had taken control. The part running through her now was deeper and older.

She released his hand. "Conner, you need to take this seriously. That's a real opportunity. A lead pastor position at a church that size, offered by a friend who knows your work and believes in you. That matters."

"I know it matters," he said. "But my heart is here."

"Don't turn it down because of what's happening here. Take time with it. Remove me from the equation. Ask yourself honestly whether Serenity Crossing is where you belong if I'm not part of the answer."

"Rebecca, I already know where I belong."

"Then take another day and make sure." She bent down and picked up her bag from where she'd set it near the wall. She straightened and looked at him, but she held his gaze for only a second before shifting her eyes to the space just past his shoulder. "Don't follow me. Don't reach out tonight. This isn't me wanting you to come after me. This isn't me testing you. This is me giving you room to think clearly."

She slung her bag over her shoulder and walked to the door, pushed it open, and stepped through without looking back. The heavy metal door swung shut behind her, and the sound echoed through the empty recreation hall.

The parking lot was dark, and the March air carried the particular chill of a Tennessee evening caught between winter and spring. She crossed the pavement to her car with measured steps, her keys already in her hand. She unlocked the door, set her bag on the passenger seat, and sat behind the wheel.

She didn't start the engine right away. She sat with her hands on the steering wheel and her eyes fixed on her windshield and let the quiet close around her. Her jaw ached from the effort of holding it steady. Her fingers were tight on the wheel.

She knew what she'd just done. She knew it wasn't a test. At eighteen, it had been a test, even though she wouldn't have called it that at the time. She'd ended things with Conner and waited for him to come running, and when he didn't, she'd spent a decade telling herself a story built on that silence. But this was different. She wasn't testing him. She was trying to give him something honest: the space to make a decision without her standing in front of him, pulling at the answer. If he chose Serenity Crossing, she wanted him to choose it because God had planted him here, not because she was in the room with everything she felt written on her face.

That was the intention. It was mature and loving.

But it felt as if she were eighteen all over again.

Chapter 26

Conner's legal pad was open to Wednesday night's lesson notes. The closing statement he'd delivered to the youth group sat near the bottom of the right-hand column, underlined once. *You are not invisible.* He'd written those four words for a room full of teenagers, and they'd done exactly what he'd hoped they would do. But sitting at his desk today, a day and a half later, the words carried a meaning he hadn't planned for.

Thursday had been long. He'd made a hospital visit in the morning to see Earl Patterson, who was recovering from a knee replacement at Smoky Mountain Medical Center in Pigeon Forge. Earl was in good spirits, already complaining about physical therapy. Conner sat with him for forty-five minutes and prayed with him before he left. The afternoon had been administrative work at his desk, answering emails about Sunday's service schedule and reviewing the budget notes Warren had left in his inbox. Normal tasks on a normal day, and beneath all of it, Rebecca's exit the previous night had played on a quiet loop he couldn't shut off.

He'd called her Thursday evening around seven. She picked up on the third ring. Her voice was warm enough to tell him she was still there, still present, still willing to answer when his name appeared on her screen. But there was a boundary in her tone that he could hear. She was holding herself at a careful distance.

They talked for a few minutes. She told him about her day at the salon. A bride-to-be had come in for a consultation about wedding hair, and she and Jenna had spent an hour going through styles and pinning test curls. He told her about Earl Patterson's knee and Earl's insistence that the hospital Jell-O was a war crime against the state of Tennessee. She laughed at that. They talked about the weather turning and whether the weekend would bring rain. Small things. Safe ground. And then she said good night, but neither of them said the thing sitting between every sentence.

This morning he'd sent her a text at eight forty-five asking if she'd like to have dinner tonight, maybe at Minnie's. Her reply came minutes later. I'll meet you there at six. She'd agreed, and that mattered. She wasn't disappearing.

Conner set his pen on the desk, picked up his phone, and scrolled to Bill Stevenson's number.

Bill answered on the second ring. "Conner Delaney. I'm glad you called. How are you?"

"I'm good, Bill. Really good." Conner leaned back in his chair. "I've spent the past couple of days sitting with your offer. The fact that you'd put my name in front of your elder board means a lot."

"I meant every word of it," Bill said. "You're the real thing, Conner. I've known that for a long time."

"Thank you." Conner looked out his window, at the blue sky above the oaks. "But my answer is still no. I'm staying where God planted me. Serenity Crossing is my home, and the ministry I'm building here is the ministry I'm called to."

Bill was quiet for a moment. "Can't say I'm surprised. When we talked on Wednesday, there was something in the way you described that town and your church that told me you were right where you belonged."

"I am," Conner said. "But I'm glad you asked me to sit with your offer. You deserved a considered answer, not a knee-jerk one."

"I appreciate that. And I respect the decision. Serenity Crossing is lucky to have you."

"Bill, I want to give you a name. A friend of mine from my Richmond years. Paul Kessler. He's been serving as an assistant pastor at a church in the Shenandoah Valley, and he's been praying about a lead role for over a year. He's solid. Good preacher, strong with families, the kind of pastor who remembers every member's name by the second Sunday. I think he'd be worth a conversation."

"Paul Kessler," Bill said. "You have his number?"

"I'll text it to you after we hang up."

"Good. Thank you for that," Bill paused. "So how's everything else? Claire keeps asking about you. She wants to know if you've found a girl in that small town of yours."

Conner smiled. "Tell Claire she's not subtle."

"I've been telling her that for eight years. She doesn't care," Bill laughed. "Listen, we'd love for you to come visit us in Guatemala if you can swing it. The school we're scheduled to build will be something special."

"I'd like that. I'll be praying for both of you. And tell Claire her Spanish is going to be better than the barista's by June."

"She already thinks it is. Take care of yourself, Conner. And take care of that church."

"I will. God bless you both."

"You too, brother."

The line went quiet, and Conner set his phone on the desk beside his Bible. The Charlotte chapter was closed. He'd made this decision on Wednesday afternoon, sitting in this same chair, before he ever told Rebecca about the offer. Calling Bill just now was a formality.

But his mind went right back to Wednesday night. To the recreation hall after the kids had left. To Rebecca standing in front of him with her hand in his, telling him he'd made her want to be known, and the warmth of that moment wrapped around him. And then to the shift. The word Charlotte landing and the expression on her face had changed instantly. The slight tightening around her eyes. The way she released his hand with a precision that told him the release was deliberate. The measured, controlled sentences she'd delivered about removing herself from the equation and about not following her.

The woman who walked out of that room wasn't running from him. She removed herself as a variable because she loved him enough to refuse to be the reason he stayed.

He admired the courage it took to walk away from a man who was holding your hand and telling you his heart was yours. Then look him in the eye and tell him to take you out of the equation.

But she was wrong about one thing. There was no equation without her. She was the equation.

He'd spent ten years learning what silence costs. He'd spent a decade carrying two letters in his Bible.

Conner pushed back from his desk and walked down the hallway toward Warren's office.

Warren's door was open, and he sat behind his desk reading through a stack of sermon notes, his wire-framed glasses low on his nose and a pen in his right hand.

Conner knocked on the doorframe, and Warren looked up over the rim of his glasses.

"Come on in." He said as he set his pen down and gestured toward the chair across from his desk.

"I called Bill this morning," he said. "I gave him my final answer, and I recommended another pastor for the position."

Warren nodded, his expression carrying the quiet satisfaction of a man who'd expected exactly this. "Good." He studied Conner's face for a moment. "Now, what else is on your mind? Because you didn't walk down here to tell me something I already knew."

Conner looked at the bookshelf behind Warren's left shoulder. A framed photo of Warren and Mary on their thirtieth anniversary sat between a Greek lexicon and a volume of Spurgeon's sermons. Mary was laughing in the photo, her head tilted back, and Warren was watching her.

"I want to tell you something about the Chosen series I used with the youth group," Conner said. "Not the content. You know the content. I want to tell you what it did."

Warren removed his glasses and set them on his desk. He folded his hands loosely across his midsection and waited.

"Every lesson I taught on Wednesday nights turned around and landed on me and Rebecca," Conner said. "Week after week. I'd stand in front of those kids and teach a lesson about identity or worth or invisibility, and then the room would empty, and Rebecca and I would end up talking about the exact same thing. Except we weren't talking about teenagers anymore. We were talking about us."

"The first lesson was 'Do I Even Matter?' I wrote it for kids who feel overlooked. But that question was the one Rebecca had been carrying since she was eighteen. She sat on her bed in this town waiting for phone calls that came later and shorter, and the boy she loved never asked himself whether she still mattered to him." Conner's voice was steady. "That was me. I was that boy."

Warren didn't interrupt. His hands stayed still in his lap.

"The comparison lesson exposed something I hadn't let myself see clearly. I poured myself into school and ministry, and everything that was opening up in front of me. I left Rebecca standing in the life I'd walked out of without once looking back to see what it was costing her. She watched my world expand while hers stayed exactly the same, and I never noticed."

He leaned forward in the chair, his forearms resting on his knees. "Lesson Five was 'What If You've Been Overlooked?' I underlined that word on my legal pad. Overlooked. Because it described exactly what I'd done to the woman I loved. I overlooked her. I didn't see her. I didn't fight for her. I let her walk away because it was easier than admitting I'd failed."

"Lesson Six cracked something open that changed the story Rebecca had been telling herself for years," Conner said. "She didn't know I called her the morning after the breakup. I sat on the edge of my dorm bed and dialed her number, and she didn't answer. Five rings, and I hung up instead of leaving a voicemail. I told myself she didn't want to hear from me, and I never called again." He shook his head. "For ten years, she believed I accepted the breakup and moved on without looking back. That one conversation, after that one lesson, rewrote a decade of what she thought she knew about me."

He sat back. "And Lesson Seven. 'Letting People See the Real You.' That discussion between us changed many things as well and touched us both deeply."

Conner looked at Warren. "I didn't design the curriculum for this to happen between us. I built this curriculum for teenagers in a church basement in Richmond years ago. I chose to present it here to the youth in our church because I thought it was the right material for this group of kids. And it was. Those kids grew. Hannah Caldwell walked into the first session barely able to make eye contact, and this past Wednesday night she told a room full of her peers she was going to talk to her mom about being lonely. The curriculum worked." He paused. "But God used it for something I never planned. He took the same lessons and began healing the two adults standing at the front of that room at the same time He was healing the kids sitting in the circle."

"That's how God works, son," Warren said. His voice was quiet and sure. "Not on your schedule. Not the way you planned it. But right on time."

"I know that, but what I witnessed these past few weeks... wow. It really is amazing when you think about it."

Warren picked up his glasses from the desk and turned them slowly in his hands.

"In thirty years of ministry, I've watched God take the thing a person built for one purpose and use it for something the person never imagined. A sermon I wrote once ended up being the thing that saved a marriage in the third-row pew of this very church. I didn't even know they were struggling. A Bible study Mary led for young mothers became the place where a woman found the courage to leave a situation that was hurting her children." He put his glasses back on. "The curriculum you presented was the vessel. What God poured into it was bigger than an eight-week series for teenagers. He used it to bring two people back to each other. That's the kind of thing that keeps an old pastor like me showing up day after day."

Warren was quiet for another moment. Then his gaze sharpened, and he looked at Conner with the direct attention of a man who could read faces the way some people read weather.

"So what's troubling you?" he said. "Because a man who just declined an offer, he's at peace with and described God rebuilding something beautiful doesn't walk into my office looking the way you look right now."

Conner rubbed his thumb along the crease of his jeans. "Wednesday night after youth group. After the kids had left. Rebecca took my hand. She told me something honest about what the Chosen series and our time leading it had meant to her." He paused. "And then I told her about Charlotte. I told her everything. Bill's call. The offer. The church in Charlotte. And I told her my answer was no. I told her that my heart is here. I told her Charlotte was never a real question." Conner looked at the bookshelf and then back at Warren. "I watched her face change the second the word Charlotte left my mouth."

"How did it change?"

"A tightening around her eyes. A pull at the corners of her mouth so small that most people wouldn't have caught it. But I caught it. And then she let go of my hand." He rubbed his palms together slowly. "She told me to take real time with the decision. To remove her from the equation. To ask myself honestly whether Serenity Crossing is where I belong if she's not part of the answer. She picked up her bag and told me not to follow her, and she walked out."

Warren took his glasses off and cleaned them with the edge of his shirt. He held them up to the window, checked the lenses, and put them back on.

"I didn't chase her," Conner said. "She asked me not to. And I respected that, because ten years ago I confused respecting her decision with giving up, and I spent a decade paying for it. This time I know the difference. She asked for something specific and honest, and I honored it."

"But?" Warren said.

"But I called her Thursday evening. She picked up. We talked for a few minutes. Present but pulled back. She didn't mention Charlotte. I didn't push. We said good night." He looked at his hands. "This morning she agreed to meet me for dinner tonight at Minnie's. So she's not walking away, but there's a wall up that wasn't there before Wednesday evening, and I put it there by telling her the truth."

"No," Warren said. "You didn't put it there. The truth put it there. And there's an important difference."

Conner met his eyes.

"Think about what Rebecca was actually doing Wednesday night," Warren said. "Not what it looked like from your side. What she was doing from hers."

Warren leaned forward and rested his forearms on his desk. "Rebecca heard Charlotte and whatever else you said, and it fueled her thinking before her mind could override it. She wasn't running from you. She was trying to give you something she couldn't give you at eighteen. A clean choice. She took herself off the scale because she loves you enough to not be the thing that tips it." He held Conner's gaze. "If you stayed here because of her, and it went wrong down the road, I can safely guess that she assumes it'd destroy both of you or you'd hold it against her."

Warren tapped his desk once with his index finger. "That's not a woman pulling away. That's a woman who's terrified of being the reason someone stays and then the reason someone regrets staying. She's not punishing you. She's protecting both of you." He paused. "The only thing she got wrong was not hearing the answer you'd already given her. Fear stepped in."

"Mary did something similar once," he continued. "Early in our marriage. I was considering a church in Knoxville. Bigger congregation, better salary. Mary told me to go visit without her. She said she didn't want her feelings about leaving Serenity Crossing to influence my decision. She wanted me to walk into that church and see it clearly, without her standing beside me coloring the picture." He adjusted his glasses. "She was trying to love me well by stepping back. I drove to Knoxville alone and sat in an empty sanctuary for an hour and realized that every good thing I wanted was back here, including the woman who'd sent me to find that out for myself."

Conner looked at the anniversary photo on the bookshelf. Mary laughing. Warren watching her.

"So what are you going to do?" Warren asked.

"The ten years I spent away from Serenity Crossing, I built a decent life," he said. "I served a church I cared about. I had a congregation I enjoyed and friendships I valued. It was a decent life, and I'm grateful for it." He looked at Warren. "But there was a piece missing, and I knew what it was the entire time. I knew it at twenty-two when I couldn't name it. I knew it when I got engaged to a woman I cared about but never loved the way I love Rebecca. I knew it every time I opened my Bible and two letters Rebecca had written to me were sitting in the front cover, staring back at me like a question I kept refusing to answer."

He leaned forward. "She's the piece. She always has been. I don't want a version of my life where I come home to an empty parsonage every night knowing the woman I love is a few miles down the road, and I didn't have the courage to say it plainly. I'm done being careful, Warren. She needs to hear me say it."

Warren looked at Conner across the desk with an expression that carried satisfaction and something close to pride. "Then be that man. Not tonight at dinner. Tonight you show up, you're present, and you let her set the pace. But when the time comes, and you'll know when it comes, you say what you just said to me. You say it to her. Every word."

Conner nodded.

Warren grinned as he picked up his pen. "Now get out of my office. I've got to work on these Bible study materials, and Mary's expecting me home for lunch in two hours, and if I don't have something written down by then, she's going to ask me what I did all morning, and I'd rather not tell her I spent it counseling a lovesick assistant pastor."

Conner stood. "Lovesick?"

"I call it like I see it." Warren sat back down and pulled his notes toward him. "Go on. You've got some heavy things to think more on and a prayer or two that need praying before you walk into Minnie's tonight."

Conner stepped toward the door and stopped at the frame. "Warren."

Warren looked up.

"Thank you."

Warren held his gaze for a second and then waved Conner out. "Go."

Conner walked back down the hallway. His footsteps were the only sound in the building, and the quiet felt different from how it had when he'd walked to Warren's office. Clearer. Like a room where the windows have been opened, and the air has shifted.

He sat down behind his desk and bowed his head.

Lord, thank You for the clarity. Thank You for bringing me home. Thank You for the ministry You've built through ordinary Wednesday nights in a room full of teenagers and two adults who needed healing. I know where I belong. I know what You've called me to.

Be with Rebecca. Give her the courage to hear what I've already said and to believe it. Help her see that the man in front of her isn't the boy who left. Give me wisdom tonight and give me patience that doesn't become silence. And when the time comes, give me the words.

Chapter 27

Rebecca pulled into the church parking lot and parked beside Conner's truck.

She picked up her purse, opened her door, and stepped out into the cool March air.

She pulled the heavy wooden door open and stepped inside. The foyer was still. The bulletin board held announcements for the monthly church dinner in April and a sign-up sheet for the Faith Foundations mentorship program. The coat rack near the entrance stood empty. She passed Warren's closed office door. The hallway stretched ahead of her toward the end of the building where Conner's office sat.

His door was open, and Conner looked up from his desk as she entered. His Bible was open in front of him, his legal pad beside it. His sandy brown hair was pushed sideways, and he wore a flannel shirt with the sleeves pushed up to his forearms. When he saw her, his pen stilled against the legal pad. His shoulders drew back from the forward curve of his reading. His eyebrows lifted, and his lips parted, and for a full second he simply looked at her with an expression that held surprise and something deeper.

"Rebecca," he said.

She closed his office door behind her. She crossed the small room to the chair across from his desk and sat down.

She set her purse on her lap and looked at him.

She didn't say hello.

She didn't explain why she was here in the middle of the day.

She didn't apologize for showing up without calling first.

She reached into her purse and pulled out the coupon book.

The small booklet of heavy cardstock, roughly the size of a greeting card, bound with twine through two holes punched along the left edge. His compact handwriting on the cover: Coupon Book. No expiration, good for a lifetime.

She set it on his desk between them.

Conner looked at the booklet. Then he looked at her.

Rebecca opened the coupon book to the first page. His handwriting filled the card, neat and compact.

One Saturday morning breakfast at Minnie's Diner. I'm buying. You pick the booth.

"I want to redeem this one," she said. Her voice was steady and clear in the quiet office.

She turned the page.

One hike to anywhere you choose. I'll pack the water and the snacks.

"And this one." She touched the edge of the cardstock with her fingertip.

She turned the page.

One evening of your Netflix picks. Zero complaints. I promise.

"This one, too."

She turned to the next page and pointed.

One batch of chocolate chip cookies, from scratch, delivered to the salon on the day of your choice.

"This one."

She kept turning. Her fingers moved with care across each page, the cardstock thick and textured beneath her touch, the twine pulling gently against its binding as she went.

One quiet walk around town.

One run on a trail.

One long break from work for coconut cream pie.

One midweek lunch break, no errands, no rushing, just sitting together.

She turned each page with the same unhurried certainty, her voice quiet and sure.

She reached the pages near the end and slowed down .

One trip to Henderson's Hill to act like kids again and go sledding.

"I want this one," she said. "Next winter. First real snow."

She turned the page.

One evening where I plan everything. You just say the word.

"And this one."

She turned to the next page, and her fingers rested on it.

One slow dance, wherever we happen to be.

She looked at the words on the card. His handwriting. The promise he'd made her on a Valentine's Saturday at his kitchen table with candles burning low and a whole coconut cream pie between them.

She turned to the last page.

Revolving coupon: One chance every day to show you what you mean to me.

Rebecca traced the edge of the final card with her thumb. The booklet was open flat on his desk now, every page turned, every coupon claimed. She looked up at Conner.

His pen lay forgotten beside his legal pad. His hazel eyes were fixed on her, and the expression on his face was something she'd carry with her for the rest of her life. His jaw was set, but not tight. His eyes were full, and the fullness had nothing to do with tears. He was watching the woman across from him reach for every single thing he'd offered, and she could see what that meant to him in the way his hands had gone still on his desk and his breath had slowed and every part of him was focused on her.

Conner reached across the desk and laid his hand over hers on the open booklet. His palm was warm and steady against her fingers. She looked down at his hand on hers and then up at his face.

"I want this, Conner," she said. "All of it. Every coupon and every promise. Every ordinary Tuesday and every quiet Sunday. I want a life with you in this town, in this church, in the place where we started. I want what's written on these pages, and I'm reaching for it with everything I have."

She turned her hand beneath his and laced her fingers through his on top of the open booklet.

"I was wrong on Wednesday night," she said. "You told me about Charlotte, and you told me your answer was no, and you told me your heart was here. I heard "Charlotte," and I heard "lead pastor," and my mind built a story. A bigger life somewhere else. A world that expands beyond me. I stopped listening to what you were actually saying because the old story was louder, and I let it drive me out of that room."

She held his gaze.

"I spent a day and a half sitting with what I did. And I realized I gave you the same exit at twenty-eight years old that I gave you at eighteen. Different words, same thing. I stepped back. I removed myself. I told myself I was being selfless, but the truth is I was afraid." She tightened her fingers around his. "I'm done being afraid, Conner."

His thumb moved slowly against the side of her hand.

"There's something else I need to say," Rebecca said. "And this is the part that's harder than the rest." She straightened in her chair and kept her hand in his. "For years, I've held onto Serenity Crossing as if leaving this town would mean losing myself. My salon, my family, my apartment above the shop, and my life here. I built my whole identity around this place because this place was the one thing that stayed the same when you left. When everything else shifted and my world got quiet, Serenity Crossing was still here. So I made it my anchor. I made it my safety net. And somewhere along the way, I made it a condition. I made it sound like loving me means staying here. Like Serenity Crossing is part of the price of admission."

She shook her head once.

"That's not how two people who love each other live. And I won't do that to you or to us."

She leaned forward in her chair.

"If God calls you to Charlotte, or to any other church in any other city, I will follow you. I will leave my salon and my family and this town, and I will stand beside you wherever you go. Because I'd rather build a new life with you somewhere, I've never been than stay in the only place I've ever known without you. I know I'm thinking toward the future, and I'm not trying to rush what's building between us. But you need to know this, Conner. Wherever you go, I go. That's my answer. It's the answer I should've given ten years ago, and I'm giving it now."

Conner stood up from his chair. He came around the side of his desk, and when he cleared the corner, the barrier between them was gone. He stopped in front of her and reached for both her hands. She gave them to him, and he drew her to standing so they were facing each other in the small space between his desk and the door.

He placed his finger gently under her chin and tilted her face up so she was looking at him.

"I called Bill this morning," he said. "I turned the job down and recommended another pastor for the position."

Her eyes filled with tears, and she didn't try to stop them.

"There is no equation without you, Rebecca. You told me to remove you, and I couldn't, because you are the equation. My calling is here. Warren, this church, my family, the ministry. All of it rooted in this soil. But you're the reason this place feels like home instead of just a town with my name in its history."

She looked at him through the blur in her eyes, and he held her gaze.

"I want to tell you something Warren said to me this morning," Conner said. "We were talking about the Chosen series. About what it did for us. And Warren said something I can't get out of my head. He was referring to God's timing and what's happened and been happening in our lives." He paused. "Not on your schedule. Not the way you planned it. But right on time... those were his exact words."

Rebecca closed her eyes for a second and let the words land.

Right on time.

"God had plans for us all along. He led us down separate paths for a reason and brought us back together when it was time. I believe with everything in me that he has even greater plans for us if we're willing to follow his lead."

Conner lifted his hand and traced his thumb along her jaw. His touch was careful and warm, and she felt it in every part of her.

"I came home for a lot of reasons," he said. "But you were the first one. You've always been the first one."

He leaned down. She rose to meet him. His lips touched hers, soft and brief and sweet, and the ten years and the silence and the letters and the missed phone call and the coupon book and every mile of road that had brought them back to this room collapsed into a single, quiet point of arrival. His hand cupped her face. Her fingers curled into the front of his flannel and held on . They stayed there for a few seconds, his mouth against hers with a tenderness that carried no urgency, only the steady, certain knowledge of two people who'd finally arrived at the same place at the right time. They separated just far enough to look at each other, and the tears on her cheeks were warm and good and earned.

He pressed his lips to her forehead. She closed her eyes and let him hold her there, his breath warm against her skin. She leaned into him, and he wrapped his arms around her, and they stood in his small office at the end of the church hallway while the building settled quietly around them.

After a while, Rebecca stepped back. She wiped her cheeks with her fingertips and looked at his desk. She reached for the coupon book and flipped through the pages until she found the one she wanted.

One slow dance, wherever we happen to be.

She turned the booklet around and held it up so he could see it. "I'd like to redeem this one."

Conner looked at the coupon. He looked at her. A slow grin spread across his face, wide and unguarded. The grin she'd fallen in love with when she was seventeen.

He took her hand. His other hand settled gently at her waist. She rested her free hand on his shoulder, and his flannel was soft beneath her palm.

And in his office at the end of the hallway at Serenity Crossing Community Church, on a Friday afternoon in March, with no music and no audience and no sound except the quiet of a building that had held a thousand prayers, they danced. Slowly and close, turning in the small space between his desk and the door, her head against his chest and his chin resting on her hair. The coupon book lay open on the desk behind them. His Bible was beside it. The legal pad with his compact handwriting.

Two people who'd loved each other since they were seventeen and broken apart at eighteen and spent a decade becoming the people who could sustain what they'd always had. A man who chose to stay. A woman who chose to reach. And on a Friday afternoon in a small room at the end of a church hallway, where they turned slowly with no music, because the music had never been the point.

Chapter 28

Conner stood at the pulpit with one hand resting along its edge and looked out over the sanctuary. March sunlight came through the tall windows in wide, angled shafts that warmed the wooden pews. The sanctuary was full. Families filled rows they'd claimed for years, their Bibles open or closed on their laps, children tucked between their parents with varying degrees of patience. Warren sat behind Conner on the platform, his wire-framed glasses on and his Bible across his knees.

Conner's gaze moved across the congregation and found Rebecca in the front row. She had walked past the row where her parents and the rest of her family were seated, and she had kept walking until she reached the front pew and sat down beside the parents of the man she loved.

Conner smiled at her. A small, specific smile that belonged to the two of them, even in a room full of people. Rebecca held it and felt the warmth of it settle against her ribs.

"Good morning," Conner's voice carried through the sanctuary with a warmth that filled the room without straining against it. "For those of you keeping track, the last time I stood behind this pulpit I was twelve years old. Pastor Warren let me read the Scripture passage on Youth Sunday, and I was so nervous I read the entire thing in about eleven seconds and sat down before he could thank me."

Laughter moved through the room behind Rebecca, soft and affectionate.

"My mother told me afterward that she couldn't understand a single word I said, but she was very proud of my speed." Conner glanced at Loretta, and Rebecca heard her quiet laugh beside her.

"So I want to start by saying thank you," Conner said. "To Pastor Warren, for trusting me with this pulpit and for being the kind of mentor every young pastor hopes for, and few are lucky enough to find. And to all of you, for welcoming me home these past few weeks. I grew up in these pews. I gave my life to Christ in this building. And standing here this morning, looking out at faces I've known since I was a boy, means more to me than I have the words for." He paused. "I'll do my best not to read this sermon in eleven seconds."

Another ripple of laughter, and Rebecca watched him from the front row and saw the way his shoulders had settled, the way his hands rested on the pulpit with ease

"For the past couple of months, I've been spending Wednesday nights with our youth group, working through a series of lessons I called Chosen." He opened his Bible on the pulpit. "We started with a question that didn't feel simple once we got into it. Do I even matter?" He looked up. "And I'll be honest with you. It didn't take long to realize that question doesn't belong only to teenagers. It's the same question sitting in most of us. It just gets quieter as you get older. We learn how to carry it without saying it out loud."

"We talked about comparison," Conner continued. "About the labels people carry. About what it feels like to believe you're falling behind while everyone around you seems to have things figured out. And by the end of the series, we landed somewhere that sounds simple but is harder to live than it is to say."

He looked down at the open page of his Bible. "First Peter, chapter two, verse nine. 'But ye are a chosen generation, a royal priesthood, a holy nation, a peculiar people, that ye should shew forth the praises of him who hath called you out of darkness into his marvelous light.'"

He let the verse sit in the room for a moment before he looked up.

"That word. Chosen. It gets used a lot. But I don't think we always stop to consider what it actually means. Because most of us, if we're honest, don't live like we believe it."

Rebecca's hands were folded in her lap. She was watching his face, the way his eyes moved across the congregation with a steadiness that didn't rush and didn't perform. The same steadiness she had seen on Friday afternoon in his office when he stood in front of her and said there was no equation without her.

"We live like we're still trying to earn our place," Conner said. "Like we're waiting for someone to notice us. Like if we just get a little further, do a little more, hold things a little tighter, then maybe we'll feel like we belong where we are."

He shook his head once.

"That doesn't disappear when you graduate high school."

A few quiet chuckles from the pews behind her.

"It just changes shape. It shows up in your work. In your family. In the way you measure your life against someone else's without even realizing you're doing it. You look at what somebody else built, or what somebody else has, and you run the math in your head, and you come up short. And after a while, you start to believe something that isn't true. That your worth is something you have to prove."

He lifted his Bible from the pulpit and held it in one hand.

"Scripture doesn't talk about worth that way. It says you were chosen. Not after you got everything right. Not once you reach a certain point. Not because you earned it."

Not after you got everything right. The words pressed against something in Rebecca's chest that had lived there for a long time. A decade of proving. A decade of showing up and smiling and giving and holding everything in place so that no one would look at her life and see a gap where something was missing. She had tried to earn her place in every room she entered, and the trying had become so automatic she'd stopped recognizing it as effort.

"Chosen first," Conner said. "And I think that's where a lot of us get stuck. We hear that truth, and part of us believes it. But we keep living like it's still up for debate."

He set his Bible back on the pulpit and rested both hands on its edges.

"So we carry things we were never meant to carry. Words people spoke over us years ago. Expectations we didn't meet. Decisions we wish we could go back and make differently. And those things start to shape how we see ourselves. They stop feeling like memories and start feeling like facts." He paused. "But they don't get to decide who you are. God already did that."

Rebecca kept her eyes on him. The man at the pulpit was the man who had held her face in his hands two days ago in his office at the end of this hallway. The man whose lips had touched hers with a tenderness that carried no urgency. The man who had danced with her in a small room with no music because the music had never been the point. He was standing in his calling, and his calling was not the thing that had taken him from her. It was the thing that had made him this. She could see it now with a clarity that filled her instead of frightening her. The boy who left at eighteen had needed every mile of that road to become the man standing at this pulpit, speaking truth to a room full of people who needed to hear it. And she was sitting in the front row, not because she had to be, but because there was nowhere else she wanted to be.

"When Scripture says you're chosen," Conner continued, "it's not describing a future version of you. It's not a promise that kicks in once you get your life sorted out. It's describing who you are right now. Today. With every imperfect thing you're carrying and every question you haven't answered yet."

He smiled.

"Living from that truth doesn't mean everything suddenly falls into place. It doesn't mean the hard things disappear or the questions stop. But it changes how you walk through them. You stop trying to prove something that's already been settled. You stop measuring your life against someone else's timeline. And you stop questioning whether you belong where God has placed you."

He looked out over the room.

"Because if He chose you, then you're not here by accident. You're not overlooked."

Overlooked. She had spent ten years believing she had been overlooked by the one person whose attention she wanted most, and then she had spent those same ten years overlooking herself. Making herself small. Making herself easy. Making herself the woman who held everyone else up and never asked anyone to hold her.

That woman was still sitting in this pew. But she was different now. She was sitting in the front row beside the mother of the man who loved her, listening to the truth she had needed to hear at eighteen being spoken aloud in the same church where she'd been baptized, and she was letting it land without flinching.

"You're not behind. You're not trying to catch up to something you missed. You're exactly where you need to be for what God is doing in your life. And when you start to believe that," Conner said, "not just hear it, but actually live from it, it changes the way you show up. It changes how you treat people. It changes how you see yourself when things don't go the way you planned.

Because you're no longer asking the question. You already know the answer."

He rested his hands on the pulpit one last time.

"Let's pray."

Conner bowed his head. "Lord, thank You for this morning. Thank You for this church and for the people in this room who show up week after week to seek You. Help us carry this truth past these doors and into the ordinary days ahead. Remind us that we were chosen before we earned anything, and that our worth was settled before we ever questioned it. Give us the courage to live from that truth instead of toward it. In Your name, amen."

Amen moved through the sanctuary in a low, gathered murmur, and the stillness broke gently into motion.

Conner lifted his head from the pulpit. Before the congregation stirred fully, before the pews creaked and the conversations began and the room shifted into its Sunday rhythms of rising and greeting and moving toward the fellowship hall, his eyes found hers.

Not a glance. A look. Quiet and unhurried, and specific. The same steadiness she had seen in his office on Friday when he told her she was the equation. The same eyes that had watched her turn every page of a handmade coupon book and reach for everything he'd offered. He looked at her the way a man looks at the woman he loves when he has just finished saying the truest thing he knows, and the truest thing he knows is also about her, even though he never said her name.

Rebecca held his gaze from the front pew. Loretta was closing her Bible beside her. Warren was rising from his chair on the platform. The sanctuary was waking up to its familiar Sunday noise. And she sat still in the center of it, looking at the man at the pulpit, carrying the quiet certainty that the girl who had asked 'do I even matter' ten years ago had just heard the answer spoken aloud in the church where she grew up, by the man God had spent a decade preparing to say it.

She didn't need to go anywhere. She didn't need to prove anything. She was exactly where she was supposed to be.

Leave A Review

If you enjoyed this book, please consider leaving an honest review on Amazon

Visit Our Website:

www.tarabaisden.com

Visit Our Amazon Author Page HERE

Find Us On Social Media:

Facebook

Facebook Author Page

Instagram

Scan the QR code above to sign up for our newsletter!

Afterword

Writing contemporary Christian romance means stepping into stories that feel close to home—places and people that reflect the world we live in today, with all its beauty, challenges, and quiet, everyday moments. These are stories about ordinary lives touched by extraordinary grace, where faith is not always loud or perfect, but steady, growing, and real.

My desire in every book is to portray characters who wrestle honestly, love deeply, and learn to trust God in the middle of life as it unfolds. Their journeys are not meant to be flawless, but faithful—shaped by hope, forgiveness, and the kind of love that calls us forward.

Scripture reminds us in Lamentations 3:22–23 that "the Lord's mercies are new every morning" and in Jeremiah 29:11 that "His plans for us are filled with hope and a future." These promises are at the heart of every story I write.

Thank you for spending time in these pages and for allowing these characters and their journeys to become a small part of your own.

With heartfelt gratitude,

Tara Baisden

Also by Tara Baisden

<u>Serenity Crossing: The Hartwell's Series</u>

#1 Hometown Sweethearts

#2 Hearts Restored

#3 The Art of Starting Over

#4 Love in God's Timing

#5 Wildflower Heart – coming June 5, 2026

#6 Brave Enough to Love – coming July 3, 2026

<u>Laurel Ridge Series</u>

#1. Season of Hope

#2. Finding Grace

#3. His Perfect Plan

#4. Love Redeemed

#5 Snowbound Blessings

#6 Sheltered Hearts

#7 Restoring Faith

#8 Love Rekindled

#9 Where She Belongs

#10 Shelter in His Arms

#11 Where Love Stands

#12 The Pieces We Mend

#13 Where Love Grows

#14 Where Hearts Heal

#15 Harvest of the Heart

#16 Heart of the Season

#17 Season of Forgiveness

#18 Threads of Grace

Riverbend Valley Series

#1 A Cowboy's Second Chance

#2 Wanderlust & Wild Horses

#3 Heartstrings on the Horizon

#4 Runaway in Riverbend Valley

#5 Mended Hearts

#6 Healing Hearts

#7 Home to Lost Creek

Mistletoe Falls Series

#1 Whisk Me Under the Mistletoe

#2 Once Upon a Christmas

#3 The Mistletoe Express

#4 Candy Canes & Sweet Dreams

#5 Wrapped Up in Christmas

#6 Jingle All the Way Home

About The Author

Tara Baisden is a contemporary Christian inspirational romance author who proudly calls the beautiful state of West Virginia her home. Nestled on a sprawling mountainous property, she is surrounded by the peace and serenity of nature. Her days are happily spent in the quiet of country life, writing heartwarming stories of love, faith, and second chances. Tara also enjoys quilting, working in her garden, tending to her beloved pets, and soaking in the beauty of her surroundings.

With deep roots in West Virginia, family is everything to Tara. One of her favorite pastimes is gathering on the front porch with loved ones, sharing stories, laughter, and enjoying the simple, meaningful moments that life offers. When she's not crafting her novels, Tara can often be found exploring the rich history of her home state, visiting local historical sites, and, of course, stopping by every bookstore she passes! Her passion for reading and discovery always fuels her next adventure.

Tara is the author of the Laurel Ridges series of novels, as well as the Riverbend Valley series of novels, of which have been beloved by fans of inspirational romance. Her novels reflect her love for faith, family, and the timeless beauty of the world we live in.

Known for her sweet and clean romances, she creates characters that feel like family and settings that make readers want to visit again and again.

You can find out more about Tara and her latest releases at www.tarabaisden.com or follow her on social media for updates and behind-the-scenes glimpses of her writing process. Stay connected—you won't want to miss the heartfelt stories of love and family she has in store!